"Rose, you can't be here."

"On the beach?" she asked.

"Yes, on the beach. I'm naked," the earl bit out.

"I don't understand the fuss. Half of London has seen you naked." Rose snorted. "The female half, anyway."

"You haven't."

"Until today. You have to appreciate the irony of this, Dawes. The infamous, unequivocal Don Juan of London suddenly shy about a little nudity."

"Because it's not proper! For you to be here when I am less than..." He stalled.

"When have you ever cared about propriety? You sound like a ninety-year-old nun."

Eli remained silent, his body rigid. "I care when it comes to you."

ACCLAIM FOR KELLY BOWEN

A DUKE IN THE NIGHT

"If you read one historical romance this year, make sure it's this one. I cannot wait to see what comes next in this series. Final Grade—A."

—FictionVixen.com

"4½ Stars! Top Pick! What a way to start the Devils of Dover series! Bowen strikes all the right chords with readers: touching emotional highs with powerful storytelling. This is a book not only to savor, but a keeper that will stay in your heart."

—RTBookReviews.com

BETWEEN THE DEVIL AND THE DUKE

"The fun, intrigue, and romance crescendo in a whopping plot twist. Bowen's Regency romances are always delightful, and this is one of her best yet."

—*Publishers Weekly* (starred review)

"Bowen again delivers the goods with this exquisitely written historical romance, whose richly nuanced characters, unexpected flashes of dry wit, and superbly sensual love story will have readers sighing happily in satisfaction."

—Booklist (starred review)

A DUKE TO REMEMBER

"This isn't a Regency comedy of manners. It's way better. This bright, surprising romance sets aside the intricate social rules and focuses on forging trust and love even when it seems like the whole world is against you."

—The Amazon Book Review
(Best Romance of August selection)

"*A Duke to Remember* has everything you want in a romance....A truly satisfying happily ever after that will leave you misty-eyed."

—BookPage.com

DUKE OF MY HEART

"Bowen's irresistible Regency is like the most popular debutante at the ball: pretty, witty, mysterious, and full of coquettish allure. From the first line to the happy dénouement, Bowen builds enough romantic heat to melt midwinter snow."

—*Publishers Weekly* (Best Books of 2016 selection)

"In her latest, Kelly Bowen offers up a vibrant, clever heroine in Ivory Moore—think Olivia Pope in a corset. The romance here is deeply satisfying, and Bowen excels in writing secondary characters and scenes. What's more, the nooks and crannies of this book are delightful, much like those in our real world, perfect to be discovered alongside true love."

—*Washington Post*

YOU'RE THE EARL THAT I WANT

"This story has it all: romance, suspense, wit, and Bowen's trademark smart and slightly quirky characters. Bowen's thrilling plot, spot-on pacing, and savvy characterization will delight her current fans and seduce new ones."

—*Publishers Weekly* (starred review)

"4 stars! Bowen is at the top of her game, and all readers could desire is more."

—*RT Book Reviews*

A GOOD ROGUE IS HARD TO FIND

"Where have you been all my life, Kelly Bowen? If Julia Quinn, Sarah MacLean, and Lisa Kleypas were to extract their writing DNA, mix it in a blender, and have a love child, Kelly Bowen would be it."

—HeroesandHeartbreakers.com

"Bowen's impish sense of humor is expressed by lively, entertaining characters in this wickedly witty Regency. This is pure romantic fun."
—*Publishers Weekly*

I'VE GOT MY DUKE TO KEEP ME WARM

"With this unforgettable debut, Bowen proves she is a writer to watch as she spins a multilayered plot skillfully seasoned with danger and deception and involving wonderfully complex protagonists and a memorable cast of supporting characters...a truly remarkable romance well worth savoring."

—*Booklist* (starred review)

"4 stars! In this delightful, poignant debut that sets Bowen on the path to become a beloved author, the innovative plotline and ending are only superseded by the likable, multidimensional characters: a strong-willed heroine and a heart-stealing hero. Get set to relish Bowen's foray into the genre."

—*RT Book Reviews*

Last Night
With the
Earl

KELLY BOWEN

FOREVER

New York Boston

Copyright © 2018 by Kelly Bowen
Preview of *A Rogue by Night* © 2018 by Kelly Bowen
Respect for Christmas © 2016 by Grace Burrowes. *Respect for Christmas* was originally published as part of a compilation entitled *The Virtues of Christmas* in 2016 by Grace Burrowes Publishing.
Cover design by Elizabeth Turner Stokes
Cover illustration by Kris Keller
Cover copyright © 2018 by Hachette Book Group, Inc.

Forever
Hachette Book Group
1290 Avenue of the Americas, New York, NY 10104
forever-romance.com
twitter.com/foreverromance

First Edition: September 2018

Forever is an imprint of Grand Central Publishing. The Forever name and logo are trademarks of Hachette Book Group, Inc.

The publisher is not responsible for websites (or their content) that are not owned by the publisher.

The Hachette Speakers Bureau provides a wide range of authors for speaking events. To find out more, go to www.hachettespeakersbureau.com or call (866) 376-6591.

ISBN: 978-1-4789-1859-2 (mass market), 978-1-4789-1858-5 (ebook)

Printed in the United States of America

OPM

10 9 8 7 6 5 4 3 2 1

ATTENTION CORPORATIONS AND ORGANIZATIONS:

Most Hachette Book Group books are available at quantity discounts with bulk purchase for educational, business, or sales promotional use. For information, please call or write:

Special Markets Department, Hachette Book Group
1290 Avenue of the Americas, New York, NY 10104
Telephone: 1-800-222-6747 Fax: 1-800-477-5925

Acknowledgments

Each book is a team effort, and I am privileged to have a talented team behind me. Thank you to Alex Logan, my editor, whose keen eye makes each story I tell so much better, and all the folks at Forever who work tirelessly on my behalf. To my agent, Stefanie Lieberman, who has offered me unerring guidance from the beginning. And to my family for supporting me every step of the way, thank you.

Chapter 1

Avondale House
Dover, England
Summer 1820

When Lady Ophelia Volante smiled, she had a face that could start a war.

Or at the very least provoke duels, enthuse poets, and empty hothouses of extravagant bouquets. A face with the sort of mysterious radiance that would have sent Rubens and Botticelli and Titian scrambling for their brushes and paints.

The old masters were long in their graves. But Rose Hayward was very much alive and indecently pleased with the image that had emerged on the canvas under her careful brushstrokes. She was almost done, and the sultry, raven-haired, green-eyed goddess who stared back at her from a palette of decadent color was nothing short of breathtaking.

Rose gazed at the portrait for a moment longer before she set her brush aside. She narrowed her eyes critically at the work, but even as hard as she was on herself, she knew without a doubt that this was one of her best. A slow grin spread across her face.

"Is it done?" Lady Ophelia asked from where she

reclined, up on the dais. She sounded hesitant and hopeful all at once.

"Yes." Rose arched her back and rubbed her neck, stretching muscles that had tightened across her shoulders.

"Can I finally see it?"

Rose looked up at her. "I would like nothing more." She moved out from behind the canvas and made her way to the dais. She plucked an embroidered robe from the back of a chair on her way and climbed up to the long settee on the raised platform. Lady Ophelia had sat up and pushed her dark hair back over her shoulders, the self-consciousness that she had worn like a shield when she had first visited weeks ago nowhere to be seen.

Rose handed her the robe and extended her arm. The young woman reached for it and pulled herself slowly to her feet. She shifted slightly to gain her balance and then slid the robe over her naked shoulders before belting it neatly at the waist. Letting Ophelia lead, Rose assisted her down the steps until they were on level ground.

Lady Ophelia released her arm, and Rose retrieved her crutch from where it had been propped against the chair, passing it to her. They moved forward, Rose matching the speed of her steps to Ophelia's uneven gait until they had almost reached her easel.

"Close your eyes," Rose instructed. "Don't open them until I tell you to."

Ophelia gazed at her anxiously. "I'm nervous," she said suddenly.

"No, you were nervous when you first got here weeks ago," Rose said lightly. "Now you are...spectacular."

The young woman smiled shyly, and Rose was again mesmerized by her beauty.

"Thank you," Ophelia said.

Rose shook her head. "Truly, there is no need to thank me for doing something that I love to do. The pleasure was all mine."

"I don't mean the painting, though I am grateful for that. I meant for your kindness." She gestured to her crutch. "For treating me as a person and not a deformed cripple. For seeing me as something more."

Rose opened her mouth to retort and then thought better of it. "Let me show you how I see you," she said.

Ophelia held her gaze for a moment longer and then nodded.

"Close your eyes," Rose repeated, and this time, the young woman obeyed. She grasped Ophelia's hand and placed it on her arm, then guided her slowly forward until they stood in front of the canvas.

"Look," Rose commanded.

Ophelia took a deep breath and then slowly opened her eyes. She made a tiny noise in the back of her throat, and her fingers tightened around Rose's arm like a vise.

The nude woman on the canvas reclined on her side amid a bed of crimson satin, her skin like the finest ivory against the lush background. Her hair tumbled over her shoulders and across her generous breasts in a glorious curtain of midnight curls. One of her hands rested lightly on the exquisite curve of her hip, her good leg slightly bent and creating a shadow beneath the subtle swell of her abdomen. Her twisted, atrophied leg wasn't hidden but simply rested beneath the smooth lines of the other.

A soft smile curved her lips, her emerald gaze focused somewhere just beyond her audience. Sultry, seductive, almost dreamlike. As though she was thinking of a lover. Or perhaps reflecting on a sensual passage in the book that was cradled in her other hand. Or perhaps simply reveling in the sheer pleasure of being a woman, confident in her strength and power.

Ophelia's throat was working. "I don't...I can't...Oh God."

Rose glanced at the young woman and saw a tear slide down her cheek.

"That's not me," Ophelia whispered. "Is it?"

"That is every inch you," Rose replied firmly.

Ophelia let go of Rose's arm and stepped closer to the painting. She simply stared, and Rose retreated slightly, giving her whatever time she needed.

Finally the woman turned her head. "I don't know what to say."

Rose tilted her head. "Say that you'll look at this painting as often as you need to remind yourself exactly how beautiful you are."

"I never thought myself beautiful. But the woman in this painting..."

"Is you."

"But my leg—"

"Is simply a part of you."

"But—"

"But nothing."

"It's never been nothing to my family. To them it's a burden. An embarrassment at assemblies. An encumbrance during social calls. A liability in a ballroom."

Rose scoffed. "Clearly you've been dancing with the wrong men."

Ophelia laughed and sniffled at the same time, wiping the moisture from her cheeks. "No one has ever had the nerve to dance with me. Save for the poor dance instructor my parents paid to do so. Though he only lasted a week before he declared me hopeless and left."

"Then it is a good thing he left," Rose said coolly.

The young woman blinked. "Yes, I suppose it is." She looked back at the painting. "Can I take this with me?"

"I have a few details left to finish on the background," Rose told her. "And it will take some time to dry properly. I'll deliver it to you in London when it's ready. Discreetly, of course."

"I don't know how I can ever repay you for this."

"Don't fret about that. Your father has compensated me very generously."

Ophelia laughed again. "He paid you for summer painting lessons from the Haverhall School for Young Ladies so he and my mother could enjoy their vacation in Dover without having to shuffle me around."

Rose grinned. "Ah. Well, my sister might have been a little vague on who would be doing the painting when she made the arrangements with your father."

"I didn't want to come at all, you know. To Dover. To Avondale House. I didn't want to take lessons in anything." The smile slid from Ophelia's face, and her expression became sober. "But your sister would not take no for an answer."

"Clara has some good ideas from time to time." Rose was still smiling. "And duchesses always seem to get what they want."

"Did she know all along? That you would do...this when I got here?"

"Yes."

"But what if I hadn't..."

"Taken a chance? Trusted me to paint you as I did?" Rose raised a brow.

"Yes."

"Then I would have given you lessons. And you would

have painted other women as I have painted you. Because there is no one perfect version of beauty."

Ophelia studied her fingers where they gripped the top of her crutch. "Do you do this for others? Like me?"

"Sometimes. Though most of the time clients seek me out. Lovers, husbands, wives, friends."

Ophelia lifted her head and stared at the painting again. She reached out and ran a fingertip along the very edge of the canvas with reverence. "I never knew."

"That's the idea," Rose replied gently. "Each painting I do is a personal undertaking for each individual. Each work of art is not meant for public consumption, to be judged and evaluated, measured or mocked by people who do not understand. By those who fear difference because they refuse to open their minds."

The young woman was silent, lost in her thoughts and the image in front of her.

"Get dressed," Rose suggested. "Take as long as you like with your painting. No one will disturb you. I'll be downstairs when you're ready to return to town."

Ophelia nodded, still transfixed by her likeness on the canvas.

Rose silently slipped from the studio, careful to close the door behind her. She glanced out the tall window at the end of the hall, noting the heavy clouds that were starting to gather on the horizon. It would rain again soon, she knew, and the darkening skies would steal the light she needed to finish the last details of the crimson satin on that canvas. But it didn't matter.

Because her work here this afternoon was done.

Eli Dawes, fourteenth Earl of Rivers, looked up at the ominous sky as he trudged onward. The clouds that hung low and heavy had broken in places just enough to allow a meager amount of moonlight through the all-consuming blackness. He'd forgotten just how much it rained along this coast, but the seemingly continuous deluge since his arrival had certainly reminded him. It seemed a fitting welcome for a dead man.

Eli had always assumed that his name had been permanently etched in the long lists of soldiers who had died in the chaos and confusion of Waterloo. Just another man lying in the morass of wasted humanity, rife with lost dreams and identities. Except his supposed death hadn't been accepted. At least not by the army of solicitors who had worked for his late father, and who presently, by default, worked for him. Somehow they had managed to find Eli Dawes, long after the guns had fallen silent.

And now here he was, back on English soil, back to face a world and a life that had long since ceased to appeal. A new reality where his appetite for the things that had once seemed so important had vanished. And for the life of him, he couldn't begin to explain what had finally made him return. A stubborn sense of duty that had ingrained itself too deep to be excised or ignored? A sense of guilt that, as the months had slipped by into years, he hadn't been able to put ink to paper to let his father know that he was alive? Eli felt the side of his lip curl, his good eye narrowing.

From the beginning his father had violently opposed Eli's decision to fight. Railed at him, threatened to disown him, swore that the only way he would have Eli back was in a pine box. He'd been a disappointment to his father for as long as he could remember, and it seemed fitting that his return should be a final act of defiance.

Just as well the old earl had died. He would never have approved of what was left of Eli Dawes anyway.

The wind had shifted, and the briny tang of the sea became more pronounced, laced with the earthy scents of the vegetation that grew along the cliffs ahead. Eli passed the familiar bulk of the castle, its outline just visible by the light of the handful of torches set along its walls, their flames dancing in the wind, but the surrounding roads were deserted this time of night. There was no one to mark his passage, and he was glad of it.

Eli hadn't been sure of his exact destination until he had stood, his boots sunk in the fine sand of Ostend, and stared across the narrow expanse of sea. The idea of London was intolerable, and he'd discarded that out of hand. He would never go back. But Dover was close, and the earldom owned a far-flung estate perched on those chalky white cliffs, a good few miles from the town proper. It was a substantial manse crafted of solid, buff-colored stone, a stoic sentinel overlooking the sea. He recalled neat rows of glittering windows punctuating the tidy facade at precise intervals, and a rolling lawn divided in half by a wide, sweeping drive. He'd been there only a few times as a young man, and the memories that lingered were of wildness and isolation. Tedious then. Exactly what he wanted now. What he needed.

If the solicitors representing his estate could manage to locate a dead man in Belgium, there was no reason they could not manage to conduct all further communication with him by post. And whatever matters might arise that needed his personal attendance—well, those lawyers could come to him. Let the rumors make their way back to the city, as they inevitably would. At least Eli wouldn't be there to listen to them.

He glanced up at the sky again. The clouds were threatening to crowd back in and obscure what little light their absence had afforded, and a dispiriting dampness hung thick in the air. It would rain again, Eli knew, and soon. As if on cue, the sky lit and flickered, and a rumble of thunder rolled in the distance, heralding the arrival of another summer squall.

He hurried on, heading for the one place where he knew his arrival would go unmarked and his presence unheeded by anyone save a handful of servants.

Avondale.

Chapter 2

It wasn't the first time Eli had broken into this house.

The rain seemed to lessen slightly as he headed for the rear, toward the servants' entrance near the kitchens. The doors of the house would be bolted, but there was a window with a faulty latch, something he had taken advantage of a lifetime ago when he would stumble back from town in the dead of night after too much whiskey. Eli gazed up at the empty windows that lined the upper floors, relieved to find that the vast house was dark and silent. Avondale would be operating with only a skeleton staff—aside from maintaining the structure and grounds, there would be little to do.

Eli slipped his fingers under the edge of the low window and tapped on an outside corner while gently pushing upward. The window inched up slowly, though with a lot more resistance than he remembered. Above his head another roll of thunder echoed, and he cursed softly as the rain once again came down in sheets. Quickly he wrested the window the rest of the way up and swung himself over the sill, then lowered the window behind him. The abrupt cessation of the buffeting wind and the lash of rain was almost disorienting.

He stood for a long moment, trying to get his bearings and listening for the approach of anyone he might have disturbed. But the only sounds were the whine of the wind and the rattle of the rain against the glass. He breathed in deeply, registering the yeasty scent of rising dough and a faint whiff of pepper. It would seem nothing had changed in the years he'd been gone.

The kitchens were saved from complete blackness by the embers banked in the hearth on the far side. Eli set his pack on the floor and wrenched off his muck-covered boots, aware that he was creating puddles where he stood. A rivulet of water slithered from his hair down his back, and he shivered, suddenly anxious to rid himself of his sodden clothes. He left his boots on the stone floor but retrieved his pack and made his way carefully forward, his memory and the dim light ensuring he didn't walk into anything. Every once in a while, he would stop and listen, but whatever noise he might have made on his arrival had undoubtedly been covered by the storm.

He crept soundlessly through the kitchens and into the great hall. Here the air was perfumed with a potion of floral elements. Roses, perhaps, and something a little sharper. He skirted the expanse of the polished marble floor to the foot of the wide staircase that led to the upper floors. Lightning illuminated everything for a split second—enough for Eli to register the large arrangement of flowers on a small table in the center of the hall as well as the gilded frames of the portraits that he remembered lining the walls.

He shouldered his pack and slipped up the stairs, turning left into the north wing of the house. The rooms in the far north corner had always been his when he visited, and he was hoping that he would find them as he had left them. At the very least, he hoped there was a hearth, a bed, and something that resembled clean sheets, though he wasn't terribly picky at this point. His stocking feet made no sound as he advanced down the hallway, running his fingers lightly along the wood panels to keep himself oriented. Another blaze of lightning lit up the hallway through the long window at the far end, and he blinked against the sudden brightness.

There. The last door on the left. It had been left partially ajar, and he gently pushed it open, the hinges protesting quietly, though the sound was swallowed by a crash of thunder that came hard on the heels of another blinding flash. He winced and stepped inside, feeling the smooth, polished floor beneath his feet, his toes coming to rest on the tasseled edges of the massive rug he remembered. This room, like the rest of the house, was dark, though, unlike in the kitchen, there were no embers in the hearth he knew was off to his right somewhere. Against the far wall, the wind rattled the windowpanes, but it was somewhat muffled by the heavy curtains that must be drawn. Eli took a deep breath and froze. Something wasn't right.

The air around him was redolent with scents he couldn't immediately identify. Chalk, perhaps? And something pungent, almost acrid in its tone. He frowned into the darkness, slowly moving toward the fireplace. There had always been candles and a small tinderbox on the mantel, and he suddenly needed to see his surroundings. His knee unexpectedly banged into a hard object, and something glanced off his arm before it fell to the floor with a muffled thud. He stopped and bent down on a knee, his hands outstretched. What the hell had he hit? What the hell was in his rooms?

It hadn't shattered, whatever it had been. Perhaps it—

"Don't move."

Eli froze at the voice. He turned his head slightly, only to feel the tip of a knife prick the skin at his neck.

"I asked you not to move."

Eli clenched his teeth. It was a feminine voice, he thought. Or perhaps that of a very young boy, though the authority it carried suggested the former. A maid, then. Perhaps she had been up, or perhaps he had woken her. He supposed that this was what he deserved for sneaking into a house unannounced and unexpected. It was, in truth, his house now, but nevertheless, the last thing he needed was for her to start shrieking for help and summon the entire household. He wasn't ready to face that just yet.

"I'm not going to hurt you," he said clearly.

"Not on your knees with my knife at your neck, I agree." The knife tip twisted, though it didn't break the skin.

"There is a reasonable explanation." He fought back frustration. Dammit, but he just wanted to be left alone.

"I'm sure. But the silverware is downstairs," the voice almost sneered. "In case you missed it."

"I'm not a thief." He felt his brow crease slightly. Something about that voice was oddly familiar.

"Ah." The response was measured, though there was a slight waver to it. "I'll scream this bloody house down before I allow you to touch me or any of the girls."

"I'm not touching anyone," he snapped, with far more force than was necessary, before he abruptly stopped. Any of the girls? What the hell did that mean?

The knife tip pressed down a little harder, and Eli winced. He could hear rapid breathing, and a new scent reached him, one unmistakably feminine. Soap, he realized, the fragrance exotic and faintly floral. Something that one wouldn't expect from a maid.

"Who are you?" she demanded.

"I might ask the same."

"Criminals don't have that privilege."

Eli bit back another curse. This was ridiculous. His knees were getting sore, he was chilled to the bone and exhausted from travel, and he was in his own damn house. If he had to endure England, it would not be like this.

In a fluid motion, he dropped flat against the floor and rolled immediately to the side, sweeping his arm up to knock that of his attacker. He heard her utter a strangled gasp as the knife fell to the floor and she stumbled forward, caught off balance. Eli was on his knees instantly, his hands catching hers as they flailed at him. He pinned her wrists, twisting her body so it was she who was on the floor, on her back, with Eli hovering over her. She sucked in a breath, and he yanked a hand away to cover her mouth, stopping her scream before it ever escaped.

"Again," he said between clenched teeth, "I am not going to hurt you." Beneath his hand her head jerked from side to side. She had fine features, he realized. In fact, all of her felt tiny, from the bones in her wrists to the small frame that was struggling beneath him. It made him feel suddenly protective. As if he held something infinitely fragile that was his to care for.

Though a woman who brandished a knife in such a manner couldn't be that fragile. He tightened his hold. "If you recall, it was you who had me at a disadvantage with a knife at my neck. I will not make any apologies for removing myself from that position. Nor will I make any apologies for my presence at Avondale. I have every right to be here."

Her struggles stilled.

Eli tried to make out her features in the darkness, but it was impossible. "If I take my hand away, will you scream?"

He felt her shake her head.

"Promise?"

She made a furious noise in the back of her throat in response.

Very slowly Eli removed his hand. She blew out a breath but kept her word and didn't scream. He released her wrists and pushed himself back on his heels. He heard the rustle of fabric, and the air stirred as she pushed herself away. Her scent swirled around him before fading.

"You're not a maid," he said.

"What?" Her confusion was clear. "No."

"Then who are you?" he demanded. "And why are you in my rooms?"

"Your rooms?" Now there was disbelief. "I don't know who you think you are or where you think you are, but I can assure you that these are not your rooms."

Eli swallowed, a sudden thought making his stomach sink unpleasantly. Had Avondale been sold? Had he broken into a house that, in truth, he no longer owned? It wasn't impossible. It might even be probable. He had been away a long time.

"Is it my brother you are looking for? Is someone hurt?"

The question caught him off guard. "I beg your pardon?"

"Do you need a doctor?"

Eli found himself scowling fiercely, completely at a loss. Nothing since he had pushed open that door had made any sort of sense. "Who owns Avondale?"

"What?" Now it was her turn to sound stymied.

"This house—was it sold? Do you own it?"

"No. We've leased Avondale from the Earl of Rivers for years. From his estate now, I suppose, until they decide what to do with it." Suspicion seeped from every syllable. "Did you know him? The old earl?"

Eli opened his mouth before closing it. He finally settled on, "Yes."

"Then you're what? A friend of the family? Relative?"

"Something like that."

"Which one?"

Eli drew in a breath that wasn't wholly steady. He tried to work his tongue around the words that would forever commit him to this place. That would effectively sever any retreat.

He cleared his throat. "I am the Earl of Rivers."

Chapter 3

Rose laughed.

It was more of a wheeze than a laugh, more like the sound she had made the last time she'd taken a tumble off her horse and found herself flat on her back, stunned and gasping. She shouldn't be laughing, she knew, given the circumstances. But perhaps it was the release of the terror that had gripped her when she had first seen the intruder silhouetted in the doorway as lightning lit up the hall beyond. Perhaps it was from relief in the knowledge that whoever he might be, if he hadn't already assaulted her, it was unlikely he would do so now. He sounded quite sane. Or at least he had, until he had made his last, absurd statement.

"Is that supposed to be a joke?" she asked before she could think better of it.

"I'm sorry?" The rough, almost raspy quality of his voice that she had noticed earlier was more pronounced.

She sniffed in what she hoped was his direction but could smell only wet wool, horse, and the scent of a man in need of a bath. "I can't smell any alcohol." Or anything else that would make an otherwise rational man believe he was a ghost, for that matter.

"You think I'm drunk?" There was a clear edge to his words now.

"No, I don't think you are." She rubbed her wrists where he had held them, knowing they would be reddened. Though he hadn't hurt her. Merely...restrained her, with a strength that she should mark. Though the fear that ought to have accompanied that thought was oddly missing.

Regardless, Rose pushed herself farther away, sliding soundlessly over the rug. She could still hear the man breathing, felt the wet spots on the rug from the rainwater that must have dripped from his coat.

"And you're sure you're not in need of medical attention?" She considered the possibility that this man was confused or insensible from a head wound, though his speech and movements seemed to lack the clumsy quality that usually came with such. But he wouldn't be the first person to have shown up on Avondale's doorstep in the middle of the night looking for her brother to patch him up. And it wouldn't be the first time Rose had been stuck assisting.

The intruder made an indecipherable noise. "I do not require medical attention," he said, sounding both impatient and confused at once.

"Mmmm."

"You think I'm lying?"

"I think you might be confused. Because the Earl of Rivers is dead," Rose said evenly. She groped around her until she found what she was looking for. She grasped the paintbrush she'd dropped, pointy end out. It wasn't enough, but it was better than nothing if it came to it. Past experience had taught her that trauma to the head could sometimes make Harland's patients act in unpredictable ways. "His Lordship was old, his health weakened, and he passed away almost a year ago. You, on the other hand, feel neither old, weak, nor dead."

The intruder was silent, only the sound of the rain against the windows filling the space. "I suppose that's something," he finally muttered under his breath.

Rose felt something stir within her. Something peculiar was raising the hairs on the back of her neck and sending gooseflesh rippling over her skin.

I am the Earl of Rivers.

He had said that. Only once, in a simple, unapologetic way. But that was impossible. Because the Earl of Rivers had died without an heir, his only son killed at Waterloo.

Not killed, a voice whispered from deep within her memory. *Missing and presumed dead.* There had never been a body to bury.

Rose swallowed with difficulty and shook her head.

No. Eli Dawes could not have survived. He must be dead. There was no other reasonable explanation for a six-year absence, no other reason Dawes wouldn't have returned to London a triumphant war hero, ready to be lauded and admired, feted by fawning friends and worshipped by willing women. The Eli Dawes she had known would never have missed out on that sort of opportunity. Certainly not by choice.

"Who are you?" The question was out again before she could reconsider.

"I already told you."

"Say it again."

Another silence. Then, "Eli Dawes, fourteenth Earl of Rivers."

A sound she didn't recognize escaped from her. "Eli Dawes is dead." She was hot and cold all at once, her heart banging against her ribs almost painfully.

"I had truly intended to remain so, trust me. But it would seem that I severely underestimated my father's resolve and his resources. Or, more accurately, his solicitors'." She thought he might have been trying to inject some levity, but it fell flat.

"I don't believe you," she lied. Because a storm of old betrayals and bitterness was starting to brew. The instincts that were pricking at her scalp and sending shivers across her skin weren't wrong. The man in this room with her was exactly who he said he was.

The intruder said nothing, and thunder rumbled again, though it was more distant this time, signaling the departure of the storm.

"Eli Dawes would not have crept like a thief into a house on the very edge of England in the dead of night," she whispered defiantly. "Eli Dawes would have had a parade along Rotten Row to herald his return from the dead."

The man in the room with her still said nothing, though she heard a slight exhalation.

Rose suddenly needed to see. Needed to see the truth of his terrifying disclosure uttered in almost total blackness. Needed to set reality to light so that suspicion could be confirmed. Because if Dawes was alive, then perhaps—

Rose left that thought unfinished and lurched to her feet, untangling the soft fabric of her robe from around her legs. She staggered toward the hearth.

"What are you doing?" The question was abrupt, and she knew he'd heard her move.

"Lighting a damn candle," she hissed. "So if you are not truly who you say you are, I would suggest that you leave this house now, quickly and quietly, and we can pretend that this entire episode never happened."

"Don't." It was harsh.

"Don't what?" Rose had reached the hearth, and her fingers found what they were looking for with a faint clatter.

"Don't light that. Not yet."

Rose paused, unsure of what stilled her hand.

"Who are you?" The question was directed at her now.

"It doesn't matter."

"I think it does."

"Why?"

"Because you know me. Or at least who..." He trailed off.

"Finish what you were going to say." Rose wasn't sure if it was the bitterness that was making her so bold, but a recklessness such as she had never experienced was coursing through her.

"Who I used to be," he finished quietly.

Rose forced her fingers to relax on the handle of the paintbrush she was still holding in one hand, realizing the wood was biting into her flesh. "I know exactly who you are." She stared into the blackness before she rested her forehead against the mantel, trying to rein in her emotions. She would not spend another second of her life reliving what she had left behind so long ago.

Rose tried to fix an objective image of Eli Dawes in her mind, the way she had last seen him. His cocky, inherently smoldering gaze that alternated between green and brown, depending on the light. His golden hair falling over his forehead—artfully styled and deliberately framing a face with sharp lines reminiscent of a Nordic warrior. Or perhaps a fallen angel. He had always dressed impeccably, favoring dark colors that had accentuated his gilded perfection. His tailoring had flaunted a lean, lithe body, something he had been inordinately proud of.

He had been only the son of an earl, and one without even the privilege of a courtesy title, but he might as well have been a king. He had been the golden boy, society's beloved. Everyone had wanted a piece of Eli Dawes. Women had wanted him for their beds or their ballrooms or both, mesmerized by his devastating good looks and legendary charisma. Men had wanted him at their clubs and card tables, to bask in his compelling presence and undeniable wit. Everyone had gravitated toward him like a moth to an open flame, if only to experience, just for a moment, the splendor that was Eli Dawes.

And now he was back to pick up where he had left off.

Outside, the rain had lessened and the wind had died, and a more pronounced silence descended. A silence that became deafening the longer it stretched.

Rose squeezed her eyes shut and opened them again, wondering if she was simply caught up in the web of an improbable nightmare. "Tell me," she said abruptly, the bitterness suddenly erupting into something more vile as she put words to the earlier thought that she'd refused to acknowledge. "Is Anthony truly dead too? Or was a dramatic homecoming something that the two of you planned together? Some ploy with which to amuse yourselves?"

The quiet that followed was charged with expectant emotion so intense it seemed to become a living thing suspended in the air.

"Rose?" he whispered, almost inaudibly.

She had known it was he, recognized the truth for what it was, but it still felt as if she had been punched in the gut. "Very clever, Dawes."

His breath was coming in harsh gasps. He moved, and

Rose felt the air stir as he reached out. His hands came down awkwardly against her shoulder and her arm, gentling immediately as if he might draw her into an embrace. She stepped back, feeling her way along the mantel, afraid that if she let go of the cool marble, she might lose the only thing that seemed to be anchoring her to this reality.

"Rose—"

"Why did you come back?" Conflicting emotions were rising fast and furious and making it hard to think.

"I never intended to."

"Why?"

"It doesn't matter. Why are you in my house?" His voice was hoarse.

"Why am I in your house?" she repeated incredulously. "*This* is what matters to you right now? This is what's important? Your house?" She lifted her head and turned in what she thought was his direction. "Well, don't worry, Dawes, your coffers are being suitably compensated for my presence."

"That's not—" There was another long silence. "You've changed."

"You can't see me."

"I wasn't talking about your appearance."

"That would be a departure for you," Rose replied, failing to keep the derision from her voice.

"What is that supposed to mean?"

Rose made a rude noise. "Are you trying to be coy, Dawes? Because it's not a flattering trait."

"When did you become so cynical?"

"When I grew up. Had my eyes opened." She paused, a suffocating tightness constricting her chest. "I suppose I have you to thank for that in part."

He didn't respond.

Rose felt her lips thin. "You never answered my question. Is Anthony really dead?"

"Yes."

Rose stared into the nothingness, fiercely glad for the darkness. Because when the death of one's fiancé was undeniably confirmed, one should publicly display some sort of suitable emotion, no matter how much time had passed. Grief. Sorrow. Regret. Some sort of measure of unhappiness. Yet all she felt was...nothing. Whatever love or respect she had once harbored for Anthony Gibson, youngest son of the Viscount Crestwood, had been brutally extinguished by betrayal and humiliation long ago.

"I saw him die. It was quick." His words were strangely flat.

Rose tried to think of something suitable to say to that but came up with nothing. She wasn't sure if Dawes was trying to make her feel better. Or, more likely, himself.

"And Giles and Prevett?" she asked instead. "Are they really dead as well?" The other half of the dashing, fearless foursome who had once been the darlings of London society.

"Yes. Both of dysentery before they ever fired a gun," he replied in that same flat tone.

Rose knew propriety demanded she say something kind. Offer him some sort of condolence. But Rose couldn't seem to conquer the bitterness that had wrapped itself around her and drawn tight. She sighed and set the paintbrush aside with a muted clatter and reached for the tinderbox again.

"Wait."

She froze. She hadn't heard him move. Hadn't heard him come so close.

"I'm done listening to you, Dawes," she said. The scent of the outdoors and wool and horse swirled around her again.

"I'm not…Just wait…"

Rose frowned at his unsteady words. They were a far cry from the confident, cavalier arrogance she remembered so clearly. "What do you want?" she demanded.

"Do you still have your knife?"

Rose sneered. "What, you're afraid I'll skewer you?"

"You tried once."

She blew out a disgusted breath. "It wasn't a knife. It was the end of a paintbrush."

She heard him mutter something unintelligible under his breath. His hand came up to graze the length of her arm before it found her wrist again. His fingers closed over her skin, his grasp warm and steady.

"I'm different," he said roughly. "From the man I once was."

"Of course you are. If the magnificent and insatiable Eli Dawes cut a swath through the boudoirs of London society before, imagine what a handful of war medals and an earldom will do for you now. You'll have women crawling about in your bed the way a hound has fleas." She didn't even try to hide her contempt.

Dawes's fingers suddenly tightened around her wrist, and before she understood what he was doing, he pulled her toward him, pressing her palm against the side of his face with his own. "Rose, please," he whispered.

"What the hell are you doing, Dawes?" Rose tried to pull away, but he held her firm, his other hand coming to rest heavily against the small of her back, keeping her securely against him. She had stood like this in his embrace many times before, she thought suddenly, the vivid, unwanted memories intruding. Only then they had been on a dance floor in some grand society ballroom, under glittering chandeliers in the middle of glittering crowds, everyone around them staring. Because people always stared when Eli Dawes danced with a woman, his vibrancy like a thrilling vortex that no one could ignore. She remembered the feeling of giddy happiness that had filled her then, secure as she was in her place in the world and secure in the care of a man she'd thought had been a good friend.

She'd been an idiot.

Rose blinked in the darkness, realizing that Dawes had never answered her. Instead he had stilled completely. His palm, pressed against the back of her hand, was rough and calloused, warming her fingers where they were trapped against his face. Dampness was starting to bleed through her robe from the front of his sodden coat. An occasional drop of icy water dripped from the ends of his hair and down her wrist.

Rose shivered, and she tried again to snatch her hand away.

The earl's hand tightened on hers, pressing her palm more firmly against his jaw. "Not yet." His voice was raw. "I need you to… You should know…"

She froze, comprehension suddenly dawning. She slid her hand down just fractionally, and Dawes made a muffled noise just before his own fingers dropped, releasing her. She could have removed her hand. She didn't. Because beneath her palm there was no longer the clean, smooth line that should have delineated the masculine cut of his jaw. The skin was textured and uneven under the pads of her fingers as she moved them upward toward his hairline. The skin there was more of the same, and she traced the subtle ridges over the bone where his eyebrow should have been. He'd been injured. Badly.

Rose closed her eyes. Absurd, she knew, because she couldn't see anything anyway, but she wanted to create a picture in her mind through touch. She did this often when she painted, as if her hands could memorize the object and help reproduce it on canvas in a way mere sight could not.

She raised her other hand to cup the opposite side of his jaw. This side was as she remembered him. Smooth skin, if a little rough with stubble. A faint hollow along the side of his cheek that denoted the contour between his strong jaw and high cheekbones.

The fingers of both her hands skimmed over his temples, testing the difference, coming to rest softly over his closed eyelids. Or at least the eyelid that remained. Beneath her touch, where his left eye should have been, was only more of the thickened, ridged skin that characterized a portion of his face below.

Rose kept her eyes closed and slid her hands back down along the side of his face, tracing the underside of his jaw and neck until they reached the collar of his coat. Dawes hadn't moved, his breathing shallow and rapid.

Rose opened her eyes. Her fingers still rested against his neck, and she could feel his pulse jumping. "And this happened at Waterloo?"

"Yes." He didn't elaborate.

She dropped her hands, and as she did so, he removed his hand from her lower back. She was left feeling strangely adrift in the darkness. "Why did you do that?" she asked, ignoring her own rapid heartbeat. "Ask me to touch you like that?"

"I didn't...didn't want to startle you. With my appearance."

Rose shook her head, trying to sort out a host of emotions that were darting through her, some too quick to identify. Pity threatened, but she squashed it as fast as it rose. He didn't deserve her sympathy. Sadness, perhaps, though for whom Rose couldn't say. So instead she settled on irritation because it was easy and familiar and fit well with her lingering bitterness. She brushed by him and felt along the mantel, finding the tinderbox and a candle.

This time, Dawes did not stop her. She lit all three candles before finally turning back to him and meeting his gaze for the first time.

Perhaps he hadn't been wrong to warn her, Rose acknowledged briefly. Because only half of the fallen angel's visage remained as she remembered. The other half of his face was a twisted, distorted landscape of scar tissue, faded with time, but leaving no doubt that his injury had been severe. The sort of injury that men do not always survive.

The scars had obscured the hollow where his left eye had been, giving him an almost piratical appearance. His left ear, where it was exposed, was mostly gone, ropes of discolored skin twisting across his jaw and down his neck, disappearing under the collar of his coat. His lips had remained unscathed, though the tightened flesh of his ruined cheek tugged at the left side of his mouth in a way that made it look as if he had just found something amusing.

"Well, then," Rose said, her verification of what she had already seen with her hands complete. "It really is you." She reached for one of the candles and glanced back in the direction of the door, considering. "I suppose I need to find you somewhere to sleep for the night. You do, after all, own this damn pile, while we are only paying guests."

A single hazel eye blinked at her. "What?"

"I'm assuming you intend to stay at Avondale. But there's no furniture in this room any longer save for what you see." She waved her hand dismissively in the direction of the dozen easels and tables that had transformed the space from a bedroom into her art studio. "Whatever was here was put into the attics and can be retrieved if that is your wish. I'll let my brother know you're back in the morning. If you have a problem with us being here, you can speak to him about the terms of our contract with your estate."

She suddenly needed to get away from him. To get away from the man who was standing in front of her, who had, in a sliver of time, torn open a festering tumult of feelings and emotions that she'd believed healed.

The earl frowned, a blond eyebrow drawing low. "What?"

"Did whatever damaged your face damage your wits as well, Dawes?" Rose asked, keeping a desperate hold on her irritation. "You can't sleep here. And whatever business you have with my family can wait until morning."

He stared at her.

"You should know that almost all the bedchambers are occupied, but I believe the room in the far southeast corner is—"

"That's it?"

Now it was Rose's turn to scowl. "What's it?"

"This doesn't..." He trailed off, but not before he gestured faintly at his face. "Don't you have anything to say about..."

She blinked. "What?"

"My face. Most people cringe. Or look away. Or stare in disgust." The words were almost belligerent, and Rose realized he was challenging her.

The utter, complete irony of this very moment was breathtaking. "Did you actually believe that your looks would be what was important to me at this moment?" she managed in a strangled voice. "Or at any moment?"

Eli didn't respond, giving her his answer.

She took a step toward him, fury obliterating her earlier bitterness. Waves of wrath coursed through her, making it hard to speak. "I will only say this once. I am not you, Eli Dawes," she hissed before she took a deep breath, trying to regain control. She was better than this.

She cleared her throat and started over, tamping down her ire with effort. "I regret whatever pain you may have suffered, my lord," she said precisely. "And any discomfort that you currently endure. My condolences on the death of your father."

Her fingers were still wrapped around the small candlestick, and with horror she realized that they were shaking. She backed away toward the door and out into the hall.

"Welcome home, Lord Rivers," she said and closed the door behind her.

Chapter 4

The smoke swirled around Eli, thick and noxious.

His eyes burned mercilessly; if there was a silver lining, it was that they hid the terrifying sight of the enemy thundering toward him. They were coming for the guns, Eli knew. Or what was left of them. Around him, shattered men and horses lay in piles, like rag dolls tossed carelessly across the field. The men still living ignored the carnage and worked feverishly, feeding the guns. Back and forth Eli ran, from the munitions cart to the cannon, from the cannon to the cart, slipping occasionally on blood-slicked grass but never stopping. There was no time to stop.

Another explosion, another cloud of smoke, another round of shot hurled toward an enemy that had pushed ever closer. The ground shook with French hooves, and the very air around him compressed and expanded with answering artillery. And then, suddenly, a horn sounded in the distance, and the thunder receded. Eli collapsed against the side of the cart, fighting for breath.

The painfully young gunner looked at him, tears from the smoke or relief or both streaming from his red-rimmed eyes and cutting tracks down his blackened face. They had been unusually blue, his eyes, the color of a summer sky washed pale by heat. Eli had never forgotten them.

"Frogs're running away," the gunner had gasped, his voice hoarse from shouting.

Why? Why had the horses and the men coming for them been called back? Eli had listened, trying to understand, but there had been only stillness. A terrible, empty stillness, sinister against the muted fighting farther across the plain.

The horn again. The boom of French guns. The unmistakable sound of round shot shrieking through the air toward them.

Eli jerked awake.

He stared motionless at the ceiling for a gut-wrenching, soul-stealing moment before he remembered where he was. It had been a long time since those memories had come back to haunt him in his dreams. He closed his one good eye again, telling himself it was a blessing that he had woken when he had.

Because it only got worse from there.

In the quiet of the morning, the faint melody of birdsong drifted in through the window, and somewhere in the bowels of the house a pail clanged as hearths were emptied and cleaned. Perhaps it wasn't too late to collect a horse and ride back the way he had come. Slip out the back and disappear again, and let his father's solicitors continue to deal with the paperwork and the processes that had already been set in motion.

Eli groaned and flung his arm over his eyes. A dull throbbing had started in his head, and his stomach growled with hunger. He would have to get up sooner or later, either way.

He wondered if anyone save Rose was even aware he was here yet.

Rose Hayward.

The fates were laughing long and loud. Of all the people who could have been planted in his path on this journey home, in this resurrection of duty and conscience and reconciliation, of all the people he could have faced first as the new Earl of Rivers...

She was the only woman he had never been able to forget. And she had never been his to remember in the first place.

The last time he had seen Rose Hayward, youngest daughter of the dizzyingly wealthy Baron Strathmore, she'd still been engaged to Anthony Gibson, the man Eli had once considered a friend. Neither Rose nor her two siblings had ever made more than a rare appearance at what might be considered fashionable society events, and until Gibson's sudden and unexpected courtship of Rose, Eli had known only what gossip he'd heard whispered behind fluttering fans on the dance floor at Almack's or behind clouds of smoke in the back rooms of White's.

That the slight, boyishly figured, plain-faced Rose Hayward was a wallflower. A bluestocking. Educated far beyond what was acceptable, though artistically gifted. Tolerated at the fringes of society only because of her charismatic and wildly popular parents. Courted only for her substantial dowry.

Anthony himself hadn't been very forthcoming about his betrothed, though Eli had known that Gibson's father, the viscount, was suffering financially. Eli had avoided asking indelicate questions that his friend had made clear he had no interest in answering. Being from a titled family, after all, did not come without its sacrifices, and Eli had naively assumed Rose Hayward was one of them.

Until the inevitable moment when Anthony had introduced Eli to his affianced.

And Eli had been instantly, irrevocably captivated.

For Rose Hayward was not like any other woman Eli had ever met. She possessed a cutting wit and a brilliant mind that fascinated him. She'd made him laugh too many times to count. Kept him on his toes with their verbal sparring. Startled him with her insights and knowledge of politics and history.

The rules of society dictated that Eli should have been suitably scandalized, but he had been too busy trying to subtly seize every opportunity to accompany Anthony and his dark-eyed, red-haired fiancée. He stole as many minutes and as many dances and as many meals with Rose as he could, and each time he left her, his hunger to see her again only grew.

He'd quizzed her on her artistic interests and discovered that they shared a keen proclivity for Renaissance art. Without a second thought, he'd given her the keys to his private collection, with instructions to his staff that she be allowed in whenever she liked, whether or not he was in residence. Though he had made sure he found himself in residence a great deal when he knew Rose Hayward would be visiting.

Occasionally she would sketch the works on his walls. More often, she would discuss and debate their provenance with a passion and intelligence he found breathtaking. And sometimes she would simply sit and gaze upon the canvases in a reverent silence, unaware that it was she who shone brightest in that room full of masterpieces.

Eli had learned that she was fiercely loyal to her family and to those for whom she cared. And that included Anthony Gibson. That she had been head over heels in love with Gibson would have been clear to even the greatest of fools. And

Eli wasn't a fool. He found himself, however, desperately jealous and aware that, if he continued like this, if he continued to covet a woman who could never be his, he would lose whatever shreds of honor he still had left.

So he'd distanced himself from Anthony and Rose and spent more time with Giles and Prevett, drinking and carousing to excess. He tried to find distraction in the lusty, voluptuous women whose company he'd once reveled in. His decadent lifestyle had become positively debauched as he'd thrown himself into assignations with bored widows, beautiful actresses, and accomplished courtesans. Women who knew all the lines of the licentious script that played out over and over with the scintillating extravagance of London society as the stage. Women who were exciting in bed and immediately forgettable out of it.

And none of them had ever made him forget Rose.

But all of that happened long before Eli had discovered that a man's character defined his fate. That was before they had all ridden off to war without a backward glance. Before he had understood the repercussions of his ignorance and self-absorption.

Before he understood that of all the regrets that had risen to plague him, Rose would be the greatest.

⌒

It was a half hour later when Eli finally dressed and stepped out of the plush bedroom he had sought refuge in last night. No one had come to disturb him, which suited him just fine, though he mourned the absence of water to wash. He felt rumpled and filthy and like an imposter in his own home. In his own life, really. All the things that surrounded him at this moment—the lavish wealth, the sumptuous decor, the presence of efficient servants—were things he had once taken for granted. Expected. Demanded, even. Now that he was back, that old lifestyle seemed to sit uncomfortably on his skin. Like an ill-fitting coat that chafed and pulled and left him feeling out of sorts.

Perhaps he had recognized that his return to England might be like this. Perhaps that was a reason he had chosen Avondale—to afford himself the seclusion and the time to acclimate to a life he'd left behind. Though that possibility had been dashed spectacularly by the presence of the Hayward family, and now he was stuck here with London as his only option.

Unless, of course, he put his tail between his legs and slunk back to Belgium. But that would be the action of a coward, and Eli still had some tattered remnants of pride. He only hoped they would be enough.

Eli had dressed in clothes that were still muddy and damp, hunger clawing at his empty stomach. He made his way down the long hall and descended the wide staircase but, mercifully, encountered no one along the way. Retracing his steps of the night before, he bypassed the opulent dining room, where breakfast had always been served, and headed straight for the kitchens. He had no interest in another difficult conversation with another Hayward. No wish to face Rose and her distrust. But servants, in his experience, would obey orders and ask no questions. They'd gossip later, of course, but he wouldn't have to listen to it.

The scent of fresh-baked bread still lingered in the air as he got closer, but more important was the blessed sound of silence. If he was lucky, the kitchens would be deserted. He could get what he'd come for and make a quick escape. Looking over his shoulder to verify no one had followed him, he hurried down the narrow hall and rounded the corner.

It took a moment for it to sink in that there was a crowd of people gathered around the large butcher block table. It took another moment, a moment in which he could have fled but remained frozen with indecision, before every single one of those people turned and stared at him directly.

Eli flinched and pivoted out of habit, presenting the side of his face that was not ruined and sliding farther into the shadow of the hall. He fought the sudden and overwhelming urge to spin and retreat the way he had come. Part of him wondered if it might not be more expedient to throw himself off the nearest cliff.

"Eli?" He heard his name from somewhere in the back of the knotted group, which seemed to be made up of women. Young women, to be precise, varying degrees of interest in their expressions.

He had woken from one nightmare only to walk into another.

There was a commotion near the back of the group, and an elderly woman separated herself and crossed the worn flagstones with an astonishing swiftness. Eli suddenly found himself caught in an embrace, looking down at a head of silver hair knotted neatly at the back. A second woman appeared at his side, this one taller but no less fervent in her embrace as she wrapped her arms around his middle as well.

"Aunt Theo?" he mumbled through his confusion. "Aunt Tabitha?"

"I can't believe you're really here," the shorter and rounder of the two said into his still-damp coat, her voice somewhat muffled.

Eli's memory struggled to reconcile the women currently squeezing the life out of him with the aunts he had barely known before he had left England. He'd met them only a handful of times growing up and hadn't given them much more than perfunctory recognition. He hadn't given them even a thought when he'd decided to come to Avondale. That being the case, he was quite certain he didn't deserve the affection that they were currently showering upon him.

They were his father's sisters, both widowed, both having chosen to live out their lives in the quiet, remote solitude of Dover. Or at least that was what Eli had assumed. But glancing up at the group of young ladies watching them expectantly, he saw that his aunts seemed to be in the thick of whatever the hell he had walked into.

"I never believed you were dead," the taller, Tabitha, sniffed as she pulled back to look at him, her cheeks flushed.

"Nor I," Lady Theodosia declared, extricating herself from the bulk of his coat to join her sister. "I never gave up hope." She gave his arm a squeeze and swiped at her eyes, which seemed to have become misty. "When our dear Rose told us of your return this morning, I knew our prayers had been answered."

"We are so thankful and happy that you're home." Tabitha's faded blue eyes skimmed over his face, his clothes, and back up, and Eli braced himself for the pity that he knew was coming. He knew exactly what they were thinking. He knew exactly what they were going to say. God knew he had heard it too many times to count—

"But you need a bath," Lady Theodosia tutted, her nose wrinkling in her round face.

Eli blinked. A bath?

"Exactly what I was thinking," Tabitha replied, nodding. "And a decent change of clothes. It looks and smells as if you've been traveling as a goatherd for a month, dearie."

"I imagine he's hungry," Theo commented.

"I'm sure he is. Goat tastes terrible."

"Not necessarily. If you spice the meat properly, it's quite palatable."

"If you put enough spice on crickets, they'd be palatable too," Tabitha sniffed. "Regardless, I can arrange to have a plate put together right away. Eggs, perhaps. And bacon. No goat meat."

"Or crickets."

"But perhaps not before we get him some hot water and soap," Tabitha continued.

"Agreed. And don't forget about clothes. He can't go wandering around here in a state of dishabille. Or whatever it is he's wearing now."

"What about a haircut?"

"If he's so inclined."

Eli was trying to follow the rapid exchange, but he hadn't quite managed to get much beyond the word *goat*. Thus far, he felt a little as if he had emerged into some alternate plane of reality where nothing was what he'd expected. He started, realizing that both women were beaming at him. Theo wiped at her eyes a second time, but not before she gave his arm another squeeze.

"I—" Eli started before realizing he had no idea what he wanted to say.

"Good heavens, dearie. Excuse my rudeness." Theo tucked herself firmly against Eli's side. "Come, I'll introduce you to the students."

"Students?"

"Why, yes." She paused. "Rose said that you were aware Avondale was leased."

"I am aware. Picnics by the seaside have ever been fashionable. I can see the allure for old Strathmore and his wife." Eli was aware that his words had a somewhat derisive tone, but this entire situation was untenable.

"The baron and baroness died three years ago, dear. Harland is the baron now." Tabitha patted his arm.

Eli cursed silently. "Rose didn't say anything."

"She doesn't often discuss it. None of the Hayward siblings do."

"But you should know that Avondale isn't leased for picnics," Theo added. "It's leased by the Haverhall School for Young Ladies."

"What?" Years ago, the Haverhall School, owned by the Strathmore family, had been the most expensive, prestigious finishing school for young ladies in London. Rose's sister, Clara, had been the headmistress. Even Eli had heard of it. Clearly it was still in operation.

"Haverhall leases Avondale for the duration of its exclusive summer program. There are a dozen students staying at the house this summer. Our Rose teaches the art program." Theo beamed up at him.

Eli hadn't walked into a nightmare; he had walked past that nightmare and directly into hell. The dull throbbing in his head suddenly became more acute. This was the last thing he needed. He was regretting his decision to return to England more and more with every passing minute.

"They are such lovely, talented young ladies," Tabitha added. "They will all want to meet you—"

"No," he snapped.

His aunts drew back.

It would appear that his years of self-inflicted solitude had stripped him of his charm and turned him into a boor. Eli took a deep breath and tried to soften his response. "That is, I do not wish to interrupt . . . whatever it is you are doing here."

"Merely casting," Tabitha supplied, giving him a long look. "Some lovely bivalve and echinoid specimens we collected earlier from the beach."

His aunt might as well have been speaking a different language for all the sense that made. "I thought you said these were Haverhall students."

His aunts both looked at him askance. "They are."

Not that Eli professed to know much about London schools for the daughters of the elite, but he was under the impression that Haverhall focused primarily on polishing one's deportment.

"Then what? Their dance instructor was late this morning? The French teacher delayed?"

He saw his aunts exchange a look that he couldn't decipher.

"No, dearie, no one was late," Theo told him.

"We just decided to go in a...different direction this morning," Tabitha added.

That still made little sense to Eli, but he was not in the frame of mind to draw out this conversation any further. What did it matter to him what Haverhall's students did or didn't do? So long as he could avoid them, he might just survive this.

He glanced over his aunts' heads at the scene in the kitchen. Only the young lady closest to them was still looking in his direction. She had dark hair and wore a faded moss-green dress that matched her eyes. Her sleeves were pushed up to her elbows and her hands and forearms covered in what looked like plaster dust. Every other student, however, had already turned back to the project that lay on the table's surface, fine bivalve specimens pressed into a plaster tray apparently far more interesting than his sudden appearance.

He knew he should be vastly relieved.

"The girls really would love to meet you," Theo said, tugging at his arm slightly. "Let us—"

"No." At least he hadn't shouted this time, but he'd rather poke out his remaining eye with a fork than subject himself to the horrified reactions of a dozen delicate sensibilities when they were presented with what he had become. Eli extracted himself from his aunt's side.

"Truly, you're not interrupting—"

"I said no. Thank you."

"Very well," Tabitha said. "Would you like to eat here? Or perhaps you would appreciate more privacy? I suspect that there will still be food laid out in the dining room, or I can arrange to have something sent up—"

"I'll look after myself."

"Very well," Tabitha said. She gave him a quick embrace again and stepped away from his side. "If you need anything at all, you just have to ask. This is your home, after all."

"Yes, and we should plan a proper dinner tonight to celebrate your return," Theo said, clasping her hands together, her eyes sparkling. "We can invite—"

"Never." It came out far harsher than he'd intended. "There will be no plans on my behalf. Not tonight. Not ever. I do not wish to see anyone."

Lady Theodosia tipped her head, the creases around her lips deepening. "Of course. My apologies."

Eli's teeth clenched. Jesus. He was still barking at two elderly women who had shown him only kindness. Bloody hell, but he didn't like himself very much right now.

He backed away. "It was...good to see you." His tongue seemed to stumble over the words, and he didn't wait for a response before he turned and fled.

Chapter 5

The late morning light was perfect.

Rose would have the crimson satin finished on Lady Ophelia's painting within the hour, a task that could be executed in blissful solitude. And for that luxury she was grateful. It had been this painting to which Rose had retreated after the sudden reappearance of Eli Dawes. It had been this painting that had reminded Rose of what was important. What was important to each and every one of the people she privately painted, and in those numbers there was a great deal of reassurance to be found.

When Rose's parents had died, they had left behind not the successful export empire that everyone believed they possessed, but one that was secretly teetering on the edge of collapse. Bad luck and bad investments had left a once-profitable shipping empire nothing but a rotting hulk of its former glory, listing badly and threatening to go under at a moment's notice. At the time the Haverhall School for Young Ladies, willed to Rose's older sister, Clara, had been the only thing that had kept the creditors at bay and the Haywards from facing complete and total financial ruin.

While her brother had struggled to rebuild the fleet and Clara had managed to keep the school running, Rose had done what she could to bring some much-needed cash to the family coffers in the best way she knew how. She began taking commissions for portraits—usually from the nouveau riche and landed gentry who, despite their astounding wealth, were unable to secure the services of the more fashionable artists who pandered to the aristocratic elite. And while Rose couldn't charge as much money as her male counterparts for a traditional rendering, she could charge obscene amounts of money for a well-executed boudoir portrait.

It had grown over the last few years, her covert business of scandalous paintings. Sometimes it was young women like Ophelia whom she painted. Often it was a wife or a mistress she painted at the behest of a husband or lover, but not always. Occasionally it was a man. A couple. Or a trio. It mattered little to Rose. Regardless of her subject, her discretion was absolute.

The financial pressure had lessened of late—Harland had managed to turn the export business around and was gaining ground, and Haverhall was as popular and prestigious as ever—but demand for Rose's skill and discretion had not lessened. If anything, it had increased, the relative privacy Avondale afforded always bringing an influx of business. The added work filled her days and brought her a deep satisfaction.

And kept her from dwelling on things she did not wish to dwell on.

Like Eli Dawes.

I'm different from the man I once was.

Well, his appearance was certainly different, she'd give him that. When Rose had first met Eli Dawes, she'd already written him off as a shallow, self-absorbed rogue. Dismissed him as a ladies' man, interested only in his next drink or his next conquest.

But the more time she had spent with him, the more he had surprised her. He'd proven to be funny, attentive, and courteous. And far more intelligent than he pretended to be under that slick, gilded exterior.

And of course, there had been his astonishing collection and knowledge of Renaissance art, both of which he had shared with her without hesitation. His collection had drawn them together in a manner that no amount of dinner parties and soirees ever could have. His gallery had become their refuge—a place where he'd seemed to delight in her opinions, asking clever questions and arguing enthusiastically, which had pleased her to no end. She'd never once felt compelled to watch her words around him. Rose had genuinely liked and admired Eli Dawes, until the day he had proven himself no better than Anthony Gibson.

But she would not dwell on that. It had already taken up far too much of her life.

Rose glanced up at the raised dais in front of her, where the empty settee was draped with satin, and picked up her brush again.

Focus on what is important, she told herself. *Focus on the things that matter.*

"Can I come in?"

Rose's brush froze, and she kept her eyes on the swath of crimson spilling across her canvas. *No*, she wanted to snap. Instead she smothered the resentment that suddenly threatened to choke her. "You own this house, Lord Rivers," she replied steadily without looking up. "You can go where you like."

"Lady Tabitha told me about your parents. I'm sorry." His voice had that same unfamiliar roughness she had heard the night before, and Rose realized that it was likely from the damage to his neck. "You should have said something last night."

She studied the tip of the brush's bristles and the brilliant color that clung to each hair. "Why?"

"I just…Because I would have offered my condolences sooner."

Rose's jaw clenched before she forced it to relax. "The packet they were on was lost in an Atlantic storm crossing to Boston."

He was silent for a long minute, and Rose had almost begun to hope that he would leave. Instead she heard the sound of booted feet advancing into the room. In a single movement, Rose set her brush aside and reached for the gauzy muslin that was tucked at the top of her easel, which she pulled down to conceal the canvas. She heard him, rather than saw him, stop just short of her easel.

"When are you leaving for London, Lord Rivers?" she asked, pleased with how civil that sounded. Reckless, knee-jerk emotion never helped anything. Her sister was forced to remind Rose of that often.

"I'm not."

Rose glanced up sharply.

Dawes was standing beyond her easel, watching her. He had angled himself slightly, the scarred side of his face turned away from her, and she wondered if he had done so out of habit. He'd bathed; it was evident from the slight flush to his face, the dampness of his hair, and the scents of lemon and sandalwood that reached her nose. He'd also found clean clothes somewhere, and the simple, if well-made, garments revealed that, along with his voice, his form had also changed. Even under his coat she could tell his chest was thicker, his biceps and forearms hinting at strength that had never been there before. The new, defined muscling in his legs was much more obvious beneath his buff breeches. It was not at all the svelte, fashionable physique of a ton gentleman he had once taken such pride in. Now he looked more like a man who earned his living on the docks or in the fields.

Rose remembered how he had held her captive last night with very little effort, and she resisted the sudden urge to rub her wrists. "You're not going to London today? Or you're not—"

"I'm not going to London ever. I plan to make Avondale my home." He crossed his arms over his substantial chest. "Permanently."

Well, hell. The last thing Rose wanted was to have to endure his presence for the remainder of the summer. "Have you forgotten you're an earl now? A soon-to-be officially dead one in the courts as I hear it, which is something you may wish to correct with alacrity. I think you'll discover you have a great many responsibilities, not the least of which is your seat in—"

"Please don't lecture me about my responsibilities. I am well aware."

"Of course." Rose looked down at her skirts, reminding herself that, above all, she did not need to pick a fight. She just needed him to leave. Forever, preferably.

"What are you painting?" he asked.

"Nothing that would interest you." Rose slid from her stool.

"You're wrong."

She managed not to scoff. "What do you want, Daw—Lord Rivers?" she asked.

"Dawes is fine, Rose. It's what you've always called me."

"What do you want, Lord Rivers?" she repeated deliberately.

He sighed. "I wanted to see you. To make sure you're all right."

"Well, you've seen me." She put her hands on her hips. "And I can assure you I am perfectly fine. Anything else?"

She held his gaze without wavering until it was Dawes who looked away, in the direction of the window. "I wanted to apologize," he said finally.

Rose stared at him. She hadn't expected that. "Apologize?"

"Yes," he replied tightly.

Rose's fingers curled, her nails biting into her palms. Did he honestly think he could simply waltz in here, utter a few words, and be absolved of what he had done? Fury started to curl through her chest, and she forced herself to take deep breaths before she spoke. "The only one who requires an apology from you is the kitchen maid who had to clean up the mud and mess you left inside the kitchen window last night."

"Rose." His voice sounded off.

Rose took another deep breath, but she was losing the battle against the anger that was still rising. "And just what, exactly, is it that you believe you need to apologize for?"

The earl looked back at her, his gaze holding hers. "Don't make this harder."

"Harder?" Her tenuous hold on her composure suddenly threatened to dissolve. "Of course. God forbid Eli Dawes should be inconvenienced."

"That's not—" He hesitated before he plunged on, as if he'd spent a great deal of time rehearsing his words. "Anthony did not treat you with the respect you deserved."

"What?"

"He told me what he had done. After we left London."

"After you all fled London, you mean."

"I—" He stopped again, looking ill at ease.

"You what? You didn't want to take responsibility for what you left behind? Anthony ran before I discovered everything. Before I could break our engagement. And you went right along with him."

"Rose, I didn't know then. I didn't know what he was doing."

"So now you're here to apologize on his behalf? It's a wee bit late for that, don't you think, given that he's dead?" A mocking quality had crept into her words that she seemed powerless to prevent.

"No. I'm apologizing for my...actions. Or my lack of them."

"Good heavens. Are you going to try to convince me that you found a conscience on the battlefields of Belgium?"

"That's not fair," he snapped, stepping closer to her.

"Things are rarely fair, Lord Rivers," she snapped back. "But believe me when I tell you I'm much more adept at recognizing that now."

"Rose—"

"I've moved on. You should too. You need not concern yourself further with my welfare, but there are others who are owed an apology."

His face was like granite. "I don't care about others, but I care about you. I will always be concerned with your welfare. I once considered you a...friend. I'd still like to."

"A friend?" Rose felt something give way deep within her. It was suddenly an effort to draw a full breath. She should stop, she knew. This conversation, this airing of bitter hurts, was something that didn't need to take place. Not now, not ever.

In her head she had already dealt with the betrayal and broken trust the best way she knew how and survived. Nothing would be changed, nothing worthwhile would come from rehashing the past, but her heart seemed incapable of listening to good sense.

"Very well, let's do this, then, Dawes. Because once, I thought you were a friend too. So let's put all our cards on the table, shall we? Speak the truth. The way *friends* would do."

She brushed past him and stalked toward the open door, then closed it with more force than was required. She had no interest in letting anyone overhear this conversation. She went to a heavy chest that sat in the corner, full of her painting supplies. With deliberate motions she opened the trunk, extracted an assortment of supplies, and withdrew a flat wooden box, the sort that might have at one time housed a pistol.

She straightened and returned to where the earl stood. "Anthony's oblivious if well-meaning mother gave this to me," she said, relieved at how even her voice sounded. Rose released the catch on the side and flipped the box open. In it lay a collection of yellowed papers, folded to form envelopes of sorts and tied with a brown ribbon. "My love letters to her son. Or at least that was what she thought they were. After we received word that he'd been killed, she wanted me to have them back. To remember him by."

Dawes was watching her warily. "I don't understand."

"No?" Rose fingered one of the papers. "You don't recognize them?"

"You're not making sense," he said. "I would never have read his personal correspondence with you. Certainly not love letters. Why the hell would you think I would recognize them?"

"Because some of their contents are addressed to you."

Dawes was frowning fiercely. "I have no idea what you're talking about."

"You really don't remember these?"

The earl threw up his hands. "No."

"You expect me to believe that?"

"Yes."

"So when you apologized earlier, you were apologizing for what, specifically?"

The earl's jaw was clenched. "Anthony's infidelity. I knew him better than anyone, and I should have known what he was doing all along. I could have—should have—intervened. I should have told you."

"His infidelity? That's what you're choosing to apologize for?"

"He was engaged to you, Rose. And yet all the while, he was carrying on with—" He stopped.

"Lady Helvers? Lady Pulsham? The actress from Sadler's Wells? Anyone who would have him?" she sneered. "Of course you didn't tell me. Your allegiance was to Anthony, not me."

"No." The word was hoarse. "Rose—"

"I'm not done." She paused, trying to keep emotion from pushing her words out in a jumble. "In hindsight, I'm surprised Anthony didn't push to marry me immediately, given how much money was on the line. Married, he could have carried on as he pleased without risking the fortune that came with my hand."

The earl's lips flattened. "You were more than a dowry, Rose."

"Oh, come now, Dawes. I thought we were dealing in truths here."

He had the grace to look away.

"I was aware of Anthony's reputation as a rake long

before he ever professed an interest in me. But he was a consummate actor. He said all the right things, did all the right things. Made me believe that I was special. Convinced me that he had changed—that I had changed him. That is my fault. That is not what you should be apologizing for."

The earl was staring at her, his one eye more green than brown in the pale wash of light. "I never wanted to see you hurt. And I wanted to apologize for it."

"It isn't I who am at issue here, Dawes. You haven't been listening. It's not me you should be apologizing to."

His nostrils flared in what looked like frustration. "I don't know what that means."

Rose spun and set the box down on a small table, knocking an empty glass jar off the edge. She left it where it lay on the rug. With precise movements she withdrew the lengths of paper, unfolding the first to reveal its contents.

She placed the first of the loose papers on the table. "Lady Abigail Spencer," she said. It was a caricature of a young woman in a garden bending down to smell a rose. Except her curvaceous rear had been exaggerated to enormous proportions, with a nattily dressed buck standing behind, leering and fumbling with the fall of his trousers. *Might Need a Map* was written underneath.

"And then, of course, Miss Emily Danvers." This was a caricature of another young woman, the beautiful freckles that spilled over her nose, cheeks, and forehead drawn as amphibious-like spots, her eyes pronounced and her mouth widened so that her face resembled that of a frog or toad. She was seated on a lily pad, and around her head a collection of flies buzzed. *Too Much Tongue* had been scrawled across the bottom.

Rose glanced up at Dawes. His jaw was set, and his hands were clenched at his sides.

"In all our time together, I didn't realize that Anthony, like you, also had an interest in art," Rose said, and the bitterness that she had so desperately tried to control finally triumphed. She slapped another drawing down on the table. This one was a picture of a woman, her narrow face elongated into an equine image, a halter buckled over it, being led out into a breeding ring, two scrawny stallions seemingly fighting in the background. "And see the note Anthony's written here along the top? There's a couple of drawings with your direction on them, but this one says, 'Eli, I thought you'd appreciate this one.' Now, I'm not sure if Anthony was referring to your own collection of art, or perhaps your love of Tattersalls, or perhaps—"

"Stop," Eli said.

"Stop? But I'm just getting started. Why, there are dozens. An entire discourse on the physical appearances of a whole collection of ladies, most young and noble and a couple who are not. And we haven't got to the crudest ones yet." She picked up another envelope from the box. "The ones that document a variety of bed sport with women he clearly found wanting. Surely you recognize them now."

His forehead was creased, his face drawn and troubled. "Maybe," he said after a hesitation.

"You sound less than sure. Shall I show you the rest to jog your memory?"

"No. Those drawings are juvenile and stupid," he said tightly. "I can't imagine you were ever supposed to see those. No one should have."

Fury hit her with such intensity that she gasped. "No one was supposed to see them?" she breathed. "Jesus Christ, Dawes, everyone in London saw them."

"What? How?"

Rose stared at him.

He looked up from the sketches. "What the hell are you talking about, Rose?" he demanded hoarsely.

"You published them. You and Anthony."

The earl lunged forward and knocked the drawings from the table. Before they'd finished fluttering to the floor, he wrapped a hand around her upper arm. "What?" His voice was as unyielding as his grip, and she could feel the tension in his body rolling off him in waves.

"The drawings. You had them published anonymously after you left London. Like *Harris's List of Covent Garden Ladies*, less the explicit sexual specialties. A booklet to be sold on every corner of London, next to the gossip sheets, meant to titillate and entertain. It was exceedingly popular. These drawings in the box are the originals, and the press and publication agreements are in here too."

Eli had gone white as a sheet, his scars standing out in stark relief. "I don't know what you're talking about."

Rose put a hand out to steady herself, a horrible suspicion starting to stir deep within her. "You did everything together," she said numbly. "You and Anthony. You were inseparable."

"Inseparable?" he repeated, the word torn from his throat horribly. "Anthony wasn't...He didn't..." Eli bent slightly, as if in pain, before he straightened again. "I had no idea that he was going to do...that."

"You didn't know," she whispered, trying to understand just what she was feeling. Trying to come to terms with the possibility that what she had believed all these years about Eli Dawes had been wrong.

The earl released her and turned away to pace by one of the long windows. "You thought I did this? That I would ever condone such a thing?"

"What did you think Anthony was going to do with the drawings?" she lashed out, anger overtaking her confusion.

He ran a hand through his hair in clear agitation. "I don't know. I never thought about it. I didn't even know there were so many."

"Well, I'll tell you what you should know." Rose's voice had risen, and she struggled for control. "You should know what those drawings did to some of these women. The destruction they wrought on their lives, when one's reputation and appearance are often the only things society puts any value on. They were shunned and mocked and ridiculed. The suggestion that all these women were tried and found wanting in ways I can't even…"

"Fuck," she heard him breathe, almost inaudibly.

"Yes, that definitely seemed to be a recurring theme throughout," Rose agreed coldly. "I never believed him to be a saint," she said. "Either of you. But I believed that at least one of you might have been a decent human being."

"If I had known what he was going to do, I would have destroyed them."

Rose bent and started collecting the scattered drawings. "Of course."

"You don't believe me." It was a statement and a question all at once.

"I believe the part about you not knowing he intended to publish them," she allowed. She didn't know what else she believed right now. Rose put the drawings back in the box with unfeeling fingers and snapped the lid closed.

"Why do you keep them?" Dawes demanded from the window. "Why haven't you destroyed them?"

She stilled and looked up at him. "To remind myself why I do what I do."

He pinched the bridge of his nose with his fingers. "I don't understand what that means either."

"I don't require you to understand anything, Dawes.

What I do require you to do is endeavor to stay out of my way." She straightened, smoothing her skirts. She felt suddenly drained, as if all the emotion that had been bottled up within her had been released and had left her limp and exhausted. After all this time, Eli Dawes wasn't the villain she needed him to be to justify six years of anger and bitterness. It left her feeling cheated somehow. Bereft.

"This is what you thought I was apologizing for," he said suddenly, breaking the silence that had fallen in the studio.

Rose didn't answer and instead returned the box to the trunk of supplies. She closed the heavy lid deliberately and carefully. "Yes," she said after a moment. "But it doesn't matter. It's done and can't be undone."

He looked away, unhappiness etched across his face. "It does matter. It matters that you thought I was capable of that. Of deliberately and publicly humiliating those women."

"Why would you care about my opinion?"

"Because I admire you. You were always too good for a man like Anthony. Like me."

Rose stared at him. "I beg your pardon?"

Dawes continued to gaze out the window and didn't answer.

Rose sat down heavily on the lid of the trunk. Everything that had seemed so clear in her mind wasn't any longer. Everything that she thought she had understood seemed alien.

"Who else knows about the drawings?" he asked suddenly. "The book? That it was Anthony who was behind it?"

She threaded her fingers together. "No one, it seems, unless Prevett and Giles mentioned it to you."

"They never said anything to me," Dawes said heavily.

"And now they're dead too. So only the publisher, I suppose."

"What about your family?"

"*No.*" Rose clasped her hands so tightly that her knuckles went white. "Do you know how awful it is to be told that the one person who you believed loved and revered you above all others had deceived you? Do you know how hard it is to explain that your monumental stupidity prevented you from seeing what sort of man he really was? No one wants to play the fool, but I was a fool of epic proportions, Dawes. I didn't see any benefit to advertising that even further."

"You are not stupid or foolish. You never were."

Rose shook her head. "Spare me the platitudes. It was a hard, but necessary, lesson for me to learn. We see whom we want to see. What we want to see. And nothing is more heartbreaking than the death of an illusion. I don't need you to make me feel better, so save yourself the trouble."

He turned toward her then, and she could feel his silent gaze settle on her. "I'm not who I once was, Rose," he finally said.

"So you keep saying. But I can't, for the life of me, figure out what that is supposed to mean. You're not who? The man who had a different woman in his bed every week? The man adored by society for his charm and dashing good looks?"

"The man who didn't do the right thing when he had the chance."

His answer caught her off guard. She'd expected him to argue. To protest. To try to paint himself in a better light. Yet he had done none of those things.

Rose rested her forehead in her palms, at a loss for a response. She knew she should say something reassuring. Something gracious. It would be the proper, charitable thing to do, especially given that her instincts were telling her that Dawes truly hadn't been aware of the cruel hatefulness Anthony had left in his wake.

Except she still wasn't feeling charitable.

Mostly she was feeling confused. Because there was a stranger standing by the window of her studio.

"I'll go." Dawes walked past her, heading for the door.

Rose offered no argument, nor did she try to stop him.

Dawes paused, his hand on the latch. He didn't turn back to look at her. "For what it's worth, I apologize for those drawings. Whether you believe me or not, I regret whatever pain they inflicted."

He opened the door and vanished.

Chapter 6

Eli leaned against the low stone fence at the base of Avondale's lawns and gardens. On the other side, grasslands filled with wild flowers rolled away before they were brought up short by the jagged edge of the cliffs. Mercifully, there wasn't another soul in sight, his only company the seabirds that soared overhead. Eli shaded his eyes with his hand and wondered if this was how he would live out the rest of his days. Trying to regain a sense of duty and conscience while avoiding everyone and everything that served to remind him just how little honor had marked his past life.

He stared out beyond the edge of the cliff at the sea, the line between cloudless sky and water difficult to distinguish in the brilliant light. The sun glittered off the surface, and where the surf met land, a spray of a thousand diamonds sparkled in the air with each muffled crash. To his right the distant outline of Dover Castle was just visible over the rise of the land, and beyond that Eli knew that the town itself would be awash in sunlight where it sat cradled in its valley beside the sea. There was a beauty to this place that Eli had never appreciated before. An empty wildness that seemed to suit him now.

Because empty was exactly how he was feeling.

Until Rose presented him with those drawings, Eli had forgotten that they ever existed. He had put them out of his mind after Anthony had shared them with him, in the back of their club amid too much brandy and too much smoke. His recollections of those nights were a little hazy, but Eli remembered quite clearly that even then, he hadn't found the drawings funny.

But he had said nothing to Anthony to convey that. He had done nothing, not comprehending how disgraceful that was. Not even considering the possibility that the pictures would ever be exploited at the expense of their targets. Not for one second considering that he should rebuke Anthony for his careless cruelty or simply toss them into the nearest hearth. His lack of consideration made him complicit and made Rose's assumptions about him not baseless, but deserved.

And he had no idea how to set that to rights.

He might have stood there for minutes or hours, left alone with only the gulls for company. But even they seemed to have ceased their never-ending laments as though they were waiting to see what he would do. Above him the sun beat down steadily, making him feel hot and restless and agitated. It had been a mistake to come back here. Or perhaps the bigger mistake had been to believe that he could come back and seamlessly claim an unfamiliar future without having to be accountable for the past. That he could claim a life he wasn't even sure he really wanted.

A shout carried on the breeze made him twist and look back toward Avondale. Someone was riding a horse up the drive, leaning low over the animal's back, gray coat flapping in the wind, dust churning under the pounding hooves. From this distance he couldn't see who it was, but the urgency was obvious as the horse rounded the back of the manor and vanished from sight. A distance behind the rider, at the top of the drive, an empty farm wagon of some sort was also turning into the drive, skidding slightly. It too barreled toward the house.

Eli pushed himself away from the fence, ignoring the small voice inside his head beseeching him to stay where he was. To avoid whatever and whoever was descending on Avondale now. But the other part of him, the part that was already irritated that his sanctuary had been invaded by a finishing school for a dozen temperamental debutantes, refused to let him turn back. The last thing he needed or wanted was more uninvited commotion. Whatever the hell was going on here at his house would be dealt with and terminated immediately.

Eli reached the lawns in front of Avondale just as a blond man drew the wagon to a sloppy stop, gravel spraying from beneath the horse's sliding hooves. He jumped from the bench and bolted around to the back of the wagon, disappearing from sight. Eli was loping across the expanse now, displeasure propelling him up the drive, past the blowing horse and around to the back of the wagon. Where he came to an abrupt halt and stared.

The empty farm wagon was not empty at all but built to conceal a compartment underneath the bed big enough to hide a man. Like the one the blond driver was now helping to his feet from the back, swaying and staggering, the front of his shirt soaked through with blood. Behind him, in the hidden space, were two wooden crates and what looked like three long leather tubes, the sort that architects used to store blueprints.

"What the hell is going on here?" Eli wasn't sure what part of the scene before him he should address first.

Both men looked up in alarm and took a hasty step back. Their reaction was expected. What Eli hadn't expected was to discover that the slight man being propped up by the driver wasn't a man at all but a boy, no more than twelve or thirteen. The youth was ashen, his face a mask of pain.

The blond driver wedged an arm under the boy. The driver had the lean edges of one who lived hard. A former soldier, perhaps. A man fallen on difficult times. Or maybe both. "The boy's been shot. He needs a doctor."

"Shot?" Good God.

"Dr. Hayward was just ahead of us. Told us he'd meet us at the front."

Eli straightened. Dr. Hayward. Otherwise known as Harland Hayward, Baron Strathmore. Rose's brother.

"I have to get...I have to take..." The youth was mumbling, his words slurred.

"Charlie, lad, I'll see everything gets where it needs to be," the driver soothed him. "I'll take care of it. And Dr. Hayward is going to take care of you, I promise. You'll be all right."

The boy opened his mouth to say something else, but his eyes rolled up in the back of his head and he crumpled, pitching forward.

The driver swore as Eli sprang forward and caught the boy. Without considering what he was doing, he lifted him into his arms. The boy didn't weigh nearly enough.

"He needs to get inside. Please." The driver had a smear of blood across the yellow detailing on the front of his faded blue jacket.

Eli frowned. "Artillery?"

The driver blinked. "What?"

"You have an artillery jacket." Worn and patched and faded, but recognizable even still.

"Third British Infantry, foot battery," the driver muttered. "But that was a long time ago—"

The front door crashed open, and a tall man with sharp features, dark mahogany hair, and a dusty gray coat stepped out. He stopped abruptly as he caught sight of Eli holding the insensible, bleeding youth. "Rivers." He didn't look pleased.

Nor did he bother to hide his clinical appraisal of Eli's face. Eli supposed he should have expected nothing else, given that the man had been a physician long before he had been a baron.

"Strathmore." He hadn't seen Harland Hayward in a lot of years. Not since before the war.

The baron turned to the blond driver. "Go, Mr. Wright. Before you are found here by people with questions I imagine you don't wish to answer. Let Mrs. Soames know what has happened and that Charlie is in my care."

Mr. Wright hesitated. "She's going to want to come here. To see her son."

"I know. But I also know that she and the girls can't afford to miss a day's worth of work. Please tell her that Charlie will be fine and that I will return him to her just as soon as he's well enough. She has my word that he'll be safe here."

"Aye. I'll tell her. Thank you, Dr. Hayward." Mr. Wright backed away from Eli and bent to close the wagon's hidden compartment. He glanced back only once before climbing up into the front of the wagon and urging the horse into a smart pace down the drive.

"Bring him in, Rivers," Strathmore said in a curt voice. He turned on his heel and strode back into the house.

Eli followed, trying not to jar the youth too much. Blood was dripping over Eli's arm to spatter on the pristine white marble of Avondale's hall floor.

"Welcome home and all that," Strathmore tossed over his shoulder. "Sorry about your floors. I'll make sure to have them cleaned."

"I don't care about the damn floors. What I'd like to know is why I am carrying a bleeding boy who's been shot into my home."

"The boy needs a doctor. Avondale was convenient. Ah, thank you, Rose."

Eli looked up to find Rose hurrying down the wide staircase with a bulky black bag clutched in her arms.

His heart thumped painfully. Was this going to happen every time he saw her?

Rose faltered as she caught sight of Eli before recovering and handing the bag to her brother. "Of course."

"I need you to fetch Rachel for me," the baron told her, barely breaking stride. "I think Clara has the students in the gardens. Use some discretion."

Rose nodded. She glanced at Eli without a word before disappearing toward the back of the house.

"If you have no objections, Rivers, take my patient to the kitchens." Strathmore was speaking in precise, clipped syllables. "Put him up on the table."

"The kitchens? Surely there is somewhere more comfortable—"

"There is an abundance of light, clean surfaces, and boiling water," Strathmore said coolly. "Your staff is familiar with the routine. This isn't the first patient I've treated here. If you wish to discuss alternative options later, I'm all ears, but I'd prefer not to tarry now, given the circumstances."

Eli felt his jaw clench, but he obeyed. Gingerly he made

his way down the narrow servants' hallway to the kitchens. The massive wooden table in the center of the room that his aunts had used for casting with their students earlier had been cleared, and Eli set the limp youth down with as much care as he could.

"Thank you for your assistance, Rivers. I'll take it from here. This no longer concerns you."

"I'll stay." Like hell was he just going to be dismissed like a scullery maid by a doctor turned baron, in his own house no less. As much as Eli mourned the loss of his solitude, Strathmore was wrong. What happened in Avondale concerned him very much.

The baron gave him a long look but didn't argue. He merely turned and began unpacking the contents of his black bag on the long counter behind him.

"Dr. Hayward." The dark-haired Haverhall student who had stared at Eli so openly this morning hurried into the room, wiping her hands on a towel she carried, and Eli instinctively turned away. But this time she barely glanced at him and went directly to the side of the boy lying motionless.

"Good afternoon, Rachel," the baron replied.

"Single shot?" she asked, setting the towel aside and inexplicably peeling back the edge of the boy's bloody shirt with quick efficiency.

"That's what I was told," Strathmore confirmed, not looking up.

"You don't have to be here, Dawes." Eli had been staring at the boy on the table and hadn't heard Rose approach. "We don't need you here."

I don't want you here. That was what he knew she meant. He turned sideways, hating the way his chest tightened. Maybe he would crawl back to Belgium. Because having

Rose this close, seeing her this often and knowing she was lost to him forever, was nothing short of torture. And he had only himself to blame.

"I already told your brother I'm staying."

"Suit yourself." Rose moved to collect a bucket from near the hearth and poured steaming water into a bowl.

The dark-haired student called Rachel had picked up a small knife and was deftly cutting the tattered remains of the boy's shirt from his body. Against the pallor of the boy's skin, the hole above his right clavicle that was still oozing blood was easily visible. She bent over the patient, her fingers prodding the entrance of the wound. The boy moaned faintly but didn't stir.

"What are you doing?" Eli snapped, unable to help himself. He wasn't sure what the hell was going on in here or what he had walked into, but he was sure that, in his absence, propriety hadn't slipped so far as this. If the young lady was indeed a student of Haverhall, she would be the daughter of a distinguished peer or someone else wealthy enough to afford the obscene tuition that Haverhall demanded. She should be in a music room practicing the pianoforte or maybe the gardens practicing her watercolors. Not poking arbitrarily at a bullet wound in a half-naked boy in his kitchens.

"Ah." Strathmore brought a roll of instruments bound in leather over to the young woman and set them on the table beside the boy's head. "Miss Swift, may I present Eli Dawes, aspiring earl. Rivers, Miss Rachel Swift, aspiring surgeon."

Perhaps Rose had been right. Perhaps whatever had damaged his face had damaged his wits, because nothing in that caustic introduction had made sense. Worse, he couldn't seem to recall any nobility with the surname of Swift, and he had once taken great pride in knowing all the right people.

Strathmore straightened. "The Earl of Rivers asks an

excellent question, Miss Swift. Please do tell his Lordship—and me, of course—what exactly it is that you are doing."

Rachel selected an instrument from the roll and considered the still form in front of her. "The bullet and all cloth fragments need to be removed from the wound. The bleeding, while initially profuse judging from his clothing, seems to have slowed, suggesting that no major vessels have been irrevocably damaged. His breathing appears even and steady, indicating that his lungs have not been compromised. I recommend widening the wound as preventative debridement, removing all foreign matter, irrigating profusely with an antiseptic. Suture in a fashion to allow drainage as it heals. Fly larvae can be introduced later if there is a need."

Strathmore looked pleased. "Very good. I concur. Please proceed."

Eli felt his jaw slacken, and it required an effort to close his mouth. "But..."

"You disagree, Rivers?"

Eli wondered if Strathmore might be mocking him. "I...no."

"Good. 'Tis a wonder all surgeons are not women," the baron mused as he moved to grasp the patient's arms. "Her sutures put mine to shame. Since you insist on staying, hold the boy's feet if you will. If we're lucky, he stays unconscious. If we're not, I have no desire to add a scalp laceration to his list of woes when he topples off the table. He's stronger than he looks."

Eli glanced at Rose, but she was busy rolling what looked like bandages. And seemed not at all surprised or taken aback that one of her debutantes sounded like a damn field surgeon.

"How was this boy shot?" Eli asked loudly, because of

all the questions that were banging away at the inside of his mind, this was the one that seemed as if it might get a real answer.

The baron frowned faintly. "Someone aimed a pistol at him and pulled the trigger."

"Who?"

"Garrison soldiers."

"Why?"

"I am told they believed him to be a smuggler."

"Is he?"

"Of course not. His name is Charlie Soames. I've treated his siblings for croup." Strathmore peered at the wound more closely. "Cut a little more on the upper edge, Rachel."

"Then why was he shot?"

"He and a colleague were moving a barrel of salted herring they had acquired in an attempt to keep their families from starving."

"Acquired?"

"I didn't ask for details."

"And his colleague was the man who brought him here? Who just left him?"

"Matthew Wright is a good man. He left because I told him to."

"A good man who had wares concealed in a wagon?"

"As I said, Rivers, I didn't ask for details."

"And I'm supposed to believe that he's not a smuggler wearing the uniform of his country—"

"What would you have him do, Rivers?" Strathmore asked evenly. "When he can't get work on the oyster boats or the fishing boats or the docks? Starve? Let his ailing father starve? Join the thousands of veterans in London who are begging on every street corner for work or a handout? You haven't been back long enough to understand that the men, the common men who fought alongside you, have returned to a country where work is scarce and the taxes levied on the average folk to pay for too many years of war have taken their toll."

Eli's hands curled into fists at the reminder of his prolonged absence. It felt like an accusation. "The soldiers who shot this boy—where are they now?"

"Who knows? But they'll show up eventually. Because people with holes in them tend to show up on my doorstep."

"My doorstep," Eli corrected him. "And will you surrender this boy to them?"

"We are not in the habit of handing over to the authorities boys whose only crime is to protect and provide for their families. Young Mr. Soames here has a mother and two younger sisters who depend on him." Strathmore was still watching Rachel's ministrations critically. "Watch the angle of your forceps, Miss Swift."

"Where is his father?"

"Dead. Quatre Bras. Along with his two older brothers. Leaving Charlie as the man of the family at the ripe old age of seven."

Eli was suddenly weary. Would there ever be a place where the shadow of so much death and so much loss did not reach?

Strathmore took the bloodied forceps from the young woman and examined the bullet caught in their grip. "Nicely done, Miss Swift. You may begin irrigating and suturing."

"Thank you, Dr. Hayward."

Rose stepped close to the table, a damp cloth in her hand. She didn't look at Eli, her eyes fixed firmly on the small form lying pale and still. "If the soldiers find him, they'll hang him."

"Jesus, Rose. He's a *child*."

Rose gently wiped a smear of blood from the boy's forehead. "He's a thief."

Eli shook his head. "He's a survivor."

She looked up at him then, studying him intently, unsmiling. "Yes. He is."

It was an effort not to reach out and touch her. Eli clasped his hands behind his back, afraid he would do just that. He looked away, watching Miss Swift prepare her needles with the same deftness with which she had wielded her knife.

The baron cleared his throat. "I'll have my patient recover upstairs in the servants' quarters for at least a few days. Discreetly. Provided that is acceptable to you, Rivers." There was an edge of challenge to that last sentence.

"This boy is the son and the brother of men who served their country. Men no different from me. Except they died and I didn't. I rather think we owe this to them, don't you?"

"I'm glad we agree on something, then, Rivers." Strathmore dropped the bullet into a glass dish with an audible ping.

"Lord Rivers?" The question came from the young woman, who was tying off a suture. "Please forgive my boldness, but I was wondering if I might inquire about the nature of your injury."

Eli recoiled. "I beg your pardon?"

Rachel Swift's needle flashed. "My family owns a foundry. Six of them, actually. Burns are common. Too common, but they are hard to avoid, especially for the puddlers and the men working the blast furnaces. I've taken it upon myself to study the best practices and courses of treatment to ensure the greatest chance of full recovery when accidents occur. As such, I am interested in how your burn was treated. It appears that the healed tissue has retained at least some of its elasticity. Your movements of your head and neck do not appear to be compromised or restricted. The loss of your eye is unfortunate, of course, but your sense of hearing seems to have been preserved on that side despite the damage to your outer ear."

Eli was aware Rose was watching him again, and he ducked his head as each horrifying component of his disfigurement was listed like an advert for a sideshow attraction. How dare this stranger, this...chit, pry into something so personal. So private. As if she had every right. It was all he could do not to release the child's legs and quit the room.

Miss Swift picked up a scissor and snipped another suture, apparently oblivious to his agony. "Do you suffer headaches because of your partial loss of vision?" She finally glanced up at him with cool green eyes as though she expected him simply to spill his innermost thoughts and his innermost pain. As though he might recount the horror of the war and everything that had come after with the same clinical detachment that she displayed.

"I'm sorry," Eli said roughly. "I can't do this." He released the boy's legs.

"I'm done anyway—"

"I can't do any of this." Eli could feel shame at his cowardice burning through him, but he didn't care. Until this moment he had forgotten. Forgotten that he was an object of morbid curiosity to be assessed or reviled. But no matter where he went or what he did, he would always be reminded.

Eli spun and headed out of the room, not looking back.

"Rivers." Eli was halfway down the servants' hallway when he heard his name.

He almost didn't stop, angry at the delay, angry at himself. "What?"

"Forgive Rachel," Strathmore said, coming to a stop

before him. "She is very passionate about what she does. Admirable, but sometimes it clouds her judgment."

Eli crossed his arms over his chest.

Strathmore's dark eyes, so like his sister's, regarded him steadily, giving away nothing. "Powder burn?" he asked suddenly.

Eli raised a hand to touch the ruined side of his face before he could stop himself. "Jesus. Not you too," he growled.

The baron shrugged, unconcerned with his ire. "I saw injuries like yours often. Though not to this extent. Usually it was the result of some panicked soul short-starting his round. The resulting explosion burns were similar, if not as severe, though significant damage to the eye was common. Your scarring suggests something much greater in scale. Like an artillery explosion."

The significance of his words distracted Eli. "You served. Were you with Wellington?"

"To the end."

"You were an officer?"

Strathmore almost smiled, as if that question amused him. "I was but a mere surgeon."

A mere surgeon who was still prying into things that were none of his business. "What do you want, Strathmore? Why did you follow me out here? And don't tell me it was to discuss artillery burns."

The baron's steady gaze was almost unsettling. "You've been gone a long time."

"Is that a question?"

"Only if you answer it." A dark brow rose fractionally.

Eli didn't owe this man any sort of explanation. About anything. He remained mute.

"When Rose told me you had returned, I wasn't entirely sure whether or not to believe her. Yet here you are, back from the dead to claim your legacy, but Dover, as lovely as it is, is somewhat removed for your purposes and interests, isn't it? I would have thought, given the petition that has already been put before the courts to declare you legally dead, you'd wish to get to London with all haste. Unless, of course, there's a reason you're avoiding the city?"

Eli could feel a muscle working along the edge of his jaw. He resented what this man was implying even if it was the truth. Perhaps because it was the truth. "My interests are my business, not yours."

"Mmmm." The baron leaned back against the wall. "Perhaps. But your interests are not the only interests at issue here."

"I beg your pardon?"

"I am sure you are quite aware by now there are currently a dozen young ladies living under your roof, ranging in ages from fifteen to eighteen, Miss Swift being one of them. And, of course, both my sisters. Is this going to be a problem?"

Eli frowned irritably. "I'm not going to renege on whatever lease agreement my father had with the school."

"That wasn't what I was concerned about."

"I beg your pardon?"

"You heard me."

"I don't like what you're implying," Eli growled.

"I'm not implying anything. I'm trying to make my position abundantly clear. Should you decide to remain at Avondale, as is your right as the owner of this estate, you will endeavor to stay away from the students. And you will stay away from my sisters." It wasn't said with malice, but the warning was unmistakable.

"I have no interest in your sisters," Eli snapped. "Nor do I have any interest in a bevy of high-strung debutantes." God, he would give them a parish-wide berth or die trying.

Strathmore leveled a long look at him. "You expect me to believe that? That your raison d'être is no longer stealing kisses from pretty maidens behind every hedge? Potted palms when a good hedge isn't available?"

"I don't care what you believe, Strathmore." The bastard.

"In my experience, a tiger rarely changes its stripes."

"This conversation is over." Eli uncrossed his arms and started down the hall.

"I would strongly suggest that, if you do intend to remain at Avondale for the foreseeable future, you make use of the dower house. It is but a short walk, and it is where both Holloway and I stay while the students of Haverhall are in residence here."

Eli paused, his memory fumbling. "Holloway? The Duke of Holloway?"

"Yes. August Faulkner. My brother-in-law."

Something lurched deep within him. "Rose is a duchess? When—" He stopped, suddenly and inexplicably unsure he wanted the answer to his unasked question.

The baron gazed at him, his expression once again utterly unreadable. "No, not Rose. Clara. Holloway is Clara's husband."

Eli looked away, suddenly limp from the relief that curled through him. "He's here too?"

"No, no. At the moment Holloway is in London doing what Holloway does best. Which is buying and selling empires for his own amusement. And ungodly profits, of course."

Eli could hear a peculiar mix of resignation and admiration in that statement.

"I would suggest, Lord Rivers, that you address whatever business brings you to Dover with all due haste and move on." Strathmore pushed his long frame from the wall. "There's nothing here for you."

Chapter 7

"What happened today?"

Rose looked up from the book she'd been reading, blinking against the brilliant sunshine that was spilling in through the long library windows. She shielded her eyes and scowled.

"Is there a reason you're standing in my light?" she grumbled at Clara, deliberately ignoring her sister's question and trying to find her place on the page again.

"Is there a reason you're hiding in the library on such a beautiful afternoon?"

"It's a lovely library." And it was. It was filled from floor to ceiling with books and maps and drawings. Treatises and manuscripts and dissertations. Plays and poetry and novels. Every subject that one could think of was represented to some degree, from science to fiction, politics to history, agriculture to art.

Maintained by an efficient staff, the gleaming, cavernous room was filled with light that flooded the room through its tall windows. Long wooden tables surrounded by carved chairs dominated the center of the room, ready for research or debates. Wide, upholstered armchairs were scattered around the edges in groups, inviting anyone to curl up with a book. Which was exactly what Rose had done.

Clara moved out of the light and took a seat in the brocaded chair next to her. Rose managed to ignore her sister for half a minute before she finally sighed and looked up. "For the record, I'm not hiding."

"Harland said he helped with Charlie." Clara propped her chin on one of her hands. "Before he fled from whatever questions Rachel was asking, looking like he wanted to fling himself off a cliff into the sea with rocks in his pockets."

There was no point in pretending she didn't know whom Clara was speaking of. Rose hadn't been able to think of anything or anyone else since Eli Dawes had stumbled into her studio in the dead of night. "Rachel might have been a little...direct."

"She is that. Though perhaps you ought to follow her example."

"I beg your pardon?"

"Harland also said that you barely spoke to the earl." Her sister paused. "You should, you know. Talk to Rivers."

"I have talked to him." Though *talk* wasn't probably the way he would describe it. *Accuse, rail,* and *censure* would be more accurate. And all based on her assumptions. Guilt pricked with an unpleasant swiftness.

Clara would have done none of those things, Rose reflected. Clara, with her flawless deportment, wouldn't have let her emotions get the best of her. She would have presented her case, confessed her disappointment, allowed him to tell his side of the story, and probably offered him tea while she was at it.

Her beautiful sister sighed, pushing her thick mahogany

hair away from her face. "I don't mean whatever exchange you had in the dead of night when you almost ran him through with a paintbrush. I mean a real conversation—"

"We've had one. And now we're done." Rose raised her book back in front of her face, but she didn't see the words.

"When?" Clara demanded.

Rose kept the book in front of her face. "Before Harland dragged Charlie Soames into the kitchens to bleed all over the place."

"And?" Fingers appeared at the top of her page and snatched the book away from her.

"And what?" Rose reached for her book, but Clara was too fast.

"You tell me." Her sister sat back and regarded Rose in that damnably calm manner of hers.

Rose looked away, staring through the windows and out into the lush gardens beyond the tall panes of glass.

"He's different, isn't he?" Clara said.

"You didn't know him well enough to say that."

"Not as well as you," Clara agreed. "But well enough to know that the man who was famous for his brazen debauchery and shameless seductions avoided my very pretty, very wealthy students as if they had all contracted the plague. Couldn't even look them in the eye. Declined any sort of social gathering to welcome him back."

"How do you know all that?"

"Theo told me."

"Aren't you just a fount of gossip today?"

"I would have had a conversation with the earl myself, except, since he's been back, he seems to be doing exactly what you're doing. Hiding."

Rose focused on a sparrow that had landed near the edge

of the windowsill, its movements nervous and watchful. "He apologized to me."

"Mmm." Clara seemed to ponder that for a moment. "For what?"

Rose pondered her response. "For not being a good friend," she said finally.

"Is that what he is to you?"

Rose gave a half-hearted shrug, unsure what the answer was.

Clara laced her fingers together, looking as though she was trying to pick her words with care. "These last years, when you thought he was dead, you've always maintained that Eli Dawes was no better than Anthony Gibson."

The sparrow on the sill wheeled away, and Rose watched it go. "I was wrong." There, she'd said it out loud. As though admitting it to another person made it more... valid. She'd believed the worst. Believed the very worst of Eli Dawes based not on proof, but on assumptions that had sprung from hurt and anger toward another.

That reality was as mortifying and shameful now as it had been when she first realized it.

"I see." Clara sounded unconvinced. "That must have been one hell of an apology."

Rose wasn't sure what was more discomfiting, the weight of her sister's gaze or the fact that Clara had cursed. Clara never cursed.

"He was... sincere."

"Then you're not angry with him?" Clara asked.

"No. Maybe. I don't know." Part of her still wanted to be angry, though for reasons that she wasn't about to reveal to Clara. When those drawings had been published, the helpless fury and betrayal she'd so desperately wanted to unleash had been cheated out of a target by French guns. Now, years later, those same feelings had been cheated of a target by the truth. "What difference does it make?"

"It makes all the difference," Clara said, and this time there was urgency in her words. "I saw what you went through with Anthony. And then... after. God, Rose, it almost destroyed you. It still affects—" Clara stopped and seemed to reconsider what she had been going to say. Which was good because Rose was not going to discuss the parts of her life that had altered and slipped away from her. The parts that she hadn't been able to get back.

"He might have apologized," Clara continued, more measured this time. "Nevertheless, Eli Dawes holds strong ties to your past. He represents a time in your life that brought you low. And I could not stand to see you go through that again."

Rose continued to stare at the spot where the tiny bird had vanished.

Clara stood and stepped in front of Rose again, forcing her to look up at her sister. "He owns this house, this property. You won't be able to avoid him, nor should you ever have to. Here or anywhere else. But you need to make sure you know where you stand. You need to make sure that whatever lies between you and Rivers is settled."

"It's settled," Rose grumbled, though it wasn't at all, really.

"Is it? You sound less than sure. Which worries me. You need to protect yourself."

"You don't need to worry about me. I know how to protect myself."

"Rose—"

"You said you believe he's different," Rose interrupted, tracing the delicate carving on the arm of her chair with the pads of her fingers.

"That was my impression," Clara replied slowly.

"Then do not forget that I am different too." Rose pushed herself to her feet so that she stood face-to-face with her sister.

"I haven't forgotten anything," Clara told her, reaching out to put a gentle hand on her shoulder. "Which is why you need to resolve whatever still remains between you and Rivers. For both of your sakes."

Chapter 8

The sun was hot against her face, and Rose was cursing her fair complexion. She hadn't bothered with a bonnet—in fact she hadn't bothered with much of anything, once she'd made her decision. She'd paced alone in the library for long minutes after Clara had departed to prepare for her late-afternoon classes. Rose would have the students in her studio tomorrow morning, and a client was arriving for a sitting tomorrow afternoon, but right now there was nowhere for her to be.

Unless, of course, she listened to Clara.

Unless, of course, she sought out the Earl of Rivers and had a conversation that did not take place in the middle of the night, shrouded with shock at the sudden reappearance of a dead man. And not in a studio, submerged in old assumptions and emotions that had simmered for too long until truth had boiled them over, making everything messy and confusing. Because, as usual, Clara was right.

She needed to hold a mature conversation with Eli

Dawes in which they would speak calmly of the future. In which she would make clear what she expected from him and what he could expect from her. It would be better to clarify everything so that when they met—and they would meet often at Avondale—they could do so without awkwardness and tension.

So now Rose found herself starting down the steep trail of the cliffs toward the small, protected cove below, rehearsing exactly what she wanted to say as she descended. Someone, at some time, certainly not in this century or even the century before, had cut a series of crude steps down the side of the cliff. Smugglers, most likely, and it was just as likely that it was smugglers who still maintained them. The passage was a natural ravine, a crevice protected by tall, chalky walls on either side covered with tufts of vegetation.

The cove was almost circular, cut out from the white cliffs. It was small, the entrance to the sea too narrow for anything larger than a small fishing boat, but the beach sloped gently and the surf only swirled and didn't pound with the same ferocity it did on the exposed shorelines. It was a place isolated from reality, protected from all eyes. Somewhere one could retreat. Somewhere Dawes could hide.

Rose continued down the narrow, twisting path. The sound of the surf and the screams of gulls became louder. The sun beat down on her head, the warmth from the sun trapped at the base of the cliff. The breeze, mostly blocked by the wall of the circular cove, did little to cool her. She reached the beach and shaded her eyes against the glare. Avondale's grooms had told her they had seen the earl heading toward the cove, but Rose wondered now if she was too late. Or if Dawes had ever come down here.

The beach was empty, but just off to the right, in the

shade cast by an overhanging cliff, she spotted what appeared to be a coat and a pair of breeches, left carelessly next to a pair of boots. Rose's eyes snapped to the water. If he had thrown himself into the depths to drown himself, at least he hadn't done it with rocks in his pockets.

There, about twenty yards out, she could just make out the figure of a man on the surface of the sea, moving with surprising speed. Rose ducked out of the sun into the shade of the overhang, watching as the earl swam for a few minutes more before stopping and floating on his back, only his head and toes visible, his face upturned to the sun. There was a grace to his movements, the unhurried effort of a person who has, for a moment, found peace in solitude.

She sat down beneath the ledge, content for a moment just to rest in the relative cool and watch the play of sunlight across the water. She knew she should probably retreat. This invasion of Dawes's privacy was not something she had planned, but now that she was here, she feared that if she left, she might just lose her nerve to say what she had come all the way down here to say. At the very least, if he was only half-dressed and dripping wet, he would have to listen to what she said before he could escape anywhere.

A movement in the water caught her eye, and Rose realized that Dawes was heading toward the beach. He was still on his back, facing away from the shore, his strokes long and lazy, letting the gentle swells carry him closer and closer to shore.

She should stand up now and wave him down. Let him know that she was here. Except she didn't move. For reasons that she didn't understand, she remained perfectly still in the shade, her eyes skimming over the long lines of his arms as they flashed in and out of the water and the breadth of his shoulders as they crested each swell. He disappeared entirely under the water for a few seconds before he suddenly stood, his back to her, the surf frothing around his thighs. Rose felt her mouth go dry.

She tried desperately to view him through the eyes of Rose the artist and not Rose the woman. Water sluiced down his body, sparkling in the sunlight as it traveled over the defined muscles of his back. Over his left shoulder she could see the whitened skin of his healed injury where the burn had afflicted the top of his arm and neck. The curve of his spine created a faint valley of shadow as it traveled from beneath his dripping hair to the small of his back, stopping just above the curve of his buttocks. And he had a glorious ass. His waist and hips were trim, a faint hollow on each buttock delimiting the hard muscle. The tops of his legs were just visible above the surface, steady against the swirl of water. Rose had not painted many men with the sharp musculature that Eli Dawes possessed, and this man, from an artist's perspective, was impressive. A model she would gladly pay for a few afternoons of his time so that she, or other artists, might practice their hand at replication and composition of truly remarkable male anatomy.

From a woman's perspective . . . Rose tried not to consider what it would be like to run her fingers over his water-slicked body and failed. The skin of his upper body glowed with color earned only by exposure to the sun, suggesting that Dawes had spent a great deal of time outdoors without his shirt on. The color ended abruptly in a sharp line at his hips, indicating that he had, at least, been wearing trousers or breeches of some sort if nothing else.

She shivered, unwelcome arousal pooling low in her belly. This version of Eli Dawes was different from the polished perfection of the man she had known long ago. Not that she had ever had cause to see him like this, in all his magnificence, but the old Eli Dawes wouldn't have looked this...real. Powerful. Imperfect.

And all the more desirable for it.

Her fingers curled into the stones beneath her, and a sharp edge pressed into her palm. She jerked and struggled to scramble to her feet, untangling her skirts from around her legs. What the hell did she think she was doing? Of all the men Rose could ogle, Eli Dawes should be the very last on her list.

She straightened hastily, yelping in pain as she hit her head on the overhanging rock above her. At the sound Eli's head whipped around, his gaze finding hers in a comical mix of shock and bewilderment and then, finally, horror. He threw himself into the water like a felled oak, sending a spray of surf into the air. After a second his head popped up, and Rose suddenly found herself battling the ridiculous urge to laugh despite the ache at her temple.

"What the hell, Rose?" Dawes demanded. He looked as though he was trying to work himself into deeper water without exposing anything below his neck, while struggling against the rolling swells.

A snort of laughter did escape then. "You look like a drunken silkie," she told him, stepping out onto the beach fully.

"Jesus, Rose, you can't be here."

"On the beach?"

"Yes, on the beach. I'm naked," he bit out.

"Yes," Rose said. "I'm aware."

From the sea Dawes cursed roundly. "And is this you coming to exact your punishment on me?" he asked. "Trapping me in the water until I freeze to death or get sucked out by the tide? Because I'm not coming out while you're standing there."

Rose sobered, and the smile slid from her face. "No," she said. With a sigh she turned and quickly retrieved his clothes and carried them across the beach. She dropped them near the water's edge. "I promise I won't look." She deliberately turned her back and returned to the shade, keeping her eyes glued firmly on the tufts of vegetation clinging to the crevices in the chalky cliffs.

After a couple of long minutes, she heard the crunch of stone behind her. She risked a peek and found the earl standing on the beach, dressed in his breeches and shirt and nothing else. His hair had been shoved back from his forehead, and the ends dripped down the side of his face and over his shoulder, leaving semitransparent spots on the linen where hints of his darkened skin showed. It was all she could do not to reach out to touch him, her fingers itching to know how all that muscle would feel under the thin fabric. She longed to yank that shirt back over his head again. A shame, Rose thought, idly, to cover up all that magnificent male perfection.

Male perfection she had no business wondering about at all. She straightened her shoulders and raised her eyes.

He had his coat balled up in one hand and his boots dangling from the other. And he looked furious. "Why the hell were you spying on me?" he demanded.

"I wasn't spying on you, Dawes," Rose replied, aiming for a light, easy tone. "Spying implies subterfuge. If I truly wanted to spy on you, you would never have known I was doing it. I was waiting for you."

"While I was naked?" he gritted out through clenched teeth.

"I don't understand the fuss. Half of London has seen you naked." Rose snorted. "The female half, anyway."

"You haven't."

"Until today."

"Damn right. You're a *lady*. And an unwed one at that."
He dropped his boots on the beach, sounding genuinely
disturbed.

Rose swallowed another sound of amusement and studied
him curiously. "A lady," she repeated, beginning to understand. "And unwed."

"Yes," he said tightly.

She swallowed the very unladylike sound that threatened
to escape. "Dammit. I missed my cue to swoon."

"You shouldn't curse."

Rose snickered. "But swooning is acceptable?"

"Are you making fun of me?" A deep groove had formed
between his eyebrows.

"Possibly. I'm also wondering if I was right earlier when
I questioned if whatever had damaged your face had damaged your wits."

"*My* wits? Jesus, Rose, we're on a beach, alone. This is
not a suitable convers—"

Rose laughed again, unable to stop herself. "Am I making
you uncomfortable?"

The earl looked away. "No."

"You have to appreciate the irony of this, Dawes."

"I have no idea what you're talking about."

"The infamous, unequivocal Don Juan of London suddenly shy about a little nudity."

"Because it's not proper! For you to be here when I am
less than..." He stalled.

"When have you ever cared about propriety? Jesus,
Dawes, you sound like a ninety-year-old nun."

Eli remained silent, his body rigid. "I care when it comes
to you," he finally growled.

Rose smothered a groan. Why was she pursuing this?

This was not the conversation she had wanted to have. "I hate to disillusion you, Dawes, but you seem to have forgotten that I'm an artist," she said, trying to inject a reasonable, matter-of-fact tone. "I see naked men on a regular basis. And naked women. Models, sculpture, portraiture."

His head swiveled back. "I beg your pardon?"

"I spent seven years off and on in Italy," she said. "Immersed in a culture that values artistry and its masters more than almost anything else. Venice. Florence. Rome."

"What? When?"

"Before I ever met you. Did you think I was guessing when I told you your triptych of the Madonna and child was a Van Eyck? Or that your *Portrait of Isabella d'Este in Red* is, in fact, not a copy by Rubens but the original by Titian?"

"You never told me that you studied in Italy."

"You never asked. But let me assure you that there is nothing you own on that body of yours that I haven't already seen a hundred times. Nothing I haven't already painted a hundred times." She managed to suppress the current of electricity that suddenly hummed through her body at the memory of what he had looked like in that surf. Not one of her models, no matter how beautiful, had ever elicited such a visceral response. Clearly she'd been out in the sun too long.

He simply stared, and for the life of her, Rose couldn't tell what he was thinking.

She shook her head again. "I didn't come down here to talk about me. Or my art," she said, unwilling to continue a conversation about his nudity any longer. Or her interest in it, academic or otherwise.

His one eye narrowed. "Then what?"

Rose took a deep breath. "I came to apologize."

Eli started. Of all the things that Rose Hayward could have said to him, that was the last thing he'd expected. But then, since its inception, this entire conversation had been utterly outlandish and unexpected. Her utter disregard for propriety and her casual references to his body had been nothing short of shocking.

I see naked men on a regular basis.

How the hell was he supposed to respond to that? He had made an effort to be a gentleman—to be what a lady like Rose deserved—and she had…laughed at him. Even more disturbing was the revelation that it was possible he had never truly known this woman at all.

"For what?" he managed to ask. "What do you have to be sorry for?"

"For believing the worst of you." She looked away from him, shadows of what looked like sadness and regret flitting across her face. "Because I once considered you a friend. I'd still like to." She repeated his own words with a wistful twist.

He tightened his grip on his coat so he wouldn't be tempted to reach out and touch her. He couldn't stand to see her unhappy, though it made her no less exquisite. Her cheeks were flushed, whether from the heat or their conversation he wasn't sure. Her hair had come loose, strawberry-blond curls cascading like fire over her shoulders and down her back, brilliant against the pale blue of her dress. She was real and honest and perfect, and he wished he could go back in time to do everything all over again.

How Anthony had never valued this woman was hard to comprehend. But then Anthony had only ever valued Anthony. How Eli had not recognized that sooner was even harder to comprehend.

"Don't be sorry. After how I failed you, I would have believed it too," he said finally, meaning every word.

"No, you wouldn't," she said, looking down at her hands. Eli shook his head.

"When I told you about that book, you wanted to believe the best about Anthony, if only for a second. If that doesn't make you an optimist, I don't know what does." She said it wryly, and he knew she meant it to make him feel better, but it only made him feel worse.

"I wasn't an optimist; I was an idiot." He heard anger and guilt echo in his words. "I only saw a few of those drawings and then never thought of them again. I was oblivious to the consequences of my actions, or in this case my lack thereof. Which makes me the same."

Rose glanced up at him, her dark eyes unreadable. "You are not the same. You never lied to me. You never were deliberately cruel."

"I chose to believe what was easy, not what was right, and ignore things that were difficult or hard. That might be worse." The truth was ugly. "At least I got what I deserved."

"What?" It was barely audible, spoken on a sharp inhalation.

He had no idea why he had said that. It was something that had lurked, dark and sinister, in the very blackest corners of his mind, loosed like a poisoned arrow at unpredictable moments. Like this one. Eli stepped closer to her, his guilt burning like salt rubbed into an open wound. He knew very well he should withdraw and wrestle his shame back to the darkness from which it had emerged, but somehow he was unable to. "You heard me. Pride goeth before destruction and all that."

Rose didn't move. "You think your injury was some sort of divine punishment?" she asked with a small frown.

"I thought you'd be more pleased."

She jerked as if he'd struck her. "You believe what happened to you makes me happy?"

Eli cursed and turned away from her, stumbling a few steps toward the water. The stones were sharp beneath his bare feet, but he ignored the discomfort. He should have retreated while he had the chance, before he managed to make it all worse. The emptiness that sat dark and hollow deep within him seemed to spread, its black edges creeping ever further, threatening to consume him entirely.

"Is that what you truly believe of me? That whatever you've suffered would make me feel...What? Vindicated?"

"No." Perhaps he should have swum for the mouth of the cove and then kept going out into the blue abyss. Perhaps he still could. He was fighting a rising tide of self-pity and self-loathing and had somehow taken it out on the only person he had managed to have a real conversation with in years. He wouldn't blame Rose if she left now and never spoke to him again.

"Why did you come back?" Her question startled him. He hadn't heard her come up beside him.

He shook his head.

She stepped in front of him then, her hands on her slim hips. "Fine. Don't answer that. Tell me why you stayed away as long as you did instead."

He shifted his weight.

"Don't do that," she said quietly.

"Do what?" He dragged his gaze from where it had been, over her shoulder, to her face.

"Turn away from me. Hide your left side."

"I wasn't."

"You were. You do it all the time. It's annoying."

"It's repulsive. Grotesque."

"It's why you didn't come back." She said it with the

finality of someone who had known the answer to her question all along.

"That's not true." It came out in a defensive snarl.

"Liar." She sounded disappointed.

"I'm not discussing this with you." He brushed by her to retrieve his boots.

"It's what friends do, Dawes. Discuss difficult things. It was you who first said you wished to call me a friend. Have you changed your mind?"

Eli could feel his teeth clench so hard he feared they might shatter. "I'm not a liar."

"You're not doing so well with the truth either."

He bent to pick up his boots, only to have them snatched away. "Give me my boots."

"No." With shoes, Rose had the advantage on the stony beach, and she skittered away. "Not until you tell me something true."

"Stop it. You're acting like you're ten."

"If I were ten, I would have thrown your boots into the sea. I still might."

"You don't understand."

"Then explain it."

"That's just it. I don't want to explain it. I don't want to have to explain how this happened." He gestured to his ruined face. "Not to you, not to Miss Swift, not to your brother. I don't want to explain every time someone looks at me with revulsion and pity. Every time a woman crosses the street to avoid me or a child ducks his head in terror."

Rose was silent for a long minute, only the sound of the surf bubbling and hissing on the beach intruding. She took a step forward and shoved his boots at his chest, and he caught them awkwardly. "You need to have done with yourself, Dawes," she said.

Eli felt his jaw slacken. "What?"

"You came back for a reason. What was it? And please, just tell me the truth."

"My father died. I had to come back."

"No, you didn't. You could have stayed dead. You could still stay dead, if you like. Disappear again. Rumors of your return might delay things in the courts for a while longer, but inevitably the outcome will be the same."

"I owed it to my father."

"Why?"

Because I disappointed him. Disappointed myself.

"Because I went to war against his wishes," he said instead. It was, at least, partially true.

"You'd hardly be the first to do that."

"But at that time, I did it for all the wrong reasons."

"And what, pray tell, are the right reasons?"

"A man should fight because he truly believes in something." He'd discovered that too late.

"Ah." She took a step back. "And this is the real reason you came back, then? To fight for something you believe in?"

Eli opened his mouth and then abruptly closed it. Was it? Or had it been a quagmire of guilt and duty that had finally broken him?

Rose gazed at him for a moment longer before she gathered her skirts and sat down on the stony beach, looking out at the water. Out in the distance, beyond the entrance to the cove, a ship had appeared, and Eli watched as its anchor was dropped.

"Where did you go? After the war?" Rose asked, sounding as though she didn't care whether or not he answered.

He turned away from the ship. "Nowhere. I simply stayed in Belgium." At least that answer was easy.

"You expect me to believe you simply wandered out of

a surgeon's tent with that sort of injury and never looked back?" She glanced up at him, skepticism stamped over her delicate features.

He almost touched his ruined face involuntarily before he caught himself and forced his hand to still. "Never made it to a surgeon's tent."

Rose seemed to absorb that, her dark eyes studying him in silence for a long moment before she returned her attention to the sea. She didn't press him further, and for some peculiar reason, Eli didn't feel nearly as relieved as he ought to. Sooner or later, he was going to have to provide rational, reasonable answers to rational, reasonable questions.

Eli sighed and lowered himself to the beach beside her. "I lived with an elderly widow. She helped me put the remnants of my face back together. When I was strong enough, I helped her put the remnants of her farm back together. War is unspeakably cruel to those who get caught in its path."

"Oh." She drew her knees up to her chest and crossed her arms over the tops. "Is she still there?"

"No. She died. Just over two years ago." Eli picked up a small stone and threw it at the surf. That he had become closer to a complete stranger than he had ever been to his father was not lost on him.

"How did you know that your father had died?" A small line formed between her brows.

Eli's hand closed around another stone, the edges biting into the pads of his fingers. "My father's solicitors hired a firm to find me. A last-ditch effort." He let the stone drop. "And somehow they did."

The dark-haired young man who had appeared in the isolated farmyard on a big-boned gelding, a rifle strapped to the side of his saddle, hadn't, on closer inspection, been a man at all, but a woman simply disguised as one. She had introduced herself only as a friend, cited the name of the earl's solicitor, and passed Eli a bound leather folder. The folder had contained a record of his father's death as well as a number of copies of documents petitioning the courts to have Eli Dawes, heir to the earldom of Rivers and all its lands and wealth, officially declared dead.

"Your father's estate has already submitted those documents to the courts, Lord Rivers," the woman had said quietly.

Eli had been too gutted and shocked to respond to either her address or her words. "How did you find me?" he had blurted like a half-wit instead.

The woman had smiled faintly but ignored his question. "I am told that there is a distant cousin in Ireland who holds legal rights to your title and estate should you choose not to contest your presumed demise. He has been found and contacted, and I have been advised that he is currently on his way to England to settle your father's affairs and assume control of the estate." She gathered the reins of her horse and swung herself up into the saddle. "So you can be reassured that the Rivers legacy won't be relegated into abeyance or simply become extinct, if that makes any difference to you. The courts will drag their feet on declaring you officially dead, but for how long it's hard to say, given the nature of your presumed demise. Especially once a living heir presents himself. I would suggest that whatever you decide to do, decide it carefully and with the urgency it deserves."

"That's it?" Eli had croaked.

"I'm not going to knock you senseless and drag you back to London, Lord Rivers," she had said with an infuriating calm. "Nor will I disclose that I've found you alive and well. From experience, I can tell you that this must be your decision and your decision alone."

And then she had simply ridden away.

"Dawes?"

Eli was jerked back into the present at the sound of Rose's voice. She was watching him with concern.

He pushed himself to his feet. The revelation of his father's death had left an awful, hollow feeling inside his chest, which had been filled instantly with an excruciating regret. That regret had never gone away. Perhaps Eli had thought he'd have more time. Perhaps he had thought that there would be an opportunity later for him to make things right with his father. Except later had come and gone and he had lost his chance.

He'd sat down to write to his father—dozens of times in that first year after Waterloo. Yet he never had, and he didn't have a good reason why, other than that he had been a coward. Afraid of the reply he might get. Or perhaps more afraid of the one he would never get.

"You can't hide here in Dover forever." Rose had risen as well and was standing beside him. "You're going to have to go to London to claim what is yours."

"I'm not hiding," he snapped.

"Says the man who let everyone believe he was dead because he isn't as pretty as he once was."

Eli felt the air rush from his lungs. "How dare you." He could barely form the words.

"I dare a lot of things these days, Dawes." Rose met his gaze, unflinching and unapologetic. "You might want to try the same. It's quite liberating."

He took a step toward her, forcing her to look up at him. He tried to gather his thoughts, tried to control the emotion that was raging through him.

"I'm right, aren't I?" She didn't give an inch.

"No," he snarled. "You're not."

"Prove it." Her dark eyes were steady.

"I don't have to prove anything to you."

"No, you don't. But I would suggest that you have quite a bit to prove to yourself." Her chin came up. "Sit for a portrait."

"What?"

"In my class tomorrow morning. Be my model."

"Have you lost your mind?" Eli was staring at her, unable to even comprehend what she was asking.

Rose's lips curled slightly, but the smile didn't reach her eyes. "Not at all, though such comments make me question the reason for your reluctance."

"Insolence does not become you."

"So I was right."

"You were not."

"Look at you," Rose snapped. "Look how you're standing even now, your scars turned away as if you still think I will... What? Cover my eyes? Run away?"

"People have."

"Then good riddance to them."

"You have no idea what it's like to be shunned and ridiculed because of your appearance." He was shouting, and he couldn't stop himself. Fury had taken hold, and he couldn't seem to shake it.

Her mouth dropped open. "I have no..." She stopped, blinking rapidly. "I have no idea?"

"Has anyone ever called you a gargoyle? Ogre? Demon?"

She looked as if she was going to say something and then changed her mind. "No," she said slowly, a peculiar expression on her face. "No, I don't suppose they have."

"Then you know *nothing*. Don't pretend otherwise."

"You know what, Dawes, do as you wish. Hide, don't hide, lie, don't lie." She made a noise of frustration and turned away from him. "I never should have come down here."

Eli let her get two steps away before he lunged forward and caught her arm. "Wait."

She stopped, not looking at him but not trying to pull away from him either.

"Rose." He tugged on her wrist until she finally faced him. "Wait."

"What, Dawes?" She sounded resigned.

"I..." God, he had no idea what he was trying to say. All he knew was that he didn't want her to leave. Not like this. Not because he couldn't face his own truths. He took her hand gently in his. "I didn't mean to yell. It won't happen again."

He saw her lips thin. "Dammit, Dawes, I won't shrivel into a quaking, weeping puddle because you raised your voice at me."

"That doesn't excuse it."

"You know, it was Clara who encouraged me to seek you out," she said suddenly.

Eli watched her, waiting for her to continue, unsure where she was going with this.

"My sister thought that I should make sure things were settled between us. That it would help me if I made it clear to you that I am not the woman you remember from the past. That I've recognized that things happen in life that have the power to make you either smaller or bigger. I'd like to think that in at least some ways, I've chosen bigger. So do your worst, Eli Dawes, because I can handle it all."

He stared down at her, her hand still clasped in his. He hadn't yet seemed to catch his breath, and his pulse was pounding in his ears, drowning out even the sounds of the surf. She was all defiance and beauty, steel and courage. So he did his worst.

And kissed her.

It was brief, a butterfly-light brush of his lips over hers. Eli felt her fingers tighten in his, felt the slight exhalation of her surprise against his skin. He raised his head and released her hand, afraid that if he didn't distance himself from her, he would pull her to him and never let go. He turned away from her then, acute regret and overwhelming desire warring with each other until they devolved into a confusion that was unrecognizable to him.

When he turned back, Rose was gone.

Chapter 9

Rose closed her eyes and set the charcoal down, realizing she had lost track of the minutes she had been standing in front of the easel.

When she had challenged the earl to do his worst yesterday, she had thought that perhaps he would yell at her again. Say something rude. Or maybe stomp down the beach in anger. She'd never thought he would kiss her. And from his expression, he hadn't either.

As far as kisses went, it hadn't been much of one, just a gentle, soft touch of his lips to hers that had lasted no more than a heartbeat. But it had left her disoriented. Left her awake all night, tossing and turning, wondering why she wasn't furious. Wondering why, instead, the idea of kissing him again was...consuming. She'd punched her pillow and stared at the darkened ceiling. For God's sake, kissing a woman was probably a spontaneous reaction for Eli Dawes whenever he found himself at loose ends. Like a nervous tic or inappropriate laughter.

Dawes had kissed legions of women, and Rose had never envied them for it before. Never even imagined or fantasized what it would be like. But now, it was all she could think of. She must be either weak or desperate. Maybe both.

Rose had finally dragged herself out of bed at dawn, irritable and restless. She never should have listened to Clara. She never should have gone down to that beach. She simply should have avoided the earl, left well enough alone, and let him think whatever the hell he wanted to think of her. Because in an effort to prevent their subsequent interactions from being awkward and tense, she had somehow managed to ensure that every meeting from now on would be more awkward and tense than anything she could ever have imagined.

"Woolgathering, dearie?" Theo's voice yanked Rose from her hopeless musings, making her realize that she had been standing dumbly in front of the easel without even the charcoal to give her a legitimate purpose.

"Something like that," Rose muttered, stepping away and moving on to the next workstation she had set up. There were a dozen easels, each with a blank canvas, each with a small table beside that held an assortment of art supplies.

"Something you'd like to share?" The elderly woman wandered into the studio, a heavily embroidered robe pulled snug around her rotund body, her silver hair streaming loosely down her back. She held a bouquet of cut roses in her hand.

Rose shook her head, trying her best to appear serene. The last thing she was about to do was confess that Eli Dawes had kissed her on a beach yesterday and she had simply stood there and let it happen. She wondered if, after everything that had unfolded in the last few days, her judgment had been compromised. If her reaction had simply been a product of a misplaced sense of compassion. She had seen the unhappiness and regret that was eating at him—understood it, even. A different man had stood before her on that beach, but who he had become was rather murky.

"Rose?"

She jerked again, realizing that she hadn't answered the question.

"No, it's nothing of import," she said, forcing a smile at Lady Theodosia.

"If you say so, dearie," the woman said, making it clear she didn't believe it for a minute.

"Why don't you go and make yourself comfortable up on the dais?" Rose asked, anxious to change the subject to anything that did not involve Lady Theo's nephew.

Theo's eyes lit up as she climbed the low step up to the settee. "About that. I know we usually do Titian's *Venus of Urbino*, but I was wondering if perhaps today we might recreate Botticelli."

"*The Birth of Venus*?"

"Yes."

Rose considered it and then shook her head. "You would be required to stand for too long."

"But it's so much more dramatic."

"So is you fainting flat on your face after standing motionless for two hours. I'd rather avoid it, if it's all the same to you."

"I won't faint."

"What about Titian's *Venus with a Mirror*?" Rose was drumming her fingers on her thigh. "You could sit for that. And for our purposes, I confess, it's rather perfect in what it represents," she said, warming to the idea. "The critique of vanity, as it were." Rose spun and retrieved a gilded mirror about the length of her arm from the corner of the studio. "We could use this."

"Hmm." Theo pursed her lips in thought. "I rather like that idea as well."

"Excellent." Rose smiled. "But before you disrobe, I'll make sure—"

"Aunt?"

Rose whirled to find the earl standing in the doorway, staring not at her but at Theo, who had set the roses aside and was arranging the crimson satin over the settee. Immediately Rose's pulse picked up speed, and a strange prickle of anticipation crackled through her.

"Eli. Good morning, dear." Lady Theodosia's face creased into a welcoming smile. "I hope you found the dower house comfortable and the staff amenable last night?"

"Yes, yes," Dawes answered with clear distraction. His mouth had fallen open slightly, his expression one of dismay. Abruptly he averted his eyes and turned his back to the room and its occupants but made no motion to leave. "What are you doing, Aunt?" he demanded. "And why aren't you dressed?"

"I'm getting ready for class, dear."

"In your nightclothes?" He sounded appalled.

Theo only laughed, and Dawes tentatively looked back, alarm written across his face.

Rose hurried across the studio. "A word, Lord Rivers?" She slipped by him out the door, pulling it shut behind them. She glanced up and down the hallway but, to her relief, found no one.

"What the hell is my aunt doing wandering around Avondale in her nightclothes?" Eli whispered, sounding aggrieved. "Is she...not well?" He gestured to his head.

Rose managed to suppress the laughter that threatened only by sheer will.

"You think this is funny?" Dawes hissed at her.

Apparently she hadn't been as successful as she had thought. "Your aunt is quite fine. More than fine. Brilliant, actually."

"Then what is she doing? Her hair hasn't even been attended to, for God's sake."

"We are studying Titian this morning and attempting to reproduce his attention to light and depth and his unparalleled handling of color. Lady Theodosia is my Venus today," Rose said, glad for the distraction that this conversation was providing. If she'd had to stand this close to him without purpose, she'd probably be staring at his mouth. Wondering if he would try to kiss her again. And wondering if she would let him again.

"Stop talking in riddles," Eli snapped. "I'm tired, and I've not the patience for it."

"Didn't sleep well?" Rose asked, and wanted those words back instantly. What did she think she was doing?

He stared down at her, and she could see the rise and fall of his chest. His gaze lingered on her face and then her mouth for a moment too long. Heat suddenly pooled low in her belly, and breathing became a chore.

"My aunt," he repeated in clipped tones. "You will explain to me why she is in your studio dressed like a courtesan."

"Your aunt," Rose managed to force out, "is my model."

"Model," Eli repeated.

"Yes. I believe I mentioned the class yesterday." *Before you kissed me.* She looked down, afraid that last thought would be written all over her face. "She will be recreating Titian's *Venus with a Mirror.* Probably my most favorite of all his works, for what it represents."

"And your students will paint her in nothing but a robe?"

The earl sounded as if he was hanging on to his patience by a thread.

Rose raised her eyes and held his. "No. They will paint her as Venus."

Eli goggled at her. "Naked?"

"There you go again, Dawes, fretting over nudity," Rose said. "Soon I am going to accuse you of being predictable."

"My aunt is a lady," Eli hissed. "She should not be subjected to such...such..."

"Veneration?"

The earl blinked.

"Your aunt does this of her own volition. She's been one of my best models over the years."

"But she's not—"

"Young?" Rose bit out. "Perfect?"

Eli stared.

"Beauty can be found everywhere, should you only look. It is not a finite commodity. It changes with time and circumstance to become something new and different, but no less valuable. Your aunt is no less beautiful now than she was fifty years ago."

"That's not what I was going to suggest."

"Good," Rose said succinctly.

"But your students—"

"Also understand that beauty goes far beyond the usual clichés. It is my job to remind them of that. Often. Expand their horizons, ensure they continue to see the world and the value they may bring to it with broader views and understanding."

"What are you saying?"

"These young women are fully aware that society most often measures them by their title and appearance, not their mind. That being different or remarkable is not something that is admired. They recognize that, while they are expected to be clever, their intelligence and wit can at no time overshadow those of their male companions."

"That's . . ."

"Disheartening? Infuriating?" Rose finished for him. "I agree."

He was frowning fiercely.

"The young women here at Avondale have been selected from the scores of wealthy and titled students that you'll find in Haverhall's regular fall and winter terms in London. Chosen because they possess something far more uncommon than an enviable listing in *Debrett's*."

"What?"

"A sense of self-worth and courage to explore it. Ambition and the daring to defy expectations. A complete disregard for the conventional and the superficial. The desire to be measured by their own merit, not by the accident of their birth."

"I'm not sure what that means."

"It means that, this summer at Haverhall, we have aspiring architects, students studying various disciplines of law, an apothecary, a gunsmith, a goldsmith, a portraitist, and of course you've already met Rachel Swift, our sole medical student this year. Each student has a local mentor. My brother is one, but there are others willing to overlook the fact that these students wear skirts and are saddled with titles and fortunes that would otherwise keep them in pretty gilded cages."

Eli looked nonplussed. "Cages."

"Miss Swift is the eldest daughter to one of the wealthiest steel barons in England. The man could buy most of Mayfair should he take the notion, and he has determined that nothing less than a duke will do when she weds."

"That's not unreasonable. It's how the world works."

"You're right. Because unreasonable would be Rachel's desire to attend medical school. Unreasonable would be her ambition to become a physician. Unreasonable is acknowledgement of her incredible skill. Skill that I am told the people in the surrounding parishes of Dover are most grateful for. Especially when it comes to bone setting and flesh wounds. And burns, of course."

"But how does any of this benefit her? She goes back to London or wherever she's from, and you can't expect me to believe that she will be allowed to continue in such a vein." He leaned back against the wall.

"She goes back to London with the knowledge that not only is she good at what she does, she is better than most. That she possesses a valuable skill worth defending and developing. And that empowers her to make decisions. Decisions about her future and how she wishes to live it."

"But her father—"

"Will have a difficult time forcing her to marry a duke. Unless, of course, she chooses to. Similar, I would hope, to the inability of your father to force you to marry."

He jerked. "How did you know about that?"

"About what?"

"Never mind."

Rose blew out a long breath, her stomach dropping strangely toward her toes. "You were to be married?"

Eli rubbed at his face with his hands.

"You never mentioned it before."

"Because it wasn't what I wanted. It was what my father wanted."

"Why?"

The earl made a rude noise. "Because he thought it would give me purpose and accountability in a life which lacked both. But you're right. He couldn't force me to do it. And then I left London, and it no longer mattered."

"Who was she?"

"That also doesn't matter."

"I rather think it does." Rose swallowed, alarmed to discover her hands were clenched in the folds of her skirts. "Especially if she still believes you're dead."

"It's just as well she believes me dead. I'm not exactly marriage material any longer."

"That's what you believe?"

"That's what I know."

Irritation swelled. "Well, I'd have to agree, then. Who would ever want to be married to a man who can't take his head out of his ass long enough to stop feeling sorry for himself?"

Two slashes of angry color appeared over Eli's cheeks. He pushed himself away from the wall and took three steps toward the tall window at the end of the hallway. "I'm not feeling sorry for myself. I'm being realistic," he said tightly, his back to her.

"Of course you are." She shook her head. "Did you even write to her while you were away? The woman you loved?"

Eli turned and stared at her, an unsettling expression on his face.

"Why are you looking at me like that?" Rose demanded. "I'm hardly being unreasonable."

His features abruptly rearranged themselves into a look of discontent once again. "I didn't love her. I barely knew her."

"She was your father's choice for you, then?" Rose asked, wondering why she couldn't seem to let this go and well aware she was relentlessly pushing him into a corner.

"Why else would I ever have reason to marry—" He

stopped midsentence. Slowly he turned around. "You think I seduced her. Compromised her."

"No." Rose tipped her chin up.

"Now who's lying?" He stepped back toward her until he was a breath away.

"Fine. But you've seduced half of London, Dawes. I've seen you do it. It's not an unreasonable conclusion."

"The women I seduced knew damn well I was seducing them and knew damn well exactly how the last act would play out."

His voice had dropped, and the low timbre scraped along every nerve ending in her body. This was a man whose skills in the bedroom had been legendary. A man who had been known for gifting the most potent pleasure before he sought his own. Whatever clever retort she'd had in mind died unuttered as she imagined the scenarios that that entailed. Deliciously erotic, lewd scenes that stole her breath and her wits.

"No matter what you think of me, Miss Hayward, I have never taken advantage of a woman who hasn't the experience and knowledge to take full advantage of me. To return the favor tenfold."

A peculiar sensation wound through her. "Is that what you wanted from me?"

He stilled. "What?"

"Why did you kiss me, Dawes?"

A muscle in his jaw jumped. "That's not— I don't— I should never have kissed you. It was impulsive, and I can only ask your forgiveness."

"You regret kissing me?"

"No. Yes." Frustration and something darker were written across his features.

"Which one?"

He looked away from her briefly, his body visibly tense. "You're different. You're not…"

"Experienced? Knowledgeable enough to take full advantage of you?"

She heard the air leave his lungs at the same time she saw his expression change. His gaze went hot, his breathing more shallow than it had been a second before. "Rose." It was a clear warning and an entreaty all at once.

"Or maybe you thought that I would be flattered by whatever crumbs of attention you cast my way?"

"No. God, no. That's not—"

"Then perhaps you thought no one else would." She was being reckless now, but she couldn't bring herself to stop.

"Jesus, Rose, what man wouldn't want to kiss you?"

"You misunderstand, Dawes. I wasn't talking about me. I was talking about you."

~⸻~

For a blinding second, Eli felt the void inside him expand, the blackness threatening to devour him whole. His chest felt as if it were on fire, and he couldn't seem to draw a full breath.

"What did you just say?" he rasped.

Rose leaned forward, so close that he could see the tiny flecks of caramel in the dark chocolate of her irises. So close he could feel the warmth of her body and smell the richness of her scent. "I asked if you believe yourself to be unkissable. Unattractive. Unlovable."

Her words fell like a series of blows, each one more painful than the last. He stared at her, at a complete loss for words. Who was this woman? The enchanting, affable woman he had once danced with, discussed art with, and attended opera with had been replaced with someone else entirely. Someone with unyielding strength and sharp edges. Someone who was ruthlessly hacking away at his defenses without apology and with all the elegance of a Viking warrior.

Or perhaps she hadn't been replaced at all. Perhaps this was just another part of her he had never truly known.

"I'm not answering that," he managed.

"Why?"

He stepped away from her, angry at his inability to answer her unyielding onslaught. He had no idea how he was supposed to answer anything.

Rose raised a slim brow and crossed her arms over her chest. "Why?" she asked again.

"Because it isn't any of your business," he snapped.

"You made it my business when you kissed me, Dawes," she said, her voice cool and caressing him like silk. "I'd like to know if you were using me to salve your own insecurities or if you kissed me for another reason altogether."

Eli felt the ground beneath him tilt, and it was an effort to remain steady. Jesus, was that what she believed? He shook his head, trying to find the right words.

Her lip curled. "That's what I thou—"

"When I kissed you, I wasn't thinking about anything except how beautiful you were," he rasped fiercely. "How wild and real and fearless you were standing on that beach. And how much I wanted a taste of that."

Rose gazed at him with that impenetrable stare of hers that betrayed nothing of what she was thinking. Finally she uncrossed her arms and stepped toward him. Her eyes traveled over his face, and for once he didn't feel the need to turn away, at least until her eyes fell to his lips. And then he was afraid that if he didn't turn away, put space between them, he would kiss her again.

"I've been seduced before, Eli Dawes," she said, and Eli's mouth went dry.

"What?"

"I've shocked you."

He wasn't shocked. Or maybe he was. It was hard to think because right now he was more aroused than he had ever been in his entire life. He felt as if he had just discovered himself on the wrong end of a bottle of whiskey, dazed and disoriented.

"I am not without experience and knowledge, Lord Rivers. And I will not abide a man who uses me for his own—"

Eli's fingers brushed her lips, silencing her instantly. He caressed the sharp angle of her cheekbone, the impossibly smooth skin at her temple. His fingers delved into her glorious mass of red-blond curls, letting the softness wrap around his touch. "That kiss was never about anything other than you," he said.

She gazed up at him, silent, and he would have given his entire fortune right then to know what she was thinking.

"Prove it."

New anger surged through his arousal. "Not this again."

"I've learned that a man should be judged on his actions and not his words. I'll ask you to do the same thing tomorrow. And the day after that. And, if you're still talking to me, the day after that. I would not call myself a friend if I did not."

"What is wrong with you?" God, he wanted to shake her and kiss her all at once.

She shrugged carelessly, her eyes daring him to do his worst, just as they had done yesterday on the beach. His anger faded as fast as it had risen, replaced again by the all-consuming need to kiss her. To possess her in every sensuous, carnal way he could imagine. He needed to kiss her the way he needed air. He lowered his head, but her own fingers came up to touch his lips, stopping him.

"You won't prove anything that way." Her voice wobbled slightly.

"Then how?" It might have sounded desperate, but at this moment he didn't care.

"A Man of Sorrows," Rose said. "To replace my *Venus of Urbino*. A Titian for a Titian. His early *Ecce Homo*."

Eli sucked in a breath. A portrait. It was what she had demanded while they stood on that beach yesterday. But he still would not do what she was asking. Could not do what she was asking. "I can't. I'm not—"

"A man of sorrows?" Her fingers slid from his lips to trail down the ruined side of his face. He thought she sounded suddenly sad. "Then maybe you can simply become a Knight of Malta," she suggested, her hand dropping to her side. "A man with the confidence and courage to defeat his sorrows."

"I can't."

"Of course you can. You won't."

Eli felt his body go rigid with frustration.

"Perhaps it's best if we forget that you ever kissed me. Pretend it never happened, before it gets too complicated." Rose ducked her head, and his fingers slipped from the softness of her hair. "Because I will always be second-guessing your motivations." She took a step back.

From somewhere downstairs he could hear the sounds of voices and the muted clatter of footsteps across marble. "Rose—"

"Those are the students on their way up to my class. Decide if what you want is worth your vanity, Lord Rivers."

"This has nothing to do with my vanity," he growled.

"No? Then enlighten me." There was an edge to her words. A final assault on the remnants of his fort of isolation.

"This is blackmail. My privacy for … whatever the hell kind of agenda you have."

"Don't be melodramatic. And it isn't my agenda in question here, but yours."

He cursed. The voices were at the bottom of the stairs now, snippets of conversation audible as they advanced. "What you're asking— It would be indecent." It sounded feeble, even in his own ears. "Your students are innocent young women. They should not be exposed to—"

"Anatomy class was last week, Dawes. Taught by my doctor brother and the local midwife with plenty of diagrams, half of them drawn by Rachel Swift. Every one of the students, if she wasn't before, is now well educated on the female body, the male body, and the bits that fit together. How they work. And all the potential consequences of that."

Eli found himself staring again, his mind struggling to process both the information and the casualness with which it had been delivered.

"You should also know that you aren't the only male model they've been asked to sketch or paint," Rose continued, as though she were commenting on the rainfall last night. "And I hate to beat a dead horse here, but half of London has seen you without your shirt."

"But they weren't just sitting and … staring at me."

Rose snorted and rolled her eyes. "Oh, I'm quite sure they were otherwise occupied with all the bits that fit together."

"Did you just roll your eyes at me?"

"Ask another stupid question, and I'll do it again."

Bloody hell. "Rose—"

"I just need a yes or a no, Dawes. I need to tell your aunt one way or another—"

"Very well," Eli said, before he could reconsider what he was doing. His anger, along with his arousal, neither of which had fully dissipated, was making him reckless. Rose had no idea what sort of game she was playing.

"Very well?"

"I'll be your *Ecce Homo*. Your Man of Sorrows. Less the thorns, if it's all the same to you."

He closed the distance between them and caught her chin in his fingers. Something shifted in her expression, and her eyes once again fell to his mouth. He moved his hand and dragged his thumb over her lower lip, the sensual softness sending an aching hunger through his body and making his pulse jump erratically. Her own hand came up, her fingers wrapping around his wrist, though she made no move to pull his hand away. Instead it seemed more as if she was simply holding on.

The sounds of feet on the stairs were clear now. Within seconds the students would reach the hallway.

"When I kiss you again, Rose Hayward," he whispered, stepping back and putting a respectable amount of distance between them, "you will never second-guess the reason why."

Chapter 10

There was a single student left in her studio.

Lady Lucy Dunleavy, daughter to the Marquess of Livingston and, at seventeen, one of the most accomplished portraitists Rose had had the privilege of teaching, was still absorbed in her work. Rose stood quietly to the side, watching her masterful application of color turn the blankness of her canvas into something astonishing. Occasionally Lucy would ask Rose a question—more of a consultation on technique, really, than anything else—but for the most part Rose simply observed.

The rest of the students, for whom art was a more casual pursuit, had already departed for luncheon. Lucy had asked for an additional hour. Rose had looked to Eli, knowing the earl had no reason to agree, but to her shock he had simply nodded. And so he remained for a third hour, still and silent, her fallen angel on a bed of crimson satin.

A fallen angel, Rose corrected herself hastily. This man did not belong to her, nor she to him, in any manner.

Her eyes slipped beyond Lucy's canvas to where he sat on the dais, and she watched him from beneath her lashes. He sat upright, his hands clasped in front of him, his gaze fixed somewhere beyond his knees. The damaged side of his face was slightly angled away from the students, as the pose required, but the earl had, surprisingly, made no effort to hide his scars as her students had filed in. He hadn't said a word to anyone and hadn't met Rose's eyes as she introduced him and thanked him for his generosity and willingness to sit for their class.

In the pale wash of light, his beauty struck her anew every time she looked at him. Her fingers twitched, and she wasn't sure if it was from her desire to paint her own version of this physically magnificent man or if she simply wished to touch him. Run her hands along the edge of his jaw, feel the broadness of his shoulders, explore the scattering of blond hair in the center of his chest, or trace the ridges of muscle over his abdomen.

When I kiss you again, you will never second-guess the reason why.

A surge of anticipation crashed through her and made her skin tighten and her nipples harden, and made her squeeze her thighs together against the dampness that instantly gathered at her core. She closed her eyes briefly, trying to rein in her arousal. She wasn't an unschooled girl, given to flights of fancy and ignorant belief in fairy tales. And maybe that was the problem.

I've been seduced before, she'd told him. But *before* had been a long time ago.

Too long ago, clearly.

"Miss Hayward?"

Rose jolted and forced her attention back to her student. She avoided looking in Eli's direction and instead focused on the canvas in front of her. Which might have been worse.

The seventeen-year-old's skill was truly extraordinary, and from the canvas had emerged a stunning likeness of the Earl of Rivers. Lucy had sketched him first and added a few washes of color, just enough to add a riveting depth to her work. But it was the expression on his face that she'd captured that made it impossible for Rose to look away. There was a stoic sadness to the portrait, a perfect representation that so many of the *Ecce Homo* portraits failed to capture.

A perfect representation of a man who had suffered betrayal and heartbreak, a man who had lost everything but found something inside that forced him onward, even when the path wasn't clear.

"I'd like to finish with the background later on, if that's all right," Lucy was saying to Rose as she cleaned her brush. "I do not wish to dominate any more of Lord Rivers's time." She flashed Rose a smile. "And, I confess, I'm rather famished."

"Of course," Rose murmured, unable to look away.

Lucy set her brush aside and stepped out from behind her easel. "Thank you, Lord Rivers, for the privilege. And for the generosity of your time and for your...progressiveness."

On the dais Eli had stirred from his pose; he straightened with a small frown. "My progressiveness?" It was the first thing he'd said in three hours.

Lucy glanced back at Rose.

"I think she means your confidence that your current state of dress could be regarded with the objectivity required for portraiture and not met with female hysterics, followed by a dozen cases of the vapors," Rose explained drily. From the corner of her eye, she saw Lucy nod.

"You are a rare man, Lord Rivers," the young woman added solemnly. "Thank you again."

Eli blinked at her, and Rose hid a smile as the young woman drifted from the room. The earl stood and stretched,

grimacing. Rose averted her gaze, the sight of all that mas-
culinity making her wonder if perhaps she had been a little
hasty in her earlier comments. Because her knees were suddenly feeling a little weak, and her breath had become
alarmingly shallow. Vapors indeed.

"That wasn't so hard, was it?" Rose asked, aiming for a
light tone, her eyes firmly on the portrait.

Eli made some sort of inarticulate noise as she heard him
move to retrieve his shirt.

"Would you like to see it?" Rose willed herself not to
raise her eyes and stare, though she could still see him over
the top of the canvas. "Lucy's work, I mean."

"No."

"Why not?"

"Because I don't." He pulled his shirt on over his head.

"She's extraordinarily talented," Rose admonished. "I
can't necessarily say the same for my other students, but
what Lucy has done here is—"

"I said no." He collected his coat from the back of a chair,
his back to her. "I did what you wanted. And now I'm done."

Rose frowned and looked up at him. "What I wanted? I
was under the impression that—" She stopped abruptly as a
commotion from somewhere downstairs filtered up.

"My lord? Miss Hayward?" The address came from near
the door. A young girl, wearing a plain dress covered by
a soot-stained apron, was wringing her hands. She glanced
at Eli, averted her eyes, and addressed Rose instead. "Captain Buhler is here, demanding to speak with someone. An'
there's a dozen redcoats in the drive outside with him," the
maid continued. "I reckon they're looking for Charlie, but
Lady Theo and Tabby are out and Dr. Hayward ain't here
and the duchess is in town and—"

"Thank you," Rose said, and cursed softly under her

breath. She'd almost forgotten about the captain, though it was faintly surprising that it had taken Buhler and his posse of garrison soldiers this long to show up. "I'll be right there to speak to him—"

"You will not," Eli said evenly. "I will speak to this officer."

"You don't need to do that. I can handle this."

"I'm quite sure you can." He turned to the maid still wringing her hands in her apron. "Have this captain put in the blue drawing room. I'll attend to the man presently."

The maid's eyes were wide and uncertain, but she raised her chin tremulously. "Forgive me, milord, but ye won't be sayin' anything about—"

"The fact that Charlie just beat me at checkers twice this morning?" Eli dropped his coat back on the chair. "No. I have a reputation to uphold. Best not to mention that such an indignity ever happened or that he was ever here, don't you agree?"

The girl stared at him before bobbing her head, relief written all over her face. "Yes, milord."

Rose turned to Eli as the maid vanished, her chest strangely tight. "You didn't tell me you had gone to see Charlie this morning."

"You didn't ask." He was rolling the sleeves of his shirt up his arms.

"Why did you?"

Eli leaned on the back of the chair, his knuckles white where they gripped the edge of the upholstery. "Because I know what it feels like to be injured and alone."

"Oh." The tightness had moved up into her throat. Rose had a sudden, overwhelming urge to touch him. To stroke the side of his face, to smooth away the sorrow touching his features.

"He was worried about his sisters. And his mother."

"What did you say?"

"I told him to worry about getting well. So that he could get home to them sooner." Eli abruptly straightened and ran a hand through his hair, leaving it a little disheveled. "Tell me about this Captain Buhler."

Rose let him change the subject. "He is...ambitious. Ruthless. Heartless. Resolute in his mission to exterminate every smuggler and thief along the Kentish coastlines, regardless of age or gender or circumstance. He craves recognition. Power. Possesses an incessant need for admiration."

Eli strode to the door. "You know this man well."

Rose shook her head. "I only know what Harland has told me. And Clara and the duke have crossed swords with him on more than one occasion."

He paused in the door frame. "Literally or figuratively?"

"Figuratively. For now, anyway. Buhler is not well regarded by anyone in this household. In this parish, really. And the feeling is mutual, I rather suspect. The captain knows, however, that he is outranked at every turn at Avondale. He resents it, just as he resents the occasions that Harland is called to the garrison by a major or colonel to consult and treat one of the enlisted men or officers."

"Why would he resent that?"

"Because Harland is a baron who does not answer to him and who is very good at what he does."

Eli looked grim. "Well, then, let's see how this captain does with an earl who does not answer to him. An earl who is also exceedingly good at what he does."

Rose stepped around the canvas. "Which is what, Dawes?"

"Scaring people away."

Eli strode down the hall to the wide staircase. He had a good idea what sort of man this captain was. He had met many men like him, and it mattered not if it had been on a battlefield or in the back rooms of White's. Men who wished to carve a name out of history for themselves by whatever means necessary, even if those means were devoid of honor or integrity.

"Dawes!" He stopped at the bottom of the stairs, realizing Rose had followed him.

"What?"

"Your coat." She was holding the garment he'd left on the studio chair out to him.

"I don't need it," he said. "If I'm going to shock this captain out of Avondale, I might as well do a proper job of it."

Rose was looking at him, worry in her dark eyes. "Are you sure you want to—"

"Do not ask me what I think you are going to ask me," Eli said. "The answer is still the same."

"Lord Rivers?" The address came from behind him.

Eli turned to find Avondale's butler approaching. Danby? Dirkley? He hadn't yet reacquainted himself with the entirety of the staff, and his memory floundered. "Yes?"

"I've put Captain Buhler in the blue drawing room," the portly man said. "As usual."

As usual? "How often does this happen?"

"More than we'd like, my lord."

"Thank you, Digby," Rose answered for him. "His Lordship will be there shortly."

"Very good." The butler paused. "I did not mention that you were in residence, Lord Rivers. I believe the captain is expecting the baron."

"Well done, Digby," Eli said. He would use every advantage he could get.

"I thought so, my lord." The butler offered him a faint inclination of his head before he pivoted smartly and withdrew.

Rose was watching him, a strange expression on her face. "Do you want me to join you?"

"No, I don't want you to join me. Do you not trust me to get rid of this captain?"

"Of course I trust you. I just thought you might want someone else on your side in there."

"On my side?"

"Yes." Rose looked suddenly flustered.

Eli took a step toward her and caught her hand in his. Without thinking about what he was doing, he raised her knuckles to his lips. That chronic, empty darkness within him that threatened to swallow him whole at times had suddenly splintered into a thousand tiny pieces.

He saw her lips part, heard her catch her breath.

And God help him, but if he didn't have a boy hidden in his attics and a captain in his drawing room, Eli might simply have picked up Rose Hayward, swept the vase of roses from the table in the center of the hall, and had his way with her right then and there.

"Thank you," he heard himself say, though it came out as an undignified croak.

"For what?" she whispered.

He had no idea. For being on his side? For believing he could be trusted? For believing in him, period?

He squeezed her fingers in his, unable to answer, and turned away. He stalked across the now-gleaming hall, the white marble as pristine as it had been before a body had been carried through it. He stopped just outside the partially closed door of the blue drawing room and straightened his shoulders, trying his best to push all lingering remnants of Rose from his mind, knowing he could not afford the distraction. Eli took a deep breath, wondering for just a moment what he was getting himself into. Then he shoved the door open with enough force that it banged against the interior wall and stepped inside.

Afternoon light poured in the windows that overlooked the long drive and lawns at the front of Avondale. The captain had been standing in front of one of them, polishing the shiny buttons on his scarlet coat, but at Eli's unceremonious entrance, he whirled.

"Captain Buhler." Eli crossed the room, his hands clasped behind his back, his boots silent on the luxurious rug beneath his feet.

The captain was a bulldog of a man with a barrel chest, thick neck, and slightly bowed legs. His boots were polished to a blinding sheen, and he held his hat under his arm. He was a good head shorter than Eli, with the dour, unhappy look of a man who found little enjoyment in life. Buhler's flinty eyes widened as Eli approached, skittering distastefully over Eli's ruined face before he sneered slightly at Eli's casually improper attire.

"I'm afraid there's been a misunderstanding," the captain said, drawing himself up to his full height but not meeting Eli's gaze. "I had requested an audience with Lord Strathmore, not his gardener."

"Indeed? I will need to reprimand my butler for his ambiguity. Allow me to introduce myself. Eli Dawes, fourteenth Earl of Rivers."

The captain's jaw slackened, and his lips worked for a moment before he was able to form a sentence. His eyes slid to the sides, anywhere but Eli's face, as if looking for an explanation. "Forgive me, but I was told that the late earl's son was dead."

Eli shrugged carelessly. "It would appear that you should

consider acquiring better sources of information. I can assure you I'm quite alive."

"Ah..."

"What is it that I can do for you this afternoon, Captain?" Eli asked, his tone glacial.

The captain's face hardened. "We are looking for a criminal. A smuggler and a thief. He was seriously wounded in our attempt to apprehend him, and we have reason to believe he was brought here."

"To Avondale? You're accusing me of harboring criminals?"

"Not exactly—"

"Again, Captain, I would encourage you to reconsider your sources of information."

Buhler had yet to look him in the eye. "My lord—"

"Do you know who I am, however, harboring here at Avondale?" Eli interrupted. "The Haverhall School for Young Ladies. A dozen tender young women and their headmistresses. None of whom can be considered diabolical offenders or vicious felons, except, perhaps, when one is forced to listen to their ghastly music lessons for more than an hour."

Buhler grimaced. "It is not necessary—"

"You know what else isn't necessary? A dozen of your men and their mounts destroying my lawns and alarming my guests. These young ladies are delicate, fragile creatures, Captain. And I will not allow them to be terrorized by you and your men."

"But my lord—"

"Do you honestly think that I would allow a criminal on my premises? Do you dare suggest that I haven't made the welfare and well-being of the daughters of some of the most influential men in England my foremost priority? While these young ladies are here, they are under my protection. Are you suggesting I am not living up to my responsibilities?"

"That's not at all what I was suggesting, my lord."

"Good." Eli spun and walked to the door, stopping and waiting expectantly. "If there is nothing else?"

The captain didn't budge. "It is your position, then, Lord Rivers, that you know nothing of the theft and illicit activities that occurred yesterday? Theft from the garrison's own stores. Theft from the king himself."

"Did you not hear a word that I just said, Captain?"

"There are persistent rumors, my lord, of smugglers using your property to land and transport their ill-gotten gains. The cove just to the northeast of Avondale, specifically. In cheating the excise men, they are cheating the king."

"And your belief is that I condone such activity?"

Buhler's expression was hard. "Let me be clear. I represent the king. I have the power to bring to justice and crush every thief and every smuggler who blackens this nation's name. Those who help them are no better. They are traitors to their country. And I will do so by whatever means necessary—"

"Take a good look at me, Captain," Eli sneered. "My service to king and country almost cost me my life. I take grave insult at the insinuation that you would suppose I was a traitor by mere rumor."

"That is not at all what I was suggesting—"

"Then I'm glad we are in agreement. I'll have you shown out."

⁓

" 'Delicate, fragile creatures'?"

Rose came to stand beside the earl, gazing out the drawing room window as Captain Buhler collected his men and departed down the drive, back in the direction of the town. She clasped her hands behind her, watching Eli out of the corner of her eye.

He had a strange expression on his face—as if he had suddenly discovered something repellant. "I saw no reason to disillusion the good captain."

"Indeed."

"You were spying on me again." He said it casually, with no venom.

"Eavesdropping," she corrected.

"You're splitting hairs."

"Possibly." The soldiers had been reduced to only a small puff of dust in the distance. "That was well done."

"What was?"

"Your dismissal of the captain. I couldn't help but notice that at no point in time did you ever actually answer a question. In fact, I don't know if you ever let him finish a sentence."

She thought she saw Eli smile faintly. "Answer a question with a question. A trick my father would use. On me, mostly. Exceedingly effective."

"It was." Her fingers twisted. "Thank you, Dawes. For doing that. For protecting Charlie. For protecting my brother and Rachel."

"It's not enough."

"I beg your pardon?"

"Your brother and Miss Swift—they do something that matters. They make a difference."

"They are very good at what they do, yes," Rose agreed slowly, unsure where he was taking this conversation.

The earl continued to stare out the window. "I've never, until now, considered what drove me to collect art the way I did." He put a hand on the window casing and leaned forward, his face a blurry reflection in the glass. "Those artists left something behind. They created something bigger and better than they were as mere individuals. I envy them that."

Rose listened.

"How did I get here?" Eli mumbled, more to himself than her.

"I beg your pardon?"

"Your brother spit in society's eye when he became a physician. Miss Swift will do the same. Defied everyone and risked censure and ridicule to do something that matters. My entire life, I have had nothing but opportunity and means to do something worthwhile. And I haven't. It's unacceptable."

Rose frowned. "Some might consider fighting for your country worthwhile. Brave. Honorable."

He fell silent again. "Do I have a carriage here?" he asked suddenly.

Rose studied his profile. "Yes."

"Good. I'm going to need it."

"Where, may I ask, are you planning to go?"

"We are going out."

"We?"

"Yes."

"Is that an order or an invitation, my lord?"

Eli pushed himself away from the window and turned to look at her. "An invitation."

Rose sniffed. "I have no idea how you managed to enchant as many women as you did, Dawes. You have the finesse of a Smithfield boar. Or was that part of your charm?"

He smiled slightly, a subtle curve to his lips. "Part of my charm, I'm sure."

Rose shook her head. "Very well, then. I accept your invitation. Where are we going?"

"I'm not entirely sure yet," he told her.

"Do I need to pack a trunk? A cloak? A parasol? A pistol?"

"A lunch."

"What?"

"Pack a lunch. Enough for three."

"I was jesting, Dawes."

"I wasn't."

"Who are we meeting?"

"I'm not entirely sure of that either."

"Is this you trying to be a mysterious rogue?"

"This is me trying to be a decent human being." His smile had long since faded, and it had been replaced by a troubled look.

"Very well," Rose said quietly. "I'll see to it. Shall I meet you outside?"

"Please. I have a few things I need to attend to before we go."

"Of course." She held his gaze for a moment longer, the light coming in from the window touching his hair with gold where it fell over the ruined side of his face. Standing there, in the light as he was, he reminded her of the charismatic, impossibly handsome scoundrel he had once been. Except that scoundrel was gone, replaced by a solemn, impossibly handsome man who had just chased an army captain away to protect a boy he hardly knew.

Impulsively Rose put her hands against his chest and went up on her tiptoes to kiss his cheek.

Too late, she realized her mistake. Too late, she felt the heat beneath her palms, the rhythm of his heart under the thin layer of linen. Too late, she heard the sharp intake of his breath in her ear. Her lips had only just grazed his skin when she felt his own hands come up to cradle her face, preventing her from withdrawing.

She stood there like that for a timeless moment, motionless, her mouth a whisper away from his. He would release her, she knew, if she struggled. If she braced herself against his chest and pulled away, he would let her go. It would be the smart thing to do.

But she did not want him to let her go.

Something had changed, shifted between them. What he had started on that beach, what he had promised in the hall outside her studio, had suddenly been placed in her power. She had told him that he was a friend. That despite everything, or perhaps because of everything, their friendship had survived. Been tested by betrayal. Strengthened by truth.

What she was considering now was far more complicated than friendship. It was a dangerous foray into the unknown with a man whose ultimate ambitions were just as unclear. If she did this, she didn't know what he would become to her. Or she to him. But right now she was having a hard time concentrating on any of that.

Because she wanted to taste him. Wanted to know what all that muscle and heat would feel like beneath her hands and her lips. Wanted to explore every inch of him. Her hands slid up and over his shoulders, her fingers tangling themselves in the thick blond hair at the base of his skull. The movement pulled her closer to him, the distance between them evaporating as her breasts pressed against his chest, her legs tangling between his. He didn't move, letting her decide exactly what would happen next.

Very slowly she tipped her head, brushing her lips against the corner of his mouth. Softly, as when he had kissed her for the very first time. She moved fractionally, this time catching his lower lip ever so gently with hers. Still he remained motionless, though she could feel the rapid rise and fall of his chest against hers, that slight friction against her breasts making desire rise, hard and fast. She wondered if he would take her here, in this drawing room, if she asked him to. Up against the windows facing the empty lawns, buried deep inside her, her legs locked around his waist. Two people surrendering to a riptide of physical attraction and letting it carry them away.

But for how long? How long before he went back to London and Rose simply joined the ranks of women who had had Eli Dawes? Who had used him to fill a lonely space in their lives for a time and moved on?

She didn't want to move on. She didn't want their future encounters to be distant and awkwardly polite, the way lovers became when they were no longer intimate. She didn't want to lose this friendship that was still so raw and imperfect, but no less precious for it. Yes, she wanted him desperately. So desperately that she ached and throbbed everywhere. The need for him to touch her, to take her, was devastating and intense, and every second of her restraint was an exercise in torture.

But she wanted a friend more.

She pulled back from him, and he released her. His eyes were heated, his breathing labored. "Rose," he whispered.

"I can't do this. I can't lose you," she said.

"What? I'm not going anywhere."

"You will." He would claim his title and rightful place in London, that she was sure of. And she could not go with him.

"No." The earl was shaking his head.

"We should go," she whispered unevenly before he said anything else. Before he did anything else that would test her precarious resolve.

He let out a heavy breath. "If that's what you wish."

Chapter 11

The equipage that came with Avondale was well maintained and well sprung, the team a handsome pair of matched bays, and the coachman who waited for him capable and efficient. Rose was already waiting for him inside, a basket of food at her feet. Eli climbed in, closed the door, and settled against the impeccably tidy interior across from her. She met his gaze, offered him something that looked like a self-conscious smile, and then averted her eyes.

Eli's body still hummed with the sexual tension that had crashed around them like a tidal wave. It had been a good ten minutes after she had left him in that drawing room before he had been able to compose himself enough to follow. Nothing he had ever experienced could have prepared him for the torrent of primal need that had nearly eviscerated him. And Rose had barely touched him.

The way she had looked at him, the way she had caught his lips with hers, had left no doubt that she felt it too. It had taken everything in his power not to haul her against him and pin her against the nearest wall. Kiss her until she couldn't speak. Couldn't breathe. Couldn't think. But he hadn't. He had let her decide what she wanted. And she had withdrawn, for reasons that he still didn't understand.

"Do you regret kissing me?" he asked bluntly.

Her gaze snapped back to his, a fetching blush rising fast and furiously in her cheeks. Bloody hell, she was beautiful.

"You asked me that once," he said at her continued silence. "And I answered you honestly. Or as honestly as I could at the time, I suppose. You will not insult me if you say yes, but I insist you answer me with the same honesty."

Rose gazed at him. He couldn't tell what she was thinking. "No," she said after a heartbeat. "I don't regret it."

"Then why did you stop?"

Rose looked away.

"You don't get to do that," he said.

"What?"

"Avoid my questions. Because friends discuss difficult things. That's something else you told me."

Her eyes came back to his. "I suppose I did."

Eli waited.

"I don't want this to be complicated," she said finally.

"This?"

"Us." Rose ran her hands over her knees. "Don't you think we're already complicated enough, without us losing our heads?"

Eli sat back with a thump. *Losing their heads?* Is that what she thought that this intense physical temptation was that rose instantly every time they were together? Something no better than some adolescent adventure or a drunken night of casual bed sport? He frowned fiercely. There was nothing casual about what he felt for Rose Hayward. If he lost his head around her, it was because he had long ago lost something far more terrifying. Like his heart.

"As strange as it sounds, in some ways you know me better than anyone," Rose said quietly. "You hold some of my deepest secrets."

"Rose, I'd never betray that trust."

"I know." She gave him a small, almost sad smile. "And that is why I stopped. Your friendship is worth more than a few moments of pleasure."

Eli realized he was still frowning and forced his face to relax. He had no idea what to say, because no woman had ever valued his friendship. All had prized his title and his fortune, some those few moments of pleasure that Rose spoke of, but none had professed to be his friend. "You don't imagine we could be lovers as well as friends?"

She didn't look away. "Do you?"

Yes, he wanted to shout. Because he wanted all of her. He had wanted all of her since the very first moment he had met her. Since the very first time he had waltzed with her. Argued with her. Laughed with her.

But she hadn't been his then, and he couldn't force her to be his now. But nor would he retreat the way he'd done before. He would not let her go. But he would respect her wishes. For now.

"The things I imagine about you and me keep me awake at night, Rose," he said in a low voice. Her cheeks flushed anew, and she squirmed, her hands pressed between her knees.

Good, he thought savagely.

"But I appreciate your honesty," he continued. "I'd hate to think you might have spent the duration of this ride pinned to the back of your seat, afraid I'd pounce on you because you'd given me the wrong idea."

"And what idea would that be, exactly?" she asked, and it sounded a little breathless.

"That you find me charming. At least more so than a Smithfield boar."

Rose laughed, and Eli stared, captivated by the sound and the sight of her merriment. Once, long ago, Rose Hayward had laughed often and easily, but this was the first time he had witnessed such unguarded amusement since his return.

Eventually her laughter faded, and they sat in comfortable silence as the carriage rattled over the rutted roads. Outside, the sea disappeared and reappeared as they traversed the rolling hills, wild flowers and long grasses bent against the stiff breeze. Far below, glimpses of the chalky white cliffs stood out in stark relief against the deep blue of the water.

Rose sat back and studied him, her eyes skipping over his dusty boots and worn breeches. "Will you tell me where we are going?" she asked as the carriage turned slightly inland.

"Hougham parish," Eli told her.

"And what, exactly, is in Hougham parish?"

"Not what. Who."

She cocked her head.

"Mrs. Soames. And her daughters, Mildred and Margret. The girls are identical twins, by the way."

Rose was staring at him. "How do you know that?"

"I asked Charlie."

"I see. Lunch for three, indeed," she murmured.

"The food is a peace offering," he said. "In case Mrs. Soames is less than...receptive to my presence."

"That's why you asked me to come with you."

"It crossed my mind. A beautiful woman is less intimidating," he admitted. "But I would never have regretted any opportunity to spend time with you."

She was giving him a strange look.

"What?"

"Nothing." She shook her head slightly. "Though I'm starting to see remnants of your legendary charm."

"It's not charm; it's the truth," he said simply.

She fell silent, regarding him with the impenetrable gaze of hers that he was starting to loathe. He couldn't tell what she was thinking.

"What is it, exactly, that you hope to accomplish here?" Rose finally asked.

"To provide Mrs. Soames with reassurance that her son is safe and well. Or as well as can be expected given the circumstances. I'd like to save a parent the grief of believing their child may be suffering. Or worse."

"Like the grief your father endured."

Eli felt his teeth clench. "I can't imagine he grieved overmuch. I was an embarrassment to him."

"You're wrong. I think your father was proud of you."

"Proud of me?" Eli asked roughly. "My father was outraged when I told him I was leaving. The military is for spares, not heirs, he said. He made it abundantly clear that if I disobeyed him and left, he no longer considered me his son."

"Do you think he perhaps spoke out of anger because he was afraid that he would lose you?"

"My father wasn't given to fits of impulsive rage. He was quite clear."

Rose studied him. "He never truly believed you were dead," she said quietly.

"How can you possibly know that?" he demanded.

"He told me."

"When?"

"Harland treated your father for his gout. Often I would go with him."

"Why on earth would you—" He stopped. "To look at my paintings."

"At first. Not as much later. I discovered I enjoyed your father's company. Almost as much as I enjoyed Da Vinci's." She offered him a soft smile.

"He never looked for me. Never hired anyone to look for me. Never did what the solicitors did."

"I think he believed you would come back when you were ready."

Eli slumped back and stared sightlessly out the window. "And I came back too late."

"For some things, perhaps. But not for others."

Another silence fell between them as the carriage rattled on. The shadow of regret and grief that followed him had suddenly become more pronounced in this carriage. The opportunities he had let slip away were staggering.

"I want Mrs. Soames to know that if she or the rest of her family require any further assistance, they may appeal to me for help," Eli said, ending any further conversation about his father and all the regrets that surrounded that topic.

Rose sighed but did not press him. "Of course," she said. "But know that pride may be the only thing Mrs. Soames has left. She may be unwilling to accept your help, however much she needs it."

Something in the way she said it caught his attention. He looked back at her. "You speak from experience."

"Perhaps." She shrugged as the carriage slowed and turned sharply before drawing to a halt altogether. It bounced slightly as the driver descended.

"Will you tell me?" he asked.

The door was suddenly opened, and a gust of wind swirled in the interior, ruffling Rose's skirts. Eli watched Rose, but it was clear an answer to his question was not forthcoming. He stepped out and offered Rose his hand. She took it without any hesitation and joined him on the ground, then released his fingers. Eli resisted the urge to snatch her hand back in his and keep her close. Instead he took a step forward and examined his surroundings.

They were in a depression of sorts, the land sloping to the sea, the shadows of the white cliffs on one side and the open water on the other. Thick reams of marsh grass rippled in the relentless wind, and the pungent odor of decaying vegetation and brackish water was overpowering. A forlorn, forgotten place home to biting insects and brooding plovers.

And people, it seemed.

Just beyond the rutted track listed a tiny, crooked cottage, if it could be called that. It was more of a shed, really, battered by the elements, with large chinks in the walls and its thatch ragged and in poor repair. A pitiful garden had been scratched out of the dirt along one side, pieces of spindly driftwood driven into the ground as stakes. A fishing net had been draped over more stakes and spread across the yard like an abandoned spider's web. There was no sign of anyone anywhere.

"Are they here, do you think?" Rose asked.

Eli shrugged. A movement near the back of the cottage, behind the garden, caught his eye. He stepped forward again. "Mrs. Soames?" he called.

There was no answer.

"I'm here about your son, Charlie." He was aware Rose had moved to stand beside him. "I mean no harm," he said loudly. "I only bring news."

"And cake," Rose added.

A head popped out from behind the cottage and then another. Two sets of pretty brown eyes stared out at them from small faces. A small, black, one-eyed mutt slunk from behind them and barked loudly before retreating back toward its mistresses.

"Good afternoon," Rose said. "Are you Mildred and Margret?"

The eyes widened. There was a flurry of whispers, and then one of the girls stepped out from behind the cottage. "How do you know our names?"

"Your brother told us," Rose answered.

"Who are you?" she demanded.

She couldn't be more than eight or nine, Eli thought, though her voice held a cynical wariness that belied her years. Her face was painfully thin but clean, her dark hair pulled neatly back from her face in a long braid. Her dress was too short, and there were patches upon the patches, but she stood straight and tall like a princess commanding her court.

Eli hung back, letting Rose take the lead. Since Mrs. Soames had yet to make an appearance, Eli assumed that only the two girls were home. And from experience Eli knew it was far more likely that the girls would speak to a beautiful woman who looked like a fairy princess than to a man who looked like the troll from the same story.

"My name is Rose. And this is my friend Eli."

Two sets of eyes narrowed in suspicion as they swung toward him. So much for remaining unobtrusive.

"Are you a soldier?" the girl asked.

"No."

"Did you get in a fight?"

"What?" Eli frowned.

"Bruno got in a fight and lost his eye. Is that how you lost yours?"

It took Eli a moment to realize that Bruno was the dog. "Sort of," Eli said slowly. "It happened in the war."

"So you are a soldier."

"Not anymore."

"Is that your carriage?"

"Yes."

"Are you rich?"

He frowned at the rapid questions. "Yes," he answered anyway.

"Where's the cake?" The twin who hadn't said anything yet spoke up.

"In the carriage," Rose told her. "I can fetch it for you if you like while we wait."

"Wait for what?" Eli and Rose both spun to find a narrow woman with the same chestnut hair and brown eyes as her daughters standing behind them.

"Mrs. Soames?"

"Yes." She took a half step back at the sight of Eli's face, but her gaze didn't falter.

"I'm here about your son, Charlie," Eli said.

"Girls, get in the house and wait for me there," she ordered without looking at them.

The twins reluctantly did as they were told, though they dragged their feet, still staring at Eli and Rose. Mrs. Soames waited until the door banged shut behind them before she spoke. "Is he dead?" Her face was chalk white, her expression hard, her body rigid as if she were braced for the worst. "Charlie."

"No, no," Eli rushed to assure her. "He's not dead. He's fine. On the mend."

Mrs. Soames closed her eyes briefly in relief before she opened them again and regarded him warily. "Who are you?" she demanded in much the same way her daughter had.

"Eli Dawes, Earl of Rivers, ma'am. And this is Miss Rose Hayward."

She looked between them, her forehead creased. "The old Earl of Rivers is dead. Everyone around here knows that."

"The man you speak of was my father. I've just recently returned to England."

She stared hard at him, as if weighing the validity of his words. "My son is under your roof, then."

"He is. I wish to speak to you about him—"

"Are you here to collect money, then?"

"What?"

"I don't have anything to pay the doctors with." Her face was pinched.

"No, I didn't come here for money," Eli said, frowning. "I came to ask if there was anything I could do to help you. Or if you wanted to see him."

She blinked rapidly at him. "I don't understand."

"I can take you to see your son if you like. It is my understanding that the doctors who treated him do not want him moved until he heals somewhat. He will be my guest until he is well enough to travel."

"Why would you do that for Charlie? For me?"

Eli's frown deepened. "Your husband and your sons, I am told, were killed at Quatre Bras. I was there too. Think of it as one soldier looking out for the family of another."

"The country my husband and my boys died for sees no need to do so, so forgive me if I have a hard time believing an earl would." Mrs. Soames's brows rose, and her eyes flickered over Eli's plain but expensive clothes and then the carriage that still waited behind them.

"Mrs. Soames, I can assure you that I only wish to help."

"Help? No one wants to help, my lord." The statement was bitter. "Look around you. Do you think I wanted to raise my children like this? Do you think it's easy putting them to bed hungry every night?"

"Mrs. Soames—"

"We had a tenancy, you know. A house, a farm. Until my husband and boys didn't come back from the war and I couldn't pay the rents any longer. So now the girls and I mend nets and sailcloth for whatever the fishermen can spare. And Charlie steals what they can't." Her shoulders suddenly slumped. "I'm afraid he'll get himself killed. And I can't lose him too."

"Tell him that yourself," Eli said, at a loss for what he could do or say at this moment that would make anything better for this family. "Come with us. Stay for dinner. Stay as long as you wish."

Mrs. Soames eyed him with renewed distrust and defiance. "I'll not be paying you anything from my back."

Jesus. Eli shifted uncomfortably.

Rose put a hand on his arm. "Mrs. Soames, it was my brother who treated Charlie," she said gently.

"You're Dr. Hayward's sister?"

"Yes. You know him?"

"Everyone around here knows the doctor," Mrs. Soames said. "He sees to everyone, no matter that they have nothing. He's a very kind man."

Rose smiled. "He is," she agreed.

"Can we go, Mother?" a small voice asked from behind them. "I want to see Charlie. And they said they have cake."

Eli turned to find Mildred, or possibly Margret, standing, the small one-eyed mutt in her arms.

"I told you to stay inside," her mother snapped.

"I was worried for Charlie." The girl's chin jutted defiantly, and the dog squirmed.

"I—"

The sound of pounding hooves interrupted whatever she was going to say next, and Eli saw a familiar blond man in a faded artillery jacket galloping across the sloped fields down toward the cottage. He reined his blowing horse to a stop, looking between Eli and Mrs. Soames, apprehension and suspicion written across his face.

"What are you doing here, Lord Rivers?" Matthew Wright blurted.

"I came to offer any assistance I could to Mrs. Soames, given her son is recuperating in my attics. Is there a problem?"

The suspicion faded, though the apprehension did not. "Buhler and his men are on their way here." His horse danced sideways. "Heard say the captain is in a rage. Seems he was at Avondale earlier." Wright was staring hard at Eli.

"He was," Eli confirmed. "I may have failed to offer the captain tea. Or any sort of welcome, at that. Most certainly no information on where he might find young Charlie Soames."

Mrs. Soames made a noise of distress. "My lord, I didn't know. I didn't intend to cause you trouble—"

"It was no trouble." Eli cut her off.

"Let me take you and the girls away from here," Wright urged the woman. "I don't want you anywhere near here when Buhler shows up if he's looking to make an example. I don't know what he might do if he thinks you're hiding…something. Someone."

"Mother? Is Charlie in trouble?" The little girl's voice was thin. "Are we in trouble?"

"Get in my carriage," Eli ordered. "All of you."

Wright shook his head. "Lord Rivers—"

"Your horse cannot carry four. Not easily, anyway. My carriage, on the other hand, is large and enclosed. And not likely to be shot at."

"Let us take you and your daughters to Avondale," Rose said to Mrs. Soames. "At least for now. You can see Charlie, and we'll bring you back here later."

"Please." Wright managed to get his horse to still. "Go with them. Just for now. Just in case."

The woman looked between her daughters and Mr. Wright and then to Eli. "I don't want to cause any further inconvenience to you—"

"Good. Then get in the carriage." Eli nodded to his driver, who hurried to open the equipage door.

"Mother? What if the soldiers—"

"Get your sister, Margret." Mrs. Soames was pushing her daughter toward the cottage. "Quickly. We will do as Miss Hayward asks, but we will return here immediately afterward."

"Can Bruno come too?" Margret asked.

"No," her mother replied.

"Yes," said Eli at the same time.

"Hurry," Wright pleaded.

Margret ran into the house, only to appear seconds later with Mildred. Both girls and the dog clambered into the carriage. Their mother followed, Rose ordering the driver back up to his post and assisting her in.

"Thank you, Lord Rivers," Wright said, worry creasing his sun-darkened face.

"It's nothing."

"It's everything." He fought with his horse for a second. "The captain and his men have become ruthless of late. I don't think I have to explain what happens when unchecked soldiers descend on unprotected women."

"You don't." Eli had seen firsthand the horror that victors could inflict on the conquered. "They're lucky to have you looking out for them."

Wright wrenched his horse's head around. "I'm not enough," he said, his anguish obvious. "And I don't know how to fix that."

Eli didn't have an answer either. "Go," he said instead, repeating Strathmore's words. "Before you are found here by people with questions I don't imagine you wish to answer." He headed toward his carriage. "I believe I'll do the same."

Chapter 12

Y ou're a hard man to find."

The Earl of Rivers started in his chair, nearly upsetting the glass of whiskey by his elbow. "Dammit, Rose." He steadied the glass and peered up at her. "How long have you been spying on me?"

"Again, Dawes, spying implies concealment. I hate to state the obvious, but my coloring prevents me from blending in with anything except, perhaps, a collection of copper cookware."

"Very funny." The deep groove between Eli's brows relaxed fractionally. He'd worn the same distracted expression on the ride back to Avondale from the pitiful cottage. Rose had watched him circumspectly as he'd readily and patiently answered Margret and Mildred's exhaustive string of questions, waving off Mrs. Soames's warnings to the girls to hold their tongues. And he had seemed perfectly content to have a dusty one-eyed dog curl up on the toes of his boots and promptly fall asleep.

But his troubled look hadn't abated even when they had arrived and his aunts had descended on the Soames family in a flurry of kind and welcoming efficiency. Eli had ordered a maid to take Mrs. Soames to her son and left instructions with the remainder of Avondale's staff that the Soames family were to be treated as valued guests. Discreet valued guests.

And then he'd disappeared.

Rose had finally found him here hours later, holed up in the rarely used study, hunched over a set of ledgers and stack of papers on the desk and frowning fiercely.

"What are you doing?" she asked.

"Trying to find a solution to the problem that is the Soames family." Eli rubbed wearily at his eye. "Bringing them here for a night or two is all well and good, but it doesn't solve anything. It doesn't help them once they leave."

Rose stilled. When she had sought him out, she had been planning to broach this exact subject. An idea had been brewing in her mind all afternoon. One that required a trip into Dover, something that she was less than thrilled about. But it needed to be done, and she had hoped that the earl would be receptive to what she would ask of him. And the fact that he had already charged headlong into the thorny issue made her want to reach out and kiss him.

Not that she would. There would never be a repeat of what had happened in the drawing room.

Rose slid off the edge of the desk and put a little more distance between them. "What do you mean?" she asked as evenly as she could.

"I want to be able to do more. I want to make a difference for families like the Soameses, not just today or tomorrow but ten years from now. Twenty years from now." He gestured at the ledgers. "I could offer Mrs. Soames money, but assuming she'd even accept it, it's a temporary fix. I could create a job at Avondale for her in some capacity, which offers a more permanent solution but doesn't necessarily provide a future for Charlie or the girls. Charlie Soames should be in school, not spending his time...acquiring things to help keep his family from starving. Margret and Mildred too. Neither one of the girls can read or write, and Charlie has only the most rudimentary of skills."

Rose already knew this from Tabby and Theo. "Your aunts told you?"

"Yes." His hand fell against his thigh. "And I know that there must be thousands of families like this. Families of soldiers who have been killed in service who are struggling just to survive. I want to do something."

"Noble."

"Necessary," he corrected grimly. "Do you have any idea what those men did? Do you have any idea what they saw? What they endured? And in the end, they sacrificed everything. If a country can't take care of its own people, can't build on those sacrifices, what have we really accomplished?"

"What do you intend to do?" Rose asked, something squeezing deep in her chest.

"That's just it. I don't know. Yet. I've been struggling with it all afternoon. And I've not been able to come up with anything worthwhile." Abruptly he shoved his chair back and stood, pacing away from her until he stopped near a set of shelves filled with ledgers. "Before I left London, nobody ever wanted or expected anything from me other than a good time. And it was easy to meet those pitiable expectations. I could rely solely on my looks. Money and charm, when circumstance required. It was all so...inconsequential."

It was Rose's turn to frown. "You may be selling yourself a bit short, Dawes, don't you think?"

"That's just it. I'm not. Six years ago, I defied my father

and went to war because three of my friends chose to do so, and I didn't want to be the only one missing out on the glory and grand adventure." He made a disgusted noise. "My ignorance and naivety were stupefying."

Rose listened, hearing all the unhappiness and regret in that admission.

"And now that I know better, now that I've seen and done things that…" He trailed off and ran a finger over the spines of the ledgers. "Now I find myself back in this life, faced with something of real consequence, something that has no solution that can be charmed or bought, and I'm at a damned loss."

Rose clasped her hands behind her back and took a deep breath. "Invite me out to dinner."

The earl gave her a look of disbelief laced with annoyance. "I beg your pardon?"

"Invite me out to dinner. With all that charm you speak of."

He was still staring at her with incredulity. "Dinner?"

"Why, I never thought you'd ask. You need to work on the charm, but I'd love to, thank you, Dawes." Rose skirted the wide desk and settled herself on the edge closest to him. "How soon can you be ready?"

He opened his mouth as if to say something and closed it again. "Just where is it that you think we're going?" he asked finally.

"Dover. A place called the Silver Swan. There are public rooms with excellent ale, an inn, and a formal dining room with a French chef and French wine. The lamb served with mint sauce is famous."

She saw him start to shake his head.

"It would be ill-mannered to back out of an invitation promised to a lady now."

"I never asked you to go anywhere with me." He strode

back to the desk and reached past her for his whiskey, then took a long swallow.

"You asked me to dinner. I accepted."

"I didn't—" He stopped and took a deep breath. "I'm not going into town."

"Why?"

"Because there is no need to go into town for dinner when there is a perfectly good cook who serves perfectly good food on perfectly good plates here."

Rose rather agreed with him. But these were extraordinary circumstances that required extraordinary measures. "Dawes—"

"And whatever the Silver Swan serves will likely kill you. I've been there before, years ago. And it's ghastly."

"Things have changed."

He was still shaking his head. "Not likely. We used to call it the Revolting Raven, what with the rotting sign that hung over the door. Even the cheap gin couldn't make it better."

"You'll be happy to know that the sign has changed and so has the owner."

"This is ridiculous. I don't need dinner. I need a solution to this dilemma."

"They're one and the same, Dawes."

"I'm not in the mood for another riddle."

"It's not a riddle. It's an answer, or at the very least an idea, and one that lies not in a pile of ledgers here but at the Silver Swan."

Eli finished his whiskey and set the crystal tumbler back on the desk with an irritated thump. "Why can't you just tell me?"

"It would be better if I showed you."

"I don't have time for this."

"You'll make time for this, Dawes. Trust me."

The earl threw up his hands. "Is this you trying to prove a point? Or trying to make me prove something to you again? First it's a portrait, now it's dinner? What's next?"

Rose considered him coolly. "Why were you never afraid of my mind? Why did my education never offend you?"

"What sort of question is that? And what does that have to do with—"

"Just answer the question."

"This is absurd."

"In all the time I've known you, I've never pretended ignorance simply because I was afraid to oppose you or because popular opinion stated that, as a woman, I couldn't possibly hope to understand."

"You can't be serious, Rose." Eli looked annoyed now. "To ask you to pretend ignorance—to pretend to be someone you aren't—would be an insult to my own intelligence."

"Most of society believes both my sister and me to be flawed because of our excessive education. I've been told too much knowledge makes a woman dangerous. Unpredictable. Threatening."

"Now you really are insulting me." The earl put his hands on the edge of the desk and leaned toward her. "Your mind, Rose, is what set you apart from any other woman I've ever known. Your intelligence, your abilities, your compassion, your convictions. I wouldn't be much of a man if I couldn't admire any of those things. If I were threatened by those things."

He was close enough that she could see the tiny chips of color in his iris, iridescent green tempered with golden brown. The heat from his body reached her, along with the rich scent of the outdoors and whiskey. Her eyes dropped to his mouth, and for a heart-stopping moment, she almost gave in to the impulse to lean forward to taste the whiskey on his lips. Rose closed her eyes, fighting the desire that was suddenly pounding through her.

"Do it," he demanded softly. "Kiss me."

Her eyes snapped open to find him watching her, the same arousal reflected in his expression. Hazily she wondered whether she was that transparent or this man simply knew her too well.

"I can't," she managed.

"Do I threaten you?" he asked. Both of them were frozen in place, neither drawing away.

"You threaten my control."

"Good." His voice was rough. He leaned toward her, and his lips grazed the underside of her jaw.

Rose shuddered. "Dawes—"

"Tell me what you want, Rose."

You, her mind hissed. *You*, her body begged. "I want you..." She trailed off, wondering what would happen if she left that fragment of truth as it was. "To take me to dinner."

The earl still didn't move. "I don't want to take you to dinner," he whispered, his breath hot against her neck. "I want to take you right here. On this desk. And then later, in my bed. Or yours. Probably both. And then in your studio on that sheet of crimson silk." His lips brushed her skin again, sending currents of electricity arcing through her. "And after that, I'll let you choose."

Rose squeezed her eyes shut again, every nerve ending in her body on fire. How did he do this to her? How, with only words and the merest suggestion of a kiss, did he reduce her to a woman disoriented and trembling with need?

"I want you, Rose. Stay with me. Here. Tonight. Just you and me. No one else."

"Dinner," she gasped, opening her eyes and stumbling back. She could not kiss him. Because if she started, she would not stop. She would kiss him and kiss him and kiss him and then beg him to do everything he'd promised. She would allow him to draw her into his bed, or perhaps she would do just as he said and draw him into hers. And she would surrender to the reckless longing that filled her, abandon caution, and embrace the all-consuming desire she harbored for this man. And everything that mattered, everything that she knew she needed to do tonight—that Eli Dawes needed to do tonight—would tumble to the side, forgotten and forsaken in a landslide of lust.

"Dinner," she repeated more firmly. "I need you to come with me to the Silver Swan."

The heat in his expression cooled, and he shook his head. "No."

"Why not?"

"Because I said no."

"That's not good enough."

"And just what will be good enough for you?" He straightened.

"The truth."

A muscle was twitching along the edge of his jaw. "You want the truth?"

"Yes."

"The last time I was in a dining room was in Ostend, on my way here. And I was asked to leave because my appearance was upsetting several women."

Rose felt her stomach fall to her toes. "That's . . . inexcusable."

"Perhaps. But it will happen again. And I refuse to allow you to be publicly ostracized and embarrassed simply because you are with me. At the very least, I can protect you from being subjected to that."

"A gallant sentiment, Dawes, but I don't need protecting."

"I didn't protect you before, when it mattered, and I won't—"

"Save your shiny armor and white horse for something better than my sensibilities," she said.

He scowled. "All I'm trying to say is that it's easier for everyone if I avoid crowds. Avoid public places altogether."

Rose, of all people, understood that feeling better than anyone. But Eli was not she. He was better. "The easy thing is rarely the right thing." She crossed her arms over her chest to keep herself from touching him. "But you already know that. You did not hesitate this afternoon when we went out looking for Mrs. Soames."

"Because it needed to be done," he said, his voice tight. "It wasn't a frivolous social call."

"Neither is this," Rose told him. Which was why she was insisting.

"Why does my appearance not repel you?" he asked suddenly.

Rose scoffed. "Now who's insulting whose intelligence here, Dawes?"

He straightened, his face grim. "I'm being serious."

"So am I. It's just skin. A part of you, just like any other. And I have a strict policy never to measure a man's merit on his scars."

He stared at her, as if gauging the sincerity of her words. "Are you trying to be funny?"

"No. Pretty is as pretty does, Dawes. Your aunts know this. Harland and Clara know this, as do the young women who are here right now. And, I hope, you know this too."

"It's not that simple."

Rose uncrossed her arms. "Your intelligence, your abilities, your compassion, and your convictions are what make you attractive. I wouldn't be much of a woman if I couldn't admire any of those things." She turned his own words back on him. "So yes, maybe I'm asking you to prove something to me. But maybe I'm trying to prove something to you too."

The earl gazed at her as the time stretched, the silence louder with each passing second. She couldn't tell what he was thinking.

"Fine," he said without warning.

"Fine?" She tried to temper the strange exhilaration that suddenly soared inside her.

"Let's go to dinner. But not before you tell me what the hell is at the Silver Swan that is so damn important."

"Not what," Rose said. "Who."

He looked down at the desk and closed one of the ledgers with a loud thump. "A man with the answers to this problem?"

Rose smiled at him. "Not a man. But a woman who will certainly appreciate one who isn't afraid of her dangerous mind."

~

The Silver Swan was located just at the edge of the busy harbor, the traffic since the end of the wars having resumed with a vengeance. Judging by the number of people coming and going and by the bustling stable yards, the inn was as popular with weary travelers as the public rooms and dining rooms were with sailors and their officers, fishermen, and locals.

The building was nothing like what Eli remembered. The dilapidated structure with its patched roof and walls had vanished under extensive repairs, and in its place stood an impeccably maintained building, the whitewashed walls turned gold in the early-evening light. Eli looked up as they climbed the wooden steps, noticing that along with the building, the signage in front had been vastly improved. A gleaming sign hung neatly on chains, a graceful swan and the inn's name carved expertly in the wood.

"An improvement since the last time you were here?" Rose asked, her arm tucked securely into his.

"Yes." She was trying to distract him, he knew, just as she had on the ride here with her constant stream of conversation.

Every muscle in his body had tensed, as if that could somehow prepare him for the stares, the whispers, the looks of pity and disgust. It was humiliating, this reaction, because he should be better than this. Rose believed him to be better than this. Yet all that reasoning hadn't made it any easier.

"Let's go in," he said abruptly, reaching for the heavy brass door handles.

Rose simply nodded and allowed him to hold the door for her, and they both stepped inside. Eli blinked a couple of times, allowing his vision to adjust to the sudden loss of bright sunlight and his hearing to adjust to the somewhat raucous din. They had entered the old public rooms, but gone were the paltry collection of crooked tables and broken chairs. Instead rows of tables and benches had been installed, and nearly every space was occupied by a patron. The air was laced with the aroma of baking bread and cooking meat and the unmistakable scent of ale. A long serving counter dominated one side of the room, and bowls of what looked like stew and tankards of ale were being consumed as fast as the women behind the counter could serve them. A few roughly dressed men turned as the door banged shut behind them, and Eli could feel the weight of their gazes, though after a few seconds, most simply turned back to their food and drink.

Eli's gaze suddenly settled on a familiar face, the man's mahogany hair pulled back in a careless queue. Harland Hayward was standing against the far wall near a narrow door, deep in conversation with several men. The baron was gesturing and speaking intently.

"Your brother is here," he said to Rose. "Are we to join him?"

She followed his gesture in time to watch as Harland slipped through the narrow door and out into the night, his companions right behind him. "No." Her eyes lingered on the door a moment longer. "Tonight I have someone else for you to meet. Come." She slipped her hand into the crook of his arm again. "There is a table waiting for us in the dining room, where it's not so loud."

Eli allowed her to lead him through the crowds and toward a door near the back. As they stepped through, the noise faded, and Eli found himself in a dining room that would not have been out of place in any well-appointed London square. A precisely ordered collection of linen-covered tables was arranged throughout the spacious room, covered in delicate glassware and gleaming silverware. Servers who could have passed for liveried footmen circulated throughout the room, quietly and efficiently seeing to the needs of the diners.

Here officers' uniforms and tailored coats replaced the rough homespun of the patrons in the public rooms. A number of bejeweled ladies accompanied expensively dressed gentlemen, the conversation subdued, and as Eli and Rose made their way to the empty table nearest the large window overlooking the harbor, many of the conversations stopped altogether. A portly woman in a feathered turban at the table closest to them made a sound of distress and turned her face away.

Eli ignored her and saw Rose seated before sitting opposite her. A server materialized at their table with a bottle of wine and, oddly enough, seemed oblivious to Eli's appearance. "Good evening, Lord Rivers, Miss Hayward," he said as he opened the bottle. "Her Ladyship is regrettably delayed, but she will be with you as soon as possible," he continued as he expertly filled their glasses. "She asked me to convey her apologies. And she also said to tell you that the lamb tonight is exceptional."

"Sounds lovely," Rose replied with distraction, glancing around the room. "Does that suit, my lord?"

Eli nodded, watching her. She suddenly seemed on edge.

"Very good." The server inclined his head in their direction, left the bottle of wine on the table, and vanished as silently as he had appeared.

Rose was still scrutinizing their fellow diners, her complexion oddly pale and her face pinched.

"Is there someone here in the dining room whom you know?" Eli asked. "Someone you need to greet?"

Her eyes snapped back to his as though he had caught her doing something untoward. "No," she replied, sounding strangely relieved. "I know no one here. No one at all."

Eli gazed out the window at the forest of masts that crowded the harbor. "Yet our server knew who I was. And that we were coming."

"Yes."

He turned back to her. "How?"

"I sent word ahead this afternoon. I wanted to ensure we had a table when we arrived."

"Before you knew I would…ask you to dinner?"

"You were always going to ask me to dinner, Dawes." She reached for her wineglass.

"You couldn't know that. I might have refused. I tried to refuse."

"And yet here we are. Because it was the right thing to do."

He had never, in all his life, wanted to touch a woman the way he did right now. Draw her into his arms and never let go. "Your confidence in me is humbling."

Her eyes held his for a moment. "But not misplaced." She smiled fully at him then, as if to dispel the somber gravity of the conversation. She lifted her glass toward him. "Perhaps a toast?"

Eli's fingers curled around his wineglass. "To what?" he asked.

"To new beginnings. And friendship that will always make difficult things less so."

Rose was deliberately putting space between them again. Shoring up the line that separated friends and lovers. And he would let her do it—let her defer to whatever it was that was holding her back, let her keep whatever secrets she held that were preventing her from letting go and taking what she wanted. But not for much longer. Because if Eli knew nothing else, he knew that he would not let the precious gift of a second chance with Rose Hayward slip away.

"Dawes?" Rose was watching him expectantly.

He lifted his glass. "To new beginnings," he repeated. "And friendship that will always make difficult things less so."

She smiled at him again, her dark eyes holding his, and brought her glass to her lips. She drew in a deep breath and closed her eyes. "And to wine that isn't English," she sighed in clear bliss before taking a slow, deliberate sip.

Rose's lashes swept over her fair cheeks, her lips parted, and her head fell slightly back to expose the graceful column of her neck. She made a small sound of pleasure as the wine slid down her throat. Eli swallowed with difficulty, his own mouth dry, and brought his glass to his lips, gulping the expensive burgundy like cheap ale.

He set his empty glass down only to find Rose watching him again, a faint crease of worry marring her forehead. "What's wrong?" she asked.

"You are so beautiful," he blurted, before groaning inwardly at the utter insufficiency of that statement. Worse, it had been delivered with all the elegance one would expect from an awkward adolescent. He knew this was the moment when he should say something witty to put her at ease. The old Eli Dawes had had an entire repertoire of smooth, clever flattery that could be produced at a second's notice. But all he could do was stare at the woman in the rich apricot-colored gown, her red-blond hair piled on top of her head, her dark eyes like pools of warm chocolate. The need to taste her—to devour her—was racing through his body like a scorching wildfire whipped by winds.

"Thank you," Rose said, her voice a little unsteady and a blush staining her cheeks. "I thought perhaps you were uncomfortable here." She glanced around, and Eli didn't miss the suddenly averted eyes of several diners.

With a start Eli realized he had forgotten that there was anyone else in this room. "No. Not at all, actually. But my words have made you uncomfortable," he said.

Rose bit her lip, her color still high.

"Would it help if I took off my shirt?" he teased in a low voice, unable to help himself. "Because you've always seemed quite comfortable with that."

Rose threw back her head and laughed, and Eli lost his breath all over again. That had been a stupid, stupid thing to say. Because now all he could think of was doing exactly that. And then pulling every stitch of her clothing away from her body so that he might feel her skin against his. And then—

"Good evening."

The address yanked him back into the present, and with some horror, Eli realized that the greeting had come from a woman standing at the edge of their table. Good God, how long had she been standing there without either of them noticing? How much had she heard?

Engrained etiquette propelled him to his feet, and he found himself facing a young woman regarding him frankly. Coffee-dark hair framed her round face, and she was dressed in a fine if simple cobalt gown that matched the color of her eyes.

Across the table from him, Rose cleared her throat. "Lady Anne, allow me to present Eli Dawes, Earl of Rivers," she said. "Lord Rivers, Lady Anne Faulkner."

Faulkner? The Duke of Holloway's sister?

"A pleasure, Lord Rivers," Lady Anne said, offering him a warm smile.

"The pleasure is all mine, my lady," Eli replied automatically, relieved that his manners were still somewhat intact, even if his wits were not.

"And I am so happy you came tonight." Lady Anne was speaking to Rose now. "I hardly ever see you outside of Avondale. I wish you would come out more often."

Eli watched as Rose shifted uncomfortably and a shadow of something he couldn't quite identify passed over her face. "I come when I need to."

Eli suppressed a frown. He felt as if he had missed something important.

"I apologize for my tardiness," Lady Anne was now saying, somewhat ruefully. "As you can see, it's busy tonight." She swiped at a strand of dark hair that had fallen across her eyes.

"It is I who need to be thanking you for making time for

us tonight," Rose responded, and whatever darkness might have lurked in her expression was gone. "Even amidst the madness."

Eli stepped forward smartly and drew out a chair for Lady Anne, comprehension dawning that this was the woman Rose had wished him to meet. Though what the sister of a duke could do to help him with the problem that was the Soames family was beyond him. As was the reason they needed to meet in a Dover dining room.

"And I am very glad to be able to offer whatever help I can." Lady Anne turned toward Eli as he resumed his seat. "Rose explained the plight of the Soameses in her message," she told him.

"I want you to tell Lord Rivers about Brookside," Rose urged. "Because I think it might be something that could work in this situation. But I wanted him to be able to speak with you directly. To be able to ask you questions that I might not have the answers to."

The duke's sister nodded. "Of course."

"What is Brookside?" Eli asked, looking between the women.

"Brookside is a boardinghouse of sorts, situated on the southern edge of London," Lady Anne told him.

"Of sorts?"

"It's paired with a textile manufacturing and import business," she continued. "Muslins, to be specific, woven on-site. It has proven quite lucrative, and allows a great deal of profit to be reinvested in the business. It's run exclusively by women whose spouses have been incarcerated in debtors' prison, and the entire model is one of self-sufficiency. Those not directly involved in the daily textile production have domestic responsibilities, whether in the house, the gardens, or the animal sheds. Most of the women have children who live with them, and they too have expectations. Aside from their chores, the children are required to attend school classes taught on-site by competent instructors."

Eli stared at her. "That sounds very..."

"Philanthropic?" Rose suggested.

"Extraordinary," he breathed. "And bloody, bloody brilliant."

Lady Anne inclined her head. "From what Miss Hayward has told me, Mrs. Soames's situation is very similar. I concur with Miss Hayward that this sort of business model would work equally well for war widows and their families."

"Yes," Eli said. "It would." What she was describing was genius. The model could also be applied to products beyond muslins. Lace, perhaps, for a society with a growing, insatiable hunger for Continental fashion. Cottons, now that the Indian markets were accessible. Sailcloth used by the navy and the increasing number of trade ships that plied the seas. Specialized fabric for military uniforms, tents, and blankets. The possibilities were extensive, should one have the capital and know-how. As an earl, he had money and power at his fingertips. As an officer, he had a working knowledge of provisional logistics. It was an expertise in the industry that he would need to acquire.

Eli drummed his fingers on the snow-white tablecloth. "Who owns Brookside? And is it possible for me to speak to him?"

Lady Anne glanced at Rose with a faint look of accusation. "You didn't tell him."

"Tell me what?" Eli shot a look at Rose, but she only offered him an enigmatic smile and sipped her wine.

The duke's sister hesitated before she met Eli's gaze again. "I own and operate it. My brother generally provides a front for me, as most men will not consider doing business with a woman, but the day-to-day decisions and operations are mine."

Eli sat back, not looking at Rose but aware of her studying him all the same. A dangerous mind indeed. "I see."

Lady Anne's fingers played idly with the handle of the silver spoon that lay on the table in front of her. "My brother is very good at a lot of things. Buying, selling, investing, reorganizing, reinventing. But managing large groups of people and their needs is not one of them. I have some skill in that regard, so he leaves that to me."

Rose snorted into her glass. "She's being modest, Dawes. Everything you see around you at this very moment is also a product of her management and skill. The Duke of Holloway may have bought the Silver Swan, but it is the woman sitting beside you who has made it so successful and profitable. It's also why she couldn't get away tonight to meet us at Avondale. She's bloody talented, and if you ask politely, she might just share some of that talent with you."

This should all be shocking, Eli knew, these...revelations of ambition and aptitude that were so far outside anything that would ever be considered acceptable in a St James's drawing room. But Eli couldn't bring himself to feel anything other than...anticipation. Admiration.

"Would you be willing to help me?" Eli asked Lady Anne.

Anne's fingers stilled. "Would you be willing to accept it from me?"

"Yes," he said with no hesitation.

Lady Anne gave him a long look with eyes that were far older than her years, as if taking the measure of his answer. "Very well. I split my time between Dover and London, and as such, I'm leaving to return to the city first thing tomorrow. Just send word to Brookside when you would like to start, and we can arrange a meeting. Though I warn you, my brother will likely insist on sitting in. He'll have some ideas as well. And as much as he can be…overbearing at times, I would counsel you to accept whatever assistance he offers."

London. The reminder of what still waited for him—of what he had yet to accomplish—reared its head, but for the first time, the lingering dread that had always seemed to accompany that thought was absent. Instead there was a feeling of resolve. Purpose.

"In the meantime, Mrs. Soames and her family would be welcome at Brookside, if that is something that they would be amenable to," Lady Anne was saying. "I can send word ahead if you wish to make arrangements for their passage to London."

"Thank you," Eli said, realizing those two words were woefully inadequate for what he was feeling. "I don't know what to say."

He glanced at Rose and found her watching him, her expression telling him that she had heard everything that he couldn't say in words. Just as she had known what would happen here tonight. Known how much he had needed this. Known him better than he had known himself.

Lady Anne shrugged. "Actions always speak louder than words, my lord," she said. "Do you have any questions for me?"

He held Rose's eyes, even as he answered Lady Anne. "Yes. Quite a few."

Chapter 13

Rose leaned against the wall of stone at her back, her sketchbook tucked under her arm, caught in that rare moment when day had not yet fully surrendered to night. The sky still had a deep violet hue that was now just deepening to indigo, and the moon was only a barely visible orb hanging low over the darkening sea. The gulls had quieted, and the only sound now was the steady lapping of the surf as it folded over on itself against the stony beach.

She had told herself that she had come here to sketch the sunset, to study the manner in which the light played off the water and the way the shadows grew long, but the book remained under her arm, the pages blank. Rose had opened it, graphite poised over paper... and created nothing. For all the beauty splashed before her, she had failed to find inspiration. Because she hadn't come here to sketch. She had come to wrestle with her thoughts.

She had listened this evening as the Earl of Rivers had plied Anne Faulkner with insightful, shrewd questions. She had watched him outline ideas and concepts, asking for estimates and opinions and suggestions. He had, in those moments when his intelligence and compassion had been so utterly obvious, never been more perfect. Never been more magnificent.

The ride back to Avondale had been dominated by a continuation of the conversation. Which was a good thing, Rose knew, because if he had let a silence fall, if he had failed to distract her with proposals of locations and technologies, Rose might have given in to the relentless need to kiss him witless. To simply take what she wanted and damn all the consequences that sort of complication would bring. Because the Earl of Rivers would be leaving soon now, she knew. He would be stepping into the role that had always been his, finally claiming position and power among his peers. Armed with ambition and compassion, he would be returning to a world that he would navigate with the same clever charisma that had once so enthralled society.

A world she had been part of, for a small window of time. And it had almost destroyed her. She could never be part of it again.

Rose sighed and gazed out across the water to the mouth of the cove. In the distance a light glowed, flickered, and then glowed again. A ship at anchor, she realized, preparing to settle in for the night. She should do the same and head back up before darkness settled fully. It would make her ascent slower—

A movement at the far end of the beach at the base of the steps caught her eye. In the pale-violet wash, his hair was more silver than gold, his white shirt almost blending into the chalky background of the cliffs behind him. Eli was picking his way easily across the stony beach, looking out toward the blinking lantern light. He stopped at the water's edge, not far from where she stood, and put his hands on his hips, an impressive silhouette in shades of charcoal and gray.

A longing so intense it was almost a physical pain coursed through Rose, stealing her breath and making her heart accelerate. The breeze tugged at his hair and pushed the pale linen of his shirt against his skin, outlining the contours of his upper body. Her fingers tightened around her sketchbook, once again itching to trace his form. She closed her eyes, memories of how his skin had felt beneath her fingers still vivid. Knowing that the failing light that had wrapped itself around this beach like a cocoon would impede sketching but encourage explorations of a more intimate nature—

Rose groaned softly, as if that would dispel the desire that was raging through her, making her legs less than steady and making her ache all over. She opened her eyes, wondering how long Eli Dawes planned to stay on this beach. Wondering if she should simply keep herself hidden until he left because right now, on a darkened beach gilded by twilight, she wasn't confident that she would say no if Eli Dawes asked her to kiss him again.

Which was ridiculous. Rose pushed herself away from the stone at her back. She had kept her head in that damn carriage, and she would not lose it now. She had once told Dawes not to be melodramatic, and it would serve her well to heed her own advice. She still had some pride.

She took a deep breath. "Thinking of swimming?"

He started and spun, peering in her direction. Rose knew it would be difficult for him to see her in the long shadows of the cliffs.

"I only ask because you have forgone a coat, and I do not want to be accused of spying on you again." She walked toward him unhurriedly.

"Rose?"

"Were you expecting someone else?" she teased, relieved at the casualness of her tone.

"I wasn't expecting anyone. What are you doing here?" He still sounded distracted.

She gestured to the book under her arm. *Trying not to think about kissing you. About how much I want you.* "Sketching. Until I lost the light." She left her sketchbook safely up on the beach and came to stand beside him at the edge of the surf, careful not to touch him. He didn't move away. Nor did he look at her. Instead his eyes stayed fixed on the light past the mouth of the cove, his chiseled profile touched with just a hint of silver.

The stars began to make their presence known, tiny pinpricks of light winking in the dark as they stood in comfortable silence. The way friends would. The way they would be able to do in the years to come.

"They burned it," Eli said into the night.

"I beg your pardon?"

"Buhler and his men. Burned the Soameses' cottage to the ground in the name of the king. As reprisal and a warning to those who would steal from their sovereign or protect those who do." Frustration and fury stained his words.

Rose's stomach clenched. "How do you know that?"

"Mr. Wright sent a message to Avondale."

She tipped her head up to the stars. "They could rebuild."

"With what? They are barely surviving as it is."

"Dawes—"

"I should have stayed behind. Perhaps I could have stopped Buhler and his men."

"You had no idea that they would do that."

The earl bent to pick up a stone and hurled it into the darkness in a fluid motion. "I should have."

"What will the family do now?"

"I will not allow them to disappear into the workhouses or whorehouses. I will not allow this to destroy the family of fallen soldiers. I've already spoken to Mrs. Soames. Sent a message of my own to Lady Anne. The Soameses will remain at Avondale until Charlie is healthy, and then they'll all travel to London and stay at Brookside. At least until I can do more."

She put a hand on her arm. "You've already done—"

"Not enough. I need to…I have to—" He stopped.

"Go to London," she finished for him.

He nodded wordlessly.

Rose withdrew her hand from his sleeve and tucked it safely back in her skirts. "I will be required to travel to London for a couple of days. I would appreciate the company on the journey." When she had come down to this beach tonight, she hadn't known if she would make that offer. But now there was no question about it. A friend—a decent human being—would take this last step. Ensure that Eli Dawes finished this last leg of a journey that had started long ago.

"Is that an invitation or an order?"

"An invitation, of course. Will you come with me?"

"Why?" he asked.

"Why what?"

"Why are you going to London?"

The light floating far off in the darkness blinked out for a second before it reappeared. "I have a completed painting I've promised to deliver to my client. He will be in London for a few days, down from his home in Nottingham." Not the raven-haired Lady Ophelia reclining on her bed of crimson satin but another one, different but no less seductively beautiful.

Eli turned to look at her. In what was left of the twilight, his face was pale, his features shadowed so that she couldn't read his expression. "What sort of painting?" he asked.

"The kind clients pay me to paint for them."

"Would you show me?" he asked.

Rose shook her head and shoved the flyaway hair from her face. Those completed paintings and the real reason she did what she did were not a topic she wished to explore with Eli Dawes. Not tonight and maybe not ever, declarations of friendship be damned. "Perhaps another time," she evaded.

"You haven't answered my question."

"You mean your invitation to accompany you to London."

"No. My invitation to a man to claim his title and fortune and, along with it, a voice and the power to effect real change."

He didn't respond. The silence stretched, broken only by the sound of the surf, and Rose began to wonder if perhaps her words had been too critical.

"I owe you a great debt," he said suddenly.

"For what?"

"For what?" he repeated. "For...everything."

Rose felt her brows knit. "I don't understand."

"For making me take you to dinner, for one," he said quietly. He reached out and placed his palm against the side of her cheek.

She shivered, afraid to move. "I've always had a weakness for French wine." She tried to make it light.

"This has nothing to do with French wine, and you know it." His fingers gently tucked a tendril of hair over her ear. "This has everything to do with making me be better. Do better."

"I can't make you be or do anything, Dawes. You are your own man."

He made an unintelligible sound. "You have no idea what you've done, do you?"

"Whatever it is that you think I did or that you think I made you do, I can assure you that it was all you. I'm just here to stab you with paintbrush ends and torture you in art class." She was babbling, she knew, but this was starting to get away from her. This was starting to slide away from the steady solidarity of friendship toward the dark, seductive abyss that was Eli Dawes, and she had no idea how to fix it.

"Did you know that sitting at that table tonight, talking to you and Lady Anne, was the first night I didn't give a fuck about what anyone thought about my appearance?" he said roughly. "Forgot all about it, in fact."

Rose blinked at the harshness of his words.

"Because for the first time, I think I finally took your words to heart in the interest of something bigger."

"My words?" she managed.

"That I should take my head out of my ass long enough to stop feeling sorry for myself."

Rose winced. "I've said a lot of things that perhaps weren't—"

"Stop talking, Rose." He took a step closer to her and brought his other hand up to cradle her face. "I will come to London with you to claim my title and a fortune. To do what I should have done a long time ago. Because you were correct. I've wasted a great deal of time, but it's not too late to do what matters. To do what is right."

⁓

There was something dangerous about touching Rose Hayward on a darkened beach. Something dangerous about touching Rose Hayward anywhere, really. Eli could feel the warmth of her beneath his palms, that simple touch sending uncontrollable heat racing through his veins. The way it had that afternoon when her casual, gentle gesture of fondness had instantly ignited into something far more carnal. The way it did every time he was near her.

"Stay with me." He had asked her that once already.

"What? Where? In London?"

"Yes."

"Don't be ridiculous. Your return will garner a great deal of attention. And I am still associated with the Haverhall School for Young Ladies. I will not do anything to jeopardize its reputation. I keep perfectly good rooms in London at the school, Dawes, attached to my studio. I'll stay there for the handful of days it will take for me to conclude my business and return to Dover."

"Don't return to Dover, then." He was not going to let this go. Not going to let her go.

"I have to."

"Why?"

Rose hesitated. "I have responsibilities here."

"Surely your sister and my aunts can manage without you."

She started to shake her head.

"A fortnight," he proposed, not caring that he might sound a little desperate. "Stay a fortnight. At least long enough for me to demand a parade along Rotten Row to herald my return from the dead."

"Dawes—"

"What about all your friends? Surely you would enjoy a visit?"

"There is no one in London I wish to visit," she said shortly.

"I don't believe that. You had many friends—"

"They were never my friends," Rose said. "They were

people who knew Anthony—who knew you—and simply became my acquaintances out of temporary circumstance."

Eli tried to think of an argument and failed. Because, he realized, those individuals who had flocked to populate his past social orbit had been exactly as Rose had described them. Acquaintances of temporary circumstance. Men and women focused entirely on indulging their own wants and needs and using those around them to do it.

"They were never my friends," she repeated, almost too quietly for him to hear.

Eli slid his fingers along her jaw and around the back of her neck. There was something she wasn't saying. "Rose—"

"I'll be back in London at the end of summer," she told him, stepping back slightly. His hand fell from her skin. "Fall always seems to bring a rash of commissions, usually for children's portraits." She took another step back. "You'll be exceedingly busy acclimatizing yourself as the new Earl of Rivers. Perhaps, once you've resettled yourself and when we both have a free afternoon, you could join me for a cup of tea at the school."

"A cup of tea? Now who sounds like a ninety-year-old nun?" he growled. Rose was suddenly slipping away from him again, and he had no idea why. Or how to stop it.

He heard her exhale. "You'll be very busy, Lord Rivers."

"Stop calling me Lord Rivers. And stop retreating." He closed the distance between them again.

"I'm not retreating."

"You are. And you know how I know that? Because you've never allowed me the luxury of doing the same. Every minute since I stepped onto these damn shores, you've challenged me. Confronted me when it mattered. Made me look inward even when I haven't liked what I've seen. And after everything, somehow, you still managed to believe the best of me."

Rose turned her head away.

"You have been the truest friend I've ever had, Rose Hayward. And I'm not letting you go. Not now, not tomorrow, not a year from now. I am not going to be reduced to an acquaintance who pops by for a cup of tea."

"Then what?" she said. "What are you going to be?"

"You tell me." He caught her chin in his hands and turned her face back toward his. "What do you want from me?"

The darkness hid her expression, but he could feel her rapid, shallow breaths against the skin of his wrist.

"Perhaps I'll tell you what I want, then." He moved his fingers from her chin, along the column of her neck and the hollow of her throat, across her chest, and down to the subtle rise at the top of her bodice. "I want you. Here. In London. Or wherever we might go. All of the days, Rose, and all of the nights." His fingers slipped farther, brushing against the peaks of her small breasts and down along her rib cage, coming to rest against the small of her back. She was so tiny, so exquisite.

"I want your mind, and I want your body. I want to be your friend and your lover." He took another half step closer and gathered her against him. He bent his head, bringing his free hand up to push the windblown tresses away from her face and neck. "I want to seduce you. And then, after I've heard my name torn from your lips, after I've watched you come apart, I want you to seduce me." His fingers slid into the hair at the back of her head, his lips a breath away from hers. But still he didn't kiss her.

He was dizzy with want, his head spinning, his body hard and heavy, his cock throbbing, every fiber in his body shaking with desire. "You're beautiful and strong and honest, and I want all of that. All of you."

"Eli." It was the first time he had ever heard her use his name, and it sliced through his tenuous control, leaving him teetering on the very edge of restraint. "There will be other women you—"

"There are no other women, Rose. There never have been."

She made a muffled noise. "I thought we had agreed to be honest with each other. I was there, remember? You had scores of women."

"Because I couldn't have you. And I didn't know what else to do."

"What?" It was barely a whisper.

"I've wanted you from the very first moment I met you. But Anthony Gibson found you first. He never deserved you. And I never fought for you then. I won't make the same mistake again." His hand tightened on her back. "Tell me what you want, Rose."

She didn't answer, but her hands came up, her palms pressed flat against his chest as they smoothed over the linen of his shirt. They dipped down, over his lower ribs and around to his back, stopping at the waistband of his breeches. And then, suddenly, she pulled the linen free, pushing it up over his back toward his shoulders. Eli ducked his head, releasing her for a second as she pulled his shirt from his body and let it fall.

He stood before her, the night air caressing his skin. She reached out and ran a delicate finger over his chest, tracing the muscle beneath his nipple and letting it travel over the ridges of his abdomen. Very slowly she stepped around him, her fingers never leaving his skin but sliding up to explore the valley of his spine. At his neck her hands slipped apart, skimming over the width of his shoulders and then down to the sides of his waist. She leaned into him, and he felt her lips graze the center of his back. Her mouth moved down lower, following the same path her fingers had. He shuddered and closed his eyes, so aroused that it hurt.

"That," she whispered against his back. "I've wanted to do that for a long time."

Her hands were moving up again, her palms sliding around the top of his waistband, coming to rest just below his navel. He trapped them beneath his own hands, held them against his skin. He could still feel her breath against his back, felt her lean into him, her lips trailing fire across his rigid muscles.

His head fell back, and he closed his eyes. Rose's hands slid from beneath his, over the sides of his hips, the curve of his ass, and then stroked the backs of his thighs. He wondered if she could feel him shaking. It had been so very long since a woman had touched him like this. And not just touched him but explored him reverently, as though trying to memorize each part.

Her hands moved again, back to his hips, only this time they delved forward over the fall of his breeches, stroking the rigid length of him through the fabric. He groaned, using every ounce of willpower not to thrust into the pressure of her palms like a green boy. He felt her exhale, felt her muscles quiver where she was pressed up against him, and that finally snapped him out of his inertia. He spun, catching her face with his hands, and kissed her the way he had always wanted to.

There was nothing soft or careful about how he claimed her mouth, just a blind, aching need to have her. And somewhere, over the roaring in his ears, he heard her whimper softly as she opened beneath him, her tongue sliding against his. Her arms wrapped around his neck, and he lowered his, embracing her and hauling her up against him. She melted against him as he took everything she gave, kissing her with an abandon and a surrender that left him dizzy.

His hands slid down to her backside, and he gathered her against him, settling her against his throbbing erection, the friction igniting a conflagration of pleasure. His hips rocked, and he groaned again, aching with want. He wanted more, wanted everything, wanted her. She made a sound deep in her throat, her fingers curling into the nape of his neck. Her mouth slipped from his, and she licked and teased her way down the side of his neck to the hollow of his throat and then across his bare chest. One of her hands slid down, her fingers brushing across his nipple. And then she bent her head and her mouth replaced her touch, her tongue swirling and sending bolts of raw desire racing through his body.

He sucked in a breath, his control fraying at an alarming rate. Two could play at this game, he thought hazily, sliding his hands up to cover the swell of her breasts. She exhaled, raising her head, arching into his touch, and he set his mouth at the center of her chest. His fingers slipped inside her stays and coaxed the bindings and the front of her dress down, exposing her breasts. He covered each easily with a hand, and his thumbs flicked over her tightened nipples. She made a sound of raw pleasure, and her hips jerked against his body.

She was quivering on the edge just as he was, he knew. He could feel it in the tautness of her limbs, the quickness of her breath, and the tightness of her grasp. With one hand he dragged her skirts up, sliding his hand over the smooth expanse of her thigh. He stroked the softness of her skin, brushing the backs of his fingers against her sex.

Rose whimpered, and he caught her mouth in his, capturing the sound. He turned his wrist and slid a finger through her folds.

"Eli," she gasped, her hips tipping instantly, giving him

more access. God, she was wet. And responsive. And utterly, completely perfect. He found the apex of her sex, and her head dropped to rest on his chest.

He slid a finger deep into her tight, slick heat.

"Oh," she breathed, her fingers digging into his skin. He stroked her, listening to the tiny sounds she was making. He bent his head and caught her lips again, kissing her deeply, pushing her ever closer to the edge. His finger slid deep once again, and just like that, her entire body tensed and strained as her climax tore through her.

He held on, waiting until she was limp against him before withdrawing his hand and letting her skirts drop. He wrapped his arms around her and held her tightly, wanting to remember the perfection of this moment.

"And I've wanted to do that for a long time," he whispered.

She stirred, pressing a kiss to the left side of his neck, the thickened scar tissue making it difficult to feel the sensation. Out of habit he almost flinched and turned before he recovered. But not fast enough.

"Don't you dare, Dawes," Rose murmured. Her hand came back up to caress the ruined side of his face. "Don't you dare hide any part of you from me."

He buried his face in her hair, holding her. Belonging completely to her. He took a deep breath, filling himself with the scent that was uniquely Rose—the exotic mixing with the tang of the sea. Around them only the sounds of the surf intruded.

"Eli," she started, but he lifted his head and pressed his finger to her lips.

"Shhh," he whispered. Because there was something else drifting on the night air now besides the sounds of the surf. The sound of a voice. A man's voice, perhaps, carried across the water or perhaps bouncing off the cliffs behind them, making it difficult for Eli to determine where it was coming from. He caught Rose around the waist and dragged her slightly behind him, away from the water's edge.

She made a squeak of surprise. "Eli—"

He slid his fingers along the edge of her bodice and set it to rights. He listened hard, but there was nothing now other than the steady sound of the surf. But every instinct he possessed was warning him that they were no longer alone on this beach.

"What is it?" she whispered near his ear.

"Men."

"Soldiers?"

"I don't know." He peered out at the water, but between the lack of moonlight and the shadows of the cove, it was almost impossible to see anything. Then, farther down the beach, a break in the line of pale surf was followed by a dull thud. Another dull thud and then splashes, and the sound of a small craft being dragged up the stony beach.

Silence descended again, and then a lantern flared to life, giving Eli a sudden glimpse of a knot of men, one of whom was instantly familiar.

"Harland?" Rose murmured.

The light suddenly swung in their direction before being snuffed and plunging the beach back into darkness. "Who's there?" someone called, and there were the sounds of booted feet advancing toward them.

Eli glanced behind him, but unless he and Rose were to scale the cliffs, there was no exit on this end of the beach. The approaching shadows would stumble across Eli and Rose eventually. He snatched his shirt from the beach and yanked it over his head, pushing Rose farther behind him. As the figures drew closer, he stepped forward.

"Strathmore," Eli said conversationally but clearly. "I didn't take you for a late-night swimmer."

The men stopped abruptly. "Rivers." There was the sound of low conversation, and then a single shadow separated to approach while the others faded back down the beach.

"How's the water?" Eli asked.

"Cold." Harland Hayward stopped just in front of Eli, his silhouette dark against the silver surf. Behind him Eli could hear the sounds of the boat being dragged back into the water, followed by the splash of an oar.

"I can see you hiding, Rose, even in this dismal light," the baron said flatly. "Your hair gives you away every time."

"I'm not hiding," Rose grumbled.

"Then what, exactly, are you doing alone with a man who has more notches on his bedpost than the sea has fish?" The baron's tone was deceptively pleasant.

"Your sister was sketching when I inadvertently disturbed her," Eli said, just as pleasantly, refusing to engage. "And she was gracious enough to allow me to keep her company. What's your excuse, Lord Strathmore?"

"Scurvy," the baron replied.

"I beg your pardon?"

Strathmore made a vague, half-visible gesture in the direction of the sea. "Half the crew of that ship."

"Unfortunate."

"Nothing that a crate of oranges won't fix." He paused. "But I'm not here with you to talk citrus. I'm here to see my sister home."

Eli heard Rose make a rude noise. "I don't need a nurse-maid, Harland," she said.

"Agreed, if only because Rivers would seduce her too."

"No one was seducing anyone," Rose snapped at her brother, and Eli wondered if she wasn't right. Because Rose

Hayward had seduced him long before he had ever stepped foot on this beach. And what he had felt for her, with her, here tonight, went far beyond mere seduction.

"Let's go, Rose." The baron was starting to lose his civility. "Now."

"That's a little autocratic, even for you, don't you think, Harland?" She didn't move.

"While I don't much care about the Earl of Girls here, I would prefer if you weren't the next body dumped on my table with a bullet hole. Charlie Soames isn't the first person to be shot by a trigger-happy soldier looking to bag a smuggler. In the dark, in this cove, they will shoot first and ask questions later." Strathmore suddenly sounded weary.

Eli felt his body tense. As much as he hated to admit it, Strathmore was right. Eli found Rose's hand in the darkness. "Go with him, Rose," he whispered.

"Not you too," she muttered.

"Your brother makes a valid point," he forced himself to say, his fingers grazing the inside of her wrist. "But we will finish this . . . conversation later."

Chapter 14

I understand you're going to London." The voice came out of the darkness as Eli entered his room.

Eli froze, though he didn't jump. Perhaps he was getting used to Harland Hayward's preferred manner of conversation by ambush.

Eli wandered to the small washstand and lit a lantern, taking his time. "Is there a reason you are skulking about in my room in the dark, Strathmore?" Eli asked evenly without turning around. "Run out of beaches?"

"I'm not skulking. I'm sitting. On an exceedingly uncomfortable chair, in fact. What the hell took you so long to get back? What could you have possibly been doing since I left you at the cove?"

Fantasizing about all the different ways I'd like to bed your sister. Imagining all the different ways I'd like her to bed me.

"Nothing that's any business of yours," Eli replied, lifting the lantern in the direction of the baron. Strathmore was sitting in the corner of the room, his legs crossed and his long fingers steepled. Only now, visible in the light that had been absent on the beach, Eli could see Strathmore's exhaustion. Dark smudges hovered beneath his eyes, and his face seemed drawn. His hair had been messily tied back, and what looked like blood was smeared along the front of his coat.

"Rose tells me that she intends to accompany you to London in a few days." There was no inflection other than one indicating a mild curiosity. Eli wasn't fooled for a second.

"Your sister, as I understand," Eli started, "has paintings that she wishes to deliver to clients currently in London. It only makes sense that we travel together in the interest of expediency and safety."

"Safety?" Strathmore repeated. "And who, exactly, will protect my sister from you?"

Eli set the lantern back down on the washstand and sat down on the edge of his bed. He would not rise to the baron's bait. "I can assure you, Lord Strathmore, I have only your sister's best interests at heart. She needs no protection from me."

The baron made a rude noise. "Anthony Gibson once claimed to have Rose's best interests at heart. You might understand why I find it difficult to believe that his closest comrade would speak any more truthfully." It was blunt and brutal.

Eli chose his words carefully. "Anthony was not the man I believed him to be. His behavior and his betrayal of Rose were despicable. He didn't deserve her."

"No, he didn't. And he is damn lucky the French got to him before I did," the baron said coldly. "Had I been in London when his treachery became the public fodder that the ton gorged itself upon at Rose's expense, I would have seen to the appropriate resolution. But regrettably, I was already abroad with my knives and saws, tasked with trying to put His Majesty's troops back together again. Not taking them apart piece by loathsome piece."

Eli watched the baron and wondered how many had made the mistake of underestimating Harland Hayward. "I understand," he said quietly.

"Do you really? Do you understand that, until Anthony, Rose had never really been a part of the cutthroat arena otherwise known as polite society? Do you understand how her engagement—how her trust in that man drew her in and made her believe that she was one of you? How her belief in his love and her place in your world left her exposed and vulnerable when that same society turned on her?"

Eli frowned. That was an odd choice of words—

"You've been gone a long time, Rivers. You weren't here to see how long it took her to heal. Between Gibson and that vile publication that came out after—"

"What publication?" Eli froze, the small hairs on the back of his neck rising.

"You wouldn't have seen it. It was a contemptible collection of caricatures, mocking the appearance of dozens of women, including—"

"No." A horrible feeling was rising from his gut and wrapping its clammy fingers around his lungs.

"So you did see it."

Eli shook his head. "No," he managed. "I didn't."

Strathmore still had him pinned beneath his dark gaze. "It was unusually cruel. Published anonymously. Gibson might have broken her heart, but that shattered what was left of her confidence. The woman I found upon my return was a mere husk of the beautiful, vibrant sister I had left. She still hasn't entirely—" He stopped, as if reconsidering his intended words.

It was everything Eli could do not to lunge to his feet and stagger toward the door. "Your sister," he said instead, speaking slowly and deliberately, an odd buzzing in his ears threatening to drown out the sound of his own voice, "is the most courageous, dauntless woman I have ever had the privilege of knowing."

The baron was silent. "She is," he said eventually. "And if you do anything to threaten what she has managed to regain, then I will happily make sure that the resolution and retribution she deserved years ago will be realized."

Eli stood, unable to remain motionless. A sickening comprehension was flooding every corner of his mind, and for a moment it felt as if he were back in a tiny farmhouse in Belgium, a piece of broken mirror lying facedown on the table before him. A moment when the need to discover the awful truth fought against the need to remain in blissful ignorance.

"Your sister has always had and will continue to hold my greatest respect and admiration," Eli said roughly. "So please, take your threats and get out."

The baron also stood, his long frame casting an eerie shadow in the flickering light. "I have never dictated what my sisters might do, who they spend their time with, or how they choose to live. I will not start now." He moved so that he was standing at the end of the bed, almost in front of Eli. "But don't ever mistake my objectivity for indifference." And then, with three long strides, he was gone.

Eli stood in the sudden silence, trying to order his turbulent thoughts. Understanding that Rose, for all her excruciating honesty, hadn't been completely truthful with him.

Eli snatched the small lantern from the washstand and extinguished it, plunging the room back into shadow. And using the darkness, his long-time ally, he slipped from the dower house.

Avondale was again dark and silent. The kitchen window was as obliging as it had always been, and Eli stole through the rooms, his direction unerring. He kept the small lantern in his hand, careful not to let it rattle as he climbed the stairs. He paused at the top, listening hard, but nothing stirred, and he made his way soundlessly down the long hall.

The studio door had been left open, and it creaked slightly as he pulled it closed behind him. The curtains on the far wall hadn't been drawn, though the moonlight outside wasn't enough to illuminate much. With hands that were surprisingly steady, he relit the little lantern and carried it over to Rose's large trunk of supplies. He set it down and dropped to his knees before opening the heavy lid.

Swiftly he withdrew packets of paper and brushes, tins of charcoal and pigment. With less steady hands now, he found the long, smooth box he was looking for. He closed the lid of the trunk and set the box on top. Releasing the catch, he revealed the stack of folded drawings that Rose had shown him.

Except she hadn't shown him all of them.

He yanked at the brown ribbon tied around the bundle, letting it fall to the ground unheeded, and began unfolding each drawing. The ones on the top were the ones he had seen earlier, and he shoved those aside. He riffled through the rest, his revulsion growing with each carefully rendered sketch, until he came to the very last one, resting on the dark velvet lining at the bottom.

Slowly he picked it up and unfolded it, smoothing the square sheet out on top of the trunk.

Anthony had captured her features perfectly—the straight line of her nose, the delicate arch of her brow, the gentle sweep of lashes at the corners of her eyes, the elegant curl of her hair. Yet there was where the likeness ended. Her petite, slight body had been drawn as an emaciated rat, every rib and joint visible and exaggerated grotesquely, a scaly tail trailing after her. One claw-like hand clutched the coattails of a gentleman who unmistakably looked like Anthony, depicted running from a church with a look of horror on his face. The rat's other hand clutched a purse that was labeled "Father's Fortune." In the background, a line of grandly dressed people pointed and laughed. *The Most Undesirable of all the Undesirables—A Plague Upon Le Beau Monde* was styled neatly across the bottom of the sketch.

Eli sat back on his heels, concentrating on taking even, steady breaths. Trying to temper the rage that was starting to cloud the edges of his vision. At that moment the hate that he harbored for Anthony Gibson was more absolute, more extreme and encompassing, than anything else he had ever experienced. And with that hate came the familiar contempt for himself, a man who had lived in a fog of obliviousness so thick and viscous that he hadn't been able to see Anthony clearly. Hadn't been able to look beyond the polished surface and see the abominable rottenness that lay beneath.

Eli tipped forward, his knees banging painfully against the hard floor. He was chilled and breathing like a winded racehorse. He glanced down and realized that he had crumpled the drawing in his fist, and with an epic effort, he uncurled his stiff fingers and set the drawing back down on the surface of the trunk. He put his hands to his face, pressing hard enough that he could feel the sensation even through the thickened, ruined skin. This was what had been left behind. This was what Rose had been left to face.

You have no idea what it's like to be shunned and ridiculed because of your appearance.

He had shouted that at her on the beach. And she hadn't said anything to him. Hadn't corrected him. Just watched him flail in a whirlpool of self-pity until she had thrown him a lifeline he hadn't deserved.

You should know what those drawings did to some of these women. The destruction they wrought on their lives, when one's reputation and appearance are often the only things society puts any value on. The suggestion that all these women were tried and found wanting...

Rose had told him, and he hadn't been listening. She'd already been regarded warily by the ton as an outsider. As someone different—someone to be feared and distrusted because there had never been a neat, proper label that could be applied to her. Eli didn't delude himself into thinking that anyone, outside of her family, would have leaped to her defense.

Eli braced his hands on the edge of the trunk, the edges cutting into his palms. He hadn't recognized the truth behind everything that she had ever said or done. When she demanded he talk about the hard things, challenged him to do the difficult things, it was because she understood. Her behavior came not from mere recalcitrance or recklessness. It came from experience.

Eli raised his head. Very slowly and deliberately, he gathered all the drawings save one that were scattered across the top of the trunk and on the floor, refolding them and binding them once more with their ribbon. The wooden box was refilled and closed and placed within the confines of the trunk. The art supplies he returned neatly to their places on top, and he lowered the heavy lid. The drawing that was left he refolded and slipped into the pocket of his coat before standing and extinguishing the lantern.

The hallway was deserted, the darkness almost absolute.

His feet made no sound as he made his way down the hall, the fingers of one hand trailing lightly along the wall. He passed the entrance to the staircase and continued until he reached the last door of the south wing. He stood for a moment, listening, but all he could hear was the sound of his own breathing and the faint rattle of a windowpane somewhere as the wind rose and died again. The door opened easily, and Eli let himself in, closing it soundlessly behind him.

Her room was as dark and silent as the rest of the house, though her warm, exotic scent instantly surrounded him. He listened, trying to detect the steady, rhythmic sound of breathing that would tell him that she was asleep.

"You'd make a lousy thief, Dawes."

Eli spun toward the window against the far wall where he thought her voice had come from. "I didn't wake you." It wasn't really a question.

"No." There was a suggestion of movement from near the window, accompanied by the sound of curtains sliding closed along their rod. "Lock the door."

Eli swallowed. "What?"

Light flared suddenly and subsided as Rose lit a candle. "As progressive as this school is, men creeping into bedrooms that are not their own is generally frowned upon. I'd prefer to avoid awkward explanations should a student make an unexpected appearance."

Eli turned and did as she asked.

"I suppose you found it."

He froze, his hand still on the key in the lock. "I beg your pardon?"

"You were in my studio. I'm assuming you found the drawing."

Eli pivoted slowly to face her. She was sitting on the edge

of the wide bed, wrapped in the same embroidered robe he had seen her in that very first night. Her hair was down, streaks of fire tumbling over her shoulders in the soft light. Her eyes were fathomless, her expression unreadable, her voice without inflection. He couldn't tell if she was angry or upset, resigned or indifferent.

He dropped his head and reached into his coat pocket, slowing withdrawing the folded paper. He held it in his fingers, suddenly unsure of what he wanted to say.

"You should have told me." He cursed silently. It sounded like an accusation, but he was still having trouble thinking clearly.

"Why?"

Eli felt his fingers ball into fists, frustrated at his inability to put what he was feeling into words. That dark emptiness within him yawned wide and precarious, but this time it seethed and writhed with a hatred and anger so acute they were making it hard to breathe. "You should have told me," he repeated, unable to come up with an answer to her question.

"So you could what? Call him out? Defend my honor? He's already dead, Dawes, and time has marched on. I told you I don't need your protection. Then or now."

"I know you don't need it, but you should have had it." Eli felt another surge of rage crash through him. "Give me the candle."

"What? Why?"

He didn't wait for her to answer, simply stalked over to where she sat and yanked it away from her. Hot wax splashed over the backs of his fingers, but he didn't care. The flame sputtered. He backed away from her until his hip hit the edge of the washstand. He set the candle down on the edge.

"What are you doing, Dawes?" She had risen to her feet. "Don't—"

He set the corner of the drawing to the flame, the paper catching and curling instantly.

Rose lunged toward him, but he dropped the burning paper in the empty washbasin and caught her fast in his arms. The fire flared and then just as quickly faded, leaving behind only pieces of blackened, smoking ash.

She stared at the faint curl of smoke. "Why did you do that?" Her voice was dull, her body rigid in his arms.

"Why didn't you?" he hissed.

She dropped her head against his shoulder, and he pulled her against him, one hand going to her back, the other stroking the hair away from the side of her face. His insides twisted in anguish because he hadn't been able to protect her from any of this. That after everything that had happened, she'd been left to face it on her own.

"That drawing is a reflection of the coward who created it, not you," he said fiercely.

She turned her head so that it rested against his chest.

"Tell me you believe that, Rose."

"I do now," she said, her words muffled. "But at the time, when that drawing was published, everyone seemed to accept it as truth. That Anthony so abhorred the idea of marriage to me, he'd rather run and forfeit a promised fortune and risk French guns than suffer a union with a woman so flawed."

He tightened his arms around her.

"There were those who saw the drawing and simply laughed at my expense. But there were those who resented me—blamed me—for driving away one of the shining stars of society. More so after word came that he had been killed. A young man with such promise, at the pinnacle of his popularity. I tried to pretend nothing had changed. I wish I could say I rose above it and ignored it all. But everywhere I went,

I heard every awful comment whispered just loud enough for me to hear, and those that weren't whispered at all. Found all the bits of greasy rodent fur that would be slipped into my hair or the rat tails that would be stuck in the back of my gown at balls or assembly rooms. Saw Clara try to hide the boxes of dead rats delivered to our house with my name on them. Watched as every person I had befriended through Anthony turned away. And all of it hurt. It made me doubt everything I once believed to be true about myself. And I hated myself even more for letting it."

Eli thought he might be ill. "Why did you keep the drawing?" he asked. "Why did you keep any of them?" He had asked her that once already, standing in her studio. And she hadn't given him an answer that he had understood.

Rose lifted her head without looking at him. Her palms rested against his chest, her forehead creased faintly. Abruptly she twisted away, as though she had come to some sort of decision. She skirted the bed to the tall walnut armoire that loomed against the far wall.

"Where are you going?" he asked.

She shook her head and instead bent to retrieve a canvas that had been leaning against its side, handling it carefully by the edges.

"What is that?" he asked.

Rose didn't answer, only laid the canvas on the bed and stepped to the side, watching him with an expression he couldn't read. "See for yourself."

Eli cautiously approached the bed. And stopped breathing.

It was a Titian, perhaps. Or a Brueghel. A masterpiece of color and decadent detail, its subject a young woman of astonishing beauty. She had been painted lying on her side against a bed of crimson satin, wearing nothing but a curtain of lustrous black hair and a soft, sensual expression that he couldn't tear his eyes from. When he did finally manage to force his eyes away, his gaze traveled over the roundness of her shoulder and the dip of her waist to the beautiful curve of her hip and down the smooth lines of her legs. Well, one leg, he realized belatedly. There was something not quite right about the leg that rested beneath her.

At the same time he realized two other things; that the painting lacked the burnish of age and, when he finally remembered to breathe, that the scent of linseed reached him.

"You did this," he whispered.

"Yes." There was no pride or meekness in that syllable, just a simple confirmation. She returned to the armoire and picked up a second canvas, this one wrapped in heavy paper. She laid it on the bed next to the first. "Open it."

Eli obeyed, pulling the wrappings away. This too was a portrait of a nude woman, far from the flush of youth but possibly even more erotic for her years. She had been captured standing in front of a long mirror, her head tilted slightly, her hair piled carelessly at the crown of her head. The play of light over the lines of her back, the curve of her spine, and the dimples above her lush buttocks had been executed with incomparable skill. But it was the woman's reflection that riveted him. She'd been caught with her eyes lowered, an enigmatic smile on her lips that made Eli believe she knew something that no one else did. One of her hands was resting between the valley of her heavy breasts, the other over a web of faint lines that marked the thickness of her abdomen.

"Jesus, Rose." The sense of wonder and reverence for these works, for their creator, was making him struggle for words that would justify his emotions. Why had he never known Rose could do this? Aye, he had known she painted, knew she was artistically gifted, had even seen a few portraits she had done of children, but this…this was over-whelming.

"You should be painting for kings," he said.

"I have no desire to paint for kings." Rose smiled a small, strange smile as she gazed down at her work. "I paint for me. And for the women you see before you." She ran a finger along the edge of the first canvas. "Lady Ophelia Volante. Twenty years old. Born with a malformed leg that never grew straight and that prevents her from walking without a crutch. She's never danced, never taken a moonlit walk through a garden, never been called anything but 'that poor cripple.' She speaks five languages, has every play ever writ-ten by Shakespeare damn near memorized, and is a gifted writer. Yet everyone is so focused on what she isn't. No one can see what she is."

"Except you," Eli whispered.

"And now, more importantly, her." Rose tipped her head. "Smart. Brave. Beautiful. In that order." She moved her hand to the next painting. "Susan Jones. Mother of six, wife and partner to a man who owns half the lace industry in Notting-ham. It was her husband who commissioned this. Because he hated how self-conscious and disparaging she had be-come about her body and he wanted her to see how he saw her. That bearing him the gift of a family had only made her more beautiful to him with every passing year."

Eli finally tore his eyes away from the paintings to find Rose watching him.

"I kept those drawings as a reminder that we are all per-fectly and inevitably flawed, and one's beauty is because of it, not in spite of it. Teaching me that lesson was the only good thing Anthony ever did."

The magnificence of Rose's work had distracted him, but the very mention of Anthony's name stopped him cold, anger and abhorrence finding a renewed purchase deep within him. Eli felt as if he were standing on a ledge, unable to go forward but unable to find a way back. "How are you not consumed with hate?" he asked. "What he did to you..."

"I was, for a while," Rose answered quietly, carefully picking up the paintings and setting them aside against the wall. "But hate is exhausting, and Anthony Gibson wasn't worthy of the effort."

"I hate him." It was out before he could stop it.

Rose lowered herself to the edge of the bed and gazed up at him, her dark eyes searching his face. The only sound in the room was the steady ticking of a clock on the mantel. "Why?" she finally asked.

"At Waterloo," Eli whispered, the words torn from his damaged throat, "he left me to die."

~

"You win," she said.

Eli laughed, but there was no humor in it, and it came out as more of a gasp. He took a step toward her and then another before he sank to his knees. She reached for him, caught his hands in hers, and held them fast.

"Do you want to tell me?"

He squeezed his eye shut. "I promised myself I wouldn't speak of it to anyone. I told myself that there was no honor in further vilifying a dead man."

"The word *honor* and Anthony Gibson have never been uttered together."

Eli opened his eye and gazed down at their entwined fingers. "I came here tonight for you. Not me. This isn't what I had intended to do. Not what I came here to say."

"But it needs to be said, I think," she said softly. "Because this is what we do, right? Discuss difficult things."

"Rose—"

"Eli. Do your worst."

He released a ragged breath. "That last day of fighting was horrific. Our advances had suffered massive losses to French cuirassiers. Horses dead, men dead or scattered. I made it back to our artillery lines, alone, on foot. They too had taken heavy casualties and were struggling to keep the guns fed. I stayed. Ran shot and fuses from the munitions cart to the gunners. I was standing next to a munitions cart when it was hit by a French round. I don't remember the explosion, I don't know how long I lost consciousness, but when I opened my eyes, everything was on fire, and the French were bearing down on our devastated line." He stopped. "The gunner—the boy—who had been beside me was still alive, but he'd lost part of his arm. There was an artillery horse trapped in its harness, and I cut it free. I was hanging on to its bridle with the boy on its back, but by then I could barely keep my feet. I thought if I could get him to a surgeon in time..."

Rose tightened her fingers around his.

"And then Anthony was suddenly there, standing in front of us. I ordered him to help the gunner."

Rose could feel the tension rolling off him in palpable waves. "And?"

"And he pointed a pistol at my head and told me to give him the horse because the French had broken through. He was running."

Rose closed her eyes, sorrow and grief spearing through her.

"I refused. Told him that the horse was for the injured boy."

She opened her eyes.

"So he shot me. He missed, mostly," Eli continued quickly, as if he were afraid that if he stopped now he would never finish. "Took whatever was left of my ear. But the horse bolted, and I fell. And from the ground, I watched a French infantryman shoot Anthony with far more accuracy than he had afforded me."

"I'm sorry," she whispered. Because she didn't know what else to say.

"I don't have a clear memory of what happened after," Eli said wearily, as if the telling of his truths had left him depleted. "It comes sometimes in dreams. I remember crawling. I remember trees and silence. And then nothing. Nothing until I woke up in a farmhouse, in a world of pain so excruciating I wanted to die, with an old woman insisting I would not."

"I'm glad she was right," she whispered.

"I don't even know what happened to the gunner. The boy I put on the horse."

"Perhaps he survived."

"Perhaps," Eli mumbled bleakly. "I want to think so."

Rose untangled her fingers from his but kept hold of his hand, turning it over to trace the lines that cut across his callused palms. "My brother is fond of saying that adversity does not build a man's character but reveals the truth of it."

Eli dropped his head. "I saw the truth of Anthony's character far too late."

"Or perhaps you saw it at exactly the right time. Perhaps what Anthony Gibson showed you was less about him and more about your own character. That his cowardice and callousness were the necessary adversity for you to prove to yourself who you were. Who you are."

"That doesn't make sense."

"Why didn't you give Anthony the horse?"

"Because the gunner was wounded and Anthony wasn't. He could have still fought."

"But he didn't."

"No." Eli's lip curled in revulsion.

"But you did."

"No." He shook his head, frowning. "I told you, I barely remember what happened after—"

"I'm not talking about after. You fought for the gunner."

He stared up at her.

"Why? Or even more to the point, why didn't you take the horse?"

"What?"

"Why didn't you take the horse for yourself? You were an officer and the son of an earl, and a grievously wounded one at that, while the boy was only a soldier. Anyone would tell you that you were, by far, the more important individual."

"This 'anyone' you speak of is an idiot," Eli grumbled. "I watched that gunner—a mere boy—sight those guns, never wavering, never retreating, even when everything was going to hell around him. His unwavering bravery in the face of unspeakable carnage was astounding. Inspiring."

"One might suggest your actions on his behalf were no different. Brave and inspiring."

Eli looked away. "I didn't feel brave or inspiring. Mostly I felt terrified."

Rose gazed at him before pulling her hand from his and standing. She stood and went to the armoire, pulling away a third wrapped painting that rested against its side. She brought it over to the bed and set it down beside him before stepping back.

"Open it," she told him.

He glanced up at her but did as he was told. The canvas and rope fell away, revealing a portrait of a man. A Man of

Sorrows. Completed, it was riveting. The detail was superb, Lucy's portrayal of Eli's power and masculine magnificence utterly striking. But it was the expression Lucy had captured that made this work unparalleled. The stoic sadness born from betrayal was still there but, beneath it, a steely resolve to stay the course. To finish what had been set into motion with honor and courage.

Eli was staring down at it, and Rose could see where his knuckles were white around a length of rope he still held. For a moment she experienced a twinge of disquiet, wondering if she had made a mistake showing him this.

"What do you see?" she asked.

He didn't answer her.

"Shall I tell you what I see?" Rose asked, not waiting for him to respond. "A man who is strong. Noble. And imperfectly perfect."

Eli reached out and touched the side of the canvas.

"It's Lucy's work, not mine," Rose told him.

"Why do you have it?" His voice was hoarse.

"I asked her if I could keep it."

"Why?"

So I can remember this moment. Remember you.

"Because it's you," was all she said.

Very slowly he stood and set the canvas aside, back against the wardrobe. The other two paintings followed. He came toward her and stopped a breath away. "Look at me."

She lifted her eyes to his.

"Shall I tell you what I see?"

Rose felt her heart banging painfully against her ribs as her throat tightened.

"I see the woman who makes me whole. The woman who knows me better than I know myself. The most brave and inspiring person I've ever met."

She could feel her nails digging into her palms, the strength and the conviction to protest battered and stripped away by his ruthless, gut-wrenching honesty of this night. He was wrong. She wasn't inspiring, and she certainly wasn't brave. But she couldn't bring herself to tell him. Couldn't bring herself to care what would happen tomorrow, or a week from now, or a year from now. Tonight would be about them. Only them.

"Stay," Eli whispered. "Stay with me."

"Yes," she said, because she was powerless to say anything else.

The heat that ignited in his gaze was a living thing, something that wrapped around her and caught her fast. Arousal roared through her, and she was torn between the need to move and the need to remain perfectly still lest she falter before she could control it. Beneath her chemise and robe, she could feel her chest rising and falling, even that simple movement setting her hardened nipples to chafing against the fabric. The ache within her pooled low in her belly, radiating to her sex, and she could already feel the dampness between her thighs.

And he hadn't even touched her yet.

Eli hadn't moved, simply looked at her, his gaze hot and dark and possessive, and Rose suddenly understood why women had fallen so willingly beneath his spell. He had the power to make her believe that she was the only woman in the world. He lifted his hand, and her skin instantly tightened, anticipating his touch. Except he didn't touch her. His fingers went to his cravat, and he slowly but deftly undid the complicated knot, pulling it from his neck.

"Turn around," he said hoarsely.

Rose released a breath that she hadn't realized she'd been holding.

"Please," he whispered.

She turned, every one of her senses straining toward him. She felt his fingers first, against her temples, gently stroking her hair away from her face and neck and setting it over her shoulders. She could feel the heat of him through the delicate silk of her robe, could feel the warmth of his breath against the side of her neck. She bit her lip, the need to face him almost unbearable.

She felt him duck his head, and now his lips were where his fingers had just been, pressing soft kisses along the side of her neck. She let her head fall back and to the side, wondering if he could feel the pulse that pounded there. She didn't want to wait. She wanted him to touch her. Wanted him to take her with the urgency and desperation she could feel building within her. To bury himself deep inside, where she needed him to be.

She tried to turn, but he caught her with his strong hands. "Not yet," he whispered. "Close your eyes."

Rose stilled, her back pressed against him. She could feel the rapid rise and fall of his chest.

"Please," he said again, and Rose complied.

She felt the softness of warm linen slide over her forehead before she understood what he was doing. The faint scents of starch and sandalwood reached her as he gently drew his cravat over her eyes.

"Eli—"

"It's been a long time," he whispered roughly against her ear. "I want this to be perfect."

She reached up, intending to draw his hands away. He still held the ends of the cravat, and as her fingers curled around his, she realized that they were shaking. Her hands stilled, and she understood then what he was asking.

"I don't need you to do this," she whispered back.

"I know," he rasped.

I need to do this. She heard the words he hadn't uttered. She let her hands fall.

Eli rested his forehead against her shoulder and then he lifted his head, his fingers tying the ends of the cravat at the back of her head. Rose felt him shift, and the heat at her back vanished as he came to stand before her.

It wasn't so different from the very first night. When she had stood close to him in the darkness as a thunderstorm had receded, excruciatingly aware of every movement and sound and scent. Except now Eli Dawes was no longer a stranger. Now he was...

Pulling on the sash of her robe. Running his strong hands along the inside edges of the embroidered silk where it had fallen open, lifting it over her shoulders and pushing it away from her body. She felt it pool soundlessly at her feet, cool night air caressing her fevered skin under her chemise, and she shivered, though she was far from cold.

He had yet to say anything, nor did he as his fingers went to work on the laces at the center of her chest. She felt the ribbons slip through their eyeholes, the gathered top loosening, and then the thin lawn slipped down her body to join the robe at her feet.

It was unnerving, to be standing thus before a man without being able to see his face. Without being able to read what he held in his eyes, to measure what he held in his expression. But she could hear the uneven cadence of his breath. She could still feel the heat of him, smell his soap, mixed now with the muskiness of arousal. An electrifying anticipation bloomed, making her breath hitch and her body sway.

Eli moved, and the air around her stirred. His fingers grazed the side of her cheek. "You are so perfect," he whispered. His fingers dropped to her jaw, then her neck, and then over the ridge of her collarbone. He pressed his palms flat against her skin, sliding down to cup her breasts, his thumbs brushing the peaks of her nipples. He bent his head, and now it was his mouth on her throat and shoulder, his lips and tongue exploring the path his fingers had taken.

Rose arched into the heat of his touch, pushing herself into his hands, a sound she didn't recognize escaping from the back of her throat. His hands slipped lower to cage her hips, and then over the slight curve of her buttocks. He was kneeling now, she realized, his breath hot against her navel as he pressed soft kisses over her abdomen. He stroked the backs of her thighs, the tips of his fingers brushing the dampness between her legs.

She put a hand down to steady herself, her fingers finding the solidity of his shoulder. This absence of sight was a torture of the most intense sort. Every touch, every sensation, every nuance was heightened. Eli's hands came around the fronts of her legs, settling against the soft skin of her inner thigh. She could feel the gentle pressure as he urged her legs farther apart and she complied, though they were no longer steady. His fingers moved upward, and he stroked her the way he had done on the beach. Slow, deliberate movements that sent spirals of pleasure ripping through her and left her panting.

But his clever fingers weren't what she wanted this time. This time she wanted him. All of him. Wanted to feel him in her, around her, possessing her so completely she would forget where he ended and she started. Her hands slid into his hair, and she pulled gently, lifting his head up.

"Take me to bed, Dawes."

Before her he was still and silent.

"Please."

She didn't hear him move, but she suddenly found herself swept up into a pair of arms and deposited on the wide bed, the coverlet cool against her back. She could hear the sounds of him undressing, the shucking off of his coat, the quiet *snick* of buttons as they were released, each sound building the agonizing anticipation, each sound amplifying the ache that was pulsing low in her belly. Her hand drifted down over the sharp ridge of her hip, over the rise of her pubic bone, and through the soft tangle of curls—

"Don't you dare, Rose," Eli snarled softly, and then he was beside her on the bed, the mattress dipping beneath his weight and rolling her toward him.

He caught her hands in his, pinning them over her head, and now there were no gentle explorations. Now he moved over her, his mouth claiming hers in a filthy, explicit kiss that was all tongue and teeth and heat. He nudged her legs apart with his knee, coming to kneel between them, his weight on his arms as he levered himself over her, kissing her relentlessly.

He lowered himself, and Rose could feel the weight of him settle over her body, the heady, intimate claim of dominance that she had craved. She could hear his harsh breathing, the scent of his soap lost now under something more primal. His chest was against hers, the mat of golden hair rubbing against her breasts and nipples and sending new currents of pleasure spiraling through her. The ridges of muscle that defined his abdomen were pressed tight against the rise of her pubic bone, and with each of his movements, the exquisite friction released a shower of sparks deep in her core. She writhed, wondering if he would undo her just like this.

She arched helplessly, tilting her hips against him, letting her legs fall open in a silent plea. He broke their kiss, and Rose whimpered at the loss, but then she felt the head of his cock hard and heavy against her entrance. He dragged himself through her slick folds once, twice, and then thrust into her, urgent and deep and full, and Rose almost wept with the pleasure of it.

He let go of her hands and set his arms at her sides, supporting himself so there was only a single point of contact between them. Rose's world dimmed, everything focused solely on the white-hot pleasure that was building from that single point. Eli flexed his hips and withdrew before thrusting himself forward again. Rose wrapped her legs around the backs of his thighs, her heels digging into the hard muscle, and he drew back and thrust again. Rose bit her lip to keep from crying out.

Eli was moving faster now, and she heard him gasping, felt the slide of their sweat-slicked bodies, smelled the scent of her arousal mingling with his. Her hands grasped in the coverlet as if trying to find an anchor in this storm of crippling ecstasy. Her release, when it came, was sudden and devastating, a torrent of pleasure that pulsed outward, crashing through her limbs with such force that it scattered any coherent thought she might have been clinging to.

Eli hissed, and he ground against her, changing the angle of his hips, drawing out each intense wave of bliss that was hurtling through her, not giving her time to catch her breath. With a ragged groan, Eli pulled out of her, and she felt him shift, one of his hands brushing against her hip as he fisted himself between them.

Rose twisted, reaching for his hand. "Don't you dare, Dawes," she whispered, and he might have chuckled, but the sound was swallowed by his gasp as her fingers replaced his. His erection was slick and hot and hard, and it pulsed as she swiftly slid her fingers up its length. She ran her thumb over the engorged head and then stroked down, and Eli made a tortured noise as his hips jerked and he came, his entire body shuddering violently, his seed spilling over her stomach.

Eli gasped and collapsed on top of her, his head buried in the crook of her neck, his chest rising and falling at a pace that matched hers. Rose wrapped her hands around him, stroking his back, feeling his tremors subside. Her skin, where it wasn't covered by Eli, cooled in the night air, and after a few minutes, he stirred, rolling to the side, and she felt the mattress dip as he shifted. His fingers were at her face then, gently lifting his cravat from her eyes and drawing it away from her face. Rose didn't move, her eyes still closed, lying still as Eli used the linen to wipe her belly. He took his time, pressing kisses against her skin as he went, until he finally withdrew and was still.

She opened her eyes to find him watching her. He had propped himself on one elbow, and with his free hand he reached out and pushed her unruly hair back from her face.

"Thank you," he said.

"For what?"

"For understanding." He crumpled the linen that had covered her eyes in his fist and let it fall beside the bed.

Rose smiled, catching his hand in hers. She turned it over, pressing her lips to the center of his palm. "I might ask you to do it again."

Eli stared down at her. "You are the most incredible woman I've ever met," he said.

Rose could feel herself blush.

"Stay in London when we go. Allow me to court you properly."

Whatever glow still lingered in her body cooled almost instantly. "Don't do this, Dawes. Not right now."

His expression was troubled. "Rose—"

"Don't ask me to do that. Not now. Please." She didn't

want to ruin this perfect moment. Didn't want the reality of the future to intrude.

She heard him exhale heavily. "I'm not going to stop asking until you say yes. You mean too much to me. I will not lose you. Not again."

Rose felt something in her heart twist painfully. They were noble words, kind words, fervent and heartfelt. They were words that should make any woman happy.

His hand moved from her hair to her cheek, tracing the edge of her jaw. "I want you to have all that you deserve. I want to take you everywhere and anywhere. The theaters, the operas, the museums. Balls, dinners, fireworks in pleasure gardens. I want all of your dances and all of your walks in the moonlight." He turned her head toward his, forcing her to meet his eye. "I want all of your days and all of your nights."

Rose was silent, knowing that she could go none of the places he was proposing. She could not be the woman the Earl of Rivers needed her to be. It was her reality, one she had learned to accept, and she had never regretted it. Until now.

Rose lifted herself up on her elbows and turned, leaning up to kiss Eli on the mouth with all the emotion that was trapped inside her. "You have this night," she whispered, because she couldn't promise anything else.

Chapter 15

The bruised clouds hung low and heavy over London, threatening rain.

Eli could smell it through the open carriage window, despite the more noxious odors of sewage, dust, and livestock. He picked out the usual landmarks visible above the riot of roofs—the Tower, St Paul's, Westminster Abbey. In some places a new building had cropped up that he didn't recall, and in others an empty space stood gaping, like a lost tooth in a row of crooked ones. After living in isolation as he had for so long, the sheer mass of humanity crammed into every space was disquieting.

As the equipage crept forward, he looked away from the passing view to study the woman sitting across from him. Rose was sitting quietly, gazing out her window, her hands folded neatly in her lap. She was wearing the sky-blue dress that set her hair on fire and reminded him what she had looked like on that Dover beach the first time he ever kissed her. And just how much he wanted to do so again.

It had been two days since he had reluctantly crept from her bed before the onset of dawn, leaving her sleeping peacefully. He hadn't asked her about London again. Hadn't wanted to taint their time with regret and refusal. But she'd withdrawn into herself anyway, even if she had tried to hide it with pleasant, amiable conversation steered always in his direction. Conversation about his plans when he reached London. How he would explain his lengthy absence. Who and what he had missed most.

Every question he'd tried to turn back on her was met with another question directed at him. Rose would have beaten his father at his own game. His father must have adored her.

The carriage stopped, and Eli glanced out the window. With some shock he realized that they were in front of the Rivers home in Grosvenor Square. He tore his eyes from the familiar facade and found Rose watching him.

"Welcome home, Lord Rivers," she said with a small smile.

He stared at her, suddenly unwilling to get out. Unwilling to leave her. As if she would be lost to him if he stepped out of this carriage alone. Which was absurd, he knew, because Rose was only continuing on to the Haverhall School and the studio and the obligations that waited for her there. Though that knowledge didn't seem to make him feel any better.

"Come inside with me," he said, before he could think better of it.

She shook her head instantly. "My lord, I don't think—"

"Do not call me anything other than Eli. Dawes if you must."

She sighed. "We're not in Dover any longer, Lord Rivers. As such, I will address you as befits your position in London—"

In a heartbeat he had closed the distance between them and crouched in front of her. "If you think that being in London changes anything, think again, Rose Hayward. You belong to me just as much as I belong to you, whether we're in London or Dover or on the damn moon."

"My lord, we've discussed this. Your focus now needs to be on the matters and duties that will—"

He leaned forward and kissed her, a demanding, searing kiss that sent desire flooding through him. God, he would never get enough of this woman. He pulled away slightly, gratified to see that she was just as breathless as he. "Matters and duties have waited for years. They'll wait a few more minutes."

She started to shake her head again. "This isn't—"

"The last time I invited you here, I had just bought a painting."

"I remember. Michelangelo's *Leda and the Swan*."

"Yes. Do you know why I bought it?"

Rose shook her head.

"Because Michelangelo painted the truth for those who cared to look closely. That it wasn't Zeus who descended to seduce Leda. Rather, he portrayed a mortal woman so incomparable that even the greatest of gods couldn't resist her." He paused. "I saw you in her. You're my Leda. Irresistible."

Rose flushed, her eyes searching his. "Eli—"

"When was the last time you visited my gallery?"

"Not since your father died. It didn't seem right."

"Would you refuse my invitation now?"

"You're using a dirty trick here."

"Yes."

"What if I say no?"

Eli leaned forward and brushed his lips against hers

again. "If you refuse, Rose, I will keep kissing you here in this carriage for as long as it takes you to say yes. I will make sure we scandalize the coachman and the neighbors and the servants and the bloody watchman who will finally come to see what is going on. Then I will carry you out of this carriage, into my house, and make love to you on the Aubusson in the middle of that gallery." His mouth grazed her ear. "I might do that anyway, my Leda."

"Eli," she breathed.

"Excellent. I'll take that as a yes." He withdrew to the other side of the carriage and opened the door.

"I didn't say yes."

"You didn't say no." He stepped from the carriage and held out his hand to her. Rose hesitated for only a moment before she sighed and took it.

The square was seemingly deserted at this time of evening—too early for the wealthy inhabitants to emerge in pursuit of evening entertainment, and too late for the servants who toiled during the day. He glanced up at the windows of the stretch of stately, pillared homes, but only the reflection of the heavy clouds stared back from the glass. He glanced down, smoothing his hand over the superfine of his coat. He'd dressed the part today. A midnight-hued coat and dove-gray silk waistcoat topped with a starched cravat. Trousers and polished boots. All things that had once been as familiar to him as breathing but now still felt slightly foreign.

He climbed the stairs, Rose at his side, and grasped the heavy brass knocker.

"You know you own this house, right?" she asked, sounding amused. "You don't have to knock."

"The last time I sneaked into a house I owned, I almost found myself skewered. I fear the servants here may be armed with something more substantial than the end of a paintbrush."

"It was the sneaking part that was problematic, Dawes. Had you used the front door and announced yourself—"

The front door suddenly swung open, and the frame was filled with the bulk of a stone-faced, silver-haired butler. His eyes went directly to Rose, and his expression thawed minimally.

"Good evening, Miss Hayward," the man intoned. "It is a pleasure to see you."

"And you, Dufour," she replied. "You're looking very well."

The man almost smiled before his mouth flattened once again. "Is there something you require that I can help you with, Miss Hayward?"

She hesitated. "Not me, exactly."

For the first time, the butler's gaze left Rose and focused on Eli.

"Good evening, Dufour. It's been a long time," Eli said, a strange sense of surrealism descending. The familiarity of all of this—it was almost as if he had never left. Almost as if the time between then and now had suddenly evaporated.

Dufour outdid himself. His face went ashen before turning an alarming shade of crimson. Though that was the only outward sign that Eli's sudden resurrection and reappearance were anything other than expected. And to his credit, his butler did not look away from Eli's injury, as if that too had been anticipated.

"Good evening, my lord," was all he said, as though Eli were back from a walk and not the dead. He pulled the door open wide and stepped smartly aside.

Eli entered and glanced around, that odd sense of simply stepping back in time intensifying. Nothing had changed since he had been here last. The marble floors still shone, the wood trim still gleamed, the crystal chandeliers hanging from the ornate plaster ceilings still glittered. The bust of a long-forgotten Greek philosopher still stared sightlessly from its perch near the grand staircase, and the matching jade vases still rested in their alcoves on the opposite wall.

"My apologies, my lord." Dufour sounded utterly composed. "But we were not notified that you were—"

"Alive?" Eli asked. Once of his first duties as earl might be to give this man a raise. He would have made a splendid general.

"Planning to be in residence," the butler corrected succinctly.

"It is I who should apologize, Dufour," he said. "For my extended absence and lack of correspondence. There were...unforeseen circumstances."

"Understandable, my lord," the man sniffed, as if that explained everything. "And I speak for everyone in offering you a warm welcome back." He paused, his heavy brows bunching slightly. "If I may be so bold, might I suggest that you and Miss Hayward make yourselves comfortable in the formal drawing room? For just a short time? I should like to advise the staff of your return so that they may...present themselves accordingly."

"Of course. A sensible suggestion."

"Thank you, my lord. I'll have refreshments for you and Miss Hayward sent in immediately." The butler bowed slightly and departed.

"You should give that man a raise," Rose murmured from beside him.

"I was thinking the same thing." He glanced in the direction in which the butler had disappeared. "Come," he said, reaching for her hand and tugging her forward.

"Where are we going? The drawing room isn't this way."

"We'll get there soon enough."

⟶

Rose climbed the grand, familiar stairs and had no idea why she'd let Eli talk her into this. She'd allowed him to obliterate all her good intentions with his clever charm and debilitating kisses, just as she was allowing him to guide her past the entrance to the ballroom that dominated the front half of the floor and to the closed door in the far rear corner.

But for all the earl's professions that she knew his strengths and weaknesses better than he knew himself, he seemed to know her weaknesses just as well. Titian and Michelangelo were difficult men to resist. Almost as difficult as Eli Dawes.

But after this she would go. Even though she'd broken the promise she'd made to herself that their shared carriage would end their time together, it would be only a fleeting concession. Because the world Eli had now returned to would soon descend like floodwaters released from a dam and carry the new Earl of Rivers away. And the mere idea of exposing herself and getting caught in that inevitability was enough to make her stomach churn and her heart flutter against her insides like a trapped bird.

But for now Rose would take this one last chance to simply enjoy something that they both revered. She was well aware that she might never get another. She watched as Eli reached up, his fingers sliding along the top of the door frame, and found a hidden key. He slid it into the lock and opened the door, pulling it wide to allow her to enter ahead of him.

Rose stepped into the room and stared.

The walls were the same chalk-gray color she remembered, best to provide a blank canvas for the masterpieces that graced them. The expensive Aubusson rug still dominated the center of the room, comfortable upholstered chairs placed in the same strategic spots to best view the art.

Except all the art was gone.

She whirled to find Eli standing behind her, his face pale and his eyes a little wild as he gazed at the bare walls, faint discolored marks the only evidence that canvases had ever hung. Rose's heart lodged in her throat. A horrible feeling was crawling across her skin, even as her mind constructed rational possibilities. The paintings had been moved. Put into storage. Wrapped for safekeeping after the death of the old earl.

"Where are the paintings?" Eli asked hoarsely, turning in a circle.

"They were all here right after your father died. That was the last time I saw them. But I haven't been here since then." She put a hand on his arm. "I'm sure that there is a good explanation." She didn't dare suggest the other possibilities that were lurking beneath all those rational ones.

Possibilities like *stolen*. Or *sold*.

The earl's gaze had fallen on the ornate mantel of the hearth against the far wall. A small object, about the size of a book, was propped up on its center, one Rose didn't recognize. In five strides Eli had crossed the room and seized it, Rose on his heels.

It was a reliquary of some ancient origin, carved from ivory, framed in gilded wood set with sapphires. A line of carved men marched across the bottom, one carrying a bucket, one scattering what looked like seed, the other with a small dog at his heels. Above them, lining the top half, were two angels, their wings unfurled, looking down at the figures below. In the center of the frame was a card, similar to one that would be presented on social calls.

However, there was no name embossed on the card. Only the image of a tiny crown, underneath which was written in an elegant scroll, *Purveyor of Fine Art.*

"Jesus," Eli swore softly.

"What?" Rose was at his side, pale and worried. "Have they been stolen?" She voiced her worst fears.

"Not exactly."

"What does that mean?"

"I know who has them." There was a muscle working alongside his jaw.

"Who? Are they safe?"

"Most likely. I—"

"My lord?" Dufour was standing in the doorway of the gallery, expressionless once again save for the faintest hint of a crease in the center of his broad forehead. "There are refreshments in the drawing—"

"When were the paintings removed, Dufour?" Eli sounded far calmer than Rose would have been had she come home to find her collection of priceless art vanished.

The butler frowned slightly. "A fortnight after your father's death, my lord," he said, as though Eli should have known that. "As per your instructions."

"I beg your pardon?"

"The written and signed instructions that you left were with your father's will and estate papers. I saw them myself, and they were quite clear. The solicitors and estate managers followed them to the letter."

"My instructions?"

"That the paintings were to be bequeathed after your father's death." Dufour looked grim. "Is there something amiss, my lord?"

Rose was looking between the butler and Eli.

"No," Eli said, waving his hand. "No, all is well."

Rose watched him, not understanding exactly what was going on.

"Would you and Miss Hayward care to retire to the drawing room now, my lord? The staff have been assembled and are—"

"My apologies, Dufour, but the staff will have to wait."

"My lord?"

"There is somewhere I need to go."

"Now, my lord? But you've only just arrived—"

"Now," Eli confirmed.

"Of course." The butler shifted. "One additional item, my lord, of pressing concern."

"What is it, Dufour?"

"Your cousin and his wife are currently in residence. Summoned by the estate's solicitors, as I understand, to deal with the matter of your—" He stopped abruptly. "Your succession and inheritance, my lord."

Eli was frowning. "They are here? Now?"

Dufour shook his head slightly. "They are out at the moment. Though in the sennight that they have been here, they have always retired quite early. I can't imagine that they will be late."

Eli's jaw was tight. "I will try to return with due haste. Should I be delayed, please assure them that I will be available first thing in the morning to address any concerns that they might have and answer the questions I know they will."

"Very good, my lord."

Eli put a hand at the small of Rose's back and guided her toward the stairs, leaving the butler standing behind them.

"What are you doing?" Rose asked under her breath as they retraced their steps.

"I'm going to get my paintings back."

"What? From whom?"

The earl didn't answer, only stalked across the expanse of his hall.

"Dammit, Dawes, you can't just appear and disappear again. Shouldn't you stay? Deal with your cousins? Your staff? You—"

He stopped without warning, and Rose almost crashed into the back of him. "And if you were in my shoes, right now, at this very moment, what would you do?"

She felt her lips press into a thin line. "I would go and get my paintings back."

He smiled, though it didn't come close to reaching his eyes. "Exactly." He spun and headed for the door.

"Will you at least tell me where you're going?" Rose demanded as he stepped out into the night.

"You'll see precisely where I'm going," Eli answered grimly, tucking the reliquary under his arm. "Because you're coming with me."

Chapter 16

A small crystal dish of cards bearing the now-familiar crown emblem sat on the edge of the massive mahogany desk. But Rose barely noticed, so overwhelmed was she with the masterpieces that graced the walls around her. An art dealer, was how Eli had described the man they had come to see, one through whom most of Eli's collection had been accrued. A man from whom anything might be had for a price. A man as famous for his fine tastes and extravagance as he was for the shadows that concealed his past.

Rose circled the room, drawn again to the wide canvas that dominated the wall across from the desk, and ignored Eli, who was pacing beside her. As a student in Italy, she'd been told that this painting had been lost. She'd seen a copy of its sister image, but that work had not possessed the aura of ... ruthless purpose that this one did. A young woman, depicted in a black dress and wearing an expression of chilling detachment, stood over a prostrate man, his mouth open in a silent scream. With one hand the woman shoved the man's head back, and with the other she severed his neck with a gleaming blade. Beside her an old woman smiled, clutching a bag and whispering encouragement in her ear.

"Do you like it, Miss Hayward?"

The question came from the doorway, and, a little unnerved, Rose turned from the painting to find a man watching her with keen interest. Beside her, Eli coiled like a panther about to spring.

"King," Eli said, his greeting lacking any warmth.

The dealer acknowledged Eli and then returned his attention to Rose. "Well?"

"It's one of his best, I think," Rose replied slowly, eyeing the man who was walking into the room. He was fair, with reddish-gold hair that was reminiscent of the early Tudors framing pale-blue eyes set in an austere face. He was impeccably dressed, one hand resting atop an ebony walking stick.

"Rubens, you mean," he said.

"No. Caravaggio."

"Ah." A red-gold eyebrow rose in approval, as though she had just passed a test of some sort. "For the record, I had the Rubens, but I sold it. This rendition of Judith beheading Holofernes is much more . . . visceral."

Rose didn't answer but merely glanced at the painting again and wondered just how this man knew who she was.

"You do not find the violence distasteful?" he inquired.

"Distasteful? Holofernes was about to destroy her home and her people. Judith did what needed to be done."

"As do we all," the man murmured. "Well said, Miss Hayward." He cleared his throat and turned his attention to Eli. "It took you long enough to get here, Lord Rivers."

"I beg your pardon?" Eli's voice was like gravel.

The man strolled across his office and settled himself

gracefully behind his desk. "I wasn't sure you were ever coming back from that miserable little farm in Belgium."

Rose heard Eli suck in a breath.

"Oh, don't look so surprised, Lord Rivers," the man chastised. "You can't honestly believe your solicitors, whose names I scrawled on those documents, actually had the wherewithal to find you."

Rose could see Eli's fingers curl into fists at his sides. "It was you?"

"Of course it was I who tracked you down. Well, I suppose that's not entirely accurate. I hired the wife of a friend. She's very good at finding people who don't want to be found."

"Why?" Eli asked through clenched teeth.

King tapped his fingers on the silver handle of his walking stick. "Your collection is not large, but it is one of the finest private collections of Renaissance art in England, Lord Rivers. After your father died, I did not want to leave it at the mercy of whatever ignorant buffoons took over your estate. There was some uncertainty over whether or not you were actually dead. And I abhor uncertainty."

"So you stole them?"

A shadow of cold impatience flickered across the man's face. "I am going to choose to assume your manners have slipped during your sabbatical and ignore whatever slur you may have just made upon my honor. If I had intended to steal them, Rivers, I simply would have taken them. I would not have gone to the expense and trouble of verifying your survival."

He leaned back in his chair and gestured at the reliquary Eli had left on the desk. "I would never have left you my card to find if and when you decided to return. Or left a paper trail of finely forged documents that even a child could follow." He paused. "Now that you've finally chosen to live out the rest of your days as an earl and not a swineherd, you'll have your paintings back. I merely kept them safe for you until your return."

"You expect me to believe you did this out of what? Kindness?"

"Kindness," King repeated silkily. He chuckled, as though he found that amusing. "It's good business, Lord Rivers. You have always been one of my best and most discerning clients. You're worth far more to me alive and in control of your fortune than you are penniless and scraping shit out of a pigsty."

Rose stared, disconcerted by the emotionless manner in which that sentence had been delivered. She understood why this man revered the Caravaggio hanging on the wall behind her as much as he did. She rather suspected he might share a disturbing kinship with Judith.

Eli swore under his breath. He put his hands on King's desk, his knuckles white around the edges. "And if you'd discovered that I was dead?"

"Only then would I have redistributed your collection to places where their worth would have been appreciated."

"You would have sold them again."

"Of course I would have." There was no apology in his reply. "Art does a dead man no good."

"Where are they?"

"Secured. I will have them delivered first thing tomorrow." He paused. "Unless, of course, you feel the need to verify their condition before then. I am assuming that is why you decided to bring Miss Hayward with you this evening."

Eli straightened and stepped back, his body partially shielding Rose. "Perhaps."

"I take no offense, Lord Rivers. In fact, I applaud your insight. I can't say I wouldn't have done the same. Miss

Hayward's reputation as an authority on such pieces precedes her." King smiled an empty smile and pushed himself to his feet languidly.

Rose stiffened. "With all due respect, you do not know me," she said.

"On the contrary," King murmured. "I know a great deal about you. I know where you've studied. I know that you are too gifted to be spending your time rendering likenesses of insufferable children and intolerable lapdogs. I've seen your work."

"Competent portraits of children do not make one gifted," Rose said evenly. "They make one able to pay bills."

He came around the side of his desk until he was facing her. "I'm not talking about those portraits, Miss Hayward. I'm talking about the ones so superbly sinful they possess the power to rob a man of breath and stir his blood. The ones that uncover everything extraordinary about a woman who might once have believed herself to be less than ordinary."

Rose could feel the color drain from her face. Against her, Eli tensed and shifted.

King studied her. "Mmm. You think that's a threat."

"Is it?" The content of each of those paintings was her insurance that privacy was guaranteed for both artist and client. In all the years that she had been painting them, there had never been so much as a whisper. Yet that hadn't kept her from being inordinately careful. She'd left no signatures, no clues, nothing that could ever be traced back to her in the event that one of her paintings should come to light.

It wasn't herself she took those steps for. The reputation of Haverhall School was still tied to the Hayward name, and she had known from the beginning she could do nothing to jeopardize that. Rumor was a cruel and merciless adversary. Rose understood that better than anyone.

"Have a care, King," Eli said in a voice that sliced through the silence and could not be mistaken for anything but a threat.

The man facing them stroked his chin, seemingly immune to Eli's anger. A bloodred ruby on his little finger glittered in the light. "I am not in the habit of threatening those whom I hold in great esteem, Rivers," he said, leaning his walking stick against the desk. "It serves no purpose, especially when I require something from that individual."

"What do you want?" Eli demanded.

"Only Miss Hayward's valued opinion." The man stopped near a covered canvas, resting against a towering bookcase, that Rose hadn't even noticed.

Rose eyed him suspiciously. "My opinion?"

"I've recently come into possession of something that I think will interest you both greatly," he said, grasping the edge of the fabric covering the canvas.

Eli's hand curled around her shoulder. "I've endured too much, I think, to suffer any more of your manipulations. We'll take our leave."

"I would consider it a favor. And I wasn't asking you, Rivers. I was asking Miss Hayward. I'm quite certain she can speak for herself."

Rose extracted herself from Eli's side, curiosity edging out her better judgment. "My opinion on what?" she repeated, stepping closer to the bookcase.

"This." King flicked his wrist, and the cloth slid from the painting it had concealed.

Rose stood rooted where she was, unable to tear her eyes away from the canvas. It was a masterpiece of sumptuous color, the nude woman seated against a background of midnight, a robe of rich garnet draped over her legs. Her fingers skimmed the single strand of pearls around her neck as she turned to gaze at her reflection in a mirror supported by two winged cherubs.

Rose wasn't aware she had moved until she dropped to her knees in front of the painting.

"*Venus with a Mirror*," she whispered. She leaned closer, studying the intricate detail and composition of each figure.

"Yes," King agreed, stepping back slightly. "And not, I think, a copy by Rubens or Van Dyck. Or anyone else, for that matter."

"No." Rose shook her head. "I've seen copies. This is his. This is Titian's. The version he did for the Spanish king."

"As I thought."

Rose slowly got to her feet, unable to look away. "It's . . ." She couldn't even come up with a word that would adequately describe the value of the treasure before her.

"It's rather poignant, don't you agree? The . . . appraisal of one's own appearance. Reflections are complicated things, are they not?"

She remained silent, unwilling to acknowledge the deliberate calculation of his words and unsure if they were aimed at her or Eli. "Has someone bought it?" she asked, if only to divert the conversation into less treacherous waters.

"No," King said after a brief hesitation. "At least not yet. Though I do have someone in mind. There aren't many who could afford such a prize." He tapped a finger on the head of his walking stick. "Why do you ask, Miss Hayward?"

She gazed at the portrait. God, what she wouldn't give to possess this. But a Titian was far beyond her means. "A work this exquisite should go to someone who cannot just afford it but who will appreciate its significance. Understand the narrative."

"I couldn't agree more," King murmured. "Tell me what you see. What you hear."

Rose studied the woman in the painting, her voluptuous beauty of a type that had been extolled by Renaissance poets over centuries. Fair skin flushed pink, soft blond hair, delicately arched brows, and red, generous lips. "This is a woman who has been told over and over that she is beautiful," Rose said quietly. "The cupid is holding up the mirror so that she may admire her perfection. But she chooses not to. Her eyes are focused not on herself but on something— someone else. Someone who is not in the picture but is of greater importance to her than her reflection."

"Perhaps the artist himself?" King asked.

"Yes. I've always liked to think that Titian was in love with this woman, whoever she was. And she with him. And this was his way of expressing his belief that a great love can eclipse all earthly vanities."

"Hmmm. You have a way with words, Miss Hayward." King stepped closer to the painting again. "I see his influence in your work, you know. Titian's. This one in particular. Yet I believe you may be that rare case of a student surpassing the master."

Her eyes flew to King's, and she found him watching her again with the same unsettling intensity he had shown before.

"You capture the very essence of each soul. Their secret wants and desires, all there to see, should one only take the time to look carefully."

"Thank you," she managed, feeling uncomfortably adrift under this man's scrutiny and praise. As if he were peering into her soul and all the secrets she kept there. "Where did it come from?" Another question to deflect attention away from herself.

King hesitated, as if weighing his answer. "The French have been almost as accommodating with their recent wars as they were with their revolution," he finally said, gathering the cloth and draping it once again over the painting with unhurried movements. "All the treasures that their ambitious emperor...collected in his travels across the Continent have ended up in the most unexpected places now that he's no longer here. I traded a crate of inferior brandy for this painting in a brothel in Marseille."

Rose watched as he straightened and then finally turned back to Eli, who had remained silent during their exchange.

King was gazing at Eli, a strange glint in his pale eyes. "You see, Lord Rivers, what is lost when one does not understand what one possesses?"

Chapter 17

T hree days.

Three days of meetings and paperwork and appointments. Three days of traipsing back and forth between the courts and offices and his home. Three days of assuring a staggering number of clerks and lawyers and magistrates that he was exactly who he said he was while avoiding and deflecting the inevitable questions that followed. Eli endured the expected stares and whispers, though it was difficult to tell if that was because of his appearance or because he had, in effect, risen from the dead.

When faced with his cousin who had, until very recently, been poised to inherit an earldom, Eli had braced himself for conflict. But to his astonishment, Horace Dawes had nearly wept with relief at the sight of Eli. Armored in thick woolen clothing, thick silver whiskers, and a thick Irish accent, Horace had immediately confessed that he wanted nothing to do with any of it. He was a simple country man, given to simple pursuits, and he had come to London only because his conscience and sense of familial duty would not allow him to do otherwise. Horace and his wife had had their bags packed and passage booked before the sun set that evening. They left the next day, wishing Eli well and beseeching him to get married and have sons.

As many as possible and as quickly as possible.

Eli wearily rubbed his hands over his face. Outside his gallery window, the day had slipped away and darkness had fallen. He gazed up at the painting now restored to its rightful place above the mantel. A survivor of the many religious bonfires of centuries past, secreted away and finally rediscovered. A little like himself, he thought with no little irony.

It possessed the clean contours so characteristic of Botticelli's work, and the centaur and the maiden he gazed up at had been painted as if caught in the dying rays of a sunset. The woman, dressed in a gossamer gown, had one hand on the beast's back and the other on the bow the centaur clutched. She looked surprised, as if she had just discovered something unexpected and wasn't entirely sure what to do next.

Not unlike how Eli felt after his disturbing visit with King.

Of course it was I who tracked you down.

Eli had turned King's words over and over until he realized that dwelling on them was pointless. Whoever had found him and whatever their motivations, it didn't change the present. Eli had, however, continued to second-guess the wisdom of bringing Rose with him. He had underestimated King's cunning. He should have known that the man would know as much about Rose Hayward as he seemed to know about all those who might call themselves allies or enemies. And there had been muddy undercurrents churning beneath that entire conversation that Eli hadn't understood or liked one bit.

Not that he could talk to Rose about it. Eli hadn't seen her since that night. She'd made him promise to take this time for himself. To get his affairs in order and to devote his full attention to the birthright that was now his. His days would be hectic and exhausting, and her presence, she had said, would only be a distraction.

She had been logical and gentle and practical, and he had detested all of it. In the end she had been right. His days had been hectic and exhausting and had required all his attention.

But she'd been wrong too. Because her absence during those days, and even worse, the nights that followed, was more than distracting. It was becoming all-consuming. Eli had sent messages to her at Haverhall, brief accounts of his progress and longer descriptions of just how much he missed her. But words written neatly on a paper to a woman he couldn't touch did not even begin to fill the chasm that had opened within him or assuage the need that was growing with every passing minute. The polite, encouraging responses he got back were not enough. Promises be damned, he wasn't going to survive another hour if he couldn't see her. Touch her. Be with her.

"My lord?" Dufour's rich baritone reverberated from the doorway.

Eli looked up. "Yes?"

"The Duke of Stannis is here. He has requested a moment of your time." The butler made a small moue of distaste, the duke's prominence seemingly no match for the impolite hour at which he had chosen to call.

There had been a handful of callers already who had left cards, curious or courteous or both, but all no doubt anxious to get a look at a newly undead earl. Stannis was the first to catch him at home, and Eli was quite sure the hour had been chosen deliberately.

"Shall I tell him you are unavailable, my lord?" Dufour asked.

"No. No, that's fine." Eli stood and retrieved his coat from the back of his chair. One did not cut a duke, no matter the hour.

"One of the duke's sons is with him, my lord."

Eli frowned and made his way out of the study. It had been his father who had known Stannis, not Eli, and he could only assume that the duke was here out of deference to the late earl. Eli could not remember ever meeting any of the duke's sons, the family choosing to reside on its northern estates. So why they were here, in London, in his formal drawing room, and at a peculiar hour, was a little baffling.

Eli's boots rang across the marble hall, and he pushed wide the drawing room door that had been left slightly ajar. "Good evening, Your Grace," he started, but that was as far as he got.

A pair of eyes the color of a summer sky washed pale by heat met his. Though on this day they weren't exhausted and red rimmed or set into a soot-blackened face. On this day they were clear and steady and set into a face with a strong nose and a wide jaw, topped by a shock of sandy-brown hair.

Eli set his hand on the edge of the door as if that would keep him steady.

"Good evening, Lord Rivers," greeted a heavyset older man who was standing ramrod straight near the hearth. "It is my honor to welcome you home. I believe you have already met my youngest son."

"Lewis Linfield." The young man inclined his head, his eyes fixed on Eli. "Your servant, my lord."

Eli's gaze slid down Linfield's finely tailored coat, stopping abruptly where his left hand should have been, his cuff pinned neatly back just below the elbow. "Jesus," he croaked. "You survived."

"Because of you."

Eli let go of the door, taking a careful step farther into the room. A bubble of what felt like joy and relief was expanding, pressing up into his chest, and making it difficult to draw a full breath. He reached out and touched Linfield's shoulder, as if to make sure that he was real. "You stayed on that damn horse."

Linfield nodded, his summer-blue eyes suspiciously bright. "I still have that damn horse. Brought it home with me. When it bolted, it bolted straight north. Straight back behind our lines. Surgeons got to me in time." He glanced down at his empty sleeve. "I don't know that there are words that will ever be adequate to thank you. You have no idea how many times I've replayed that moment over and over in my head. How many times I wondered why you did what you did. Why you chose to save me and not yourself." He looked up at Eli again, a dark anguish twisting his expression. "I saw you fall."

Eli looked away, memories sending cold tendrils creeping through the joy and relief. "As it turns out, I don't kill very easily."

"You let everyone believe you were dead." It wasn't an accusation.

Eli closed his eyes briefly. "Some wounds take longer than others to heal."

"'The private wound is deepest,'" Linfield said softly. He caught Eli's look. "It's from *The Two Gentlemen of Verona*. Shakespeare," he said, almost apologetically. "I didn't mean to—"

"No," Eli murmured. "You are exactly right."

Behind his son, the duke cleared his throat. "My son is right. There are no words that can adequately express our gratitude. Nothing that will ever be able to repay a debt such as the one I owe you for saving my son."

"I didn't know he was your son—"

"I am aware. No one did." The duke pinned both Eli and Linfield with a hard look. "He should never have been on that damn field," he said. "He defied me, fled in the night, and joined the artillery corps with an invented name."

Despite himself, Eli felt his lips twitch.

The duke glared at him, though the effect was ruined by his obvious pride. "You did something of the same, I understand. Your father and I commiserated with each other over our willful, honorable sons. And how we would throttle you both when you returned."

Eli swallowed with difficulty, his throat suddenly thick. *I think your father was proud of you*, Rose had told him. He hadn't really believed her until now. Hadn't let himself believe it.

"I hope the two of you are each blessed with a dozen boys," the duke was saying. "Each one more headstrong and reckless than the both of you combined."

Linfield turned to Eli. "I didn't tell anyone about...the circumstances of what happened," he said, looking uncomfortable. "Not even my father. Not until now. Not until I heard that you had come home." He searched Eli's face. "I knew who you were. And I heard you call the other officer by name. The one with the pistol. The one who..."

"Shot me?"

Linfield's throat worked. "Yes." He glanced at his father. "And I didn't know how I could ever justify or explain..."

"There is no justification or explanation for such cowardly actions," Stannis growled. "And to give them any additional attention serves no purpose. But your actions, Lord Rivers, will not go unheralded. Or unrewarded."

Eli drew back. "Your Grace, your son's survival is all the reward I require. There is nothing else I need."

"Don't be daft, Rivers. Despite your modest professions, there will be something, sometime, that you will need. And when you do, you will come to me, and I will make it happen. Is that understood?"

"Yes." Eli nodded, knowing it was pointless to argue.

"We will be hosting a ball in your honor at our London estate a fortnight from today. I know that it is not exactly the pinnacle of the social season, but as the new Earl of Rivers, you will wish to renew as many acquaintances as possible in the coming weeks. Reestablish connections and regenerate relationships. From experience I can tell you that the faster you can do that, the easier it will be to regain your footing."

"I can assure you, the extravagance of a ball is not necessary," Eli protested.

"It was my wife's idea," Stannis said with an ominous expression. "So if we're talking assurances, then let me assure you that it's very necessary."

Eli glanced at Linfield. The young man gave him a helpless shrug.

"Additionally, you will come to dinner tomorrow," Stannis informed him with the authority of a man used to being obeyed. "The duchess has invited a number of our closest family and friends, if only so that you'll have some familiar faces in the crowds that you'll face in the weeks and months to come."

"Your Grace, that is too much. I can't impose—"

"Save your objections for an argument you can win, Lord Rivers."

Eli shook his head ruefully. "In that case, it would be my honor to accept your invitation to dinner."

"Much better," the duke grunted. "You may be a humble man, Rivers, but you might as well prepare yourself to be properly welcomed home as the hero you are."

Chapter 18

Rose was wrong.

He would have made a fabulous thief, Eli thought, as he levered himself silently through the window that had been left open to the warm night air. He had no idea what time it was when the Duke of Stannis and his son had left his place, but he didn't care. There was nothing and no one that existed in this world that would have kept him from coming directly here.

Something had broken deep within him and soared free this night. Seeing Lewis Linfield standing tall and proud before him had changed something. Perhaps it was the proof that what Eli had done had made a difference. That his actions had not been in vain. He wanted to tell someone that. Stand on the rooftops and shout it into the night. But he didn't. Because there was only one person he really needed to see—one person who would understand everything. The way she had always understood him.

Which was why he found himself slithering through a half-open window of the cottage that housed both Rose's studio and her rooms, perched on a far corner of Haverhall's expansive grounds. He needed to see Rose, promises of distance and work and space be damned. He was certainly not going to wait until the morning.

"Don't move." Her voice came out of the blackness as he straddled the sill awkwardly, the tip of something cold and sharp against the side of his neck. He froze, and the bulky box he had brought with him dropped to the floor with a dull thud.

"If that is another paintbrush, Rose, I'm going to be disappointed."

There was a beat of silence, and then the pressure at his neck disappeared.

"Dammit, Dawes, what are you doing here?"

"I would have thought that was obvious."

He heard her curse softly. "Hurry up, then."

Eli swung his other leg over the sill, then yanked his muddy boots off and left them beneath the window. He couldn't see her in the darkness, but through the faint scent of turpentine, he caught the exotic, warm fragrance that he would always associate with Rose.

"You shouldn't be here," she said quietly, lighting a candle and setting it aside on a tiny table.

Eli glanced around, taking in the simple furnishings in the small, shadow-filled room. A bed covered in plain gray sheets, rumpled because she had been disturbed. An unornamented armoire, a plain wooden washstand and chair. A small jar of white roses, their fragrance mingling with hers. "I'm sorry. I should have used the kitchen window."

"I don't mean my bedroom, Dawes. I mean here. At Haverhall. You promised me that you wouldn't—"

"I lied." He turned back to her, her hair shining like fire in the candlelight, her eyes dark, unfathomable pools. In a single step, he closed the distance between them and brought his mouth down hard on hers. He felt her stiffen, and then in the next heartbeat she melted against him, kissing him back with the same desperation that was pounding through him. His hands cupped her face, his lips devouring hers. She tasted faintly of wine and that perfect, intoxicating sweetness that was Rose. She opened beneath him, and his tongue swept hers, exploring all of her velvet heat.

His hands dropped to her back, pressing Rose more tightly against him, as if that could bind her to him forever. "I've missed you," he whispered against her mouth.

Rose kissed him again, one of her hungry kisses that made him wonder why he had ever let her leave him, if only for three days. She was *his*, he thought fiercely. No other man would ever hold her like this. No other man would ever draw her clothes from her body, worship her with his hands and his tongue, and hold her as she shattered in ecstasy. He wanted her. Needed her. Loved her. Mind, body, and soul. She belonged to him. Now and forever.

Eli pulled back slightly, breathing hard with the staggering certainty of that thought. He loved her. More than he'd thought it possible to love someone. And it wasn't a new love born of mere lust and attraction, the sort of infatuated love that skated over the polished surface and was afraid to look too closely at what might lie beneath. No, this was a love that had started before he understood what it was. A love that had faced every difficult thing and had endured.

"Are you all right?" Rose whispered.

Eli squeezed his eye shut, his scars tugging. "Yes." He'd never be more all right than he was now. He opened his eye and stared down at her. "He survived," he said.

In his arms Rose stilled. "I beg your pardon?"

"The boy. The gunner I put on that horse. He stayed on

that horse and somehow made it back to our lines. His name is Lewis Linfield. Youngest son of the Duke of Stannis." His throat tightened again, and it was suddenly difficult to speak. "They came to my house. And when they left, I came here."

She slid her arms around his neck and kissed him softly. "Then I'm glad that there is someone else who saw what I see now, Eli Dawes."

He exhaled, a shaky, ragged sound. "And I can't hate him anymore," he managed. "Anthony." With those words he had finally identified what had broken in him. That hatred and despair that had followed Eli back from the battlefield had evaporated, replaced by hope and a belief in something better. And Rose was part of that.

"Good," she said. And if she had anything else to say, she never got the chance because he was kissing her again. The first kiss, he thought ardently, of what would be a lifetime of kisses. A lifetime of confessions and debates and laughter and lovemaking.

His fingers tightened in her hair as he teased her lips open, his tongue dueling with hers. The coals that had been smoldering since he had first pulled her into his arms roared to life, an inferno of longing that he was powerless to stop. Everything around him seemed to recede, this connection between them the only thing that mattered. He deepened the kiss, a prologue to and a promise of what would come next.

He felt Rose's hands at his throat, her fingers tugging on his cravat. He pulled back, allowing her space to work. The linen fluttered to the floor, followed by his coat and waistcoat. And then her fingers were on the buttons of his trousers, and they too slipped down his legs. His cock surged free, heavy and hard, covered by the hem of his shirt. Flames licked across his skin, and he shuddered at the sensation.

Rose stepped closer, releasing the single button at his

collar. With slow, agonizing movements she drew his shirt over his head and let it drop carelessly to the floor. He heard her make a small sound of approval as she reached out to touch him. She ran her fingers down the center of his chest, over the ridges of muscle that marked his abdomen, and stopped just shy of his erection.

"I want to paint you like this," she said, and her voice sounded a little hoarse.

"Not right now, you won't," Eli growled, dipping his head to nip at her jaw.

"No," she gasped. "Not right now." Her hand slipped down, and she wrapped her fingers around the base of his cock, sliding them up until they found the bead of moisture that had gathered at the head.

Every muscle in his body hummed with pleasure, his blood roaring in his ears.

Rose released him and pushed him back until he could feel the edges of the bed against the backs of his legs. Slowly he sank down onto the mattress, his hands settling at her waist. He pulled her toward him, his thighs caging her own legs, his body straining toward her.

"You're wearing too many clothes," he murmured.

Rose's hand drifted to the sash of her robe, then tugged on the loop and released it. Her robe slipped open, and Eli realized she wore nothing underneath. He let go of her waist and pulled the robe to the side so that she was standing before him wearing nothing but the glorious mass of fire that trailed over her shoulder.

Eli's hands came back to her body, and he stroked the ivory skin at her shoulders, her throat, and then lower, circling but not quite touching the gentle swells of her breasts. She shivered and arched her back in a silent plea. He covered her breasts with his palms, capturing their perfect weight, and then caught her nipples between his fingers, tugging and squeezing gently.

"So gorgeous," he whispered.

Rose's breath faltered, and her eyes fluttered closed. Eli leaned forward, and his mouth replaced his fingers, licking, sucking, teasing. He heard her moan, and his hands dropped over the curve of her hips to cup her ass, and he hauled her up onto his lap. She was straddling him now, her knees braced on the edge of the bed, his cock trapped and throbbing between them. He let his fingers slide lower over her buttocks and around, until they found her hot, slick center at the juncture of her legs. He pushed a finger into her heat, and her head tipped back in abandon.

She looked like a goddess in the candlelight. A goddess of fire that tempted gods and brought them to their knees. His goddess.

Eli lifted one hand and curved it around the back of her neck, bringing her lips back to his, and he ravaged her mouth, setting a tempo with his tongue. Rose rocked her hips, her lower belly rubbing up against his erection, and Eli groaned as that simple friction ignited a new firestorm of pleasure. Without hesitation her small hand slipped between their bodies and grasped him, stroking his cock in time with his tongue. The edges of his vision dimmed, and he broke their kiss, wanting more than to simply rut against her hand.

"I want you," he growled against her ear. "I want all of you."

He twisted, pushing himself farther up on the bed. Rose lifted herself away from him and retrieved something on the floor near the edge before returning to kneel at his back.

"Close your eyes," she told him.

He turned his head to look at her, but she put a hand against his cheek.

"Close your eyes," she repeated.

Slowly, he did as she asked. He knew what she was doing long before he felt the soft linen of his cravat slide over his eyes. "Rose—"

"It's your turn," she whispered, binding the fabric snug.

She moved, straddling him once again. Her hands slid over his bare chest, urging him back against the pillows, and he obeyed. She bent and kissed him, picking up where he had left off, offering no quarter. Her hair fell over his chest and shoulders, a silken wave that made his skin tighten and surrounded him with her scent. He slid his hands down the length of her back, her skin impossibly smooth beneath his palms.

He could feel the head of his erection just at the opening of her sex, and now it was he who arched toward her, trying to push himself deep. Except she shifted on her knees, her lips now skimming his throat and nipping at the pulse he could feel hammering there. Eli made a sound of desperation and desire, but Rose ignored him. She slid farther back, his cock gliding through her wet folds as she moved over him, her mouth now exploring the path her fingers had taken. Every stroke, every caress, every kiss was more potent than the last.

Arousal crackled through him, gathering at the base of his spine. Her teeth grazed one of his nipples, and he groaned, his hips jerking. She paused and then did it again, deliberately and slowly. Eli gasped.

"You like that," she murmured.

"Too much," he panted.

Rose made a sound low in her throat and lifted her head, granting him his reprieve. Until she slid lower. Until her tongue traced the ridge of muscle that descended from his hips to his groin. Until her hair slid over his throbbing erection. Until her fingers cupped his balls. Until she took him deep in the velvet softness of her mouth.

Eli writhed, the blind pleasure of it almost unbearable.

"Rose," he managed in a strangled gasp, every muscle in his body straining for control. It was too much and not enough all at once.

And maybe she heard the desperation in his voice or maybe she too could no longer wait, for she withdrew and positioned her hips over his once again, her body trembling as she held herself above him. He felt her reach between them, felt her grasp the length of his cock, felt her position the head at her entrance.

And with a savage groan, Eli thrust into her.

He heard her welcoming gasp, even as his mind went blank, aware only of the tight heat that sheathed his cock. She went still, and Eli clenched his teeth against the almost uncontrollable urge to move. Her hands were at his shoulders, her fingers digging into the muscles of his upper arms, holding on to him with a desperate strength. He felt the tremor that coursed through her even as she tilted her hips just enough to allow him to slide even deeper, seating herself fully.

This time he was unable to stop his hips from tipping back and then thrusting hard.

He heard her hiss with pleasure. "Again," she whispered, and he complied.

She rolled her hips, his cock sliding from her almost to its tip, before sinking all the way back down. Eli nearly came right there, the ecstasy so perfectly devastating. His hands searched for her, finding her hips, and he guided her next movements, leaving them both panting. They moved together then, her undulations meeting each of his driving thrusts. Sweat gathered on his skin, and he could feel his climax gathering like a storm, electricity arcing through his veins.

He heard Rose gasp just before her hands slipped from his shoulders to the back of his neck. Her hips lost their rhythm beneath his hands as they ground down hard against him. Her head dropped to the side of his neck.

"Eli," she groaned. "I need..."

Eli thrust deep and held himself there. Instantly he felt her body convulse around him. Her fingers twisted almost painfully in his hair, and she cried out, her teeth grazing his shoulder. Deep inside her he could feel the ripples and contractions tighten the walls of her passage, milking him mercilessly and obliterating what remained of his control.

Eli's palms slid to her buttocks, bracing her against him as he pumped into her, feeling his own release roaring down on him. His balls tightened, and he drove into her once more before yanking himself from her heat and thrusting against the tautness of her abdomen. His orgasm slammed through him, tearing a shout from his throat and detonating blinding explosions of light behind his eyelids. Wave after wave of euphoria rolled over him, leaving him gasping like a drowning man as his hips slowed their spasms and then finally stopped.

He lay on his back, trying to catch his breath. The echoes of his release chased themselves through his limbs, leaving him shaky and limp, and unsure when he would be able to move again. Or if he ever wanted to.

Because the feel of Rose, the heat of her body covering his, her hair spilled across his chest like a silken blanket, seemed like a perfect way to spend the rest of his days.

She moved before he did, her fingers brushing his hair back from his forehead and then peeling the cravat from his eyes. He thought he might die at the beauty of her. Her lips were swollen, her cheeks reddened from exertion or chafing or both. Her hair was a wild, glorious mess, her eyes lidded with the glow of a woman well pleasured.

She wiped his seed from between them and let the linen fall to the floor, and when she would have rolled to the side, Eli caught her. "I like you right where you are," he said, his arms tight around her.

Rose didn't answer, only lay back down, tucking her head into the crook of his neck again. Eli reached over with one hand and drew the sheet over their sweat-slicked bodies.

"Why did you ask me to cover my eyes?" he asked presently.

One of her fingers traced the skin over his heart. "So you could feel everything the way I felt it when you asked the same of me."

"I think I should like to do that again," he murmured. "It heightens the senses."

He thought she might have nodded against his shoulder.

"Though there will come a day when I will watch your beautiful face when you come apart with my name on your lips."

Her fingers curled against his skin. "I'd like that too," she said, and Eli thought she almost sounded inexplicably wistful. He hugged her to him and closed his eyes, feeling her settle against him with a soft sigh.

He must have dozed because, when he opened his eyes again, the sheet was bunched at his hips and she was no longer beside him. He turned his head in alarm.

"Don't move." Her voice came from out of nowhere.

His gaze found her where she sat on the edge of the bed, her robe wrapped around her, her sketchbook in her lap.

"How long have I been sleeping?" he asked, his voice rough.

"Not long." She met his gaze in the soft light. "You looked so peaceful. I couldn't help myself. I'm almost finished."

"Finish later," he said, starting to sit up.

"No," she whispered, almost desperately. "It has to be now. Please."

Eli stilled and then lowered himself back against the pillows. It was an easy enough thing to grant her.

"May I continue?"

He nodded, and the only sound was the scratch of charcoal over the page as the minutes slipped by.

"Does this bother you?" she asked suddenly.

"What, waking up to find a woman drawing me naked?" He chuckled. "It would appeal to me a whole lot more if she were naked too."

She smiled faintly, but her eyes remained serious.

"No," he said. "It doesn't bother me." And it didn't.

"I know it was hard for you the first time I asked you to do this," she said. "To make yourself vulnerable like that. I don't think I ever thanked you properly. For what you did."

"I'd do anything for you," he said, frowning slightly at the same wistful sadness he'd thought he'd heard earlier.

Rose set her charcoal aside and dusted her fingers on the edge of the sheet.

"Can I see it?" he asked.

She nodded silently and held out the book, and Eli pushed himself to a sitting position, reaching for it. She'd drawn him as he'd slept, one hand over his abdomen, the other flung across the space where she should have been. He was reclining against the pillows, the ridges of his torso shadowed in the play of candlelight. His head was turned slightly, the details of his face so perfectly captured that it was a little like looking in a mirror. Except gone was the haunted darkness that had always stared back at him. Gone was the stoic sadness that Lucy had captured in her portrait. In its place was...peace.

Eli set the drawing aside on the bedside table.

She hesitated. "Do you not like it?" she asked.

"It's perfect," he replied. "But it's missing something."

"What?"

"You." He rose to his knees and caught the back of her neck with one hand, kissing her deeply. He wrapped his other arm around her waist and dragged her up against him. He settled back against the pillows, pulling her with him. "I don't want to wake up without you by my side anymore," he murmured, tucking her against him. "I want you right here."

Rose rested her head on his chest again, though she remained strangely silent.

"Did you know," he said, "that I heard a rumor yesterday that my prolonged absence was because of a woman? A forbidden love, apparently, and one that ended tragically when she died bearing my child."

"That's an awful rumor."

"It is, isn't it? Luckily, the bulk of the rumors that have reached me have presumed that I have been working for the crown in some regard. Something covert and dangerous that I can't reveal. Though there was some speculation that it was amnesia that kept me from returning for so long. What with the obvious blow to my head and all."

Rose rolled to her side, and Eli let her go. He could feel her eyes on him. "And what did you tell them?"

"Nothing. Where I was and why I was there is no one's business but mine." He propped his head up on his arm.

"They won't stop asking anytime soon."

"Then perhaps I'll fall back on the covert option. Or maybe the amnesia." He reached out and stroked her cheek.

"Hell, perhaps I could be a spy who lost his memory. Who needed the love of a woman to regain himself. That sounds very...dashing and romantic."

He saw a smile ghost over her lips before it vanished. "And ridiculous."

"Except for the last part." He paused. "The last part is true."

Rose's eyes dropped from his, and he put a finger under her chin, forcing her head and her gaze back up. He couldn't read what was in her eyes.

"I have a gift for you." He slid from the bed and fetched the box he had brought with him.

"As I said, Dawes, you would make a lousy thief." She said it lightly, but there was a strain that made her words sound forced. "Thieves do not bring gifts."

Eli put the box on the bed and sat down beside her. "Tonight it was I who was gifted with the most incredible joy and happiness, lessened only by the fact that you were not with me at the time to share it. Tonight I understood that there is no world that I will accept that doesn't have you by my side. You have stood by me through the very worst, and now you deserve to share the very best. If I live to be a hundred, I cannot ever repay you for the courage you've shared with me. But perhaps this might be a humble start."

Rose knew what was in this box. Once, long ago, she'd had boxes just like this delivered, as had Clara. As had any lady who had ordered a gown from a certain Bond Street modiste.

"Open it," Eli urged.

Slowly Rose undid the ribbon and lifted the lid off the box, then let it drop to the floor. She peeled back layers of delicate paper and lifted the gown, catching her breath as she did. The gown was ice-blue silk, vivid and dazzling. Over the silk was layered a gossamer, ethereal muslin that stirred with even the slightest of movements. Tiny crystals had been embroidered along the edge of the bodice, like the glittering spray from the ocean. It was a gown fit for a princess. It was a gown fit for the finest ballroom or court in England, sewn with exquisite care to impress the most discerning, critical eye.

"It's the color you were wearing the first time I kissed you," he said.

Rose's heart stuttered.

"Invite me out to dinner, Rose."

"Dinner?" A dark dread instantly ignited. This was why she had kept her distance from Eli. This was why she should have kept her distance tonight. Because he shouldn't be bringing her gifts like this, believing that there would be a future for them.

"I never thought you'd ask. You need to work on the charm, but I'd love to, thank you."

"Eli, I can't—"

"Back out of a promise. You've already taught me how this conversation ends. And because of that, you should know that you can't win."

Rose shook her head. "That was different—"

"I want you to meet him." Eli's voice was thick with emotion, all traces of teasing gone.

"Who?"

"Linfield." He reached out to stroke her hair. "I want you to see that everything was not for nothing."

Her heart cracked.

"The duke and duchess have invited me for dinner. I want you to come with me. I want you beside me."

Rose wanted to crawl into a hole. He had no idea what he was asking her to do. She wanted to turn away so that he could not see the irrational trepidation and weakness that were crowding through her. "Eli—"

"I'm not taking no for an answer."

She squeezed her eyes shut, sharp anxiety overwhelming her. And with it the old shame and embarrassment that were never far behind.

I cannot ever repay you for the courage you've shared with me.

Eli Dawes was wrong. She hadn't shared her courage; she had just helped him find the courage he had always had.

Because Rose didn't have any courage of her own.

If she had courage, she wouldn't be nauseated at the thought of facing throngs of London society. If she had courage, her heart would not be racing at the thought of encountering every judgmental stare and critical, disparaging whisper. If she had courage, the thought of another rat carcass being delivered, or another amputated rodent tail being shoved into the back of her gown, would not leave her shaky and sweating and gasping for breath.

Whatever this weakness was that she suffered, it was, without question, absolutely and wholly devoid of courage.

She opened her eyes and let the dress fall back into the box, hating herself.

Hating her weakness.

"Rose? Is something wrong?"

Everything was wrong.

"Of course not." She tried to offer him a reassuring smile.

"Is it the dress? Do you not like it?"

She hated the confusion in his voice most of all.

"The dress is beautiful," she managed. Because it was. "It's not the dress."

"Honestly, I was trying to do a better job of asking a lady to dinner than I did the last time."

When he had accompanied her to the Silver Swan. When he had trusted her and done as she'd asked, even though he had wanted to refuse. Even though he'd had every reason to refuse.

"I owe you a dinner, Rose. Please say yes."

He was still wrong, she realized. He owed her nothing. It was she who owed him this. She who owed him her trust.

It was she who owed it to him to at least try.

Rose would be gone the day after tomorrow, their paths diverging as they must. She would retreat back to her life in Dover and the quiet safety it provided, while Eli would go on to claim his place in the tumult and glitter of society and politics. Somewhere Rose could never go. Something she could never do.

But she could go to a private dinner with him. As he had once done. As a friend would do.

This invitation wasn't to the assembly rooms at Almack's or the season's opening ball. There would be no swarms of London elite, honing their tongues with the sport of gossip. It would not be an ocean of people angling to see and be seen, making sure that the stage upon which they stood presented them in the best light, even at the expense of others.

It would be a small, private dinner with a duke and his family. A family who owed Eli the life of their son.

Rose took a few deep breaths, letting that knowledge slow her heart. "You did have clothes on the last time you asked me to dinner."

"I'll put on my shirt if my nudity offends you, but then I might accuse you of sounding like a ninety-year-old nun." His words were teasing again, but his eyes were still searching hers.

"Dinner sounds lovely." She lifted her chin and forced herself to say the words. "It would be my honor."

"Will you wear this dress?"

"Of course."

"Thank you, Rose. For this. For everything."

"I'm the one who is supposed to be thanking you." Rose swallowed with difficulty and reached to pick up the blue silk. "I'll try it on."

"Not right now you won't." Eli snatched the box away and set it aside. "It will fit. The modiste already had your measurements in her records." He rolled onto the bed, catching her lips with his, his fingers working at the sash of her robe. "Right now I've got a much better idea."

He was distracting her, she knew, even if he didn't.

And because she was weak and desperately in love, she let him.

Chapter 19

The Duke of Stannis's London home blazed with light.

In the encroaching twilight, it spilled out of every window and onto the zealously manicured gardens that surrounded the grand building. Lanterns had been lit along the edge of the large circular driveway at the front of the house, their light reflected off the gleaming row of carriages that were lined up, disgorging their passengers in a steady stream.

Women in brilliantly hued evening gowns, on the arms of men dressed in dark splendor, milled in the gardens. Their chatter and laughter drifted back on the breeze, interspersed with the classical sounds of a pianoforte being played somewhere in the house. The entire atmosphere was one of festive elegance.

It was Rose's worst nightmare.

"I thought this was just a dinner," she said from inside the confines of Eli's carriage as it crept toward the top of the driveway.

"It is."

"Who are all these people?" Her words came out as an undignified wheeze.

Eli shrugged. "Friends and family of the duke and duchess. And probably friends of Linfield and his brothers."

Rose stared out the carriage window, fighting the suffocating breathlessness that was clawing at her. "There are so many people. You didn't tell me that there would be so many."

Eli leaned forward from his seat across from her and caught her hand. "There can't be more than two dozen. Besides, who cares how many people the duchess invited? You're here and I'm here and Linfield is here, and that is all that really matters."

"I can't...I just—" She couldn't put together a rational sentence because none of what she was feeling was rational. And no matter how she tried, she couldn't seem to fix it. Couldn't seem to control the fear and the weakness that were once again consuming her. "I've changed my mind."

"You're shaking." He was staring down at their intertwined fingers.

She snatched her hand away. "I'm not."

The carriage came to a halt. The door was opened by a liveried footman who stepped back smartly, waiting for Eli and Rose to descend. Beyond the open door, a group of women had stopped near the entrance, their eyes on Eli's carriage. From behind the fluttering fans that they carried, the sounds of their laughter rose.

"This isn't my place, Eli. I shouldn't be here. I'm sorry." She hadn't eaten anything all day, but her stomach churned and sweat pricked her temples.

"Close the door," Eli snapped at the footman. "And tell the driver to make another circle of the drive."

The footman merely nodded and did as he was told, and the carriage lurched as it rolled away.

"I shouldn't be here."

"What are you talking about, Rose?"

"I have to return to Dover."

"What?" He was looking up at her, his face awash in confusion. "Now?"

"Yes." It was barely audible. "You need to go on without me. I apologize for the inconvenience. But this night is about you. Not me. I don't need to be here."

"You're not making any sense, Rose."

"You'll be quite fine on your own—"

"I know I'll be fine," Eli said. "But I won't be complete. Not without you. I want you here because you are important to me. Because you mean everything to me." He reached up and caught her chin with his fingers. "I want you here, Rose, because I love you."

His words stopped time.

And shattered her heart into a million pieces. Eli could not love her. Loving her would clip his wings. She should never have let this get this far. She should have told him to leave the second he'd come through her window last night. She should have refused this dress, this invitation, and left for Dover a long time ago.

Her breath hitched, and the back of her throat tightened. "You don't," she said.

He drew back. "I don't what?" he asked roughly.

"You don't love me."

His fingers dropped from her face. "What?"

"You needed me, Dawes, when you came back. If only to make you see what I saw. And perhaps I needed you too in my own way. But don't confuse need with love."

He pushed himself away from her, back onto the squabs.

"I haven't confused anything. I love you, Rose, just as I need you. In all the days and weeks and years ahead."

"You don't love me, and you don't need me." She sat up to face him, clutching her reticule so that she wouldn't touch him. "Not anymore."

"You have no idea what I need." He sounded angry and hurt and confused.

"But that's just it, Eli. I know exactly what—whom—you need." The backs of her eyes were burning, and she was fighting to keep her voice even. "You need a woman who possesses a substantial title and all the influential connections to help you wield your power in a way that will make a difference. A woman not only comfortable in society but one who can command it. One who can manipulate it to your advantage and further your ambitions on behalf of you and the people who are depending on you. Including the families of fallen soldiers. The stakes are too high now for anything less." She stopped, trying to catch her breath. "I will always support what you do, but the woman you need isn't me, Eli. I can't do those things. I can't be who you need."

His fists clenched where they rested on his knees. "I don't want any woman who is not you, Rose."

She looked helplessly at him.

"Marry me, Rose."

Oh God. Her fingers twisted painfully in the silk cord. She felt a tear slide down her cheek. "I can't."

"Of course you can. You won't."

She was shaking her head. "You don't understand."

"What are you afraid of?" he demanded.

Rose looked away from him. "I'm not afraid of anything."

"You're lying."

"I'm not."

"Then you're not doing so well with the truth either."

She had said that to him once, and he had answered her with the truth. She owed him nothing less. "No," she agreed. "I suppose I'm not."

"Is this about Anthony?" he demanded.

"This has nothing to do with Anthony. This is about me."

Eli relaxed his hands, visibly trying to corral his emotions. "Then explain it to me, Rose, because right now I don't understand anything."

"Before I was ever engaged, I had my art and my family and I was happy. And then I was drawn into your world and discovered that there was never a place for me. And now I have my art and my family and I am happy again. Even more, I have a purpose to my art that brings me joy."

"Rose, I would never let anyone ever do anything to—"

"You can't protect me from myself, Eli," Rose said without meeting his eye.

"You're talking in riddles again."

She unwrapped her fingers from the cord of her reticule and looked down at the red welts forming across her knuckles. "There was a day, after everything, when I stood alone on the edge of those white cliffs and stared down at the surf below. And in that moment, I couldn't think of a reason why I shouldn't simply step off." She took a shaky breath. "I can't ever go back there, Eli. I can't go back to a society and a life that almost took everything from me. I can't ever risk putting myself back in a place so dark that I might not find my way out again."

He was studying her, as if he could see through her. "You haven't forgiven them, have you? All those insignificant fools."

"This has nothing to do with forgiveness."

"You don't have to forget to forgive, Rose. I understand that more than anyone, I think."

"I know that. I'm just trying to make you understand that I have finally found happiness in the place I'm at. Why I can't go where you're going." Grief was burning through her. "Sometimes one must simply cut their losses."

"Like me? Am I one of those losses?" His confusion and hurt had faded, and anger had taken hold.

She shook her head miserably. "Eli—"

"And I'm supposed to believe you're happy alone?"

"I'm not alone. I have the clients who seek me out solely for my talent and nothing else. Save my discretion, of course. I have my summer students. I have Clara and Harland and Theo and Tabitha. I am far from alone."

"But you're telling me that there isn't a place for me in your world." He was staring at her hard.

"There will always be a place for you, Eli," Rose said, swiping angrily at her eyes. "You are my friend. But there is no place for me in your world. I know my limitations, and I have accepted them. And I will not allow them to limit you. I will not allow you to sacrifice all your ambition, all your compassion, all the good you will do as an earl because of me. I should never have let this—us—go this far. This is your chance to become the man you have always been."

"You didn't accept my limitations," he said harshly. "You didn't let me hide. You didn't let me do what you're doing now."

"I'm not hiding. I'm doing what I must."

"That's a little hypocritical, don't you think?"

"No."

"Then why didn't you let me do the same? Do what I thought I must?" he snarled. "If I had had my way, if you had let me, I'd still be at Avondale. *Hiding.*" He shook his head. "Is this what you tell your clients to do? Clients like Ophelia Volante? Did you tell her to hide?"

"I don't tell any of my clients to do anything. They must do what's best for themselves."

"Yet you always seemed to know what was best for me."

"Was I wrong?"

Eli's lips thinned. "You couldn't have known you were right."

"Yes, I could. Because you're stronger than I ever was. You have more courage than I will ever have."

"That's horseshit, Rose, and you know it. You're the strongest person I know. It's one of the reasons I love you."

Rose closed her eyes, feeling another tear scald its way down her cheek. "You don't love me, Dawes."

"Do you love me?"

She stared at him, an awful cold seeping into her very soul.

"Answer me, Rose."

Yes. It was right there, on the tip of her tongue. It was what he wanted to hear, what he deserved to hear. Because it was the truth. But it would tie him to her. She would become the weighted chain that would forever hinder him. And eventually, no matter his declarations, he would come to resent it. Resent her.

The tears were coming faster now, and she hated them. Hated this feeling of helpless desolation that was smothering her. But she couldn't change, no matter how much he wanted her to. "No," she said. "I don't love you."

"You're lying."

"I care about you, Eli, I do. And I'm so proud of you. But I don't love you. And it would be best for us both if we said goodbye here."

The carriage came to a halt again. There was the sound of booted feet on the gravel, and then the door was opened once more by the same footman.

"Then go, Rose. Go back to Dover." Eli gazed at her for a moment longer and then climbed from his seat and stepped out into the night. He turned and braced himself against the frame of the carriage. "I did everything you asked. Proved myself over and over. And I would have done anything for you." He straightened, his expression remote. "No matter what happened, the next time you found yourself at the edge of a cliff, lost and afraid, I would have been right beside you to pull you back." He paused, grasping the door. "Just as you did for me."

Chapter 20

The Duke of Holloway, my lord."

Eli started, jerking in his chair. His gaze swiveled to the doorway where Dufour was standing, looking sour. "Pardon?"

"The Duke of Holloway is here to see you, my lord," his butler sniffed with a pointed, censorious look at the tall clock in the corner, much the same way he had done when Stannis had appeared. Eli followed his gaze with bleary eyes and blinked at the late hour. He didn't remember when it had gotten so late.

"Show him in," Eli said, and his butler vanished.

He stood and moved out from behind his desk, stretching stiff muscles. He'd been crouched far too long over this damn desk, fighting through the mountains of correspondence that had avalanched onto its surface. But it had provided the necessary distraction he needed, not unlike the duke's sudden appearance. He would embrace any distraction, no matter how mundane it was or how late it might arrive, to keep himself from dwelling on Rose.

Just the tiny reminder sent shards of pain and anger, frustration and regret, lancing through him.

I don't love you.

He'd spent an agonizing week second-guessing every nuance of that last conversation. He should have been more understanding. Or perhaps he should have pushed her harder, the way she had always pushed him. Perhaps he should have given her an ultimatum. Or perhaps he should have promised that he'd wait forever. There were a thousand different things he could have done or said or promised, and he had no idea which one would have been right. Which one would have changed her mind and kept her with him.

He hadn't asked her to change. He didn't need her to abandon her quiet life in exchange for an endless parade of parties. He didn't need her to command anything, much less all of society. But he needed her by his side. And he had tried so hard. Tried to tell her, tried to show her how much he loved her. But it was like throwing himself against a stone wall. He couldn't make her love him.

He had started a dozen letters to her, finishing only one. Not that he would send it. It was rambling and sad and addressed to a woman who had never truly been his. He simply added it to the pile of letters he'd written to her in France and Belgium. Letters he'd also never sent because she hadn't been his then either.

And now Rose was gone, back to Dover, and Eli was here in London, surrounded by all the luxury and privilege he could imagine. And he had never been more miserable in his life.

And that was saying something indeed.

"The Duke of Holloway, my lord," Dufour announced formally.

Eli spun, finding the duke and his butler standing at the

door of his study. Dufour departed again with one last long-suffering look at the duke's back, leaving Eli to study the man who filled the better part of his doorway. He could immediately see the resemblance between August Faulkner and his sister. Except that while Anne's face was round, Holloway's was a collection of sharp angles. He had the same coffee-dark hair, the same blue eyes, but there was a restless intensity to him that his sister lacked. Eli hadn't known Holloway well—he hadn't even been a duke yet when Eli had left London, but he had heard the rumors. That August Faulkner had grown up on the streets of London and survived. That he was ruthless and ambitious and that only fools underestimated him.

"Good evening, Your Grace," Eli said as the duke entered. He didn't miss the way Holloway's sharp blue eyes flickered around the room, taking measure of his surroundings. They returned to Eli, and he found himself measured also without apology.

"My sister was correct," the duke said matter-of-factly, examining Eli. "You really are fortunate to be alive."

Eli gazed at the duke steadily. "Yes. I am."

"Welcome home."

"Thank you." He gestured to a pair of chairs close to the hearth. "Would you care to sit? Something to drink, perhaps?"

"This isn't a social call, Rivers, so I'll save you the trouble of the formalities." The duke carefully placed a long, rolled paper on Eli's desk and withdrew a leather folder from under his arm. It was one that Eli recognized instantly because he had written every word on every document that was inside. A preliminary business plan, compiled after Eli had spent countless hours plying customs officers and importers and weavers and merchants with questions and after Anne had given him a tour of Brookside.

It had been what Eli had thrown himself into and found solace in after Rose had left.

Holloway placed the folder on the desk next to the roll with the same deliberate precision, and Eli idly wondered if Holloway ever made social calls. Somehow he doubted it.

"Lady Anne shared that with you, I must assume," Eli said.

Holloway gave him a long look. "She did. She made her own notes before passing it on to me. I took the liberty of reviewing it."

"And?" Eli asked. "I'd be obliged if you'd share your thoughts."

"Tell me, Rivers, how serious are you about this venture?"

"I beg your pardon?"

"This crusade of yours to assist the families of fallen soldiers. How committed are you to it?"

"Are you questioning my honor?" Eli kept his voice even.

"I'm trying to gauge your sincerity," Holloway said. "And, possibly, your resilience. You'll be criticized for your involvement in industry. You will be told a man of your stature and wealth should never need lower himself to such."

"And what do you tell them, Your Grace?" Eli replied.

The duke smiled faintly before his eyes grew cool once again. "I don't know you well, Lord Rivers. But what I remember was a man who was exceedingly popular for his looks and his charm and his wit. Which is not a criticism, necessarily. But your ambition, insight, and wisdom were a bit more ambiguous. If I am going to contribute my time and expertise and, possibly, capital, I'd like to know whether or not it is doomed before it even begins. I despise failure."

It wasn't unfair. If Eli were standing where Holloway stood now, he might have asked the same. "I think, Your Grace, that you should review my plan with me and decide for yourself."

"Mmm." The duke straightened and wandered over to the hearth, stopping to gaze up at an uninspired hunting scene that hung over the carved mantel. "Cotton," he said to the painting.

Eli wasn't sure if that was a question or a confirmation. "Yes," he said, answering both.

"Premade garments." The duke turned from the hearth. "Why?"

Eli hid a frown. The duke would have read Eli's arguments in his plan. "Because demand for both cotton fabric and premade garments has been steadily increasing," he answered anyway. "And will continue to do so, especially now with access to cotton from India, and access to new weaving technologies. I intend to utilize both."

"And this premium product you speak of in your notes?"

"A small but valuable percentage of my planned output. Underclothes. Chemises, shirts, petticoats, and the like. Adding embroidery and accoutrements such as lace and ribbon to an otherwise plain product will add value and expand our market. It will also allow me to utilize the specialized skill sets of a number of women and older girls who will be part of the business."

"You've put thought into this."

Eli leaned back against his desk and crossed his arms over his chest. "I should hope that was evident in my plans."

The duke's sharp blue eyes bored into his. Eli didn't waver.

"Your sister has very generously offered her assistance, Your Grace. May I count on yours as well?" Eli asked, still not looking away.

"And if I said no?"

"Then I would do it anyway. Granted, it would likely not go as smoothly, and it would certainly take longer, but I would find a way."

Holloway watched Eli for a moment more before he abruptly left the bookcase and returned to the desk, as if he had come to a decision. He stopped just shy of Eli.

"You will spend some time in Liverpool," Holloway said. "I own two factories there that handle and weave raw cotton. Learn the processes, study the technology, and for God's sake, hire someone trustworthy who knows how to maintain both." He paused. "I can arrange for my foremen to take you on and show you what you need to know."

"I'd be much obliged."

"Don't thank me yet. When you go, you will go only as Mr. Dawes, and you will do what they tell you. You can leave your fancy clothes and fancy manners in London. You will not be the earl of anything during your tenure there, or you won't learn a damn thing."

"I would expect no less." Eli rather thought he was starting to like this duke.

"Over these next days, you will spend time with my man of business, my distributors, my builders, and at least one of my fleet captains to advise you on other matters related to this enterprise. Your research was thorough but incomplete in places. I've already spoken to these people, and they will be expecting you. My sister will best advise you on the building plans," Holloway continued. "How you wish to set up the kitchens, gardens, sleeping quarters, and laundry. Common spaces and classrooms. All of that."

"Of course."

"I will be traveling to Dover on the morrow to join my wife," the duke told him, and just like that, Eli's stomach clenched, and his body went rigid. Dover. The wild isolation to which he had lost Rose. Damn it, he had to pull himself together. Holloway and Lady Anne were bending over backward to help him, and all he could think about was—

"Is there a problem, Rivers?" Holloway asked, his sharp eyes seemingly missing nothing.

"No." Eli uncrossed his arms and forced his hands to relax.

"Is the timing not to your liking?"

"No, the schedule you have proposed is fine."

"You having second thoughts about working with my sister? Me?"

"No. Of course not."

"Ah." The duke brushed an imaginary piece of lint from his sleeve. "Then perhaps you have a message you'd like me to take to Miss Hayward in Dover?"

Eli tried not to react. "I beg your pardon?" What the hell did Holloway know about what existed between Rose and himself? Or, more accurately, what didn't exist?

"My sister indicated that you and Miss Hayward are close. That it was Rose with whom you've spent the bulk of your time since your unexpected return. And that it was she who encouraged you to develop this." He tapped a long finger on the surface of the leather folder. "I must assume that her return to Avondale has left you...out of sorts?"

Eli pushed himself away from his desk and circled it to put more space between Holloway and himself. As if that pitiful distance could keep this man from peering right through him and could give him space to think. "Miss Hayward has been a good friend since my return to England."

"Then you're a lucky man," the duke commented. "She doesn't trust easily."

"Yes. I am lucky." Eli wasn't sure if that had come out with the detachment he was aiming for.

"There is nothing that you'd like me to pass along? Nothing you wish to say?" Holloway prompted again.

Perhaps Eli hadn't succeeded in hiding his sorrow. Or perhaps the duke was just being polite.

Eli thought of the pile of unsent letters addressed to Rose stacked in his desk drawer that attested to just how much he wanted to say. Letters that he would never send because, even when he had told Rose how he felt—that he loved her—face-to-face, it hadn't been enough. Sending them now would be pointless.

Not that he would ever tell that to a man he barely knew, no matter how benevolent he might be.

"Perhaps you could ask Miss Hayward if she might consider attending the Duke of Stannis's ball with me," Eli replied, even knowing as he said it that it would change nothing. But he had to say something.

A dark brow lifted. "Ah. The ball being held in your honor. Yes, I heard about that. All of society will be there. Anyone who is anyone. I understand that some people are even coming back to London from their summer estates for the occasion."

All except one. All except the only one who really matters.

"I also heard that you saved Stannis's son."

"A series of fortunate circumstances in the chaos of war. Nothing more," Eli said. He had no interest in getting into a discussion about what had happened on that field.

"Now, that is not how I heard it told."

Eli shrugged. What difference did it make? The end result was all that mattered. "You'll pass on my message to Miss Hayward?" He tried to steer the conversation away from Waterloo.

"No."

"I'm sorry?"

"No, I'm not going to ask Rose to do something that she cannot," Holloway said, his brows drawing together. "It serves no purpose."

"You mean something that she will not," he mumbled.

"You have no idea, do you, Rivers?"

"No idea about what?" Confusion was competing with irritation.

Holloway picked up a decorative glass paperweight, turning it over in his hand in careful contemplation. "In my wife's last letter, she relayed that it appeared that you had come to care deeply for Rose, and she for you. And Anne told me that the Silver Swan, or at least its dining room, was in danger of going up in flames with the way you two were looking at each other." He held the weight up to the light. "So I am going to tell you this because I have to believe you have Rose's best interests at heart."

"Of course I do," Eli said with a frown, thinking that the duke sounded suspiciously like Strathmore.

"Rose Hayward hasn't gone to a fashionable London event in five years. Balls, assembly rooms, dinners, any affair really, that is infested with the titled and entitled crowd you were once so popular with."

Eli stared at him with incomprehension. "I don't understand."

Holloway set the paperweight down with a muted thump. "You are aware of the horrific publication that came out not long after—"

"Yes," Eli interrupted shortly. "I'm aware."

"And are you aware of the treatment she endured after?"

"She told me." But Eli was beginning to wonder if she had told him everything.

"It had a profound effect on her."

"But that was a long time ago. Surely, she—"

"She freezes in those crowds now. Gets nauseous, goes pale and shaky, is often short of breath, and can barely focus. It's as if a debilitating anxiety overwhelms her. She avoids them at all costs."

"That's impossible." The Rose he knew, who was so full of conviction, was totally at odds with what the duke was describing. That was not his Rose, his unyielding Viking warrior. That was not his Rose, his pillar of unwavering strength and courage.

You're shaking. He'd held her hand in that carriage until she'd snatched it away.

And he hadn't reached for her again.

"She's not proud of it," Holloway said. "Deeply ashamed, in fact, if I'm going to be blunt."

Eli was still struggling to understand. "But it was Rose who took me out to dinner at the Silver Swan. To meet your sister."

"She took you to a dining room in an inn on the edge of England," Holloway said. "Where the chance of running into hordes of the ton who once crucified her was almost nonexistent."

"But her involvement with Haverhall—"

"My wife is the face of Haverhall. She handles the school's clients. Even the initial applications for the summer program. Rose simply plays a very minor role, most of which is limited to Avondale."

"I..." He trailed off. He had no idea what to say.

"She's not a recluse, Rivers. She's a woman who has chosen to surround herself only with people whom she trusts. A woman who has dealt with her own private wounds in the best way she knows how. I can't condone or condemn what she has done because who am I to judge how anyone keeps themselves whole?"

Eli sat abruptly in his chair, a dull drone filling his ears.

"The private wound is the deepest."

It had been Linfield who had said that to Eli, and Eli had agreed. But he had been focused on himself at the time, and when Rose had said the same thing, though not in so many words, he hadn't heard her.

I can't go where you're going.

Those were the words that she had said to him, though she had tried. Tried to do what he had asked of her. The truth of it all had been there for him to hear if only he'd been listening. He had accused her of hiding. But what he had really been accusing her of was surviving in the only way she knew how.

I don't love you.

He ran a hand over his face. There was a horrible, gut-wrenching certainty that what she had actually meant was, *I can't love you.*

Rose had helped him regain everything that he had believed lost. Given him everything that was in her power to give to make him the man who was sitting behind this damn desk at this moment. And in return he had left her behind when it mattered most. He thought he might be ill.

The duke cleared his throat. "Perhaps you'd like to reconsider the message you'd like me to bring to Miss Hayward, if any?"

"Yes," Eli managed.

"Very good. I'll be leaving at nine on the morrow. You have until then." The duke's tone was curt but not unkind, and Eli was grateful for it.

He nodded, not trusting himself to say anything.

"There is one other issue of import that should be addressed before I depart," Holloway said, the topic of Rose Hayward apparently concluded. The duke reached for the rolled sheaf of paper and drew the leather tie from it, and a map of London spilled across the surface of the desk. "Acquiring the land needed for such an operation. I noted that you did not name a location in your plan."

Eli forced himself to pay attention to the duke's words. "I don't have one yet. I will need to purchase the land."

Holloway pulled the map toward him. "You'll be best served by a waterway for bringing in raw materials. A location with reasonable access to both the canal and road systems if you intend to distribute. You'll need a sizable parcel of land to support both the industrial and domestic buildings, and that land additionally needs to be of a quality that can sustain small agriculture." He stabbed a finger at a point on the map. "This section of land would be perfect," he said grimly.

Eli followed the duke's finger and found it planted on a location just outside the boundaries of London, one side running along the Thames, the thick web of roads immediately to the south and east of London almost touching the outer perimeters of the piece. Holloway, or maybe someone else, had circled it in red ink.

"You don't sound pleased," Eli remarked. "Is it occupied?"

"By hedgehogs and crickets and weeds," Holloway grumbled. "I've tried to buy it myself numerous times. But the stubborn sod who owns it refuses to sell. To me or anyone else. He's not stupid. He knows the potential of it just as well as I."

"Who owns it?"

The duke gave him a long look. "The Duke of Stannis."

Eli stared at the red ink that enclosed the land, like a circular rivulet of blood that had spilled across the paper.

"I'll have a word with Stannis tomorrow," he said.

Holloway nodded in knowing satisfaction. "I thought you might say that."

Eli trudged up the stairs toward his bedroom, the house dark and silent around him.

The Duke of Holloway had left hours ago, but Eli had stayed at his desk. He couldn't say he had achieved anything, other than staring at the paper in front of him, watching ink blots form as he tried to put his scattered, fevered thoughts to paper. The candles at his elbow had finally burned down to nothing, and Eli had been left sitting in the dark, acrid smoke curling around his head.

He'd gathered the bundle of letters from his desk drawer, the latest attempt on top, and shuffled, exhausted, out of his study. He had no idea what he could say to Rose. What he could say to her to make her believe that he finally understood. Make her believe that his love for her, a love that had survived so much, for so long, would survive this too.

He reached the partially open door of his bedroom, and a chilled breeze lifted the hair on his forehead. Eli froze. The windows in his bedroom were never left open at night. Every window was locked at sundown, something that his father had always insisted upon and that Eli hadn't bothered to change. He stepped silently to the side, the only illumination coming from the gaslights in the square below.

Someone had been, or was still, in his room.

Silently Eli pushed the door open, every muscle in his body tensed, but the room was seemingly empty, any thieves or intruders long gone. Eli shoved the door wider, then tossed the letters on his bed and retrieved the poker leaning against the empty hearth. He moved forward silently, listening hard, but nothing stirred. With efficient motions he lit the candle on the washstand, both reluctant and anxious to discover what was missing.

A quick perusal of the room showed that nothing seemed disturbed. He held the candle above his head with one hand

and the poker with the other and approached the shadows of his dressing room.

And froze as he saw the woman.

She was nude from the waist up, her skin the palest ivory in the soft light, a strand of white pearls fastened around her neck. A robe of rich garnet was draped over her legs, and she had turned slightly to gaze at herself in a mirror.

Eli set his candle down with fingers he realized were trembling and approached the painting. It was a long time before he remembered to breathe. It was even longer before he realized that there was a folded card propped on the top of the canvas.

Slowly Eli reached for the card, the tiny emblem of the crown visible on the front. He turned it over, smoothing it flat with his fingers and reading the precise, eloquent words.

I have chosen to offer this piece to you, Lord Rivers, because the narrative of it seems to suit you more than any other. By my doing so, I trust that you have come to understand what you possess.

Underneath those words a number had been scrawled. The price, Eli realized, of this painting. Which he would pay. Because whatever value King had assigned to this canvas was irrelevant.

This painting represented something far more priceless.

Chapter 21

T hinking of swimming?"

Rose closed her eyes and then opened them. "No."

Clara came to stand beside her, shading her eyes with her hand and peering out at the mouth of the cove. There was a ship anchored just beyond the entrance today, its dark color standing out in stark relief from the brilliant blue of the sea and the sky beyond.

"Perhaps you should. It would be better than what you are doing now."

Rose glanced at her sister. "And just what, exactly, am I doing now?"

"You tell me."

Rose focused her gaze back on the ship, another wave of the never-ending sadness swelling and pulling her under again despite her best efforts. She had thought retreating to Dover would make leaving him easier. Instead it had made it harder. Because everywhere she looked in this place were memories of Eli Dawes.

"I'm enjoying the scenery," she said dully.

Clara bent and picked up a stone, turning it over in her fingers. "You're not enjoying anything. You're miserable. You've been miserable since you returned from London."

Rose remained silent, arguing pointless. She might be able to hide her unhappiness from her students, but not from her sister.

"This morning, Harland finally asked me what happened between the two of you," Clara said. "You and Rivers."

Rose watched the waves as they raced forward and receded. Apparently she hadn't fooled her brother either. "What did you tell him?"

"Nothing. Because you haven't said anything to me." Clara threw the stone in her hand into the foaming surf and turned to Rose. "But you should know that Harland is probably sharpening his knives and bone saws right now."

Rose tried to smile and failed.

"What happened?" Clara asked. "Because whatever Rivers did to make you so unhappy—"

"He told me that he loved me," Rose blurted before she could reconsider.

The only discernable reaction that let Rose know Clara had heard her was a minute arch of her brow. "Indeed?"

"And then he asked me to marry him."

"I see." Clara's perfectly composed face betrayed nothing. "And what did you tell him?"

Rose looked away from Clara, back at the relentless curl of the water against the beach. "I told him I couldn't marry him."

"Ah. And the other?"

"The other?"

"Did you also tell him that you didn't love him?"

"Yes."

"You lied."

Rose kept her eyes fixed firmly on the water, unable to meet Clara's gaze. "Yes."

Above them the gulls wheeled and shrieked.

Clara bent, and it was a moment before Rose realized her sister had discarded her half boots and that she was in the process of unlacing her day dress.

"What are you doing?" she asked, distracted.

"Going for a swim," replied Clara. Her dress puddled at her feet, and she stepped neatly over it.

"What?" Rose's eyes darted down the beach and along the edge of the cliffs, but they were, mercifully, deserted. "Have you lost your mind?" Clara did not do impulsive, rash things like this. Clara could be counted on for her calm and decorum at all times.

Clara had undone her stays and was now standing in the sunshine clad only in her chemise. "Not at all."

"You can't swim," Rose wheezed.

"But you can. You'll save me if I need saving." She flashed Rose a grin and then yanked her chemise over her head.

"Dammit, Clara," Rose mumbled as she yanked at the ties of her own dress. Her sister was already picking her way over the stones toward the water's edge. Naked.

Clara stopped as the surf splashed against her pale legs. "It's freezing," she reported over her shoulder and waded in deeper.

Rose tossed her own clothes aside and stumbled after her sister, who was standing in the water up to her waist now. Because of the cove, the surf was gentle here, devoid of dangerous undertows, but that did not mean that Rose did not have a healthy respect for the power of the sea.

A slow-moving wave crested and broke over Clara's shoulders, and her sister suddenly laughed like a lunatic.

Rose struggled forward through the water, taking too long to close the gap. Another wave crested, and Clara ducked under, coming up spluttering and giggling. Rose dove into the wave, surfacing smoothly beside her sister.

"What the hell are you doing?" she gasped, wiping the water from her face.

"Swimming."

She grasped Clara's hand and pulled her toward the beach. "Let's go back."

"Not yet."

"You'll sink."

"I'm not going any deeper than this."

"Someone might see us." Maybe that would snap Clara out of this insanity.

"So?"

Rose stared at Clara. "Who are you and what have you done with my sister?"

"Why haven't I done this sooner?" Clara giggled, ducking as another wave broke over them.

Rose tightened her hand on Clara's. "Because you might drown?" she suggested when they came up.

"I'm not going to drown. You're right beside me." Clara sighed. "Perhaps I'll get you to teach me to swim. It feels glorious, does it not?"

Rose raised her face to the sun as the water caressed her skin. "Yes," she admitted.

"Though perhaps it is a bit chilly."

"Your lips have gone blue," Rose confirmed.

"Let's go warm up."

"You don't have to ask me twice."

A few minutes later they sat side by side on the beach, clad only in their chemises, their hair dripping down their backs, letting the sun warm their skin.

"Why did you do that?" Rose asked presently. Because Clara didn't do anything without a reason.

"Swim naked?"

"Yes."

"Because it's good to shock yourself from time to time, I think. Do something that you scares you once in a while." She paused. "Why did you tell Rivers you didn't love him?"

Rose felt something deep in her chest twist painfully. She should have known Clara would come back to this. She drew her legs up and rested her chin on her knees. "You know why," she mumbled.

"I want to hear it from you."

"Because I can't ever be his countess."

"I don't think Eli Dawes was asking you to be his countess. I think he was asking you to be his wife."

"They are one and the same."

"I don't think so, Rose."

"He asked me to dinner. At the home of the Duke and Duchess of Stannis," Rose said bleakly. "And I couldn't even give him that."

"Did you tell him why? The truth?"

"No."

"Why not?"

"Because the why makes no difference."

"Perhaps he should be allowed to decide that?" Clara asked gently.

Rose closed her eyes briefly in helpless frustration. "He is angry with me."

"Funny," Clara remarked. "Because I remember, not so long ago, you were angry with him. You were angry with him for years, in fact."

"That's because I didn't know that—" Rose stopped abruptly.

"Exactly," Clara said. "Whatever it was, you didn't *know*. And now you've put him in the same position."

"It's not the same."

"Would you have pulled me to safety if I had found myself in over my head just now?" Clara asked suddenly. "Out of my element in the sea?"

"Don't be obtuse. Of course I would have." Rose scowled at the seemingly random, inane question.

"Why?"

"Because you're my sister and I love you."

"Do you love Eli Dawes enough to believe that he would do the same for you?"

I would have been right beside you to pull you back.

Eli's last words echoed through her, making her insides tilt and her chest ache.

"Regret is a far worse fate than fear," Clara said quietly. "It will last a lifetime. If you truly love your earl, you owe him the chance to prove that he is the man you believe him to be." She found Rose's icy fingers with her warm ones. "The Duke and Duchess of Stannis are hosting a ball in Rivers's honor in two days' time."

"How do you know that?"

"Because Tabby and Theo are invited. So are you." Clara squeezed her fingers. "And you should go."

"I can't." It was immediate.

"What do you have to lose?" Clara asked.

"I couldn't even get out of the carriage when he took me to dinner," Rose said brokenly. "In my head, I knew it was stupid and irrational, but I froze." She tried to pull her hand away from her sister's, but Clara held fast.

"Tell me what happens if you freeze at that ball," Clara said with an infuriating calm.

"You mean, what happens if I'm not branded a

madwoman? Or hysterical? Because people have been committed to Bedlam for less."

"Will he run?"

"What?"

"Will the Eli Dawes you fell in love with run? Turn away from you?"

I would have been right beside you to pull you back.

Rose drew back, swallowing hard. "I'll humiliate him," she whispered.

"More than you did when you lied to him and told him that you didn't love him?"

"I had no choice."

"You had every choice. You still do. There is nothing perfect about true love, Rose, and I say this from experience. It will be messy and terrifying and hard. It will make you do things that you never thought you'd do."

Rose stared down at their interlocked fingers.

"Let him love you, Rose. Let him in."

There was a tiny kernel of...something stirring deep within her, and it took her a moment to identify what it was. Hope. Fragile and tenuous, but it was still there.

"What if I can't?" Rose whispered.

Clara gazed at her. "What if you can?"

⌒

The Duke of Holloway caught them in the hall.

He stopped abruptly, almost sliding on the polished marble as he stared at them. His eyes went from their damp, tousled hair to the crumpled stays each held in her hands. "What the hell happened?" he demanded, looking as though he couldn't decide whether to be incredulous or worried.

"August," Clara breathed before she launched herself into his arms.

The duke caught her and kissed his wife with such searing passion that Rose blushed and looked away.

"Why are you half-dressed?" he asked after a moment, drawing back to examine Clara. "And why is your hair wet? And where are your students?"

"The students are with Theo and Tabby," Clara told him, her arms still wrapped around his neck. "And I was swimming."

"In the *ocean*?"

"No, in the fountains." She made a face. "Of course in the ocean."

"You don't swim." His dark brows had lowered like thunderclouds.

"Today I did. I don't know why I haven't done it before now."

"You could have drowned."

Clara released him and gave Rose a piercing look with dark eyes so like her own. "I was perfectly safe. Rose was with me."

The duke transferred his attention to Rose. "Good afternoon, Rose," he said belatedly. "And my thanks, it seems, for saving your sister from herself."

"I think I was only returning the favor," Rose murmured. The hope that had germinated down on the beach had grown, spreading tiny, tentative roots. The easy thing is rarely the right thing, she had told Eli. Perhaps it was past time for her to heed her own words.

Clara smiled softly, and Rose nodded. Holloway looked back and forth between them, but no further explanation would be forthcoming.

He turned his attention to his wife. "When will your students be back?"

"Not for hours. It's why I didn't bother with these." Clara held up her stays. "I was planning on changing."

Without warning Holloway swept his wife into his arms, ignoring Clara's startled gasp. "Just as well," he growled. "It will save me some time." He started up the stairs, only to stop halfway up. "I almost forgot. Lord Rivers sent something along for you, Rose," he said over his shoulder. "I had it put in your rooms."

Rose knew what it was before she pulled the thick protective fabric away from the canvas with shaking hands.

She stumbled back and sank down on the edge of the bed. In front of her, the beautiful blond woman still gazed into her mirror, alone and silent.

"Oh, Eli," she whispered. "What have you done?"

There had been a satinwood box delivered with the painting and left on the end of her bed. It wasn't large, perhaps something that had once been used as a tea caddy. Rose reached for it and pulled it onto her lap, opening the inlaid top. Inside lay a bundle of letters, clearly written over a long period. Some were travel stained, frayed and torn along the edges, and some were still crisp and unmarred, but all were clearly addressed to her. On top of the bound bundle lay a single folded sheet of paper. Rose lifted it out of the box and opened it, Eli's neat cursive blurring as her eyes stung.

You once asked me why, in all the time I was away, I never wrote to the woman I loved. I did, though it seems it has taken me longer than it ever should have to post these letters. Just as it has taken me longer than it should have to truly understand what I once possessed.

Rose sniffed, wiping at her eyes with the back of her hand.

I will never ask you for anything you can't give. But know that I have loved you from the moment I saw you and I will love you until my last. My love for you is a great love that will forever eclipse all earthly vanities.

Rose set the paper aside and clutched the bundle of Eli's letters to her chest. Her eyes found those of the woman who gazed back at her in the mirror, eternally searching for her love, and Rose knew deep in her heart that her own search was over. And the proof of it lay not in the priceless masterpiece that sat before her but in the collection of battered, dusty papers she held in her hands.

And knowing, in that moment, what she needed to do.

Chapter 22

Eli used to love balls.

Any sort of extravagant entertainment, really, where the music was excellent, the food superb, and the spirits plentiful. This display of lavish excess would have, at one time, delighted him. The orchestra was expansive and talented, the tables positively sagged under the weight of all manner of delectable offerings, and footmen appeared and disappeared like wraiths, making sure one's glass was never empty. The fact that all of it was in his honor would have once made him giddy.

He was certainly grateful. Appreciative of the time and the expense that Stannis had gone to on his behalf. But time had changed his perspective, and he found himself trying and failing to keep a low profile in the crush. A ball held in honor of a dead man was a novelty. A ball held in honor of a man who had risked his own life, suffering dire injury to save the son of a duke, was an even bigger draw.

Somehow, Eli's appearance had become a badge of honor

and bravery. His ruined face belied not a monster to be es-chewed but a hero to be embraced, and the irony of that was not lost on him. The charming rogue everyone had once adored had returned, now a triumphant conqueror, tested and proven. And Eli had been subsequently and enthusiastically swallowed back into the glittering world as though he had never left.

The guest list had been exhaustive and there had been no shortage of men who had wanted to talk about the wars. Most he found he already knew, others he was introduced to. He accepted condolences on his father's death. Danced with daughters and debutantes under the cynical gaze of marriage-minded mamas delighted with his newly acquired fame and, even more, his newly acquired title and fortune. He'd fielded subtle and not-so-subtle questions about his de-lay in returning to England. As the hours had dragged on, he answered what he wished to and ignored the queries he didn't.

And tried not to think about the fact that the only person he really cared to see was missing.

He knew Holloway would have kept his word and deliv-ered the painting and the letters to Rose. But she had sent nothing back by post. Not a word. He'd thought that giv-ing her a modicum of privacy, a small measure of time and space, would be best, but as of tomorrow, he would be on his way back to Avondale and damn whatever consequences that might bring.

Eli placed his empty glass on the tray of a passing foot-man and headed toward the tall terrace doors that had been pushed open at the end of the ballroom. He couldn't leave, but he could escape, if only for a few minutes. The dark night air beckoned him forward, offering him respite from the stuffy ballroom and the tiring if well-meaning masses.

He had reached a row of potted orange trees that had been placed by the doors, checking his surroundings surreptitiously to make sure no one had followed him, when a haunting sense of recognition froze him in his tracks. A young woman with raven hair and wearing a pale-green dress sat against the wall on the other side of the spindly trees, a wistful smile on her face as her fingers tapped against her knee in time to the music. She was alone, as far as Eli could tell, with nothing save the abandoned crutch that leaned against her chair for company.

Abruptly, without considering what he was doing, Eli altered his course until he was standing directly in front of her.

"Good evening, Lady Ophelia," he said.

The young woman started, emerald-green eyes ringed with sooty lashes widening as she gazed up at him.

"Lord Rivers," she managed smoothly, as if strange, battle-scarred earls addressed her without warning every day.

"Good, you know who I am," he said easily. "I suppose that saves me the need to introduce myself. Or alternatively, drag our illustrious hostess over here to do it properly."

Lady Ophelia tried to hide a smile and failed. "I won't tell if you don't. My mother went to fetch us a refreshment, and there's no need to give her an apoplexy." She paused, meeting his eye. "This is your ball, my lord. Everyone knows who you are. But I'm not sure how it is that you know who I am."

Eli found himself grinning back at her. "It would seem," he said, "that we have a mutual friend in Miss Rose Hayward."

"Indeed." A hint of pink crept into her cheeks.

"I understand that you have been taking painting instruction from her?"

"Yes," the young woman replied slowly. "Painting instruction."

"Excellent. Miss Hayward is quite extraordinary."

She gave him a curious look and opened her mouth as if to say something before changing her mind. "Yes. She is," was all she said.

"I'm sure you learned quite a bit."

"You have no idea."

"Ophelia?" The question snapped her head around.

A short, expensively dressed woman with two glasses of punch in her hands was looking suspiciously between Eli and her daughter.

"Mama," Lady Ophelia said, her eyes darting to Eli and back.

Eli offered the woman a slight bow. "Good evening, my lady," he said airily. "My apologies if I've intruded."

"Not at all," she murmured, uncertainty and confusion adding to her existing suspicion. "A wonderful welcome tonight, isn't it, my lord?" she offered, clearly at a loss as to why the guest of honor was speaking to her daughter and what she should do about it.

"It is, isn't it," Eli agreed. "And the only thing that would make it even more so is if your daughter would be so kind as to grant me a dance. With your permission, of course."

The woman's mouth fell open. "She can't."

Ophelia was blinking at him.

"Why ever not?" he asked stonily.

"She's...she's...She simply *can't*."

Eli frowned. "Do you not believe my intentions honorable?" he asked, a clear edge to his words. "I can assure you, I've danced with many lovely women tonight, and not one has questioned my honor."

"No, of course not," she sputtered.

"Well, then, that settles it." He extended his hand toward Ophelia. "If you would grant me the privilege, my lady." He cocked his head. "It sounds as though they are getting ready to play a waltz."

Lady Ophelia put her hand in his, and he could feel her hesitation. She reached for her crutch with her other hand.

"You won't need that," Eli assured her. "We're dancing. Not running a lap at Epsom Downs."

He saw her bite her lip.

"Trust me, my lady."

Lady Ophelia nodded and stood. He tucked her hand through his arm, making sure he was on her weak side, simply replacing her crutch with himself. He ignored the horrified huffs from her mother.

Her hand clutched his arm. "My lord..."

"You do know the steps?" he asked, letting her set the pace as they moved toward the dance floor.

She nodded. "But..."

"But what?"

"No one has ever asked me to dance."

"Their loss."

"Did Miss Hayward put you up to this?" she asked.

"No," he answered honestly. "She most certainly did not."

"You don't have to do this," she said quietly as they stepped out on the dance floor. "I'll embarrass you."

Eli threw his head back and laughed. "Impossible."

"But—"

"I tried using that excuse once with Miss Hayward. It didn't work on her either."

"What if I stumble?"

"Then I'll catch you." He placed her hand on his shoulder and took her other firmly in his. "Lean on me. We'll go as slow and as carefully as you need."

"Everyone is already staring."

"Good. They should be. I'm dancing with the most

beautiful woman in the room." Around them the music started. "Shall we?"

Ophelia took a deep breath. " 'Cowards die many times before their deaths; the valiant never taste of death but once,' " she mumbled to herself.

"Good Lord, I hope you're not planning to die on me halfway through this dance," Eli teased. "Because that would make explanations to your mother terribly awkward."

Ophelia suddenly laughed, and Eli could feel the tension drain from her body. "It's from *Julius Caesar*. And I'm not planning on doing anything but dancing."

"I'm glad to hear it." Eli smiled down at her and took the first step.

It would never have been considered a perfect waltz, and often they fell out of time with the music with their shortened steps. But it didn't matter because Lady Ophelia's eyes were shining, and she was smiling like a fool. Eli enjoyed every second of it until the music finally reached its crescendo and ended.

He grinned at Lady Ophelia. "How did I do?" he asked. "Think you might grant me the honor of another dance one day?"

"That was— You were superb," she said breathlessly, allowing Eli to tuck her hand back into the crook of his arm. "And it will always be my honor, my lord."

"I suppose I should return you to your mother," Eli said. "There's only so much scandal she might be able to handle in one night."

"I suppose." Ophelia sounded less than enthused.

Eli ignored the gawking stares and slowly led the extraordinary young woman back in the direction of her mother, who was wringing her hands and pacing along the wall. He stopped suddenly. "On second thought, I have a better idea."

Eli didn't give Ophelia a chance to answer but angled them away from her mother and toward a man standing alone, just beyond the terrace doors, staring out into the night.

~

Rose had been ready to flee until she saw them dancing.

She had fought the smothering panic that had risen with each forced step that took her farther into the stifling ballroom. She had tried to control the breaths that came in ever-shorter gasps. Ignored the rising nausea that pressed up into her throat as she ventured into the crowd.

Around her, people jostled and bumped, fans and silks and evening coats turning into a dizzying blur. The conversation seemed inordinately loud, shrill laughter punctuating the unintelligible cacophony. Critical eyes set in powdered faces with rouged cheeks and lips turned her way, and she cringed each time, unable to stop herself from reacting.

She hated that she had allowed this part of herself to become diminished. Lost. In her head she knew she was being unreasonable. In her head she understood that the people who had been ruthlessly cruel would have moved on. Found other targets and probably forgotten all about her. In her head she knew that she should have been able to rise above such vindictiveness, then and now, if need be. But that knowledge had done nothing to stop her heart from hammering or the icy beads of sweat from sliding down her spine.

She had finally come to a stop near the edge of the dance floor, at a set of tall terrace doors, close to a row of potted orange trees, as if their tiny trunks could afford her cover. Her ice-blue gown was suffocating her, and the flowing skirts might as well have been constructed of lead. The walls had started to close in on her, and Rose's eyes had seized on the doors that led out to the stone terrace and the gardens beyond. A promise of escape, she had thought a little wildly. Because no matter how badly she had wanted to do this, no matter how much she wanted to prove to herself that she was stronger and braver, doubt and fear had seized her hard in their grasp.

And that's when she had seen them.

They had started their waltz not far from where she stood behind the orange trees, Eli holding Ophelia in his arms, lending his strength to her. Their movements were far from fluid, and other couples spun past them. But none of that mattered. Because as the music ended, Ophelia was, on that ballroom floor, the woman Rose had painted. Her cheeks were flushed, her eyes a little dreamy, her smile uninhibited. Her crutch was nowhere to be seen.

Eli had never looked more devastatingly resplendent. He was dressed in all the trappings of wealth, his dark evening clothes perfectly tailored to accentuate his strength and bearing. But it was the ease with which he carried himself that made him stand out from all others. A man who had walked through fire and emerged on the other side, fiercer and more resilient than anyone could have imagined.

And Rose forgot where she was standing. Forgot about the crowd and the crush and simply stared, drowning in her love for him.

~

"Linfield," Eli greeted as the Duke of Stannis's youngest son turned. Eli watched as his eyes slid to Ophelia and widened.

"Lord Rivers," Lewis Linfield replied, though his gaze never left Ophelia. "I trust you are enjoying yourself?"

"Your parents have outdone themselves." He paused. "Lady Ophelia Volante, may I present Mr. Lewis Linfield, son of His Grace the Duke of Stannis. Linfield, the Lady Ophelia Volante, daughter of the Marquess of Kerwith."

"A pleasure." Ophelia dropped into a curtsy, her hand tightening around Eli's arm for balance.

"The pleasure is all mine," Linfield replied, tucking his empty sleeve against his abdomen and bowing.

"It struck me that the two of you might have something in common," Eli said casually.

Linfield looked at him sharply, finally pulling his eyes away from his beautiful companion. Beside Eli, Ophelia's fingers curled into his sleeve, and she dropped her gaze, her cheeks flushing.

"*The Two Gentlemen of Verona*," Eli said into the taut silence. "And *Julius Caesar*."

Linfield blinked, and Ophelia's head came up.

"I beg your pardon?" Linfield said.

"You've both quoted Shakespeare in our recent conversations. A shame, really, because I am no scholar, and the finer merits are probably lost on me," Eli continued guilelessly. "I was thinking that, in each other, you might find a partner far more worthy of your academic acumen than I."

Linfield's startling blue eyes were once again fixed firmly on Lady Ophelia's face. "Indeed?"

Ophelia was smiling shyly back.

"Perhaps, Lady Ophelia, you would care to join me on the terrace for a spell?" Linfield asked.

Eli smothered a grin.

"I'd like that." Ophelia glanced up at Eli, a shadow of uncertainty touching her face. "Perhaps I should fetch my crutch before—"

Linfield moved with smooth grace, and Eli found himself

replaced as Ophelia's escort. "That won't be necessary," he said to Ophelia. "So long as you're comfortable with me?"

She nodded.

"Excellent. Enjoy the rest of your evening, the both of you." Eli turned smartly, leaving neither the chance to respond as he headed back into the ballroom. The grin he had cloaked now split his face as he lifted his head. And froze.

For a terrifying moment, Eli wondered if he was imagining her.

Wondered if she would vanish like smoke in the wind if he blinked or moved or even breathed. She was wearing the gown he had given her, her hair caught up loosely on the crown of her head, curls drifting down to brush her shoulders. She was unusually pale, making her dark chocolate eyes seem huge in her delicate face.

And then he saw her take a deep breath and lift her chin.

The joy that surged through him was complete and disorienting in its intensity. And on the heels of that came a wave of deep longing and a feeling of impossible, perfect love.

Rose's eyes met his. "It would seem, Lord Rivers, that it was I who had one more thing left to prove."

Chapter 23

She was hot and cold all at once, the way she had felt in a darkened studio on a stormy night in Dover. Only this time, when he caught her hand, she didn't pull away. Instead she wrapped her fingers around his and held on for all she was worth, anchoring herself with his strength.

"Rose," he said hoarsely, and somewhere in her name was a question.

"Sorry I'm a little late," she managed with a tremulous smile.

"God, Rose." His eye searched hers, and he pulled her toward him. He crushed her to his chest, seemingly uncaring who might be watching. "Come," he said, wrapping her hand under his arm, holding on to her as if he was afraid she might let go.

She let him pull her into the night, down the wide terrace steps, and onto the gravel paths that wound through the manicured gardens. Rose took deep gulps of the cool night air, an odd, restless energy humming through her, every fiber in her body attuned to the man at her side. They drew near a fountain, the sound of the orchestra inside still audible over the musical splash of water.

And then he stopped and she was in his arms and he was kissing her until she was breathless and delirious. "I've missed you," he whispered against her lips.

"I love you," she whispered back.

Eli rested his forehead against hers, his arms tightening around her. "You didn't have to come here," he said.

"Yes, I did." She pulled back.

"You don't have to stay."

"Yes, I do."

"You don't have to prove anything else to me, Rose. I love you just as you are."

"I had to prove it to myself," she said. She studied his face in the weak light that filtered into the garden from the ball-room windows.

"Tell me you didn't come alone."

"No, your aunts came with me. To support me. And you too."

"Why didn't you just tell me?" He waved his hand in the direction of the terrace and the ballroom beyond. "Why didn't you tell me that this was hard for you?"

Rose felt her cheeks heat, but she answered him with the truth anyway. "Pride? Vanity? I was so ashamed, Eli. I told you to have done with yourself when I couldn't do the same. If that isn't the height of hypocrisy, I don't know what is."

"Rose—"

"I didn't want you to think me weak, foolish."

"I would have thought you human."

"You were right, you know. When you said I was hiding. I was. And you were right to say so—"

"I didn't understand." His hands slid up her back. "But I do now. And I don't need you to change for me."

"I know that. But I need me to change for me. And I need to trust you to help me do it. The way you trusted me." She bit her lip. "I needed to trust that a great love would eclipse all earthly vanities."

He bent his head and kissed her softly. "You once told me that I was brave and inspiring. I think that describes you tonight, Rose Hayward."

"I don't feel brave and inspiring," she said, laying her head against his chest and hearing the echo of his own words from so long ago. "Walking through that crowd, mostly I felt terrified."

"But you survived. And now you're here. Right where you're supposed to be."

"As are you." She smiled.

"I only made it as far as I did because of you, Rose."

"Then I suppose that makes us even."

"I suppose it does."

She was quiet, listening to the steady beat of his heart. The heady scent of roses eddied around them, the breeze gently rustling the foliage. From the terrace, strains of another waltz drifted over the gardens.

Rose ran her fingers down the lapel of his coat. "I saw you dancing. With Ophelia."

He chuckled, the sound rolling through his chest. "I don't imagine her mother has recovered yet."

She lifted her head. "It was—"

"Only a charming scoundrel angling to dance with the second-most-beautiful woman in the room," he said. "Though I may have lied to Lady Ophelia and told her she was the most beautiful woman. But you should know that that was before I was aware you were here."

Rose smiled. "I'll overlook it this once," she teased.

"You should also know I plan to take full credit should Linfield decide that he cannot live without her," Eli continued. He tenderly pushed a curl back over Rose's ear as he had done so many times before. "In the way that I cannot live without you."

"So marry me," Rose whispered, wrapping her arms around his neck.

"Is that an invitation or a command?"

"A command, I think. I'm done with invitations for a while."

He kissed her and then looked at her seriously. "I don't need you to be anyone other than who you are."

"I know. But you have and you will continue to make me a better version of myself, Eli Dawes."

The warm, fragrant air swirled around them, still carrying the sounds of the music. Eli slipped from her embrace and bent low over her hand. "May I have the privilege of this dance, Miss Hayward?"

"I'd thought you'd never ask."

He moved to take her in his arms, but she put her hand against his sleeve. She looked up, searching his eye in the filtered light.

"I think," she said slowly, "that if I am to be the Countess of Rivers, we'd best go inside to dance."

"Are you sure?"

Rose reached up and cupped the sides of Eli's face, feeling the perfect imperfection of the man she loved beneath her palms. "I've never been surer of anything in my life."

Chapter 24

London, England
Spring 1821

T he horse had been turned into a unicorn.

And not only a unicorn, but one with a ruby-red mane and tail, its hooves churning up rainbow-colored dust as it raced across the paper. Rose clasped her hands behind her back and hid a smile as Margret Soames bent her head in concentration. She'd asked the dozen children who sat in the classroom to paint the wooden horse statue that she'd set up in the center, and on Margret's page this had been the result.

Rose was rather delighted.

"I'm done," Margret announced.

Her sister hopped down from where she had been sitting next to her to peer over her shoulder. "That's not a horse," Mildred commented, her nose scrunched up in her small face.

"'Er Ladyship never said what it had to look like," Margret retorted.

Mildred turned to give Rose a dubious look. "She didn't follow the rules."

"Ah, but this is art class," Rose replied. "There are no rules in art class. Here you are free to create whatever it is that you see inside your head. There is no wrong answer."

Margret brightened considerably. "No rules," she repeated with satisfaction. "And no wrong answer."

"Just in this class," Rose reminded her. "Arithmetic is completely different."

"Exactly," Mildred said with the same sort of satisfaction. "Which is what makes arithmetic so much fun. Because there is a right answer every time." She put her hands on her hips.

Margret opened her mouth to argue, but Rose interrupted. "You can debate this later," she said with a laugh. "But your mother is waiting for you out back. There is a garden out there that won't plant itself."

The twins departed, followed by the rest of the students, and Rose picked up the painting of the unicorn. She would hang this among the other artworks that covered the newly whitewashed walls in this room—

"Is that a goat?"

Rose turned with a grin to find Eli leaning against the door frame, his arms folded across his chest. His face was flushed and his hair windblown, as though he had just come inside. At his feet a small black one-eyed dog collapsed with a huff. Bruno had taken to following Eli everywhere.

"If you must know, it's a unicorn," Rose sniffed, setting the art aside and advancing toward him.

"Ah," he said, catching her by the waist and pulling her against him. Rose tipped up her head, and Eli claimed her lips with his. "It's delightful," he murmured. "Almost as delightful as finding my wife in an empty room, all to myself." His hands dropped to the curve of her backside.

Rose laughed and extricated herself with some reluctance. "An empty room with no door," she reminded him. "And a houseful of families who might happen by at any moment."

"I should have had the classroom doors installed a long time ago," Eli muttered.

Rose plucked a bit of cotton off the back of his sleeve. "I think you had the right of it when you gave the looms priority," she said.

"Second shipment of the finished garments is loaded and ready to be delivered," he replied. "Charlie is coordinating with the merchants."

"Is that where you were just now? In the warehouse?"

Eli shook his head. "Actually, I was in town." He caught her hand, an almost diffident expression suddenly shadowing his features. "I want to show you something."

Rose nodded and allowed Eli to lead her through the maze of hallways, passing more classrooms, common rooms, and the massive kitchens. The scent of new lumber still lingered in the air even now, months after the completion of the house. Eli pushed open the wide front doors, and they stepped into the spring sunshine. To her left, set back from the house, the weaving shed, mill, and warehouse were a hive of activity. And on this day a row of wagons was lined up in front, all in the process of being loaded. Along the other side of the house, stretching back to the river, the extensive gardens that would supply the kitchens had been plowed and were in the process of being planted.

Eli pulled Rose across the drive to a sturdy cart hitched to a dozing gelding. Two men built like pugilists jumped from their perches and greeted the earl. One pulled the back board of the cart down and pushed aside a battered piece of burlap from a bed of straw, revealing a long, flat piece of cut stone. It was buff colored and polished smooth, and EMANUEL HOUSE had been expertly carved across the surface.

"I thought my father would be proud to have his name on something that mattered," Eli said gruffly. "It's to go at the entrance."

"Oh, Eli." Rose reached forward and ran her hand over the cool stone. She stared at it a moment longer before turning away and slipping her arms around Eli. "What you've accomplished here is extraordinary."

"I had help. Lots of it."

Rose smiled. "Even so. Your father would be just as proud of you as I am." She went up on her tiptoes and brushed a soft kiss across his cheek. "The name is perfect."

"Your brother thought so as well."

She looked up at him. "When did Harland see this?" she asked.

"I ran into him in town. Caught him just before he left."

"Left for where?" she asked, confused.

"Dover." Now it was Eli who looked confused.

"Again?"

"You didn't know he was leaving?"

Rose shook her head. "No." Harland had done this with increasing regularity—left abruptly with no warning. And he had been evasive when questioned afterward, mumbling something about doctoring. But Rose wasn't sure she believed him any longer. "When is he coming back?"

Eli shrugged. "Didn't say, though he seemed to be in a dashed hurry. He mentioned that Miss Swift would be available to cover any medical needs that we may have here while he's away." Eli gathered her hands in his. "I wouldn't worry," he said. "If I've learned anything about your brother, it's that he can take care of himself."

"I know he can." Rose sighed. There was nothing she could do about Harland's absence now.

"Come," Eli said. "We should go. We don't want to be late to the theater. Linfield and Lady Ophelia promise me it will be a good one, if only because Byron has his trousers in a twist over something about the play. The staging, I think."

"The play doesn't start for at least five hours, Dawes."

"Exactly." Eli tugged on her hands. "Just enough time for us to get home and get changed."

"It doesn't take me five hours to take a dress off and put another on."

"Who said anything about putting another one on?" Eli lowered his head to her ear, his lips grazing the side of her neck. "Unlike here, dear wife, the rooms in our house have doors," he whispered, his breath hot against her skin. "With locks."

"Then by all means, dear husband," Rose whispered back. "Take me home."

Enjoy more of the Devils of Dover when Harland Hayward, an intriguing combination of doctor and baron, finally reveals his biggest secret and meets his perfect match.

Please turn the page for a preview from *A Rogue by Night*.

Available Spring 2019

Chapter 1

Dover, England
July 1821

The bullet wound, as far as bullet wounds went, was not dreadful.

The bullet had caught him at the top of the shoulder, punching a messy hole in flesh and muscle but not shattering bone. The cold of the sea had slowed the bleeding, and the fact that her patient had been shirtless at the time meant no remnants of fabric would be caught deep in the tissue. More concerning was the long gash that ran across the muscles of his upper back. The gaping, ragged edges were still oozing blood, and the wound would require a substantial number of stitches. Katherine Wright increased the pressure she was applying to the gash, watching as the linen turned scarlet in the pool of lantern light.

"Jesus, Kate, are you trying to kill me all over again?" It was an angry question, accompanied by a groan.

"Maybe I should." She kept her voice steady, though inside she was shaking with fury. "If only to keep the damn soldiers from having the satisfaction of doing so."

From the front corner of the cottage, her father wheezed, his laughter made ominous by the rattling in his lungs. "Stop your whining, lad, or your sister might just decide to get careless with her wee knives."

There were a couple of snickers from the rest of the men who had carried her brother into their tiny abode. Most of the men she recognized, a couple she had never seen. Katherine glared up at them, and the snickers faded. She wished she had drawn the heavy curtain she'd put up in the center of the cottage for those times when she and a patient needed privacy.

"Get out," she ordered the lot of them.

They shuffled their feet and looked uncertainly between Katherine and her patient in response.

From where he lay facedown on the table, her brother lifted his head and tried to look back at her. "There's no call for—"

"Stop talking, Matthew, or I'll let one of these logger-heads sew you up. And then you'll have a scar the likes of which you don't want to consider."

Matthew's forehead came to rest on the table again. His dark-blond hair was still wet, and twisted strands fell forward against the sides of his face. "I'm told women like their men with scars."

"Women like their men safe," she gritted out through clenched teeth, still glaring at the assembled crowd. "Not shot and at the wrong end of a blade."

Matthew grunted. "Kate—"

"Off with you, then, lads," her father said, his voice like gravel. "Let her do her work. Go home, keep your heads down, and let the soldiers chase their tails for the rest of the night. Matty will be right as rain by morning."

The men muttered but obeyed the order, and one by

one they vanished soundlessly into the darkness. Katherine knew they would each go a different direction, slipping through the blackness like wraiths in the night, evading the blockade men and patrols that hunted the coast for prey. Since she'd been a child, she had watched as smugglers deliberately scattered, men with generations of experience behind them. She had watched her father do it. Watched her brother do it. When she had gotten older, she had done it as well.

But occasionally they weren't as invisible as they thought. And the proof of that was still bleeding all over her table.

"They didn't follow you here, did they?" Katherine asked her brother. "The soldiers?"

"Don't be daft."

"I'm not being daft, I'm being careful. Something you might want to do more of." She peeled back the linen and grimaced at the gaping wound, though the bleeding was starting to ebb. She despised deep cuts like this. Forget the deeper damage to the muscle tissue, wounds like this could fester.

"We lost them in the tunnels." Matthew's words were muffled against the table.

"You're sure? If you were bleeding, you'd have left a trail—"

"I'm sure, dammit."

"How did they know you'd be in that cove?"

"Someone must have tipped the patrols off," her father answered.

Katherine glanced up at her father. The light from a small candelabra set near his side illuminated his wizened profile as he stood. He pulled back the curtain covering the small window at the front of the cottage, peering out into the darkness. Wrapped as he was in a bulky blanket, he almost looked like his brawny former self. Before he'd been shot. Before his lungs had weakened and deteriorated.

"What was it tonight?" she asked Matthew. "Silk? Tea?"

"Brandy. From Boulogne," he replied. "The patrols were hidden on the beach, waiting for us to retrieve it. Didn't see them until it was almost too late."

"Almost?" Katherine asked angrily. "Dammit, Matt, do you have any idea what your back looks like?"

"It was hard to run in the surf, at least until I got deep enough to swim. But I drew them out, and they couldn't run either. The other boys got away clean, and that's all that matters."

"You matter. Your life matters. And you almost lost it—"

"Those men, those boys, are my crew, Kate. My responsibility. What kind of leader am I if I don't lead?"

"You said that you would stop doing this, Matt." Katherine pulled a candelabra closer and reached for her suture kit. "You promised me."

Her brother mumbled something unintelligible into the table.

"What was that?"

"He asked how you think we're all to eat if he stops," her father said harshly from his post at the window. "How we're supposed to keep a roof over our heads and coal in the hearth in winter. How we're going to pay for the medicine you keep stuffing down my throat every time you get the chance. That all takes coin, lass."

Katherine set her kit aside. "I earn—"

"You earn the occasional chicken," her father said wearily. "A handful of carrots, or a measure of dried herring if you're real lucky."

"I can't not help someone who needs me," she snapped.

"Aye, I know that. And you've a rare gift for healing, and this parish and its people desperately need you, especially now. But they have nothing, and thus, neither do you."

"You almost died at the hands of the king's men, Father. Five inches is all that kept Matthew from dying tonight from another soldier's bullet. You—" She stopped, trying to keep her voice from rising. "You speak of having nothing. If the two of you die for the sake of a bale of smuggled tobacco or a tub of brandy, then I'll truly have nothing."

"I'm not so easy to kill." Her father was still looking out into the darkness.

"And neither am I," Matthew added irritably from the table. "French artillery and guns couldn't do it. A handful of leftover Englishmen with inferior weapons and high-strung horses will not be able to do what the French could not."

Katherine suppressed the urge to throw something. "Are you not hearing what I'm trying to say? I—"

"Douse the light," her father said, his voice hard with urgency. "We've company."

Katherine immediately blew out the candles surrounding the table as her father did the same to the candles near the window. She reached for the lantern hanging above her head on its hook and extinguished that too, fear spiking and making her pulse pound. "Soldiers?"

"Can't tell." Her father shuffled across the darkened space, illuminated now only by the dim light flickering from the hearth. He stopped beside the only other window in the cottage, on the far side of the door, and eased back its covering.

Katherine set the lantern on the floor off to the side. She moved slowly around the table, reaching for the long curtain that hung from a rope across the center of the cottage, and drew it closed. The heavy fabric concealed the rear of the cottage from the view of anyone at the door, but it would be a poor solution in the face of a regiment of soldiers hunting for a smuggler.

There was, however, a space beneath the floor, big enough for a man to crouch in, accessible from a trapdoor. She eyed the corner of the bed that her father and brother shared, just visible in the gloom. It would need to be pushed away from the wall, and the threadbare rug would have to be peeled back, if she were to get her brother hidden.

She took a step closer to her brother. "You need to hide."

"There's not time. Get me the rifle." Matthew staggered to his feet, swaying slightly and reaching for the edge of the table to steady himself. His breathing was shallow and labored.

He kept a rifle near the cottage door, always loaded with fresh powder. Though Katherine doubted very much that Matthew would be able to manage the heavy weapon in his state. And she knew that her father couldn't.

Without considering what she was doing, she slipped past the curtain, stole across the dimly lit space, and snatched up the gun.

"Single horse and rider," her father warned from the window.

That was better than a posse of soldiers, but it still didn't bode well.

"Bring that damn gun back here," her brother whispered weakly. She saw the curtain behind her twitch and knew he was watching her.

Outside, the sound of boots on the packed earth was faint but unmistakable.

Katherine swallowed hard, raising the gun to her shoulder and leveling the muzzle at the door.

"Jesus Christ, Kate, get away from that door and bring me the gun." Matthew's demand was both faint and desperate.

"Do what he says, lass," her father pleaded.

"Sit down before you fall down, Matthew," Katherine murmured in a voice that sounded surprisingly steady to her own ears. "You've lost a lot of blood. Keep the curtain closed. And you stay where you are, Father."

There was a soft tap on the door, and the latch creaked. Katherine felt her brows draw together, even as she adjusted her grasp on the stock. Soldiers would not have knocked first. At least not that quietly.

"Mr. Wright?" The voice was low and male. The door swung open a little farther, and a tall figure carrying a bulky bag of some sort ducked carefully into the cottage. "Mr. Wri—" He stopped abruptly, and Katherine guessed he had finally seen her silhouetted in the firelight. And the gun she was holding.

From the side of the room, her father muttered something under his breath and moved from the window. He ducked past the man and shoved the door closed, though not before he scanned the darkness beyond. "Dr. Hayward," he said by way of greeting, "welcome."

"Mmm," the doctor replied drily, gazing at Katherine. "I'm not so sure I am."

Katherine lowered the gun and set it back against the wall. She put a hand out to anchor herself, the tension abruptly broken and leaving her a little more wobbly than she'd like. She tried to will her heart back into a normal rhythm.

Not a soldier, but a doctor. One she knew spent his summers in Dover and saw to a great deal of the county's medical needs while he was here. Katherine had never actually met him in the short time that she'd been back, but she'd seen him at a distance, usually accompanied by a pretty young woman who seemed to hang on his every word. Which wasn't surprising because Dr. Hayward, she had been told, was not only a doctor but a baron as well. A wealthy, widowed baron. Which was surprising.

And made no sense to Katherine at all.

Because rich, titled men did not labor in such professions. They did not lower themselves to toil in a trade marked by disease and blood and gore. They didn't spend time worrying about people who did not possess an address west of Haymarket, London. And they certainly didn't prowl the back roads of Dover in the dead of night when the air was heavy with the promise of rain.

Which, all together, made the baron's sudden presence here inordinately suspicious. She wasn't about to test the doctor's discretion. Who knew what Harland Hayward—Baron Strathmore—did or didn't know about what went on along the shores of Kent County? And where his allegiances might lie? With king and country or with the peasants who struggled to survive both? Baron Strathmore was a grand lord, after all.

He was certainly not one of them.

Katherine deliberately did not look back to where her brother remained concealed. "What do you want?" It was abrupt and rude, but with Matthew still bleeding behind her, she needed this baron turned doctor to leave.

"Miss Wright, I presume?" The baron hadn't moved from where he stood in the shadows. Nor did he sound the least bit offended by her utter lack of decorum. "Your father has told me a lot about you."

Katherine's eyes narrowed. Well, her father certainly hadn't returned the favor. She hadn't even realized that he knew the baron. She shot a glance in her father's direction, but he ignored her, concentrating on relighting the candles, though not fast enough for Katherine's liking. She wanted—needed—to see this Lord Doctor clearly, to read his face and the nuances of his expression.

"Yes," she replied finally into the silence, acknowledging her identity but ignoring his assertion that he was familiar with anything about her. "Again, I'd ask what you want—"

"He's come to help you, lass," her father grumbled as he bent to retrieve the lantern and set to lighting it again.

"If you need it, of course," Strathmore added, sounding merely pleasant and polite.

Katherine was not at all prepared with a story to explain Matthew's bullet wound to his Lordship, any more than she was prepared to trust Strathmore with the truth. "I have no idea what you're talking about—"

A crash reverberated through the room, and Katherine spun. The table behind the curtain had fallen over and torn the fabric from its moorings. On top of the heavy wool, caught in the table legs, Matthew was inelegantly sprawled.

"That," the baron said in that annoyingly calm way of his. "I was talking about that."

Katherine jerked into action, cursing under her breath and hurrying forward. She dropped to her knees beside Matthew. In the soft light, she could see that his eyes were closed, his face pale, but his chest moved up and down steadily. A dark, rusty stain was smeared over the surface of the wool where it had come into contact with his wound as he fell. She cursed again and pushed the crumpled fabric away from where it had bunched across his hips.

On the other side of the overturned table, her father hovered above her with the lantern, a worried expression on his face. "Is he all right?"

"He's merely fainted because he came in here bleeding

like a stuck pig." Katherine put her fingers beneath Matthew's chin, searching for his pulse, relieved to find that it still beat steadily beneath her touch. She withdrew her hand. "Which is why I told him to sit down before he fell down."

"Brothers," came a voice by her ear, "rarely do what they're told. At least that's what my sisters tell me."

Katherine started, not having heard Strathmore crouch beside her.

"Bullet or blade?" he asked almost conversationally.

"Both," she said with a frown, not taking her eyes off Matthew.

The baron leaned forward, his long, graceful fingers sliding over Mathew's scalp in sure movements, searching, Katherine surmised, for any lumps that he might have suffered in the fall.

The baron has incredible hands, she thought. They were not the hands of a soft, pampered peer, but the capable hands of a man used to working. Hands that were used to communicate and discover and touch— She averted her eyes. She could not be noticing a man's hands while her brother languished insensate and bleeding in a pile at her feet.

Those hands had stopped, and the baron pushed the wool farther away from Matthew's shoulder. "Ah. Yes, I see the exit wound now. He was lucky. Minimal damage, more bruising to the muscle than anything else, I think. This the only bullet wound?"

"Yes."

"Mmm. And the laceration? That is on his back, then?"

"Yes." She couldn't really see Strathmore's face, his thick, dark hair falling carelessly over his ears and concealing his features. She tried not to notice his nearness or the warmth she could feel from his body.

"Has it been sutured?"

"Not yet." Katherine studied the back of his head. The baron wasn't asking the obvious questions. Like how her brother had come to be shot and wounded. Or why Katherine had greeted him at the door with a leveled gun. He hadn't asked any question that wasn't clinical in nature. He hadn't even expressed surprise or dismay or disapproval. She really didn't understand this man at all.

And she didn't like what she didn't understand.

The baron rocked back on his heels and pushed himself to his feet. "Well, then. Let's get him back up on the table so we can get his laceration sutured, shall we? I need to examine the severity of the wound."

Well. The baron might not be asking the expected questions, but he was certainly giving the expected orders.

"*You* don't have to do anything, my lord," Katherine said coolly. "I can assure you that my brother is in good hands under my care." She had lost count of the number of times that a physician or surgeon—a male physician or surgeon—had inserted himself into a situation, dismissing her and her talents amid a fog of condescension. That was not about to happen here. Not when it came to her own brother.

She got to her feet and turned to face the baron in the light for the first time.

Her mouth went dry.

Viewed from a distance, he had struck her as attractive. Standing as close as he was in the soft light, Katherine realized he was not merely attractive, he was striking. He was long limbed and lean, his simple clothes doing nothing to hide the strong lines of his body. His hair was a rich mahogany, pushed carelessly away from a face crafted of impeccable angles—sharp cheekbones, a straight nose, a strong jaw. His eyes were dark beneath his brow, and they were watching her without expression.

Her insides did a slow, horrifying somersault, and she could feel a flush start to creep into her cheeks. No wonder he had women hanging on his every word. At another time in her life, a time long past, perhaps she might have been one of them.

"*Doctor* is fine," the baron said.

"I'm sorry?" Katherine had lost her train of thought.

"My title, I find, is more of a hindrance than a help when I'm attending my patients."

"He's not your patient, my lord." Whatever unwanted and unwelcome reaction she had just suffered was instantly cured by a considerable dose of irritation. "He's mine."

Strathmore held her eyes for a moment longer before looking down at her brother. "Of course."

Katherine blinked. He wasn't going to argue?

"Though perhaps you might need help getting him up?"

She blinked again, wary of his motivations. The Lord Doctor was being far too reasonable and agreeable. But he was also right. Her father, still hovering with the lantern, didn't have the strength to lift such a deadweight. And alone, neither did she. Matthew was not a small man.

"Yes, thank you." She swallowed her pride with effort and tried to sound at least a little gracious. "I would appreciate it."

Strathmore nodded and bent, carefully pulling the table away. As he heaved it upright, Matthew groaned, and his eyes fluttered open. He stared up at the ceiling, his brow furrowed, before his eyes found Katherine.

"You fell over," she said before he could speak.

Matthew winced and raised his head.

"You really should have listened to your sister," Strathmore added as he settled the heavy, wide table back in place.

"Hayward," Matthew grunted and let his head fall back. "You don't need to take her side. I've had a trying night. Have a little sympathy."

From the far side of the table, her father barked out a laugh, and the shadows from the lantern light danced off the walls.

Katherine scowled. She did not see the humor. And was everyone in her family on familiar terms with the Lord Doctor? Something that they'd failed entirely to mention?

The baron straightened from the table. "How are you feeling?"

"Like I've been bloody well shot." Matthew grimaced and struggled to push himself to his good side. "Help me up."

Strathmore glanced at Katherine. "You take a side, I'll take the other. We'll try not to do any more damage than what's already been done."

Katherine sighed and did as she was instructed because to argue for the sake of argument was petty and ridiculous. Between them they helped Matthew to his feet and eased him back onto the table so that he was once again lying facedown. A sheen of sweat had broken out on Matthew's forehead, and he hissed in pain as he moved.

"Well, that is a bit of a mess." Strathmore bent slightly to peer at her brother's upper back.

"I've been told." Matthew rested his forehead on the table.

"A jealous husband, was it?" The baron sounded amused now. "Didn't get out that window fast enough?"

"Something like that," Matthew mumbled.

Katherine eyed Strathmore. He seemed happy to accept Matthew's nonanswer.

"Well, are you going to fix him up, lass, or are you going

to stare at the doctor all night?" Her father laughed again, though it quickly dissolved into another round of coughing.

Katherine would have been incensed had she not been so worried about the sound of his chest.

"Why don't you come sit back down by the hearth, Mr. Wright?" the baron asked easily. He glanced at Katherine in question, and she gave a him a curt but grateful nod.

She busied herself retrieving the basin of water and the clean towels she had set aside earlier, though she watched Strathmore out of the corner of her eye the entire time. The Lord Doctor took the lantern from her father and hung it back up on its hook in the ceiling. He was now settling her father back in his chair, tucking his blanket around him with an endearing gentleness that made her heart turn over. She could hear the baron murmuring something to her father, and though she couldn't make out the words, she saw her father nod a few times.

Are you going to stare at the doctor all night?

Katherine snatched up her suture kit, turning away from Strathmore. She wasn't going to stare at him at all. Because the Lord Doctor was not endearing. He was unwanted.

She set to cleaning up the new blood that had leaked from Matthew's wound and fetched the bottle of brandy from the sideboard behind her. Smuggled French brandy. Ironic that she should be using it on wounds earned in acquisition of the damn stuff.

She returned to the table, stuffing towels along the edge of Matthew's torso before opening the bottle. "This might sting a bit," was all the warning she gave to her brother before she poured half the contents over his wounds.

Matthew jerked and choked, his hands gripping the edge of the table so hard his knuckles were white. A loud string of curses exploded.

"You could have given him more warning."

Katherine almost dropped the bottle. She hadn't heard Strathmore approach her side. Again.

"Better to just have done with it," she said as her brother wheezed and cursed under her touch. "Better too if he never had cause for me to do it in the first place," she said more loudly.

Matthew groaned.

She poured a measure of liquor into a cup and dropped her needles in, then wiped her hands on the brandy-soaked towels. "You don't have to stay," she said to the baron without looking at him.

"I've nowhere else to be." He reached for the brandy bottle. She could hear him inhale. "Good stuff, this," he said with a note of approval. "Cases of this sell for a bloody fortune in London."

That was exactly the problem. And that was also why Strathmore wasn't endearing. Because comments like that encouraged her brother and, for that matter, her father. Convinced them that their fortunes could be found in contraband.

The brandy wasn't good stuff at all, any more than the tobacco or the tea or the silk was.

Because one day, they were going to get her family killed.

About the Author

RITA Award–winning author Kelly Bowen grew up in Manitoba, Canada. She attended the University of Manitoba and earned a Master of Science degree in veterinary physiology and endocrinology.

But it was Kelly's infatuation with history and a weakness for a good love story that led her down the path of historical romance. When she is not writing, she seizes every opportunity to explore ruins and battlefields.

Currently Kelly lives in Winnipeg with her husband and two boys, all of whom are wonderfully patient with the writing process. Except, that is, when they need a goalie for street hockey.

Learn more at:
   http://www.kellybowen.net
   @kellybowen09
   http://facebook.com/Kelly Bowen

Henrietta Whitlow is leaving behind the life of a very successful courtesan in hopes of making peace with her family in the shires. Newly a baron, Michael Brenner is trying to settle a debt of honor involving Henrietta when he instead loses his heart and learns an important holiday lesson.

For a bonus story from another author that you may love, please turn the page to read

Respect for Christmas by Grace Burrowes.

Respect for Christmas

To those who spend the holidays with family members who will never *get it*. When it comes to family, the season of miracles is 365 days long, or sometimes 366.

Chapter One

My Dearest Brenner,

You will forgive a friend of long-standing for not using your newly acquired honorific. Old habits die hard, though I suppose even an Irish barony is due an occasional nod. In ten or twenty years, perhaps, I will acquire the habit of addressing you as my lord. Perhaps not. In any case, I hope this letter finds you well and anticipating the holidays—or the holiday wassail—with much joy.

The time has come for you to repay that small favor I did you several years ago—the favor that resulted in you eluding capture, torture, and death at the hands of our then-enemies. My request is laughably simple to accomplish for a man of your skills, which is fortunate, for the matter has become urgent. My solicitors tell me I'm in want of a wealthy wife. One must approach the matrimonial lists confident that no stain *will mar one's bachelor escutcheon in the eyes of prospective in-laws.*

Did I ever tell you that I deserve sole credit for raising the celebrated Henrietta Whitlow from the status of bumbling housemaid to consort of dukes and nabobs? The tale impresses even me, who more or less wrote it…

Henrietta Whitlow—a bumpkin's name, of a certainty—joined my domestic staff shortly after I came down from university. A more shy, unworldly, backward creature you never met. She took pride in blacking the andirons and in polishing the candlesticks. She took pride in shining the windows until every parlor reeked of vinegar. She took a painful degree of pride in every domestic chore imaginable, but no pride whatsoever in herself. I changed all of that, though it was a thankless and tedious chore…

I tell you, John Coachman, there is no room at this inn!" The innkeeper banged a palm on the counter, as if knocking down goods at auction.

The coachman, a substantial specimen of middle years, leaned forward so he was nose to nose with the innkeeper.

"Your stable is nearly empty," he said, a Scots burr in every syllable. "Your common room boasts exactly one gentleman awaiting a meal, and you *will* find accommodations for my lady."

Lord Michael Brenner, Baron Angelford, the gentleman in question, sat before the common's largest window, which was close enough to the foyer that he heard every word of the argument between the coachman and the innkeeper. Beyond the window, an enormous traveling coach with spanking yellow wheels and four matched chestnuts stood in the yard. The horses' breath blew white in the frigid air, and one of the wheelers stomped a hoof against frozen ground.

No crest on the coach door, but considerable fine luggage lashed to the roof. Why would an innkeeper with rooms aplenty turn away a wealthy customer?

"I'm expecting other parties," the innkeeper said. "Decent folk who expect decent accommodations."

A woman emerged from the coach. She was attired in a brown velvet cloak with a cream wool scarf about her neck and ears. She was tall and, based on her nimble descent, young. The second woman, a shorter, rounder specimen in a gray cloak, emerged more slowly and teetered to the ground on the arm of a footman.

What self-respecting innkeeper refused accommodations to two women, at least one of whom was quite well-to-do? Michael waited for a drunken lordling or two to stagger from the coach, or one of London's more notorious gamblers—he knew them all—but the footman closed the coach door.

The taller woman removed her scarf and wrapped it about her companion. Michael caught a glimpse of flaming red hair before the awning over the inn's front door obscured the women from view.

Ah, well then. The puzzle began to make sense.

"If you're expecting other parties," the coachman said, "they won't be underfoot until sundown. My lady needs a room for only a few hours, while I find a blacksmith to reset a shoe on my off-side leader."

"My guests might arrive at any moment," the innkeeper shot back. "The sky promises snow, and I don't give reserved rooms away."

The front door opened, an eddy of cold air reaching even into the common room.

"He's being difficult, ma'am," the coachman said to the

red-haired woman. "I'll make the cheating blighter see reason."

"Mr. Murphy's difficult demeanor is one of the reliable institutions on this delightful route," the lady said. "Rather like the potholes and not quite as inconvenient as the highwaymen. Fortunately, Mrs. Murphy's excellent house-keeping is equally trustworthy. How much, Mr. Murphy?"

The woman's tone was cultured and amused, but also just a shade too low, a touch too knowing. Had the common been full of men, every one of them would have eavesdropped on the conversation because her voice was that alluring.

"No amount of coin will produce an extra room," Murphy retorted. "Your kind think everything can be bought, but I run a proper establishment."

"*My kind* is simply a cold, tired traveler far from home and willing to pay for warmth and privacy. A room, please."

Coin slid across the counter. Murphy watched the lady's gloved hand and then studied the gold glinting up from the worn wood.

"I told you after your last visit, Henrietta Whitlow, you are not welcome here. Now be off with you."

"And you call yourself an innkeeper," the coachman sneered. "A woman willing to pay you good coin for a short respite from the elements, and you send her back out into the cold when anybody—"

"Excuse me," Michael said, rising from his table and joining the group at the front desk. "I couldn't help but over-hear. Miss Whitlow is welcome to use my rooms."

"But, sir!" Murphy expostulated. "You don't know to whom you're offering such a kindness. I have good, sub-stantial reasons for not allowing just anybody to bide under this roof."

Michael well knew to whom the innkeeper was being so rude.

He passed Miss Whitlow's coins to the coachman. "The holidays are upon us, Mr. Murphy, which means the weather is unpredictable, and travel is both dangerous and trying. The lady and her companion are welcome to use the parlor connected to my bedchamber. The hospitality extended is not yours, but mine, and as my guests, you will please show them every courtesy. Miss Whitlow."

He bowed to the redhead, who executed a graceful curtsey in response. Her companion had come inside and watched the goings-on in unsmiling silence.

"My thanks," Miss Whitlow said. "Though to whom am I expressing my gratitude?"

"Michael Brenner, at your service. Mr. Murphy, the ladies will take a meal and a round of toddies in your private parlor once they've refreshed themselves above stairs. John Coachman and madam's staff will similarly need sustenance and hospitality. Do I make myself clear?"

Murphy scowled at Miss Whitlow, who regarded him with the level stare of a cat deciding whether the menu would feature mouse, songbird, or fricassee of innkeeper.

The scandal sheets and tattlers didn't do Henrietta Whitlow justice. Her features were just one degree off from cameo perfection—her nose a shade too aquiline, her mouth too full, her eyebrows a bit too dramatic, her height an inch too grand—and the result was unforgettable beauty. Michael had seen her from a distance at the theater many times, but up close, her impact was…more than physical.

Duels had been fought over Henrietta Whitlow, fortunes wagered, and her amatory skills had become the stuff of legend.

"Mr. Brenner, might I invite you to join us?" Miss

Whitlow asked. "You are our host, after all, and good company always makes time pass more pleasantly."

The invitation was bold but, at a coaching inn, not outlandishly improper.

"I was awaiting my own midday meal," Michael said. "I'll be happy to join you."

Michael's day had been laid out according to a careful plan, but plans changed, and opportunities sometimes came along unlooked for. A man didn't have a chance to share a meal with London's most sought-after courtesan every day, and Michael had been growing damned hungry waiting for Murphy to produce a bowl of soup and some bread.

Nothing about Lord Angelford's demeanor suggested he expected Henrietta to repay his kindness with intimate favors, though she knew better than to trust him. British gentlemen were randy creatures, particularly wealthy, titled British gentlemen.

His lordship had chosen not to mention that title. Henrietta and Angelford hadn't been introduced, but Michael Brenner would soon learn that newly minted barons had almost as little privacy as courtesans.

His lordship was tall and handsome, though not precisely dark. His hair was auburn, and his voice bore a hint of Ireland overlaid with plenty of English public school. He was exquisitely attired in tall boots, breeches, brown riding jacket, and fine linen, and his waistcoat was gold with subtle green embroidery vining throughout.

Newly titled, but a lord to the teeth already. Such men took good care of their toys, from snuffboxes, to hunters, to dueling pistols, to mistresses.

Henrietta was heartily sick of being a well-cared-for toy.

Lord Angelford ushered her into a cozy parlor with a blazing fire and a dining table set for four. Lucille trundled along as well—she was fiercer than any mastiff when it came to Henrietta's safety—and passed Henrietta her scarf.

"If madam will excuse me," Lucille said, "I'll step upstairs for a moment while we're waiting for a meal."

"Take your time," Henrietta replied, then fell silent as Lucille bustled off. A courtesan excelled at conversation, Henrietta was exhausted, however, and fatigue predisposed her to babbling. A self-possessed quiet was always a far better course than babbling.

"May I take your cloak?" his lordship asked.

"Of course." She passed him her scarf, then undid the frogs of her cloak and peeled it from her shoulders. In London, Henrietta would have made sure to gild the moment with a brush of fingers or a lingering gaze, because a courtesan never knew who her next protector might be.

London, thank the Almighty and John Coachman's skill, was many snowy miles to the south. Henrietta hoped never to see its smoky, crowded, noisy like again.

Nothing in Angelford's gaze lingered—another small mercy. After he hung Henrietta's cloak and scarf on the hooks on the back of the door, he held a chair for her.

"Have you far to go?" he asked, taking the opposite seat. He'd put Henrietta closest to the fire, and the heat was heavenly.

"Another day or so, weather permitting. What of yourself?"

The distance Henrietta wished to travel, from the pinnacle of the demimonde clear back to respectability, was far indeed. Some had managed, such as Charles Fox Pitt's widow, but she'd taken years and years to accomplish that feat and had called upon a store of charm Henrietta could only envy.

"I am traveling to my estate in Oxfordshire," his lordship said, "and tending to some business along the way. Will you celebrate the holidays with family?"

Henrietta's brothers and their wives hadn't cut her off, but Papa was another matter. "My plans are as yet unconfirmed. Have we met before, Mr. Brenner?"

She wanted the dangling sword of her former occupation either cut loose from over her head, or plunged into her already bleak mood.

Damn the holidays anyway.

"We have not been introduced, though I'm sure we have mutual acquaintances. The Duke of Anselm and I have invested in the same ventures on occasion."

Henrietta's last protector, and the best of a curious lot. His Grace was married now, and happily so.

The varlet.

"Then you are aware of my reputation, *your lordship*. If you'd prefer my maid and I dine without you, I'll understand." Henrietta wished he'd go strutting on his handsome way. Men either wanted something from her, or reproached her for what other men paid handsomely to take from her. The hypocrisy was as stunning as it was lucrative.

"Miss Whitlow, I make it a habit not to judge people on the strength of reputation. Too often, public opinion is based on hearsay, anecdote, and convenience, and when one meets the object of gossip in person, the reality is either disappointing or dismaying. The beef stew here is above reproach, though I've sustained myself mainly on bread, cheese, and ham."

A serving maid brought in a tray of toddies, and the scent alone nearly made Henrietta weep. She was cold, exhausted, angry, and should not be taking spirits, but these toddies would be scrumptious.

"I asked you to join me for the meal," she said, "so Murphy would not serve me boiled shoe leather with a side of week-old cabbage. You mustn't think me hospitable."

His lordship set a steaming toddy before her. "I think you tired, chilled, and in need of a meal. As it happens, so am I. Happy Christmas, Miss Whitlow."

He touched his glass to hers and waited for Henrietta to take a sip of hot, sweet, spicy heaven. The spirits were good quality—not fit for a duke, but fit for a retired courtesan. When his lordship launched into a discourse about the potential for increased legal trade in Scottish whisky—of all the undrinkable offenses to pleasurable dining—Henrietta wondered if the baron might be that rarest of specimens, the true British gentleman.

~

Michael was already engaged in thievery, a skill he'd hoped never to rely on again. He was stealing the trust of a woman who would doubtless prefer he take her last groat or the clothes off her back. He didn't need her money, and he didn't want her trust.

The yearning to remove the clothes from her back filled him with a combination of self-loathing, amusement, and wistfulness.

"Happy Christmas, your lordship," Miss Whitlow said, taking a sip of her toddy. "Why did you introduce yourself without the title?"

He hadn't noticed that blunder—for it was a blunder. "Habit," Michael said, which was the damned sorry truth. "My last employer was of such consequence he could command favors from the sovereign. A barony was the marquess's way of thanking me for years of loyal service, or so he claimed."

Miss Whitlow held her drink in both hands, and even that—the way she cradled a goblet of hot spirits with pale, unadorned fingers—had a sensual quality.

"You refer to the Marquess of Heathgate," Miss Whitlow said. "A refreshingly direct man, in my experience, and he hasn't a vain bone in his body. My path hasn't crossed his for years."

Arrogant, Lord Heathgate certainly was, but the lady was right—the marquess was not vain. "What you call direct, others have deemed shockingly ungenteel. I suspect hanging a title about my neck was Heathgate's way of getting even for my decision to leave his employ. A joke, by his lights."

She traced her finger about the rim of her glass, and Michael would have sworn the gesture was not intended to be seductive.

"The marquess's jest has not left you laughing, my lord."

If he asked her to call him Michael, she'd probably leave the table, if not the inn. "When I turned in my notice, the marquess wasn't laughing either." Though Heathgate had probably known Michael was contemplating a departure before Michael had admitted it to himself. They'd been a good fit as lord and lackey, a rarity for them both, particularly prior to the marquess's marriage.

Miss Whitlow took another leisurely sip of her drink. "Is this where you lament the terrible burden placed upon you by wealth, consequence, and the sovereign's recognition?"

Mother Mary, she was bold, but then, a courtesan had to be. "I was born bog Irish, Miss Whitlow. You could hang a dukedom on me, and the stink of peat would still precede me everywhere. I respect coin of the realm as only one who's done without it can, but I don't give a counterfeit farthing for titles, styles, or posturing."

The maid intruded again, this time bearing bowls of steaming soup, a small loaf of bread, and a tub of butter.

She'd bobbed half a curtsey and headed for the door when Michael thought to ask, "Would you like a pot of tea, Miss Whitlow? Or chocolate, perhaps?"

"Tea would be lovely. Gunpowder, if it's available."

He would have taken her for a hot chocolate sort of a woman, but he liked that she'd surprised him. So few people did.

"If titles, styles, and posturing don't earn your respect, what does?" she asked.

Michael knew what she was about, turning the conversation always to him, his opinions, his preferences, and yet, he liked even the fiction of interest from her.

Which was not good at all.

"I admire honesty, courage, learning, and determination." *Says the man bent on deceiving a woman who's done nothing to deserve the slight.* "What about you?"

She tore off a chunk of bread, there being no serrated knife on the table. "Honesty is too often counted a virtue, even when it causes an unkind result, and education is largely a privilege of wealthy men. I value compassion, tolerance, and humor. Determination has a place, provided it's tempered by wisdom. Would you please pass the butter?"

A lady would have waited until somebody produced the proper sort of bread knife and recalled to pass her the butter rather than make do and speak up. Such ladies likely endured much needless hunger and unbuttered bread.

"I'll trade you," Michael said, passing over the butter and appropriating the rest of the loaf. "Where do you suppose your companion has got off to?"

Miss Whitlow dabbed a generous portion of butter onto her bread, considered the result, then added more.

"Lucille is exhausted from packing up my household, getting the new tenant settled, and organizing my remove to Oxfordshire. I suspect the poor dear is fast asleep on the sofa in your parlor. I can fetch her down here, if you would rather we have a third at the table."

She turned the same gaze on him she'd treated the innkeeper to: feline, amused, and subtly challenging. No wonder princes and dukes had vied for her favors.

"I'm sure, Miss Whitlow, that my virtue, or what's left of it, is safe in your hands. Unless you're concerned that my behavior will transgress the bounds of your tolerance, we can allow Lucille her rest."

She popped a bite of bread into her mouth. "Your virtue, and the virtue of the male of the species generally, is safe from my predation. I've retired from that game, not that I ever had to stalk the poor, defenseless male. Behave how you please, provided you don't expect me to allow the soup to get cold."

Henrietta Whitlow had retired? Michael belonged to several clubs, though not the loftiest or the most expensive. He owned gaming enterprises among other businesses, rubbed shoulders with journalists and Bow Street runners, and remained current on all the gossip as a matter of business necessity.

Also, old habit, and he'd heard nothing of her retirement. "Am I the first to learn of this decision?" He'd known she was journeying to Oxford for the holidays, as she had every year for the past five, but not that she'd removed from the capital entirely.

She gestured dismissively with the buttered bread. "My comings and goings are hardly news. The soup is good, compared to some I've had. Mr. Murphy apparently respects your custom."

"Or my coin," Michael replied, taking a spoonful of steamy beef broth. "May I ask what precipitated your decision to quit London?"

He ought not to have inquired. The question was personal as hell, and a criminal's professional detachment was integral to achieving Michael's objective.

"I'm not simply quitting London, my lord, I'm quitting my profession. My reasons are personal, though boredom figured prominently among them."

She took a dainty spoonful of soup, when Michael wanted to salute her with his drink. She'd been bored by the amatory attentions of aristocrats and nabobs? Bored by the loveliest jewelry the Ludgate goldsmiths had on offer? Even the king had expressed an interest in furthering his acquaintance with Henrietta Whitlow, without apparent result.

On behalf of the male gender, Michael acknowledged a set-down all the more devastating for being offered with casual humor.

"Maybe you aren't bored so much as angry," he suggested.

Miss Whitlow drained her toddy. "My upbringing was such that my temper is seldom in evidence. I do find it tedious when a man who barely knows me presumes to tell me what sentiment holds sway over my heart. Boredom and I are intimately acquainted, my lord. I try to keep my distance from anger."

She wrinkled her nose at the dregs in her cup.

Michael suspected Henrietta Whitlow's temper could cinder London, if she ever cut loose, and every red-blooded male over the age of fourteen would line up to admire the spectacle at peril to his own continued existence.

Men were idiots, as Michael's four sisters constantly reminded him. "Shall I order more toddies?"

"The tea should be along shortly, and my appreciation for a hot, sweet cup of pure gunpowder rivals my love of books."

Another surprise. "Books?"

"You know," she said, dipping her buttered bread into her soup. "Pages, printing, knowledge, and whacking good stories. Growing up, my brothers were given free run of my father's library. I was limited to sermons, lest my feeble female brain become overheated with Mr. Crusoe's adventures. I'll have the rest of the bread, if you don't care for it."

An Irishman treasured fresh bread and butter almost as much as he favored a good ale. Michael passed her the remains of the loaf.

"What's your favorite book?"

As they consumed their meal, Miss Whitlow gave up a small clue to her soul: She knew her literature, as did Michael. He'd come late to his letters and had studied learned tomes as a way to compensate for a lack of education. Henrietta Whitlow had a passion for books that had probably stood her in good stead among Oxford graduates and comforted her on those occasions when the Oxford graduates had proven poor company.

The maid arrived to clear the plates, a half-grown boy on her heels bearing a tray.

"Mrs. Murphy sends along the plum tarts with her compliments," the maid said, setting a bowl down before Miss Whitlow, then a small blue crock of cream.

"How very gracious of her," Miss Whitlow said as the maid served Michael his portion. "The soup was excellent, and the bread perfect. Please thank everybody from the scullery maid who churned the butter to Mrs. Murphy. The kitchen here is truly a marvel."

From across the table, Michael watched as Miss Whitlow offered the maid a smile so purely warm-hearted, the half-grown boy nearly dropped the tray and the serving maid's curtsey would have flattered a queen. That smile made all right with the world and gave gleeful assurances of happy endings just waiting to come true.

Harmon DeWitt, Viscount Beltram, still spoke fondly of that smile, even as he plotted against the woman who bestowed it.

"My thanks as well," Michael said. "Would you be so good as to ensure that Miss Whitlow's maid has some sustenance? She's enjoying a respite in the parlor adjoined to my bedchamber."

"Certainly, sir. Come along, Gordie."

The lad tried for a bow, but kept his gaze on Miss Whitlow the entire time. She winked at the boy as he backed from the room.

"You'll spoil him for all other ladies," Michael said.

The smile faded into a brittle light in Miss Whitlow's eyes. "Good. We should all exercise the greatest discernment when choosing with whom to share our time and our trust. If I've preserved him from a few scheming chambermaids—for chambermaids are not to be trusted where juvenile males are concerned—then he's better off."

Nothing in her tone suggested even mild annoyance, and yet, Michael sensed reproof again—no creature on earth was less of a threat to anybody than a harried chambermaid—or... something sadder.

Bitterness, perhaps. Well-earned, entirely appropriate bitterness.

Happy Christmas, indeed.

Chapter Two

...*Seducing a housemaid ought to be the work of an evening, one doesn't have to be a peer to grasp that fundamental truth. Henrietta had a deceptively strong will, however, and her morals did not yield easily to seduction. After much importuning and not a few stolen liberties, some of which might have borne a slight resemblance to threats to her livelihood, insight befell me.*

What the poor thing wanted more than a good tumble was simple attention. She wanted my company, not my cock, for she'd been raised in the household of some selfish old Puritan and a pair of equally gormless brothers. For all her awkward height, her unfortunate red hair, and her Cyprian's form, she thought herself invisible.

And thus, to many she was. But being a man of discernment, I saw her potential...

Baron Angelford did not conform to Henrietta's expectations, though it took her half the soup and most of the bread to recognize the source of her annoyance. He was supposed to steal a glance at her breasts, then smile at her, as if his leering were not only a compliment, but a clever, original compliment.

He should have stolen a sip from her drink then treated her to a smug grin, as if in the history of the male gender, no other fellow had ever been so subtle in his overtures, or so worthy of her notice.

He might have at least accidentally brushed his boot against hers under the table.

Instead, he'd confided that he memorized Shakespearean insults in an effort to impress the English boys with whom he'd gone to school.

"Did that work?" Henrietta asked around a mouthful of plum tart.

"Not exactly. A two-hundred-year-old insult usually falls flat, but I gained a reputation for knowing the Bard, and thus earned extra coin tutoring those upperclassmen unequal to the subtleties of *Hamlet* and *Othello*."

"I would have given much to read those plays as a girl," Henrietta said. "I bought myself a complete, bound edition when I'd been in London for less than a year. My first Christmas token to myself."

She still had that gift and had spent many a night at the theater longing to be home with the Scottish play, rather than smiling at some randy earl.

"What would you like for Christmas this year?" his lordship asked.

What Henrietta wanted was impossible. A succession of titled, wealthy men and her own choices had seen to that.

"Books are always a good choice," she said, "though they come dear. Good tea, and I'm perilously fond of warm stockings." The toddy on top of the fatigue had pried that bit of honesty from her.

Or perhaps she could blame his lordship's ability to truly listen to a conversational partner.

"We can agree on the stockings," he said. "I have four sisters, and I value their knitting skills almost as much as their abilities in the kitchen. I'm fond of a good Irish whiskey, particularly in a cup of strong coffee with a healthy portion of cream."

"Sounds like a waste of good cream." Henrietta liked knowing his lordship had somebody to fuss over him and keep him in good stockings. Truly, she'd consumed her spirits too quickly. "You're letting that plum tart go to waste, my lord."

"I'm not fond of plums, while you appear to relish them." He passed his bowl across the table, and for Henrietta, the moment became fraught with bewilderment. Men stole a bite of her sweets, they did not offer their own, whole and untouched.

"Take it," his lordship said. "I cannot abide food going to waste or a smoking chimney."

Henrietta took a bite of his tart. "What else can't you abide?"

In the course of the meal, he'd become less the titled gentleman and more the hungry fellow enjoying good fare. How had he gone from bog Irish to baron? The journey had doubtless required calculation and daring, much like becoming a wealthy courtesan.

Henrietta had decided by the end of her first year in London that the appellation "successful courtesan" was a contradiction—what female could consider lost virtue a hallmark of success?—but "wealthy courtesan" ought to be a redundant term.

"I'm not fond of winter travel," his lordship said. "For business reasons, I undertook many journeys on the Continent when wiser men would have remained at home, far from war or wintertime coach trips."

Those journeys had doubtless been lucrative, but they'd clearly taken a toll as well.

"All of that is behind you," Henrietta said. "You're titled, wealthy, have all your teeth, and know some excellent insults. The holidays find you in possession of many blessings."

Teasing men was the natural result of having grown up with an older brother and a younger one. *Tease and be teased, lest Papa's sternness suck all the joy from the marrow of life's bones.* Henrietta wasn't teasing her companion, though. She was offering him the same philosophical comfort she offered herself.

It's in the past. No use crying over spilled virtue. You'll never know want or have to step and fetch for another man. Never.

"You look wistful," the baron said. "My mother used to detest the holidays. I can't say all the folderol is much to my taste either."

"Is that why you're repairing to your family seat rather than remaining in Town?"

His smile was crooked, charming, and entirely unexpected. "It's not my family seat, is it? It's simply the real estate I purchased in hopes my great-grandchildren might think of it as home."

Lord Angelford was a bachelor. Henrietta kept track, because she had never, ever shared her favors with engaged or married men.

"To have great-grandchildren, you'll first have to acquire a few children, my lord. Perhaps next Season you'll start on the prerequisites for that venture."

Bride-hunting, in other words. Year after year, Henrietta had watched the marriage machinations from the outer periphery of polite society, half-affronted on behalf of the young ladies, half-envious of the respectability that was the price of admission for the race to the altar.

"If I seek a bride," his lordship said, "the social Season won't have much to do with it. In addition to four sisters, I have two brothers, and one has obliged me with three nephews. They are naughty, rambunctious, entirely dear boys, and any one of them would make a fine baron."

"I have nephews." Another unplanned admission. "They both have my red hair, and the youngest..." Henrietta had a niece as well, though she'd never met the child.

At some point, his lordship had shed his jacket—the room was toasty—and he'd turned back his cuffs. Each departure from strict propriety made him more attractive, which ought not to have been the case. Henrietta had learned to appreciate—and mentally appraise—masculine tailoring down to the penny.

What lay beneath the tailoring was usually a matter of indifference to her.

"Those small boys are why you quit London," the baron said. "You love them madly."

"A courtesan doesn't love, my lord. She adores, treasures, or is fond of." Eventually. At first she loved, and then she learned to be more careful.

"You love those children. My youngest nephew is a terror. The child scares the daylights out of me, and I can only guess at the prayers my sister-in-law has said to keep his guardian angels ever vigilant."

"You're a Papist?"

"Church of England, though my mother has likely haranguing the Deity to correct that mistake since the moment she gained her place next to St. Patrick."

His tone said he'd been fond of his mother, and worse yet, he missed her. Henrietta had been missing her own mother for more than twenty years.

"I used to dress in widow's weeds and slip into the back of St. George's on rainy Sundays." Only Lucille knew this, though Henrietta was certain her secret was safe with his lordship. "I missed services, though my father would say my attendance was blaspheming."

His lordship patted Henrietta's hand. "Papas are the worst. My mother often reassured me of that, and I pass the sentiment along to my nephews."

His touch was warm and surprising for its pure friendliness. The contact must have taken him aback as well, because when the maid bustled through the door, his fingers yet lingered on Henrietta's knuckles.

"Madam's coachman is come back," the maid said. "He be cursing something powerful in the common, and I do believe it's starting to snow again. The smithy's gone off to Oxford to spend the holidays with his sweetheart's family. Murphy could have told John Coachman as much. Don't know why he didn't."

She piled dishes on a tray as she spoke, and Henrietta's sentimental reminiscences collided, as sentiment so often did, with hard reality.

"I'll have to bribe Murphy into renting me a room," Henrietta said, taking a last sip of tepid gunpowder. "You will excuse me, my—"

She'd started to rise, but the baron stayed her with a raised hand. "My room is available to you, should you wish to tarry here for the duration, though you might be weeks waiting for the smithy to return."

One of the greatest pleasures of falling from grace was learning to curse. Henrietta instead fell back on the words of one of her few old friends.

"Blasts and fogs upon this weather. I cannot take your rooms from you, my lord. I'll probably end up buying a horse before I can journey onward, and it will be the most expensive nag this village ever sent limping onto the king's highway."

"You quote *King Lear*," the baron replied. "And you need not tarry here at all. I'm traveling on in the direction of Oxford, and you're welcome to share my coach. I can see about hiring you a spare horse when we reach the next coaching inn."

He offered assistance, with no apparent thought of anything in return.

Years of disappointment made Henrietta cautious. "I will pay for any horses myself, my lord."

"Will you at least accept my company as far as the next coaching inn?"

She shouldn't. She really truly should not, but he'd surrendered his plum tart and understood the desperation with which she loved her nephews.

"As far as the next coaching inn," Henrietta said. "No farther."

⁓

"Mordecai MacFergus, as I live and breathe. What are you doing so far south of a proper Scotsman's home?"

Despite the cold, the stingy innkeeper, and the dodgy off-leader, MacFergus's heart lifted at the sound of his native Strathclyde accents.

"If it isn't wee Liam Logan," he said, extending a hand and striding up the aisle of the stable. "How long has it been? Two years since I laid eyes on your ugly face?"

Logan shook hands and offered his flask. "At least, and we were on the Great North Road, God rot its ruts to hell. Tell me how your family goes on."

In the relative warmth and privacy of the stable, they caught up, as two coachmen will, passing the time happily with news of home and news of others who plied their trade. Like most coachmen, Logan was a healthy specimen, his cheeks reddened by the elements, his face weathered, and his grip crushing.

"So who's the fancy gent?" MacFergus asked as the horses munched hay and winter breezes stirred bits of straw in the barn's dirt aisle. The smell of the stable would ever be his favorite—horses, leather, fodder, and even the occasional whiff of manure.

Nothing fertilized a garden like good old horse shit.

Logan made a fancy bow. "You see before you the coach-man to Michael, Baron Angelford, and he's anything but fancy. I'm working for an Irishman, MacFergus, one with a proper estate not forty miles on and a proper title, though he's an Irishman among the English."

The English and the Scots had an uneasy tolerance for each other, while the Irish, who'd attempted a rebellion as recently as 1798, didn't fare as well on English soil. They had their peers and grand estates, but in the hierarchy of peerages, the Irish duke ranked below his English and Scottish counterparts and was seldom allowed to forget it.

"Lonely business, being Irish among the English," MacFergus said. "My lady is no stranger to loneliness. I've been driving for Miss Whitlow since she acquired her first coach and team, nearly eight years ago, and you never met a better employer."

Logan tipped his flask up and shook the last drops into his mouth, then tucked the empty flask into his pocket.

"That's always the way of it, isn't it? Them as the Quality disdain can be the most decent, while the earls and dukes will leave good horses standing in the cold for hours outside the Christmas ball."

A gelding two stalls down lifted its tail and broke wind in staccato bursts.

"Caspar agrees with you," MacFergus said. "Your baron was right considerate of my lady, despite Murphy's pernickety airs."

A barn tabby leaped down from the rafters, strutted along a beam, then hopped to a manger and to the floor. Logan picked up the animal and gave it a scratching about the ears.

"So it's like that, is it?" he said. "My Mary got by as best she could before we married. Many a village girl does when she comes to London. Many a Town girl does too, and some of the goings-on at the house parties, Morty MacFergus, would shame the devil."

Miss Henrietta did not attend house parties, and her household conducted itself properly, but for the comings and goings of the gentleman with whom she'd contracted a liaison. Those comings and goings were undertaken discreetly, which Lucille claimed was a written condition signed by both parties.

"My lady was a good girl, from what I hear," MacFergus said, "and then she went into service. Been some time since a gent treated her proper."

"A pity that, but the baron's no stranger to them with poor manners. His own family can't be bothered to join him at the holidays. He'll be all alone in the great hall come Christmas morning, and that's just not right. I've had more than a few wee drams with my lord over a hand of cards, though you mustn't tell any I said that."

Coachmen were privy to an employer's secrets. They knew who called upon whom and who was never at home even when they were clearly within the dwelling. They knew who was invited to which entertainments, who skipped Sunday services, and which gentlemen paid very-late-night calls upon the wives of friends.

A baron sharing a flask and a frequent hand of cards with his coachman, though...Not the done thing.

"My lady travels to see her family at the holidays," MacFergus said, "and they barely welcome her. She stays at an inn rather than with any of them and calls on her brothers as if she were some distant cousin. Her own father won't stay in the same room with her, though my lady never complains of him."

Lucille, usually as taciturn as a nun, ranted about Squire Whitlow's treatment of his daughter. As the holidays came closer, Lucille became more grim, for nothing would dissuade Miss Henrietta from her annual pilgrimage to Oxfordshire.

"Damned rotten English," Logan said. "My oldest—you recall my Angus?—has three girls. He'd never treat one of his own so shabbily, much less at Yuletide, or my Mary would serve him a proper thrashing and I'd cut the birch rod for her."

Quiet descended, underscored by the sound of horses at their hay and the cat purring in Logan's arms.

"Logan, we're a pair of decent, God-fearing men, aren't we?"

Logan set the cat down and dusted his hands. "You're about to get me in trouble, Morty MacFergus, like that time you suggested we put that frog in Mrs. MacMurtry's water glass."

"You're the one who came up with that idea." Always full of mischief, was Liam Logan. "Your baron is lonely, my Miss Henrietta is lonely, and they're rubbing on well enough as we speak. All I'm suggesting is that we take a wee hand in making their holidays a little brighter."

"No coachman has wee hands."

"And nobody should be alone at Christmas."

"Can't argue with that."

"We're agreed, then," MacFergus said, slinging an arm around his friend's shoulders. "I have a few ideas."

"You have a full flask as well, or my name's not Liam Patrick MacPherson Logan."

"Aye, that I do." MacFergus passed the flask over. "Mind you attend me, because we'll have to be subtle."

Caspar broke wind again as the two coachmen disappeared into the warmth and privacy of the harness room.

Most of Michael's travel on the Continent had been aimed at gathering intelligence while appearing to transact business. An Irishman, assumed to be at odds with the British crown, had a margin of safety his English counterparts did not, and Michael had exploited that margin to the last limit.

Missions went awry all the time, and this encounter with Henrietta Whitlow had just gone very awry indeed. The dratted woman had scrambled his wits, with her smile, her ferocious love for her nephews, and her wary regard for all assistance.

"Shall we transfer your trunks to my vehicle?" Michael asked.

Wrong question. Miss Whitlow tossed a wrinkled linen serviette onto the empty table. "I see no need to impose on you to that degree."

"I have sisters and know that a lady likes her personal effects about her. Even if the next coaching inn is more obliging, you might spend a few days there, depending on the availability of a blacksmith."

Michael could have reset a damned shoe, provided a forge was available. He'd been hoping his quarry would either spend the night at Murphy's establishment, where she'd broken her journey before, or bide long enough to allow a thorough search of her effects.

A loose horseshoe was a metaphor for the course of most missions—good luck mixed with bad, depending on perspective and agenda.

"I'll fetch a small valise of necessities," Miss Whitlow said. "Give me fifteen minutes to rouse Lucille and assemble our immediate needs."

Before Michael could hold her chair, she rose and swept from the room. In her absence, the little chamber became cramped instead of cozy, the peat fire smoky rather than fragrant. In future, Michael would have more respect for Mrs. Murphy's toddies, and for Henrietta Whitlow's legendary charm.

He paid the shot, summoned his coach, and gave instructions to his grooms to prepare for departure. By the time those arrangements had been made, Miss Whitlow and her maid stood at the bottom of the inn's stairs, the maid looking no less dour for having stolen a nap.

"I don't like it," Miss Whitlow's coachman was saying. "The weather is turning up dirty, yon baron has no one to vouch for him, and this blighted excuse for a sheep crossing likely hasn't a spare coach horse at any price."

"Then I'll buy one at the next coaching inn and send it back to you, MacFergus," Miss Whitlow said. "His lordship has offered to tend to the purchase if the next inn is as disobliging as Mr. Murphy tried to be."

Michael strode into the foyer, Miss Whitlow's cloak over his arm. "I understand your caution," he said to the coachman, "but as it happens, Miss Whitlow and I are both journeying to Oxfordshire, and if need be, I can deliver her to her family's very doorstep. Your concern is misplaced."

He draped the velvet cloak over Miss Whitlow's shoulders when she obligingly turned her back. The urge to smooth his hands over feminine contours was eclipsed only by the knowledge that too many other men had assumed that privilege without Miss Whitlow's permission.

"My concern is not misplaced," the coachman retorted. "See that my lady's trust and her effects aren't either."

"MacFergus, the baron has no need to steal my fripperies," Miss Whitlow said, patting her coachman's arm. "Enjoy a respite from the elements, and don't worry about me. Lucille is the equal of any highwayman, and his lordship has been all that is gentlemanly."

Lucille smirked at the coachman, who stomped off toward the door.

"I'll be having a look at the baron's conveyance," he said. "And making sure his coachman knows in what direction Oxford lies."

"Don't worry," Michael said to the ladies as the door closed on a gust of frigid air. "My coachman is Scottish as well. He tells me two Scotsmen on English soil are under a blood oath not to kill each other by any means except excessive drink. The Irish try to observe the same courtesy with each other, with limited success."

"It's the same with those of my profession in London,"

Miss Whitlow said. "My former profession. We never disparage each other, never judge one another in public. Why bother, when polite society delights endlessly in treating us ill?"

Lucille cleared her throat and stared at a point beyond Miss Whitlow's left shoulder.

"Shall we be on our way?" Michael offered his arm, and Miss Whitlow took it.

Murphy was not on hand to see his guests off, which in any other hostelry would have been rank neglect. As Michael held the door for the ladies, the serving maid rushed forth from the common with a closed basket.

"From the missus. She says safe journey."

Lucille took the basket as the girl scampered back to the kitchen.

Michael handed the women into his coach, which boasted heated bricks and velvet upholstery, then climbed in and confronted a dilemma. Lucille had taken the backward-facing seat, while Miss Whitlow sat on the forward-facing bench.

A gentleman did not presume, but neither did he willingly sit next to a maid glaring daggers at him. Michael was on the point of taking the place beside Lucille anyway, when insight came to his aid.

To eschew the place beside Miss Whitlow would be to judge her, and for Miss Whitlow to sit on the backward-facing seat with her maid would have been to assume the status of a servant.

What complicated terrain she inhabited, and how tired she must be of never putting a foot wrong on perpetually boggy ground.

"May I?" Michael asked, gesturing to the place beside the lady.

"Of course." She twitched her skirts and cloak aside, and Michael took his seat. At two thumps of his fist on the coach roof, the coach moved off.

The vehicle was warm and the road reasonably free of traffic. One of the advantages of winter travel was a lack of mud, or less mud than during any other season, and thus the horses could keep up a decent pace. Michael's objective was simply to learn where Miss Whitlow would spend the night, so that he could steal a certain object from her, one she might not even value very highly.

He considered asking to purchase the book, but coin carried the potential to insult a former courtesan, particularly one whose decision to depart from propriety had made her wealthy.

Fortunately, Miss Whitlow had failed to notice that the trunks lashed atop Michael's coach were her own.

A soft snore from the opposite bench sounded in rhythm with the horses' hoof beats.

"Poor Lucille is worn out," Miss Whitlow said softly. "She does two things when we travel any distance. Swill hot tea at every opportunity and nap."

"What of the highwaymen?" Michael asked. "Who guards you from them?"

"I guard myself."

Michael mentally translated the words into Latin, because they had the ring of a battle cry. "My barony needs a motto. That might do."

"Better if your family can say, 'We guard each other,'" Miss Whitlow replied. "My grandmother certainly tried to guard me."

Where were her father and brothers when she had needed guarding? "My grandmother was the fiercest woman in County Mayo, excepting perhaps my great-grandmother.

Grannie lived to be ninety-two, and not even the earl upon whose land her cottage sat would have gainsaid her. You put me in mind of her."

The coach hit a rut, disturbing the rhythm of Lucille's snores and tossing Miss Whitlow against Michael's shoulder.

"In mind of her, how?"

"She was independent without being needlessly stubborn, and she judged people on their merits, not their trappings. Could quote Scripture by the hour, but also knew poems I doubt have been written down. You and she could have discussed books until the sun came up."

Michael's recitation purposely mentioned no aspect of Miss Whitlow's appearance, though Gran had been ginger-haired in her younger days.

"My grandmother was rumored to be part Rom," Miss Whitlow said. "My father denied it, which only makes me think it more likely to be true."

For a woman who'd been self-supporting for nearly a decade, Miss Whitlow mentioned her father rather a lot. Josiah Whitlow lived in Oxfordshire, not five miles from Michael's property, which was what had given Beltram the idea of sending Michael after the damned book in the first place.

Three months ago, Beltram had invited himself to tea with Henrietta and had seen the tome tucked among some risqué volumes of poetry in her sitting room. With any luck, she'd tossed Beltram's scribblings into the fire when dissolving her household.

"Was your grandmother a lover of books?" Michael asked.

"She was passionate about literature, in part because she taught herself to read after she'd married. She stole out of bed and puzzled over her son's school books, then got the housekeeper to help her. She loved telling me that story."

"I learned by puzzling over my younger brother's books too, then an uncle whose fortunes had improved stepped in and off to public school I went."

Public school had been awful for an Irish upstart with no academic foundation, but Michael had guzzled knowledge like a drover downs ale at the end of a long summer march.

Miss Whitlow studied the snow intensifying beyond the window. "Will you tell me the same lie all titled men tell about public school, and claim you loved it?"

Titled men probably told her worse lies than that. "I learned a lot, and also came to value information in addition to learning. Did you know that James Merton, heir to the Victor family earldom, wet his bed until he was fourteen?"

"Wet his—? Really?" She purely delighted in this tidbit, and who wouldn't? Merton was a handsome, wealthy horse's arse who fancied himself an arbiter of fashion.

With a glance over at Lucille, Miss Whitlow leaned closer. "He's also afraid of mice. Screams like a banshee at the sight of one and has been known to climb a bedpost if he thinks one is under the—oh dear."

She sat up as straight as she could in a moving coach. "I should not have said that. Not to you, but his mistress told me that herself, and I have no reason...I should not have said such a thing. I do apologize. You must never repeat it, or a woman I consider a friend could lose her livelihood."

Mary Mother of Sorrows, what an impossible life. "I will tell no one, but Henrietta, *you have retired*, and any who hold the occasional humorous reminiscence against you are fools. What sort of man calls himself a woman's protector, then shins up the bedpost at the sight of a wee mouse?"

"He had other shortcomings, so to speak. Gracious,"—
she put a gloved hand to her lips as if she'd hiccupped in
church—"that didn't come out right."

"One suspected this about Merton," Michael said. "I hope
your friend was well compensated for the trials she endured
in his company."

"She recounts an amusing tale about him," Miss Whitlow
said, her posture relaxing, "but one doesn't joke about dis-
closing a man's foibles. His friends might make sport of
him, his family might ridicule him in public, but a mistress
must be loyal, no matter the brevity of the contract."

Not a relationship, a contract.

"So you'd never publish your memoirs?" The question
was far from casual.

"Of course not. A naughty auntie might eventually fade
from society's view, but not if she memorializes her fall from
grace for all the world to read."

"Doubtless, half the House of Lords would be relieved at
your conclusion."

Perhaps if Michael conveyed her assurances to Beltram,
the viscount might release Michael from the obligation to
plunder her luggage in search of a single, stupid book.

"Not half the Lords," she said quietly. "A grand total of
six men. We are in the middle of some serious weather."

Six? Only six men in a decade of debauchery? Heathgate
had occasionally had six partners in the course of twenty-
four hours. Michael considered himself a good formerly
Catholic boy, and even he had enjoyed some notably adven-
turous house parties.

"I detest serious weather," he said. "The going will be
difficult, and the coach will soon acquire a chill. We'd best
break out the lap robes now."

Miss Whitlow arranged a soft wool blanket over her

maid, then allowed Michael to tuck a blanket over their knees. The progress of the coach slowed, and before Michael could think up another conversational gambit, Miss Whitlow had become a warm weight against his side.

His scintillating company had put the lady to sleep. Within five minutes, her head was on his shoulder, and Michael was more or less alone with his conscience in the middle of a gathering snowstorm.

Chapter Three

Henrietta resisted my lures for weeks—weeks spent cozening her into a parody of friendship. I admired her quiet nature. I begged to sketch her hands—as if a housemaid's hands deserved that honor. I consulted her on my choice of cravat pin and other weighty matters. Never was a mouse stalked with more patience than I stalked Henrietta Whitlow's virtue, and all the while, she was honestly unaware of her peril, such was my skill as a romantic thespian. When I recall my dedication to the task, I truly do marvel at my own tenacity, for once upon a time, Henrietta Whitlow was that bastion of English respectability, the good girl...

In Henrietta's experience, men truly comfortable with their rank and fortune were good company. They neither suffered fools nor put on airs, and the best of them operated under an ethic of *noblesse oblige*. Most were well educated and well informed about the greater world, and thus made interesting conversationalists.

Henrietta had known she was at risk for foolishness with the last man whom she'd granted an arrangement, because His Grace's conversation, his wealth, his grasp of politic affairs, and his generosity hadn't appealed to her half so much as his tacit friendship.

Noah, Duke of Anselm, had truly been a protector, deflecting any disrespect to Henrietta with a lift of his eyebrow. He'd escorted her everywhere with the punctilious courtesy of a suitor, rather than the casual disdain of a lord with his fancy piece.

When he'd informed her that he was embarking on the hunt for a duchess, Henrietta had wished him well and sent him on his way with as much relief as regret. By way of a wedding gift, she'd informed him that his greatest amatory asset was...

His ears.

In the course of their arrangement, Anselm had lingered over breakfast with her, chatting about the news of the day rather than rushing off at first light. He'd never expected her to take him straight from the foyer to the bedroom, as some of his predecessors had, and he'd always approached lovemaking as a conversation. Behind the bedroom door, the taciturn, difficult duke had been affectionate, relaxed, and devilishly patient.

Not quite garrulous, but a good listener. A very, very good listener.

Michael Brenner's willingness to listen eclipsed even the duke's. He never watched Henrietta as if he were waiting for the moment when he could turn the topic to intimacies, and his gaze never strayed even playfully to places a gentleman ought not to look.

Henrietta had lapsed into tired silence mostly because further acquaintance with the baron could go nowhere. She was mulling over that sad fact—also mentally rehearsing Christmas carols with her nephews, Dicken and Zander—when the coach came to a smooth halt.

"That was a fast twelve miles," she said, struggling to sound more awake than she felt.

"Wait a bit," the baron said. "Your hair has tangled with my buttons."

Henrietta was obliged to remain close enough to his lordship to appreciate the soft wool of his cloak beneath her cheek and the scent of lavender clinging to his skin. He extricated her hair from the offending button, and she could sit up.

Lucille stirred as well. "I'll just be having a nice, hot cup of—oh, I must have caught a few winks. Beg your pardon, ma'am. My lord."

"Let's stretch our legs." Anything so Henrietta could put some distance between herself and the man upon whom she'd nearly fallen asleep. She'd shared her bed with a half-dozen partners, which meant she was ruined past all redemption, and yet she was embarrassed to have presumed on the baron's person.

The most highly paid courtesan in London, embarrassed by a catnap.

The baron handed them down from the coach amid steadily falling snow. The coachman clambered off the box, and Lucille disappeared around the side of the inn, doubtless in search of the jakes.

"Please see to accommodations for the ladies, Logan, and a fresh team, unless you're not inclined to press on."

"A bit of snow needn't stop us, my lord," Logan said. "Though you'll be wanting more bricks heated, and we'll have to unload the lady's trunks."

"What are my trunks doing on your coach?" Henrietta asked, counting a half-dozen traveling cases lashed to the roof and boot of the baron's conveyance. "I thought you understood that a valise would be sufficient for my needs." The idea that he'd made free with her possessions or countermanded her orders sat uneasily.

"I gave no order to transfer your belongings," the baron said as his coachman stomped up the steps into the inn. "Perhaps your coachman tried to anticipate your needs. We can unload your bags easily enough and have them sent up to your rooms."

Now that the moment to part was upon her, Henrietta didn't want to lose sight of his lordship. He'd behaved toward her as a gentleman behaved toward a lady, nothing more, and yet his consideration had solved many problems.

"I suppose this is farewell, then," she said.

"If you're biding in Oxfordshire, our paths might well cross again." He'd eschewed a hat, and snow dusted auburn locks that brushed the collar of his cape.

"I generally stay at the Duck and Goose in Amblebank." Henrietta's own father refused to grant her the use of a bedroom, though his manor house boasted eight. She refused to impose on her brothers lest their hospitality to her cause difficulties with Papa.

The baron reached into the coach and produced Henrietta's scarf. "I have the great good fortune to dwell at Inglemere, due east of Amblebank by about five miles. I'd welcome a call from you or your family."

Welcome a call.

His lordship spoke a platitude, but in the past ten years, no one had offered Henrietta that courtesy. She was not welcome to call on old friends and neighbors. They didn't judge her for having wealthy protectors in London, but her own family refused to openly welcome her, and the neighborhood took its cue from that behavior.

If only Papa weren't so stubborn, and if only Henrietta weren't even more stubborn than he.

The grooms led the team around to the carriage yard, where fresh horses would be put to. Abruptly, Henrietta was alone with a man who tempted her to second thoughts and if onlys.

If only she'd met him rather than Beltram when she'd gone in search of employment all those years ago.

If only she'd realized sooner what Beltram had been about.

If only her father had written back to her, even once.

Such thoughts went well with the bitter breeze and the bleak landscape. The falling snow created a hush to complement the white blanketing the steps, bushes, pine roping and the wreath on the inn's door.

The baron studied that wreath as if it bore a Latin inscription. "Will you slap me if I take a small liberty, Miss Whitlow?"

Henrietta wanted to take a liberty or two with him, which came as no little surprise. "Is it a liberty when you ask permission?"

He looped her scarf about her neck and treated her to a smile that crinkled the corners of his eyes. "Excellent point. We'll call it a gesture of thanks for making the miles pass more agreeably."

He bent close and brushed his lips over hers. In that instant, Henrietta regretted her decision to retire from the courtesan's profession. To earn even a semblance of acceptance from any polite quarter, she'd been prepared to give up all kisses, all affection, and certainly all pleasures of the flesh.

She'd thought the absence of masculine attention would be a relief, and she'd been wrong.

The baron tendered a kiss as respectful as it was surprising. His lips were warm, his hand cradling Henrietta's jaw gentle. He didn't *handle* her, he caressed, albeit fleetingly.

He'd be a devastatingly tender lover, and that realization was more sobering than all the arctic breezes in England.

"I'll wish you a Happy Christmas," Henrietta said, stepping away, "and thank you for your many kindnesses."

The door to the inn banged open, and Lucille trudged back around the side of the building. Now—*now*—the chill wind penetrated Henrietta's cloak, and a damnable urge to cry threatened. The baron made matters worse by tucking the ends of Henrietta's scarf about her neck.

"The pleasure was mine, Miss Whitlow. If I can ever be of assistance, you need only send to me at Inglemere, and anything I can do…"

Henrietta's heart was breaking, and over a chance encounter that ought never have happened.

"Godspeed, my lord."

He took out his gloves and pulled them on, and the coach returned from the carriage yard, minus Henrietta's trunks. This team was all gray, their coats already damp and curling from the falling snow.

"Begging your lordship's pardon," said his coachman, who'd emerged from the inn. "I don't think the ladies will want to bide here. There's rooms aplenty, because there's illness in the house. Half the staff is down with influenza, and the innkeeper said the cook was among those afflicted. Shall I have the lady's trunks loaded back onto the coach?"

"Henrietta?" Not Miss Whitlow, and his lordship's familiarity was that of a friend.

Henrietta's relief beggared description. "Lucille catches

every illness, and as tired as she is, she'll be afflicted by this time tomorrow if we stay here."

"And then you might well succumb yourself. The next inn is but twelve miles distant, and surely there, you should have better luck."

"Twelve more miles, then," Henrietta said, smiling despite the cold, despite everything. "But no farther."

⌒

"How many more years will we be coming here for a weekly dinner, listening to Papa's pontifications and making our wives and children listen to them as well?" Philip Whitlow kept his voice down, because he stood on the squire's very doorstep.

Thaddeus turned to shield the bundle in his arms from the winter breeze. "I promised Isabel that after the baby came, we'd invite Papa to our table rather than keep trooping over here every Sunday, but the child is nearly six months old, and here we are. Again."

Thaddeus's wife had presented him with a daughter over the summer, and Philip acknowledged a pang of envy. Dicken and Alexander were dear, and he'd gladly give his life for either boy, but Beatrice longed for a daughter.

"Papa gets worse as the holidays approach." As the oldest sibling, Philip expected a certain diplomacy of himself, but at some point, that diplomacy had shaded closer to cowardice.

"Because Henrietta insists on visiting," Thad replied. "She hasn't met her namesake. I expect they'll get on famously."

The infant in Thad's arms was Isabella Henrietta. Her mother called her Izzy. Her father referred to her as his little red hen, owing to her mop of ginger hair.

Unfortunate, that. Both of Philip's boys were red-haired, but they were boys. "Beatrice says we must do more to make Henrietta welcome."

Thad left off fussing with the blankets enveloping his daughter. "Beatrice says? I thought Bea had no patience with straying women."

Bea had no patience with families who couldn't get on with being families. "I might have misread her, somewhat." Or hidden behind her skirts, as it were, or betrayed a sibling for the sake of keeping peace with a parent.

"Isabel said if I ever treat our daughter the way Papa has treated Henrietta, she'll disown me. I do not favor the prospect of being disowned by my dearest spouse."

"If you wrap the child up any more tightly, she'll expire for want of air." How many times had Bea offered Philip the same warning when the boys were small?

Thad rubbed noses with his daughter, which set her to squirming and cooing. "Who looked after Henrietta, Philip? Having a daughter sets a man to wondering. Henrietta was six when Mama died, and my earliest memory is of Henrietta reading to me. I have no memory of our mother, but I can't forget that when Papa was too grief-stricken to recall he had children, Henrietta read to me every night."

Philip came the rest of the way down the steps. "Henrietta was a good girl. That's part of what makes Papa so angry with her."

"He's not angry, he's ashamed. Time he got over it, I say."

Thad was the family optimist, and in part because Henrietta had been such a devoted sister, his recollections of the years following their mother's death were sad but benign. Squire Whitlow's grief had expressed itself in temper and discipline with his two older children.

"People don't get over a hurt because we say so, Thad,

but for what it's worth, Beatrice and I agree with you. Henrietta asks nothing of us but some hospitality at Christmas, and she always offers to help if we need it."

Their wives emerged from the manor house, chattering volubly despite being wrapped up in scarves and cloaks.

"I wondered if Henrietta's generosity extended to you as well. I've never had to ask for help, but I'd ask her before I'd ask Papa."

"So would I." Though Philip hadn't realized that truth until he'd spoken it aloud.

"I suppose we'll see you next week," Thad said, taking Isabel's hand. "Unless Henrietta's come to visit."

Beatrice took the place at Philip's side. "Where have the boys got off to?"

"The stable, last I saw them."

"Where they will get their best clothes filthy. Come along, Philip, and prepare to be stern."

"Yes, ma'am."

Thad smirked, Isabel took the baby from him, and Philip wished the holidays weren't bearing down on them all like a runaway team on a muddy road.

One did not kiss an innocent woman and then steal from her, not if one had any honor.

Michael accounted himself in possession of a modest store of honor, and yet, he'd kissed Henrietta Whitlow, or started to kiss her. That chaste little gesture in the inn yard barely qualified as a kiss, especially when offered to a woman whose affections had been coveted by kings and princes.

And yet that kiss had been enough to set Michael to wondering.

What would kissing Henrietta passionately be like? Holding her through a long and lazy night? Waking to see that red hair in glorious disarray? What would *she* feel like wrapped around him, half mad with desire?

As the coach jostled along the increasingly snowy road, Michael set aside those speculations. He could sleep with any number of women, make love to many more, and hair was hair. What bothered him was that he wanted to know more about *her*, and not simply so he could steal from her with less risk of discovery.

What books did Henrietta Whitlow treasure most dearly?

Did she ever stay up all night reading?

What holiday token would make her smile the way she'd smiled at the serving maid?

How did she *like* to be kissed, if she cared for it at all?

"You've grown quiet," Miss Whitlow said. "You needn't worry for Lucille's slumbers. I've seen her sleep through a gale."

Indeed, the stalwart Lucille had fortified herself with two cups of tea at the last inn and was now wedged against the opposite squabs, a lap blanket tucked beneath her chin, her snoring a counterpoint to the rhythm of the horses' hooves.

"My former employer had the same ability to sleep any time," Michael replied, "though Heathgate limited himself to naps and delighted in making me think he was asleep when he was in truth eavesdropping."

"You miss him."

Michael missed his sisters. Did they ever miss him? "Heathgate and I became a good team. Ten years ago, I was the shy Irish lad willing to do anything to better myself. Heathgate was a fundamentally decent man trying to impersonate a jaded rogue. I had the better classical education and stronger organizational skills, while Heathgate had business intuition and daring. He took a modest fortune and made it enormous, if you'll excuse a vulgar reference to commercial matters."

Miss Whitlow rustled about on the bench beside Michael, tucking the lap robe around her hip.

"Patch leaf," he murmured.

Her fussing paused. "I beg your pardon?"

"The scent you wear. It reminds me of the patch leaf used to keep the moths away from Kashmir shawls. I couldn't place it and have never come across its like on a woman before."

She extended her left arm beneath his nose. "I have it made up specially. At first I was simply storing my clothing with the leaves used to protect the shawls, but then my Parisian perfumer found a way to capture the scent."

Michael turned her wrist and sniffed translucent skin. Blue veins ran from her forearm to her palm, and a single tendon stood out.

"It's different," he said, resisting the urge to taste her pulse. "Unusual."

"I don't care for it. Too exotic, too...loud. I no longer have to be loud or exotic, and what a relief that is." Her fleeting glance asked if her admission offended him, though her idea of loud was probably a healthy man's notion of a seductive whisper.

"What scent do you prefer?" he asked.

"My favorite scents are green tea and freshly scythed grass, but those would hardly do for a fragrance. My mother hung lavender sachets all about the house, from the bedposts, in the linen closets, in the wardrobes, and among the dry-goods pantries. In the new year, I will wear proper English lavender."

On her, that common herb would smell anything but proper. "Why wait until next month?"

"I am determined on an objective, my lord. I expect to fail, but I must try. My success will depend on remaining very much the woman in possession of herself, rather than the meek girl who left Amblebank ten years ago."

The coach lurched sideways, then righted itself. Logan was a first-rate coachman, and thus when he slowed the team to a more cautious pace, Michael didn't countermand his judgment.

And yet, these conversations with Miss Whitlow were driving him barmy. He wanted to kiss her, though his job was to betray her, to the extent purloining one book was a betrayal. To blazes with Beltram, favors owed, and Yuletide travel.

"I find it hard to believe you were ever a meek girl," Michael said, though he well knew she had been. Beltram damned near took pride in "making Henrietta Whitlow what she is today," as if ruining a housemaid was a rare accomplishment rather than a disgrace.

"I was a drudge," Miss Whitlow replied. "A pretty drudge, though I grasped too late how that beauty could affect my fate. I quarreled with my father over his choice of husband for me and decamped for the metropolis, as so many village girls have. The tale is prosaic and my fate not that unusual."

"Your fate is very unusual," Michael countered. "Those village girls often end up plying their trade in the street, felled by the French disease, or behind bars. You had your choice of dukes and, I hazard, are wealthy as a result."

"I am wealthy, and all that coin only makes my father hold me in worse contempt. The wages of sin are to be penury, disease, disfigurement, and bitter remorse, not security and comfort."

Two hours ago, she would not have been that honest.

"Your father's household is the objective you're intent upon?"

She tucked one foot up under her skirts, a very informal pose. "Papa refuses to enter any room I'm in, he will not say my name to other family members, and he's removed every likeness of me from his house."

And to think Michael was pouting because his sisters had declined to join him for Christmas. He did not want to know that Henrietta Whitlow was afflicted with heartaches. He wanted to believe she'd leave her London life, become an intriguing fixture among the lesser gentry of some backwater, and never miss one small volume from among her store of books.

When Christmas angels took up residence at Inglemere, perhaps.

"Why bother with further overtures in your father's direction?" Michael asked. "He deserves to have the cold comfort of his intolerance directed right back at him."

Miss Whitlow peeked beneath the shade rolled down to keep the worst of the cold from leaking through the window.

"I hope your coachman knows this road well. The weather is turning awful."

Was there any change of subject less adroit than the weather? Miss Whitlow hesitated to discuss her family, though she'd numbered her lovers without a hint of a blush.

"I hired Logan when I bought Inglemere. He's driven the route from here to London for years. We can't be far from the next inn, and you are not to worry. Compared to the Norwegian coast in December, compared to the North Sea in a temper, this snowstorm is merely weather."

She continued to gaze out at the snowy landscape, which had acquired the bluish tinge of approaching twilight.

Michael was running out of time to plunder her possessions, though tonight, as she slept secure at the next inn, he would surely see his task completed.

"I cannot give up on my father," she said, "because he gave up on me, and that was wrong of him. We are family. I will make one more effort to bridge our differences, and if he remains adamant, then I'll do as you suggest and put him—and my quarrel with him—aside."

Ten years was an infernally long time to quarrel. Mr. Whitlow was a fool to toss away a daughter with that sort of tenacity, but then, Michael was a fool too.

He'd wondered idly about how to concoct some sort of green-tea-and-scythed-grass soap to give Miss Whitlow for a Yuletide token—in a world where he wasn't about to steal more than kisses from her—when what she wanted by Christmas morning was nothing less than a miracle of paternal forgiveness.

∼

By the time the coach lumbered into the inn yard, Henrietta was tucked against his lordship, all but asleep, and half dreaming of a Christmas dinner with her family—all of her family—gathered around a laden table. Oddly enough, his lordship was present at the feast too.

"I have doubtless snored as loudly as Lucille," Henrietta muttered, righting herself. Her back ached, and her feet were blocks of ice.

The baron retrieved the arm he'd tucked across her shoulders.

"I suspect somebody keeps moving the inns along this stretch of the highway so they recede as we approach. In Ireland, we'd say the fairies have been busy."

The farther the coach traveled from London, the more a soft Irish brogue threaded into his lordship's words. In the dark, his voice would be...

Henrietta nudged Lucille's knee. "We've arrived, my dear. Time to wake up."

Lucille scratched her nose, but otherwise didn't budge.

"Tea, Lucille!" his lordship said. "Hot, strong, sweet, and laced with a dollop of spirits."

Her eyes popped open. "I must have caught a few winks. If you'll excuse me, Miss Henrietta, I'll just be stretching my legs a wee while, and...my gracious, the daylight has all but fled."

Someday, much sooner than Henrietta wanted to admit, Lucille would be old. The maid had a crease across her right cheek, and her cloak had been misbuttoned at the throat. She already had the dowager's habit of falling asleep in company.

Lucille had been in service at Beltram's, the same as Henrietta, and she'd been the first person Henrietta had hired for her own household.

His lordship climbed from the coach to hand the ladies down, and off Lucille went.

"The inn doesn't look like it receives much custom," Henrietta said. The entrance was lighted and the doors sported pine wreaths, but other than a tang of smoke in the air, little suggested the place was open for business.

"I've not had to stay here previously," the baron said. "We're but eight miles from Inglemere. I've seldom even changed teams here, though I will today."

He was traveling on, then. Henrietta hated that notion. As the coach was led away, she wrapped her arms about his lordship's waist.

"I'm taking a liberty with your person," she said. "You

will think badly of me, but then, everybody already does. I will miss you."

He drew her closer, though winter clothing prevented the degree of closeness Henrietta sought. He'd been decent to her, and she'd missed decent treatment more than she'd realized.

"I'm rarely in Oxfordshire," he said, "though I will think of you when I travel back this way."

Henrietta knew exactly how to send a man on his way smiling. She usually dropped hints that he'd been the most exciting/passionate/affectionate/inventive lover—something credible, but not too effusive—gave him looks of fondness and regret and a parting exchange of intimacies remarkable for its dullness.

Lest he second-guess his decision to part from her.

In five cases out of six, her paramours had come wandering back around, hinting that a resumption of their arrangement would be welcome. Henrietta never obliged. Anselm had come around as well, and Henrietta had taken fierce joy in the fact that the duke had called simply as a friend, albeit one with marital troubles and a wide protective streak.

She'd not even flirted with Michael, Baron Angelford, and she would miss him.

"You're being kind," she said, stepping back. "Letting me know that some Yuletide chivalry on your part will not develop into anything more. I'm usually the one who must be kind. I suppose we'd best find me accommodations and see about sending word back to MacFergus regarding my whereabouts."

Please argue with me. Please contradict my brisk conclusions, or at least express a hope that we might meet again.

"I've come to Inglemere with an eye toward selling it." His lordship used a gloved finger to brush a wind-whipped lock of hair from Henrietta's cheek. "My sisters bide in Oxford itself, so owning a town house there makes more sense. If you ever have need of me, I can be reached at the home of Clarissa Brenner, Little Doorman Street."

Worse and worse.

"I have brothers in the environs of Amblebank," Henrietta said. "They won't gainsay my father, but neither do they disdain my company. A wealthy sister is allowed a few peccadilloes."

I sound bitter.

Probably because I am bitter.

Henrietta was also tired, cold, and once again a lone female making her way against all sense on a path of her own choosing.

The coachman, Logan, came down the inn's steps. "Ye canna bide here, mistress."

"What do you mean?" the baron snapped. "Miss Whitlow has been traveling all day. She's hungry, chilled, fatigued, and due a respite from my company. You should be unloading her trunks as I speak."

Must he be so ready to get rid of her?

"I'm sorry, guv, but this inn accepts no overnight custom. The innkeeper and his wife are elderly, and they're off to await the arrival of a new grandchild in Oxford. The housekeeper says we can get a fresh team and a hamper, and warm up for a bit in the common, but there are no beds to be had here."

No beds? How ironic that a courtesan, who generally plied her trade in a bed, should be so pleased to find none available.

"What sort of inn stays in business by letting its beds go empty?" his lordship fumed. "I've never heard the like."

"Beds are a lot of work," Henrietta said, which earned

her a look of consternation from the baron. "The innkeeper would need maids to change the linens daily, laundresses to do endless washing, heaps and heaps of coal to heat the wash water, more maids to tidy up each room, every day. More coal to keep those rooms warm, and all for not very much coin. The kitchen and the stable generate most of the profit for an establishment like this."

His lordship peered down at her. "How do you know that?"

"I need investments and have considered buying a few coaching inns. Widows often own their late husband's businesses, and thus a female owning an inn isn't that unusual. It's a chancy proposition, though. Very dependent on mail routes, weather, and the whims of the fashionable."

"We can continue this discussion inside," his lordship said. "Get me a fresh team, Logan, and leave Miss Whitlow's bags on the coach. We can push on to Inglemere as soon as the moon rises."

The baron took Henrietta by the hand and tugged her in the direction of the steps, and a good thing that was. Left to her own devices, she might have stood in the snowy yard until nightfall, marveling that his lordship had more or less invited her to spend the night at his own house.

⁓

The storm had obligingly taken an intermission, and in the bright illumination of a full moon on new snow, Michael and his guests continued on their way. Lucille was at least awake, which meant he had more incentive to keep his conversation free of innuendo, overtures, or outright begging.

He wanted time alone with Henrietta Whitlow, he *needed* time alone with her trunks. Having her as an overnight guest at Inglemere would tempt him to arrange the former, when he must limit himself to the latter.

"I do believe it's getting colder," Lucille muttered. "Does that sometimes, when snow lets up. You think it's cold, then winter stops funning about. How much farther, milord?"

Too far. "We're better than halfway," Michael said. "If you'd like to continue to Amblebank, I can have Logan drive you tonight, though I'd suggest you leave your bags with me to make the distance easier for the horses." *Please say you'll go.*

Please stay.

I'm losing my wits.

"Miss Henrietta," Lucille said, "if you make me spend another minute longer than necessary in this coach, I will turn in my notice, so I will."

"You turn in your notice at least once a month," Henrietta said. "In this case, such dramatics won't be necessary. Nobody in Amblebank would be alarmed if my arrival were delayed until next week, though I do want the children to have their presents on Christmas morning."

She'd at least be spending her holiday around children. Michael would have to journey into Oxford for that privilege.

"I never know what to get them," he said. "My nieces and nephews. Two of my sisters are married and between them have a half-dozen children. I'm at something of a loss when it comes to presents. My brothers remain in Ireland, so the issue is less pressing with them." Fine spirits for the menfolk, silk for his sisters, but the children were a puzzle.

Miss Whitlow passed him the flask of tea they'd been sharing, though the contents had grown cold within a mile of the inn.

"You're at a loss because as a child, you never had presents. You had no toys, no books, no pets. My father was of a similar bent, though my mother's influence softened him somewhat."

Michael's diversion had been hard work and harder work. "We had a pig, a grand creature named Bridget Boru. If she had more than ten piglets, my father divided up the proceeds of sale from the extra piglets among us children. The birth of the Christ child was not more warmly anticipated than Bridget's litters."

But how Michael had died a little inside to see those piglets sold off, season after season, and how jealously he'd guarded his "sow bank."

"You had dreams," Miss Whitlow said. "Your nieces and nephews do too. I think of my girlhood dreams when I'm shopping for Christmas tokens."

The question was out before Michael realized how fraught the answer might be: "What were your dreams?"

She took back the flask and capped it. "The same as every other girl's: a home of my own, children, my own tea service."

"Not books?"

"My love of books came later."

When the hope of children and family was beyond her? How odd that Henrietta and he should share the same dream—a family, in all its prosaic, complex, dear, and exasperating variability. All of his hard work, all of the risks he'd taken, had been so that someday he'd be able to provide for a family, with no fear of potato blight, English prejudice, or hard winters.

"For Christmas, I want never to set my backside upon a coach bench again," Lucille said. "In case anybody should wonder."

"I was consumed with curiosity on that very point," Michael said. "Assuming your wish can be granted temporarily, what else might Father Christmas bring you?"

Lucille's gaze landed on Miss Whitlow. "Peace on earth. It was a fine aspiration back in Bethlehem, though we've yet to achieve it. Peace in Oxfordshire would be a start."

"Lucille." Miss Whitlow's reproof was weary.

"I'll hold my tongue, miss. But his lordship's bound to hear the parish gossip. You haven't done any more than many other country girls do when they're—"

"Perhaps my nieces would like a tea service for their dolls," Michael said, rather than watch the maid's defense further erode her employer's mood. The closer they drew to Amblebank, the quieter Miss Whitlow became.

"That's a lovely idea," she said. "Or a lap desk, for the older children. One with their name carved on the top."

"What about a journal?" Michael mused. "My nieces would memorialize their brothers' every transgression given a chance."

"Not a journal." Miss Whitlow tucked the half-empty flask into her sizable valise—which Michael might also have to search. "Journals can be found and their contents exposed by mischievous siblings at the worst possible moment."

Was no topic of conversation safe with her? "You speak from experience."

"Two brothers' worth. My older brother showed up shortly after my parents married, and I followed less than two years later. My younger brother waited a proper five years to come along. In any case, I learned not to keep a journal. What of you, your lordship? What would you like for Christmas?"

Her question brought an image to mind of Michael in the great hall at Inglemere presiding over a long table shared with sisters, in-laws, children, the occasional cousin, and—truly, he'd been shut up in the coach for too long—Henrietta Whitlow at the far end of the table.

He wanted a holiday full of laughter, warmth, and family.

He'd get a solitary tray in the library and a guilty conscience.

"I hope the coming days will allow me to find some rest," he said, "and peace and quiet. I'll read, catch up on my correspondence, and consider properties in Oxford for possible purchase." His sisters claimed there weren't any, though Michael suspected they'd simply got used to managing without his fraternal interference.

Henrietta was at her customary place beside him, close enough that he could see the fatigue shadowing her eyes, a bleakness in her gaze, and a grimness about her mouth.

"I know it's highly unusual," he said, "and you must feel free to refuse me, but I'd be very grateful if you'd tarry at Inglemere tomorrow. My coachman and grooms deserve to rest, and I daresay you do as well."

He was a cad, a bounder, an idiot, and very good thief. He did not need an extra day to paw through Miss Whitlow's effects.

"I don't—" Miss Whitlow began.

"What a generous offer," Lucille said. "You'll have the rest of your life to wear plain caps, miss, and endure sneers in the churchyard. Might as well get a good night's rest before we embark on your penance, aye?"

"My staff is utterly discreet," Michael said, "and I won't think of you journeying on to Amblebank tomorrow. The roads will be safer in a day or two, and you will be fortified for the challenge of dealing with family."

Didn't he sound like the voice of gentlemanly reason? Miss Whitlow ought to toss him from the coach.

"One day," she said. "One day to rest, get warm, plan my approach, and let MacFergus know what's become of me. One day, but no more."

One day—and two nights—would be more than enough for Michael to trespass against her trust, steal from her, and send her into the arms of the family who presumed to sit in judgment of her. They'd treat her like royalty if she were his baroness, regardless of her past, but he was the last man who deserved to be her baron.

Chapter Four

Even good girls grow weary of loneliness and poverty. You will realize, of course, that I might have been a tad bit misleading where my comely housemaid was concerned— or perhaps she misunderstood my overtures? Henrietta's education had been neglected in every regard except how to drudge for her menfolk, poor thing.

I didn't go down on bended knee, but I might have alluded to wedded bliss a time or two or twenty. She eventually granted me the prize I'd so diligently sought. For some while, all was not-quite-connubial bliss. Never was my candlestick so well polished, as it were…and I didn't have to spend a penny for my pleasure. I could not boast of my cleverness, trifling with the help being frowned upon, but you must admit, London's bachelors are a happier lot for my having seen to Miss Whitlow's education…

What the hell are you doing?" Liam Logan kept his voice down lest he upset horses who'd earned a ration of oats for their labors.

"I'm plundering a woman's luggage," the baron replied from the depths of a large, brass-hinged trunk. "What are you doing out and about at this hour?"

The light of the single lantern made the baron look gaunt when he straightened. Gaunt and guilty. He'd served his guests a fine dinner in Inglemere's elegant dining room, and should have been abed himself, not wandering around a darkened stable.

"I'm tucking in the boys," Logan said. "You ought to consider buying these grays. They're a good lot, and they pull well together."

His lordship went back to rummaging in the trunk. "Spare me your analogies. Henrietta Whitlow is no longer for sale. I'm not sure she ever was."

The Quality in a mood were puzzle enough, but Michael Brenner was new to his title, far too solitary, and without much cheer. Liam respected the man and even liked him— the baron was scrupulously fair, hard-working, and devoted to his family—but Liam didn't always understand his employer.

"Miss Whitlow had something on offer," Liam said, tossing another forkful of hay into the nearest stall, "to hear half of London tell it. I don't blame her for that. Dukes and nabobs are as prone to foolishness as the rest of us, and it's ever so entertaining to see a woman from the shires making idiots of them."

The baron straightened, his greatcoat hanging open despite the cold. To Liam, a horse barn would ever be a cozy place, but the baron wasn't a coachman, inured to the elements and dressed to deal with them.

"The damned thing isn't here."

"The only damned thing I see in these stables is you, sir. Care for a nip?"

Two other trunks were open, and the latches were undone on the remaining three. The baron accepted Liam's flask and regarded the luggage with a ferocious scowl.

"I was sure she had it with her. She's closed up her household in London, and these are all the trunks she's brought. Damn and blast."

"Have a wee dram," Liam said. "It'll improve your cursing."

"My cursing skills are excellent, but I try to leave them back in the bogs from whence I trotted. This is good whisky."

"Peat water makes the best, I say. My brother-in-law agrees with me. What are we searching for?"

His lordship sat on one of the closed trunks. "We're searching for foolishness, to use your word. Lord Beltram was Miss Whitlow's first... I can't call him a protector, for he ruined her. He was her first, and in the manner of besotted men the world over, he wanted to immortalize his conquest. Somewhere in Miss Whitlow's effects is a small volume full of bad poetry, competent sketches, and maudlin reminiscences. Can I buy some of this whisky?"

"I'll give you a bottle for Christmas. Miss Whitlow is not in the first blush of youth, if you'll forgive a blunt observation. Why has Lord Beltram waited this long to fret over his stupidity?"

The baron sighed, his breath fogging white in the gloom. "He's decided to find a wife—or cannot afford too many more years of bachelorhood—and this book is a loose end. When they parted, Miss Whitlow asked to have only this book—not jewels, not a bank draft, not an introduction to some other titled fool. All she wanted was this silly journal. Beltram passed it along, thinking himself quite clever for having ended the arrangement without great expense or drama."

Liam tossed a forkful of hay into another stall, working his way down the row. "So Beltram is a fool, but why are you compounding the error with more folly? Miss Whitlow has had years to blackmail the idiot or publish his bad verse. Why must you turn thief on his behalf?"

The baron took up a second fork and began haying the stalls on the opposite side of the aisle. Horses stirred, nickered, and then tucked into their fodder.

"Once long ago," the baron said, "in a land not far enough away, with which we were at war, Beltram's silence saved my life. I promised him any favor he cared to name and only later realized my silence had also saved his life."

"So he took advantage of an innocent maid, and now he's taking advantage of you," Liam said. "And you wonder why the common folk think the Quality are daft. You're not a thief, my lord."

The baron threw hay with the skill of one who'd made his living in a stable once upon a time.

"Unless you've been poor as dirt and twice as hopeless," he said, hanging the fork on a pair of nails when the row was complete, "you don't know how an unfulfilled obligation can weigh on your sense of freedom. Every time I crossed paths with Beltram, I knew, and he knew, that I'd put myself in his debt. I cannot abide being in his debt, cannot abide the thought that ten years hence, he'll ask something of me—something worse than a little larceny— and I'll be bound by honor to agree to it. I gave the man my word."

"Honor, is it? To steal from a woman who's already been

wronged?" MacFergus would have a few things to say about
that brand of honor, and as usual, this plan gone awry had
been his idea.

"I've considered stealing from her, then stealing the book
back from Beltram so I can replace it among the lady's
belongings."

"Clever," Liam said, wondering what Mary would make
of all this nonsense. "Or you might tell Beltram you simply
couldn't find the thing. I daresay lying to his lordship won't
meet with your lofty idea of honor either."

"If I can't find it, if I honestly can't find it, then I'll tell
him that."

"That you wouldn't lie to a nincompoop makes it all better, of course. I'll wish you the joy of your thievery, sir. I'm
for bed. Pleasant dreams."

"Go to hell, Logan. If the book isn't here, the only other
place it could be is in Miss Whitlow's valise."

Which was doubtless resting at the foot of the lady's cozy
bed. "And Happy Christmas to you too, my lord."

His lordship hadn't come to Henrietta's bed last night.

He'd lighted her up to her room, offered her a kiss on
the cheek—the forehead would have provoked her to quot-
ing the Bard's more colorful oaths—and wished her pleasant
dreams.

Her dreams had been tormented, featuring an eternity
racketing about naked and alone in a coach forever lost in a
winter landscape.

"You're already dressed," Lucille said, bustling through
the door without knocking. "I bestir myself at a needlessly
early hour and find my services aren't required. The baron

had chocolate sent up to my room. Fresh scones with butter, and chocolate, kept hot over a warming candle."

Henrietta knew how that chocolate had felt, simmering over the flame. She decided to leave her hair half down, the better to light the baron's candle at breakfast.

"What is wrong with me, Lucille?" She shoved another pin into her hair. "I swore off men more than six months ago and in all that time wished I'd made the decision years earlier." Before she'd met Anselm, in any case. Her memories of him had been a little too fond. "You don't have to make the bed. The baron has an excellent staff."

An excellent, cheerful, discreet staff who appeared genuinely loyal to their employer.

"I cannot abide idleness," Lucille said. "All that feigning sleep in the coach yesterday taxed my gifts to the limit."

Were pearl-tipped hair pins too much at breakfast? "You were feigning sleep? That was a prodigious good imitation of a snore for a sham effort."

"Mostly feigning. You and his lordship got along well. These are the loveliest flannel sheets."

For winter, they were more luxurious than silk, which was difficult to wash. Henrietta had never thought to treat herself to flannel sheets, but she would in the future.

"The baron and I got on so well that after supper he left me for the charms of his library. Perhaps I retired in the nick of time." Was that a wrinkle lurking beside her mouth? A softness developing beneath her chin?

Henrietta had never worried about her appearance before—never—and now . . . "I have left my wits somewhere along the Oxford Road."

Lucille straightened, a brocade pillow hugged to her middle. "This is what you put the gents through, Miss Henrietta. This uncertainty and vexation. They didn't dare approach you without some sign you'd welcome their advances. Do you fancy his lordship, or merely fancy being fancied?"

"Excellent question." Henrietta began removing the pins she'd so carefully placed. "I fancied being respectable. I know that's not likely to happen for the next twenty years, but I can aspire to being respected. Then his lordship goes and treats me decently, and I'm...I don't care for it as much as I thought I would."

The respect was wonderful. The insecurity it engendered was terrifying.

She cared *for him*, for the boy who'd had no toys, the wealthy baron who didn't know how to entice his sisters to join him for Christmas dinner. She cared for a man who'd not put on airs before a cranky maid, who regarded Henrietta's past as just that—her past.

But she also desired him, which was a fine irony.

"He did invite us to bide here today." Lucille smoothed thick quilts over the sheets. "Have you seen his library?"

"I have not. After supper, he brought me straight up to bed, and I confess I was happy to accompany him. Then off he went, and I'm all in a muddle, Lucille."

"Fallen women get paid for accommodating a man's desire," Lucille said. "Un-fallen women aren't immune to animal spirits. They simply know how to indulge them without being judged for it. I wasn't always a plain-faced, pudgy old maid, you know."

"You are not plain-faced, pudgy, or old. I have it on good authority that men like a substantial woman between the sheets."

Thank God. Though maybe Michael Brenner preferred the golden-haired waifs and blue-eyed princesses of the Mayfair ballrooms, drat their dainty feet. Henrietta's feet were in proportion to the rest of her. Her father had called her a plow horse of a girl, and the baron might see her as such.

"I hate this uncertainty," Henrietta said. "I'm wondering now if men value only the women they must pay for."

Lucille tossed the brocade pillows back onto the bed, achieving a comfy, arranged look with casual aim.

"You have it all wrong, miss, which is understandable given your situation. What the men value, what they respect, is a reflection of what we value in ourselves. You did very well in London because after Lord Beltram played you so false, you never allowed another man to rule your heart or your household. Respect yourself, and devil take the hindmost. You told me that years ago. What are you doing with your hair?"

Henrietta's hair was a bright red abundance she'd refused to cut once she'd arrived in London. She'd also refused to hide it under a cap, and her bonnets had been more feathers than straw.

"I'm braiding it for a coronet. I used to favor a coronet, though my father said that only accentuated my height."

"He didn't like having a daughter nearly as tall as he was," Lucille said. "What will you do about the baron?"

Henrietta finished with her braid, circled the plait about her crown, then secured it with plain pins.

"I'd forgotten my little speech to you all those years ago, but I was right then, and you are right now. I respect myself and will regardless of how the baron regards me. I also respect the baron, though, and hope when we part, that's still the case. With all the other men…"

Professional loyalty to past clients warred with the knowledge that Henrietta was no longer a professional. Society might never note the difference, but Henrietta suspected that six months ago, she would not have given Michael

Brenner a second look. A mere baron, merely well-fixed, *merely decent*.

What a sorry creature she'd been.

"With all the others," Lucille said, standing behind Henrietta at the vanity, "your respect was tempered by the knowledge that they paid for your favors. You were compensated for putting up with them, and they knew it, and still sought you out."

The arrangement between man and mistress was as simple on the surface as it was complex beneath. The usual bargain was complex for the mistress and simple for the man. Henrietta finished with her coronet—adding a good two inches to her height—and draped a shawl about her shoulders.

"I know two things," she said, facing the door. "I do not want his lordship paying me for anything, and I'd rather he spent tonight with me than in his library with his books. I'm not sure what that makes me, but breakfast awaits, and I'm hungry."

"Desire for the company of a man you esteem makes you *normal*," Lucille said, tidying up the discarded pearl-tipped pins. "I daresay he's a normal sort of fellow himself. Be off with you, and if you need me, I might be back in bed, munching scones and swilling chocolate. Or I might suggest the staff do a bit of decorating. The holidays are approaching, after all."

Many a day, Henrietta would have regarded lazing about in bed as a fine reward for her exertions the evening before. Today, she wanted to spend as much time with Michael Brenner as she could, either in bed or out of it.

Normal wasn't so very complicated, though neither was it for the faint of heart.

"I think I'm in love," Miss Whitlow said, taking another book from the stack on the table beside her.

She'd spent most of the day in Michael's library, and he—with a growing sense of exasperation—had sat at his desk, watching her write letters or read. When she looked up, he made a pretense of scribbling away at correspondence or studying some ledger, but mostly, he'd been feasting on the simple sight of her.

When he ought to have been rummaging in her valise.

She wore gold-rimmed spectacles for reading. They gave her a scholarly air and gave him a mad desire to see her wearing only the spectacles while he read *A Midsummer Night's Dream* to her in bed. She favored shortbread and liked to slip off her shoes and tuck her feet beneath her when a book became truly engrossing.

Would she enjoy having her feet rubbed?

The worst part about this day of half torment/half delight was that Michael's interest in the lady was only passingly erotic. He wanted to learn the shape of her feet and the un-spoken wishes of her heart. He wanted to introduce her to his horses—which was pathetic—and memorize the names of her family members.

Heathgate would laugh himself to flinders to see his ef-ficient man of business reduced to daydreaming and quill-twiddling.

Michael and his guest had taken a break after lunch, and he'd shown her about the house. Inglemere was a gorgeous Tudor manor, just large enough to be impressive, but small enough to be a home. The grounds were landscaped to show off the house to perfection, though, of course, snow blan-keted the gardens and park.

Michael had shown Miss Whitlow his stables, his dairy, his laundry, and even the kitchen pantries, as if all was on offer for her approval.

He wanted to be on offer for her approval, and yet, she never so much as batted her eyes at him. Smart woman.

"You are in love?" he asked, rising from his desk. He probably was too, but could not say for a certainty, never having endured that affliction before.

"You haven't merely collected books for show," she said, hugging his signed copy of *The Italian* to her chest. "You chose books that speak to you, and the result is...I love books. I could grow old reading my way through this library of yours, Michael Brenner."

Not *my lord*. "Have you no collection of your own?"

She set the novel aside and scooted around under the quilt he'd brought her. "I patronized lending libraries. They need the custom, and they never cared what I did for my coin. They cared only that I enjoyed the books and returned them in good condition. Perhaps, when I purchase a home, I'll fill it with books."

While her protectors—Michael was coming to hate that word—had treated her bedroom like a lending library. She'd been well compensated, but he still wished somebody had made her the centerpiece of a treasury that included children, shared memories, and smiles over the breakfast table.

And wedding vows, for heaven's sake.

Michael settled in beside her on the sofa. "You're in the market for a house?" He could help with this, being nothing if not well versed in commercial transactions. He'd searched long and thoroughly before settling on Inglemere for his country retreat.

"I'm in the market for a home," she said. "This is another reason I'm determined to reconcile with my father. All the family I have lives within a few miles of Amblebank, but if he refuses to acknowledge me, then settling elsewhere makes sense."

I'll make him acknowledge you. The only way Michael could do that was by marrying her.

"Give it time," he said, patting her hand. "Family can be vexing, but they'll always be family." Witness his sisters, who had no more time for the brother who dowered them than they did for Fat King George.

Miss Whitlow turned her palm up, so their fingers lay across one another. "You are very kind."

He was a charlatan. "One aspires to behave honorably, though it isn't always possible."

Her fingers closed around his, and Michael felt honor tearing him right down the middle of his chest.

"I have a sense of decency," she said, "as unlikely as that sounds. I've sworn off sharing my favors for coin. I'd like to share my favors with you for the sheer pleasure of it. Lucille has reminded me that the coming years will be..."

She fell silent, her hand cold in Michael's. In another instant, she'd withdraw her hand, the moment would be lost, and he'd be reduced to asking her about Mrs. Radcliffe's prose.

"Lonely," he said. "The coming years will be lonely. The coming night need not be."

Michael drew Henrietta to her feet and wrapped his arms about her. The fit was sublime, and for a moment, he pitied all the men who'd had to pay her to tolerate—much less appear to enjoy—their advances. That she'd offer him intimacies without a thought of reward was more Christmas token than he'd ever deserve.

And in return, what would he offer her?

"I'll take a tray in my room," she said, kissing his cheek.

"You can come to me after supper, after I've had a proper soak."

She'd taken a bath the previous evening, as had Michael. He suspected hers had been a good deal warmer than his.

"You don't need to fuss and primp," Michael said. "I don't care if you bear the scent of books, or your hair is less than perfectly arranged. I'd rather be with you as you are."

She drew back enough to peer at him, and they were very nearly eye to eye. "I insist on toothpowder. That's not negotiable."

God, what she'd had to put up with. "I insist on tooth-powder too, and I generally don't bother with a nightshirt. Shall we surprise each other with the rest of it?"

"You think you can surprise *me*?"

She'd had a half-dozen lovers, probably not an imaginative bone in the lot, so to speak. "I know I can." Her patch-leaf fragrance was fainter today, as if she'd forgotten to apply it, though the aroma yet lingered on her clothes. Michael bent closer to catch the scent at the join of her neck and shoulder. "Shall we go upstairs now?"

Darkness had fallen, though dinner was at least two hours off. Michael was famished, and food had nothing to do with his hunger. He'd regret this folly, but he'd regret more declining what Henrietta offered.

And if he was lucky, Beltram's damned book had been tossed in the fire years ago.

⁓

Henrietta stepped behind the privacy screen, aware of a vast gap in her feminine vocabulary. No man had sought to share intimacies with her for the simple pleasure of her company. From Beltram onward, all had regarded her as a commodity to be leased, though Beltram had masked his agenda as seduction.

Michael had cast her no speculative glances, assayed no "accidental" touches, offered no smiles that insulted as they inventoried. Any of those, Henrietta could have parried without effort.

His honest regard might have been a foreign language to her.

"Shall I undress for you?" She was tall enough to watch over the privacy screen as Michael added peat to the fire.

"Not unless you'd enjoy that," he said, setting the poker on the hearth stand. "Perhaps you'd like me to undress for you? Can't say as a lady has ever asked that of me."

A lady. To him, she was a lady. "It's a bit chilly to be making a display out of disrobing." Some men had needed that from her, had needed as much anticipation and encouragement as she could produce for them—poor wretches.

"Burning peat is an art, and my staff hasn't the way of it," he said. "I keep the smell about to remind me of the years when a peat fire was the difference between life and death. Your hair is quite long."

Henrietta had undone her coronet, so her braid hung down to her bum. "I might cut it. For years, I didn't." Because long hair, according to Beltram, was seductive. By his reasoning, ridiculously long hair was ridiculously seductive.

Though Beltram's opinion now mattered... *not at all.*

"That is a diabolical smile, Miss Whitlow."

"You inspire me, and if we're to share a bed, you might consider calling me Henrietta."

"I'm Michael." He draped his coat over the back of the chair by the hearth. "After the archangel. Have you other names?"

"Henrietta Eloisa Gaye Whitlow. Is there a warmer to run

over the sheets?" Warmed flannel sheets would be a bit of heaven.

"I'll be your warmer."

They shared a smile, adult and friendly. Henrietta decided that her hair could be in a braid for this encounter, and to blazes with the loose cascade most men had expected of her. She'd always spent half the next morning brushing out the snarls, half the night waking because she couldn't turn without pulling her hair loose from her pillow first.

Michael-for-the-archangel removed his clothing in a predictable order, laying each article over the chair in a manner that would minimize wrinkles. He pulled off his own boots, and used the wash water at the hearth with an emphasis on the face, underarms, privities, and feet.

He was thorough about his ablutions, and his soap—hard-milled and lavender scented—was fresh.

"You are not self-conscious," Henrietta said. A surprising number of men were, if the gossip among courtesans was to be believed. Several men might cheerfully aim for the same chamber pot while the port was consumed, but they'd do so without revealing much of their person, or overtly inspecting any other man.

"I was one of eight children sharing a one-room sod hut," Michael said. "Growing up, privacy was a foreign concept."

While hard work had doubtless been his constant companion. Michael had the honed fitness that came from years of physical labor and constant activity. Some wealthy men came by a similar physique by virtue of riding, shooting, archery, and pugilism. Michael had a leanness they lacked, a sleekness that said he eschewed most luxuries still and probably always would.

"Growing up, my modesty was elevated from a virtue to an obsession," Henrietta said. "I like looking at you."

He wrung out the wet flannel over the basin, arm muscles undulating by candlelight. "Does that surprise you?"

"Yes." Henrietta hadn't chosen her partners on the basis of appearance, not after Beltram. He'd been a fine specimen, also selfish, rotten, deceitful, and lazy. She hoped whatever woman he took to wife could match him for self-absorption and hard-heartedness. He'd come by months ago to tell her he'd be wife-hunting, as if his eventual marriage might dash some hope Henrietta had harbored for years.

What a lovely difference time could make in a woman's perspective.

Michael laid the cloth over the edge of the basin and crossed to the bed. "Won't you join me, Henrietta?"

What need did the Irish have of coin when they had charm in such abundance? Michael sat on the edge of the bed wearing not a stitch of clothing, his arm extended in invitation. He was mildly aroused, and his smile balanced invitation with...hope?

Henrietta kept her dressing gown about her. She had no nightgown on underneath—why bother?—but neither did she want to parade about naked, and that too was a surprise.

"I'm all at sea," she said, taking the place beside Michael on the bed. "I know how to be a courtesan. I know what a courtesan wants, how she plies her trade. But this..."

A courtesan never confided in her partner. She managed every encounter to ensure he would be comfortable confiding in her, and what a bloody lot of work that was. The physical intimacies were so much dusting and polishing compared to that heavy labor.

Michael took her hand and kissed her knuckles. "If you're at sea, allow me to row you to shore. This is being lovers. You don't need to impress me, please me, flatter me, or put my needs above your own. We share pleasure, as best we can, and then we share some sweet memories."

"How simple." How uncomplicated, honest, and wonderful—so why did Henrietta feel like crying?

Michael slid his palm along her jaw and kissed the corner of her mouth. "Simple and lovely. Will you get the candles? I'll start warming up these sheets."

How many times had Henrietta made love with the candles blazing? She couldn't fall asleep that way—lit candles were a terrible fire hazard—though her partners had succumbed to slumber following their exertions with the predictability of horses rolling after a long haul under saddle.

She blew out the candles one by one. Michael had three sheaths soaking in water glasses on the bed table, and he'd already informed Henrietta that she was to notify him of any consequences from their encounter.

She suspected she was infertile, a courtesan's dearest blessing, and for the first time, the idea bothered her. A baron needed an heir, not that Michael's succession was any of her business.

"Come to bed, love," Michael said as candle smoke joined the scent of peat in the night air. "Mind you don't trip over that valise."

Considerate of him. Henrietta hefted her traveling case onto the cedar chest at the foot of the bed, then shed her dressing gown and climbed into bed with . . . her first lover.

⤙

Hot wax dripped onto Josiah Whitlow's hand and woke him. He'd fallen asleep at his desk for the third time in a week, or possibly the fourth. His housekeeper had given up scolding him for leaving the candles burning.

"Candles cost money," he muttered, sitting up slowly, lest the ache in his back turn to the tearing pain that prevented sleep. The fire in the hearth had burned down—coal cost money too—and the house held the heavy, frigid silence of nighttime after a winter storm.

"You left me on such a night," he muttered, gaze on the portrait over the mantel. Katie had died in March, after a late-season storm that had rattled the windows and made the chimneys moan. Josiah had known he was losing her since she'd failed to rally after a lung fever more than a year earlier. She'd never quite regained her strength after the birth of their younger boy.

"He has a daughter now," Josiah said, draining a serving of brandy he'd poured hours before. "Poor little mite is cursed with your red hair, madam."

He saluted with his glass. "Apologies for that remark. Ungentlemanly of me. Christmas approaches and I . . . am not at my best."

Every year, Christmas came around, and Henrietta did too. Every year, Josiah found some excuse to lurk in the mercantile across from the inn at Amblebank, until he caught a glimpse of his tall, beautiful daughter.

Henrietta resembled her mother, but every feature that had been pretty on Katie was striking on Henrietta. Katie had had good posture, Henrietta was regal. Katie had been warm-hearted, Henrietta was unforgettably lovely. Katie had known her Book of Common Prayer, and Henrietta—according to her brothers—quoted Shakespeare.

Accurately.

"I kept her from the books," he said, experimentally shifting forward in his chair. "Didn't want her to end up a blue-stocking old maid."

Josiah pushed to his feet, though the movement sent

discomfort echoing from his back to his hips, knees, and feet. Not gout, except possibly in one toe. Gout was for the elderly.

"Which I shall soon be, God willing."

Katie remained over the dying fire, smiling with the benevolence of perpetual youth. Josiah was glad for the shadows, because his wife's eyes reproached him for the whole business with Henrietta.

Girls fell from grace, Katie had once said, when a man came by intent on tripping them. Lately, Josiah had begun to suspect that Katie's point was not without validity, from a mother's perspective. Henrietta had been sixteen when she'd fled to London, and Josiah had been sure she'd come home within the week, chastened, repentant, and forever cured of her rebellious streak.

Instead, she'd shamed her family, set a bad example for her brothers, and broken her father's heart.

"She made her bed," Josiah said, blowing out the candles on the desk. "She can jolly well lie in it. And—with a damned aching hip—I shall lie in mine. Good night, madam."

The portrait, as always, remained silent, smiling, and trapped in pretty youth, while Josiah steeled himself for the growing challenge of negotiating the main staircase at the end of the day.

In Michael's wildest imaginings, he could not have anticipated the sheer joy of making love with Henrietta Whitlow. She was like a cat in a roomful of loose canaries, chasing this pleasure, then that one, then sitting fixed while fascinated with a third, until leaping after a fourth.

She wanted to spoon with Michael's arms snug around

her, then she demanded to lie face to face and touch every inch of his chest, arms, face, and shoulders. Just as he was having trouble drawing a steady breath—he'd not realized his ribs were ticklish—she'd rolled to her back.

"Now you touch me," she said, and Michael had obliged with hands, mouth, and body.

She gave him the sense that she'd never before permitted herself an agenda in the bedroom other than: Please *him*. Accommodate *him*. Make *him* happy. Her own wishes and dreams hadn't mattered enough to any of the men in her bed—or she'd been that skillful at hiding them—and thus those wishes hadn't been allowed to matter to her.

They mattered to Michael. *Henrietta* mattered.

She liked the sensation of his breath on her nipples, he liked the ferocious grip she took of his hair. Then she wrapped her hand around another part of him, and Michael sat back, the better to watch her face by the firelight as she explored him.

"If women were as proud of their breasts as men are of their cocks..." she muttered, tracing a single fingernail up the length of his shaft.

"There would be more happy women, and happy men," Michael said. "Perhaps more babies too. Would you please do that again?"

She obliged, more slowly. "You ask, you never demand."

"I'll be begging in a moment."

Her mouth closed around him, and for long moments, Michael couldn't *even* beg. He could only give silent thanks for these moments shared with Henrietta, while he tried to ignore the itch of guilt from his conscience.

Her valise sat at the foot of the bed, a reproach every time he opened his eyes. When Henrietta smiled up at him, he shifted over her, so she filled his vision.

"Now?" he asked.

She kissed him, framing his jaw with both hands, wrapping her legs around him. Her movements were languid and—he hoped—self-indulgent.

"I want to be on top," she said. "This time."

Michael subsided to his back, and she straddled him. He used her braid to tug her closer. "Like this?"

With no further ado, Henrietta tied a sheath about him, then sank down over him and joined them intimately. "More like this."

Michael struggled to locate a Shakespeare quote, a snippet, any words to remark the occasion. "Move, Henrietta. Move now."

She smiled down at him. "He demands. At last he demands."

"I'm begging you."

Her smile became tender as she tucked close and *moved*.

Chapter Five

All good things must end, or at least be paid for, and Henrietta the Housemaid eventually realized that her station in life had changed. I had the sense she might slip back to the shires, given a chance. I was forever finding her in tears over some draft of a letter to her martinet of a papa. No matter how often she wrote to him, he apparently never answered.

Having no recourse, when I offered to put my arrangement with her on professional footing, she accepted, and thus the career of London's greatest courtesan had its origins in my family parlor. Delicious irony, that, but for one small detail, which I must prevail upon you to tidy up...

Michael Brenner had needed a woman.

Or maybe—Henrietta wasn't quite awake, so her thoughts wandered instead of galloped—he'd needed *her*? Somebody with whom to be passionate, tender, funny, and honest. Maybe he'd needed a lover, an intimate friend with whom to be himself, wholly and joyfully.

Henrietta had needed him too. Needed a man who wasn't interested in tricks and feats of sexual athleticism, who wasn't fascinated with the forbidden, or bored with it, but still fascinated with his own gratification. Making love with Michael had been so *easy*, and yet so precious.

She'd been needing him for the past ten years.

To join with Michael had felt intimate, invigorating, and sweet. Surely the Bard had put it better, but Henrietta couldn't summon any literature to mind. The hour was late, and she was abed with a lover.

Her first lover.

She reached beneath the covers and found warmth but no Michael. Her ears told her he wasn't stirring about behind the privacy screen, which meant...

Nothing for it, she must open her eyes.

A page turned, the sound distinctive even when Henrietta's mind was fogged with sleep. Michael had pulled a chair near the hearth and lit a branch of candles. He sat reading a small book, his hair tousled, his dressing gown half open. His expression was beautifully somber, suggesting the prose on the page was serious.

Foreboding uncoiled where contentment had been.

"You'd rather read than cuddle?" Henrietta asked, sitting up. She kept the covers about her, and not because the room was chilly. Michael's expression was anything but loverlike.

"I'd rather cuddle, but I couldn't bear..."

"What?" Couldn't bear to remain in bed with her?

He closed the book and stared at the fire. "I couldn't bear to further deceive you. I have misrepresented myself to you, Miss Whitlow, in part. I've also been honest in part."

Miss Whitlow? *Miss Whitlow?*

"You've been *inside* me, Michael. Several times. Don't call me Miss Whitlow." *And don't remain halfway across the room, looking like a fallen angel on the eve of banishment to the Pit.*

"This book is the reason we met," he said, holding up the little volume. "Lord Beltram wants it back, though legally it is entirely your possession. He's begun searching for a bride and realized what a weapon he'd given you."

No flannel sheets, no cozy quilts, no secure embrace could have comforted Henrietta against the chill Michael's words drove into her heart.

"You *seduced* me to get Beltram's bloody book, and now you're confessing your perfidy?"

"I hope we seduced each other, but yes, my original intention was to steal this book from you." He thumbed through the most maudlin collection of bad verse and inferior artistry Henrietta had ever seen.

She rose from the warmth of the covers, shrugged into her night-robe—and yes, that made her breasts jiggle, and what of it?—and Michael looked away.

"Are you disgusted with the woman you seduced?" she asked, whipping her braid free of the night-robe. "Was bedding me a great imposition, my lord? What hold does Beltram have over you that you'd make a sacrifice of such magnitude with his cast-off mistress?"

"Miss—Henrietta, it's not like that."

Henrietta had a temper, a raging, blazing, vitriolic temper that had sent her from her father's house ten years ago and sustained her when it became apparent that Beltram was exactly the handsome scoundrel every girl was warned against.

She'd learned to marshal that temper in the interests of professional survival, but she was *no longer a professional*.

And she might not survive this insult. "It's never like that," she snapped. "Good God, I thought I knew better. Never again, I promised myself. Never again would a man get the better of me, no matter how handsome, how charming, how sincere..."

Michael rose, tossing the book onto the empty bed. "Henrietta Whitlow, I am not ashamed of you. I could never be ashamed of you. I am ashamed of myself."

"For sleeping with me?" She would kill him if he said yes and then burn his house down, after she'd carted away all of his books.

"I am ashamed of myself," he said, hands fisting at his sides, "for lying to you. For being an idiot."

"Idiot is too kind a term, Michael Brenner. I am Henrietta Whitlow. I turned down the overtures of the sovereign himself and scoffed at carte blanche from countless others, then gave you what they'd have paid a fortune to enjoy. I swore I'd never again... Why am I explaining this to you? Get out and take the damned book with you."

He stayed right where he was. "I should have asked you for the book, straight out. I apologize for not using common sense, but I was too long a thief, a spy, a manipulator of events. I could not simply steal from you, and I've left my honesty too late."

"Which means now you're a scoundrel," Henrietta said, though he seemed to be a contrite scoundrel. "You have exceeded the bounds of my patience, sir. Be off with you."

So she could cry, damn him. Henrietta hadn't cried since her last cat had died two years ago.

"Why have you kept Beltram's book all these years, Henrietta? Are you still in love with him?"

Through her rage, humiliation, and shock, Henrietta's instincts stirred. Michael had what he'd come for—so to speak—and Henrietta's feelings for Beltram ought to be of no interest to him.

At all.

"I kept his awful little book because I didn't want him publishing it and making me the laughingstock of the press and public. Beltram is selfish, unscrupulous, mean, and not to be trusted." And he had clammy hands. "Possession of that book was my only means of ensuring he'd not trouble me after he'd turned me from a housemaid to a whore."

Still, Michael remained before the fire, his expression unreadable. "Why not destroy the book?"

She might have confided that to him an hour ago. How dare he ask for her confidences now? "I will join a nunnery, I swear it, rather than endure the arrogance of the male gender another day."

"You kept that book for a reason. Were you intent on blackmailing him?"

With the room in shadows, Henrietta could believe Michael Brenner had been a spy and a thief. He hid his ruthlessness beneath fine tailoring and polite manners, but his expression suggested he'd do anything necessary to achieve his ends.

He made love with the same determination, and Henrietta had reveled in his passion.

Now, she'd do anything to get him out of her room, even confess further vulnerability.

"I kept the book because I wanted the reminder of what a gullible, arrogant idiot I'd been. Beltram laid out my downfall, page by page. He sketched me in my maid's uniform, adoration and ignorance in my gaze. He sketched me the first night he'd taken down my hair—for artistic purposes only, he assured me. He sketched me after he'd kissed me for the first time. It's all there, in execrable poetry and amateur sketches. My ruin, lest I forget a moment of it."

Michael crossed to the bed, and Henrietta stood her ground. He snatched the book off the bed, and she thought she'd seen the last of him. A convent in Sweden, maybe, or Maryland. If Borneo had convents, she'd consider them, provided they had enough books.

"Henrietta, I am sorry." Michael stood close enough that she could smell his lavender soap. "Beltram did, indeed, have a hold over me. I've fulfilled my part of the bargain and removed the book as a blackmail threat. I have no excuse for insinuating myself into your affections. I'm sorry for deceiving you. My coach will take you to Amblebank in the morning."

"You've insinuated yourself right back out of my affections, my lord. No harm done."

If she'd slapped him, he could not have looked more chagrined. "There's been harm, Henrietta. I know that. I'll do what I can to make it right."

Not more decency, not now when he'd betrayed the trust Henrietta hadn't realized she'd given.

"Comfort yourself with whatever platitudes you please, my lord, but leave me in peace. I'm tired and have earned my rest."

He considered the book, Beltram's exercise in lordly vanity and a testament to feminine vulnerability.

"This book means nothing to you?"

"It's reproach for my folly," Henrietta retorted. "I loathe the damned thing and the man who created it."

Michael threw the book straight into the fireplace, landing it atop the flaming peat.

Henrietta watched her past burn, incredulity warring with loss. As long as that book had been in her hands, she'd had proof—for herself, anyway—that once upon a time, she'd been innocent.

"Did Beltram force you, Henrietta?"

Nobody had asked her that, but Henrietta had asked the question of herself. "He took advantage of my ignorance and inexperience—I'd been chaste before I met him—he misled, he betrayed, he lied and seduced. He did not force. His actions were dishonorable, not quite criminal."

"Then I won't kill him."

Michael stood beside her until the book was a charred heap, its ashes drifting up the flue, and then he stalked from the room.

Henrietta gathered up the pile of fine tailoring Michael had draped over the chair, brought it into bed with her, and watched the flames in the hearth far into the night while her nose was buried in the scent of lavender.

Michael rose to a house made brilliant by sunshine on freshly fallen snow, though his mood could not have been blacker.

He'd committed two wrongs. First, he'd agreed to thievery to settle his account with Beltram. Stealing was wrong, and neither starvation nor the security of the realm provided Michael any room to forgive himself.

Second, he'd made love with Henrietta Whitlow. Not for all the baronies in Ireland would he regret the hours he'd spent in her bed, but he'd go to his grave regretting that he'd betrayed her trust.

"You will notify me if there are consequences, Henrietta."

He stood with her by the library window, waiting for the coach to be brought around. His house now sported wreaths on the front windows, cloved oranges dangling from curtain rods, red ribbons wrapped about bannisters, and an abundance of strategically placed mistletoe.

The holiday decorations Lucille had inspired were enough to restore Michael's faith in a God of retribution.

"Last night, you called me Miss Whitlow, and I insist on that courtesy today, if you must annoy me with conversation."

Last night, he'd called her his love. "I am annoying you with a demand. If taking me as your lover has consequences, you will inform me, and we will make appropriate accommodations."

Had she grown taller overnight? She certainly seemed taller, while Michael felt once again like that grubby youth clawing his way up from the peat bogs.

She regarded him from blazing green eyes down a magnificent nose. "You must be one of those Irishmen who longs for death. I don't fancy such melodrama myself, but I will cheerfully oblige you with a mortal blow to your cods if you don't cease your nattering."

He leaned closer. She smelled of neroli—orange blossoms—this morning rather than patch leaf, and he was daft for noticing.

"Kick me in the balls, Henrietta, if that will ease any of the hurt I've done you, but we shall marry if you're carrying my child."

She drew in a breath, as if filling her sails for another scathing retort, then her brows twitched down. "Not your child. *Our* child."

The coach came jingling around the drive from the carriage house, for some fool had put harness bells on the conveyance.

"You'd marry me?" Henrietta asked as the vehicle halted at the bottom of the front steps.

"Of course I'd marry you."

"Out of pity? Out of decency? Don't think I'd ever allow you into my bed, Michael."

"I'd marry you in hopes we might put the past behind us, Henrietta. I have wronged you, and I'm sorry for that, but I would not compound my error by also wronging my—our—child. If you closed your bedroom door to me, I'd respect that, for I respect you."

"Perhaps you do," she said, her gaze unbearably sad, "but your version of respect and mine differ significantly. If you'll excuse me, I'll be on my way."

"Henrietta, *I'm sorry*."

She paused by the door, her hand on the latch. "Would you have stolen from me if I'd been Beltram's sister rather than his ruined housemaid?"

"To get free of that man, I'd have stolen from the bishop of London on Christmas Eve."

Henrietta crossed back to Michael's side, kissed his cheek, and remained for one moment standing next to him. "If there's a child, I'll tell you."

She hadn't agreed to marry him, but Michael was grateful for small mercies.

⁓

"There's no room at the inn," Henrietta said, crossing her fingers behind her back. "I've come home for a visit, and you will either make me welcome, or take yourself off elsewhere."

Papa had aged significantly in ten years. His shoulders were stooped, his hair had thinned, and his clothing hung loosely on his frame. Henrietta steeled her heart against the changes in his appearance, because the jut of his chin and the cold in his eyes promised her no welcome. The housekeeper had tried to show her to the formal parlor, but Henrietta had scoffed at that bit of presumption and let herself into Papa's library.

He stood in the doorway, still apparently unwilling to be in the same room with her. "Madam, you are not welcome in this house." Even his voice had grown weaker.

"Too bad," Henrietta retorted, "because I was born here, and I've nowhere else to go. The least you could do is ring for tea, Papa. Traveling up from London has taken days, all of them cold, and the dratted coaches nearly rattled my teeth from my head."

"Your mother never liked——" He caught himself. "Be gone from this house. Immoral women must fend for themselves."

Stubborn, but then, Henrietta had learned to be stubborn too. "I've given up being immoral. I content myself now with garden-variety wickedness. When I burn my finger, I use bad language. I forgot to say grace before breakfast today, but I was anticipating this joyous reunion. I haven't had a duke in my bed for months, Papa."

"Henrietta!"

Had his lips twitched?

"Well, I haven't." One handsome baron, for a few hours. That hardly mattered. "Unless you intend to scorn me for the rest of my life—or what remains of yours—then you will endure my company over the holidays."

Please, Papa. Please… She'd tried pleading once before, and he'd not bothered to reply to her letter.

His gaze strayed to the portrait over the mantel. Mama's likeness needed a good cleaning, something Henrietta's brothers would never dare to suggest.

"There isn't a single bed available at the inn?"

The inn had never once been full, in Henrietta's experience. "Not that I know of. You're letting out all the heat from the fire."

He took two steps into the room and closed the door

behind him. "You have grown bold, Henrietta Eloisa. I do not approve of bold women."

"I do not approve of hard-hearted, cantankerous men." Or thieves or liars.

Papa had always had a leonine quality, and his eyebrows had grown positively fierce. "I'll not tolerate disrespect, Henrietta."

"Then we understand each other, because *neither will I.*"

That earned her a definite twitch of the paternal lips, though she'd never been more serious.

Then Papa drew himself up, into a semblance of the imposing man he'd been in Henrietta's childhood. "Tomorrow, you will find other accommodations. You may stay the night, but no longer."

One night? He'd toss his own daughter out into the snow come morning? Henrietta was tempted to remonstrate with him, to air old grievances and trade recriminations until he admitted his share of responsibility for ten years of rejection.

She was *sorry* she'd disobeyed him and had apologized for her transgressions in writing. She was about to remind her father of those salient facts when she recalled Michael, apologizing with desperate sincerity in the cold morning sunshine.

"Thank you, Papa. I'll have one of my trunks brought in and introduce my maid to your housekeeper."

"You travel with a maid?"

"Of course, and I usually take my own coach and team, though on the way up from Town I had a mishap." *I fell in love, but I'll get over it.*

He settled into the chair behind his desk, his movements slow and gingerly. "You have a coach and team. My daughter. Racketing about England in the dead of winter with her own..."

"And a maid too."

"Whom you will see to now," Papa said. "Be off with you, Henrietta. I have much to do, and your brothers will want to know of your arrival. Send them each a note, lest they hear of your visit from some hostler or tavern maid."

Be off with you, not five minutes after he'd stepped into the room. When Henrietta had taken herself away to London, he'd not spoken to her for ten years, now she was to *be off with herself*.

"You can write those notes to my brothers," she said. "My travels have exhausted me, and I'm in need of a hot cup of tea. Shall I have a tray sent to you as well?"

Papa scowled at her as if she'd tripped over a chamber pot. "I prefer coffee."

"Coffee, then. I'll let the maid know." If Henrietta brought him that tray, she might dump it over his head. "It's good to be home, Papa."

She left him in his comfy chair in his cozy study, before she started shouting. For Christmas, she'd longed to have his respect. They were speaking to each other, mostly civilly, and he'd granted her shelter from the elements, albeit temporarily.

That was a start, and more than she'd had from him for the previous decade.

⁓

Five days went by, during which Michael rehearsed enough apologies and grand speeches to fill every stage in Drury Lane. On Friday, he received a holiday greeting from Lord Heathgate that was positively chatty.

Heathgate, once the greatest rogue in Britain, maundered on about his daughters' intrepid horsemanship and his sons' matchless abilities at cricket. The paragraph regarding his lordship's marchioness was so rife with tender sentiment that Michael had nearly pitched it into the rubbish bin.

Instead, he took himself for a long walk and ended up in the stables.

"You again," Liam Logan said. "I'd thought by now you'd be traveling into Oxford to see those sisters of yours."

Michael joined him at a half door to a coach horse's stall. They still had the grays from the last inn Michael had stopped at with Henrietta.

"I thought by now my sisters might see fit to pay their brother a holiday visit," Michael said. "But sitting on my rosy arse amid a bunch of dusty old books hasn't lured my family into the countryside."

"Then you'll want to go into Oxford to purchase tokens for the Christmas baskets," Logan said, reaching a gloved hand to the gelding nosing through a pile of hay.

"My staff has already seen to the baskets. Didn't I give you leave for the holidays, Logan?"

The horse ignored Logan's outstretched hand and instead gave Michael's greatcoat a delicate sniff. Horse breath on the ear tickled, but Michael let the beast continue its investigations.

"That you did, sir, but here I am."

"I won't have much use for—"

The horse got its teeth around the lapel of Michael's collar and tugged, hard. Michael was pulled up against the stall door, and—with a firm, toothy grasp of his coat—the horse merely regarded him. The domestic equine was blessed with large, expressive eyes, and in those eyes, Michael detected the same unimpressed and vaguely challenging sentiment Henrietta had once turned on him.

"Ach, now that's enough," Logan said, waving a hand in the horse's face. "Be off with you."

The same words Henrietta had used.

The horse, however, kept its grip of Michael's greatcoat. If the beast could talk, it might have said, "I weigh nearly ten times what you do, my teeth could snap your arm, and my feet smash your toes. Ignore me at your peril."

I'm to fetch Henrietta home to Inglemere, and to me. For ten years, Henrietta had bided in London, probably longing for her family to fetch her home, because that's what families were supposed to do when one of their number strayed. The idea had not the solid ring of conviction, but the more delicate quality of a hope, a theory, a wish.

Which was a damned sight more encouraging than the cold toes and insomnia Michael had to show for the past week's wanderings.

"Have the team put to," Michael said, scratching the gelding's ear. "We're for Amblebank."

The horse let him go.

"Thank God for that," Logan said. "But you'd best change into some decent finery, my lord. The ladies are none too impressed with muddy boots."

"I'm not calling on a lady," Michael said. "But you're right. The occasion calls for finery."

And some reconnaissance. A comment Henrietta had made about her brothers had lodged in Michael's memory, and the comment wanted further investigation. Henrietta's family was merely gentry, not aristocracy, and life in the shires ran on more practical terms than in Mayfair.

Michael dressed with care, explained the itinerary to Logan, and made only one brief stop on the way to Amblebank. Less than two hours after making the decision to go calling, he was standing in Josiah Whitlow's study, sporting his best Bond Street tailoring and his most lordly air.

Henrietta's father put Michael in mind of an aging eagle, his gaze sharp, the green of his eyes fading, his demeanor brusquely—almost rudely—proper.

"To what do I owe the honor of this call, my lord?" Whitlow asked.

"We're neighbors, at a distance," Michael said. "My estate lies about five miles east of Amblebank, and I've had occasion to meet your daughter."

Whitlow stalked across the room and stood facing a portrait of a lovely young redhead. His gait was uneven, but energetic. "For ten years, I had no daughter."

Whose fault was that? "And now?"

"I've sent her off to her brothers. She tarried here for five days, made lists for the housekeeper, the maids, the footmen, put together menus, hung blasted greenery and mistletoe from—she's no longer here, and I doubt she will be ever again."

Her name is Henrietta. Henrietta Eloisa Gaye Whitlow. "If you've driven her from her only home permanently, then you are a judgmental old fool who deserves to die of loneliness."

Whitlow turned from the portrait, his magnificent scowl ruined by a suspicious glimmer in his eyes. "Do you think I haven't died of loneliness, young man? Do you think I haven't worried for the girl every day for the past ten years? And what business is it of yours? You seek to entice her back to wickedness, no doubt, as if coin can compensate a woman for discarding her honor."

Michael advanced on Whitlow. "Your oldest was born six months after your wedding vows were spoken. Your first grandchild arrived five months after his parents' union. I stopped at the church and leafed through the registries. If

I'd had the time, I'd have gathered similar information on half your neighbors. Order a tea tray, Mr. Whitlow, and stop feeling sorry for yourself. You're a hypocrite at best, and possibly a poor father as well."

"You are a very presuming young man."

Stubbornness must be a defining trait of the Whitlows, but the Brenners had clung to life itself on the strength of sheer stubbornness.

"I will not lie—ever again—and say that I've been entirely honorable where Henrietta is concerned, but I promised her I'd do what I could to atone for the wrong I've done. She seeks a rapprochement with her family, and I'll see that she gets one."

Whitlow hobbled over to the desk and dropped into the chair behind it. "I cannot condone immorality, you fool. So she sits down to Christmas dinner with us. If she takes up with the likes of you again, then I want no more to do with her. She deserves better than you strutting young popinjays with your coin and your arrogance. If she can't see that, I'll not stand by and smile while she waltzes with her own ruin."

Michael's father would have understood this version of love. *I'll shame you to your senses*, the argument went. The difficulty was, two people could engage in a mutual contest of wills that had nothing of sense about it.

"Henrietta never wants to see me again," Michael said. "And from everything she's said, she feels similarly about the popinjays, dukes, and even the king."

Whitlow put his head in his hands. "The *king*?"

"Turned him down with a smile. Wouldn't do more than share his theater box for any amount of money."

"Good God. My little hen . . . and the king." Whitlow's expression suggested he was horrified—and impressed. "She wasn't just making talk about dukes, then?"

"She had her choice of the lot," Michael said. "Dukes, princes, nabobs. She never had dealings with men who were married or engaged. Not ever, and she demanded absolute fidelity from her partners for the duration of any arrangement. The titled bachelors of London will go into a collective decline at her retirement, and she gave up all that power and money just so you could behave like a stubborn ass yet again. I'll not have it."

Whitlow produced a plain square of soft, white linen. "Who are you to *have* anything? Henrietta made choices. She was stubborn. You don't know how stubborn. I had a match all picked out for her. A decent chap, settled, respectable. She flew into hysterics, and then she was gone."

Michael appropriated the chair opposite Whitlow's desk, because the man apparently lacked the manners even to offer a guest a seat.

"You chose one of your widowed friends, I'd guess. A man at least twice Henrietta's age, with children not much younger than she. Her fate would have been to give up drudging for you and her brothers for the great boon of drudging for some middle-aged man and his children. What sixteen-year-old girl with any sense would be flattered by that arrangement?"

Elsewhere in the house, a door slammed, though Whitlow didn't seem to notice. Perhaps he was hard of hearing as well as of heart.

"She was growing too rebellious," he said. "I had to marry her off, or she'd…Sixteen isn't too young to be engaged. I'd talked Charles into waiting until she was eighteen for the wedding, and that would have been in the agreements. Henrietta said in two years the damned man would probably have lost the last of his teeth. She cursed at me. My own daughter, cursing."

"And because even cursing didn't get your attention, she ran away rather than bow to a scheme that would only make her miserable. What else was she to do?"

Whitlow had had ten years to convince himself that he was the wronged party, and yet, Michael still saw a hint of guilt in his eyes.

"In time, she would have been a well-fixed widow," Whitlow said. "Many women would have envied her that fate."

"In twenty or thirty years? Assuming your friend and his children didn't spend his every last groat first? You are blind, Whitlow, and Henrietta was too. She went to London, a complete innocent, a young girl who thought men were selfish, irascible, and high-handed, but not her enemies. She went into service, glad to have employment in the house of a titled family, prepared to work hard for a pittance.

"She had no inkling that her virtue was at risk. She'd been trained to wait on the men of her family, to see to their every need, to put their welfare before her own, and by God, you trained her well. She had no grasp of her own beauty, no sense of what men might do to possess it, or how to defend herself from them. That is your fault as well, and no other's."

Whitlow erupted from his chair, bracing his hands on his desk blotter. "How dare you lecture me about the daughter I raised in this very house? How dare you presume to make excuses for a girl who knew right from wrong as clearly as I know noon from midnight?"

"Better you should ask how dare her employer ruin her and suffer no consequences for his venery," Michael said. "Read this."

He tossed Beltram's letter onto the desk, where it sat like a glove thrown down to mark a challenge.

"What is it?"

"A letter to me from the man who destroyed your

daughter's good name, but not, fortunately, her self-respect. He plotted, he schemed, he lied, he charmed, and he made empty promises of matrimony. He behaved without a shred of honor and left Henrietta broken-hearted, ruined, and alone at the age of sixteen. She took the same risk her mother did—granted favors to a man promising matrimony. Her mother is enshrined over your mantel for that decision, while Henrietta was banished from your household."

This was not the speech Michael had rehearsed, but he should have, for the recitation nearly broke his heart, while Whitlow appeared entirely unmoved.

"Henrietta's failing was that she trusted the wrong man," Michael went on more softly. "*She trusted you* to forgive her for straying into the wrong pair of arms, and in that, she erred. I'd guess she wrote to you, asking permission to come home, and you denied her. Read that letter, Whitlow."

Whitlow subsided into his chair, regarding Beltram's letter like the foul excrescence it was.

Michael rose and leaned across the desk. "Read it, or I'll read it to you loudly enough that the whole house will hear me. Then I'll read it in the tavern. I'll read it to her brothers. I'll read it in the church if I must, or the village square. I'll read the damned thing in the House of Lords, and then all will know of your shame. Not hers. Beltram's—*and yours*."

Whitlow read the letter, then sat unmoving, his gaze on the portrait over the mantel.

"Will you apologize to your daughter, Whitlow?"

He nodded once, a tear trickling unchecked down his weathered cheek.

"Then I'll wish you the joy of the season and take my leave."

Chapter Six

I don't regret a moment of the time I spent making Henrietta Whitlow what she is today, though she's never thanked me for the effort I put forth, peeling her grip from the dust mop and rags of propriety. When our paths cross now, she adopts an air of subtly injured dignity, though I can't imagine she'd ever want to go back to dreams of wedded contentment, or a quiet life in the shires.

She's had the pleasure of my protection, after all, and I'm nearly certain when I ended our affair, her heart was broken for all time. I did her a very great favor, if so, for what woman plying the oldest trade has any need for tender sentiment or permanent attachments?

She has your hair, Henrietta," Isabel said, taking a seat across the kitchen table. "I think Thad is pleased by that. Philip's two got it as well."

Henrietta stroked the downy head pillowed on her shoulder. "The little ones all have Mama's hair. I hope the children got Mama's sweet nature too."

Isabel searched through a bowl of whole cloves. "You have a sweet nature."

"You're being kind." Both brothers, and their wives, and even Alexander and Dicken were being kind, treating Henrietta with the unfailing cheer of those on nursing duty in a sickroom. She was sick—at heart—but her family need not know that.

"I'm being honest," Isabel said, jabbing a clove into an orange. "If you'd been less sweet, the squire would never have been so daft as to think he could marry you off to Charles Sampson. Those oldest three sons of his have gambled away half his fortune, and the second Mrs. Sampson is rarely out of childbed."

The kitchen was perfumed with cloves and oranges, and the baby was a warm bundle of joy in Henrietta's arms. Isabel's words were an odd sort of comfort too.

Henrietta *had* been sweet, far too sweet. "I didn't know Mr. Sampson had remarried."

"Mrs. Sampson got a procession of runny noses and lazy housemaids. You got London and the company of dukes, from what I hear."

Isabel selected another clove from the dish, her focus overly intent.

"Only two dukes, Isabel, and they're much like any other man. One of them snored a bit and had a cold nose, which he delighted in nuzzling against my neck. The other fretted endlessly over his three sisters and had a fondness for chocolate."

Isabel popped the clove into her mouth. "No orgies, then?"

"Not a one. I would have sent any man who suggested such foolishness on his way with a flea in his ear."

"And they would have departed on your whim," Isabel said. "You're not sweet, biddable Hen anymore. Has that child gone to sleep?"

A quiet slurping near Henrietta's ear suggested otherwise. "Not quite. How many cloves will you stick into that poor orange?"

The hapless fruit resembled a beribboned mace from days of old. Isabel set it aside and plucked another orange from a bowl on the table and measured off a length of red ribbon.

"So what now, Hen? You've made your fortune, turned your back on Sodom, and here you are. The whole shire knows you bided with the squire for most of this week, and we'll drag you to services on Sunday if you like. If you were here to make a point, you've made it."

"I am here to enjoy my family's company over the holidays," Henrietta said, though also, apparently, to make a point. "Attending services needn't be part of the bargain. Papa allowed me to bide with him, but he might as well have been billeting a French prisoner of war for all the hospitality he extended."

The squire had barely spoken to her, had barely acknowledged her at meals. Henrietta had been tolerated under her father's roof because to toss her out would have created more scandal than to allow her a few days at her childhood home.

And that tolerance had been more hurtful than all his years of distance, oddly enough.

Isabel cut the red ribbon with a single snip of the shears. "Do you believe that if you attend services, then you can't go back to your old life? Is waking up in the middle of the night to a duke's cold nose pressed to your neck that thrilling? I can suggest a few dogs who'd be as obliging, though they might not pay you in any coin but loyalty and devotion."

The baby sighed, and no exhalation was ever softer than a baby's sigh.

"She might be falling asleep now," Henrietta said.

"Good. I suspect the poor thing is getting ready to present us with a few teeth, and that's always an occasion for misery."

Isabel wrapped the ribbon about the orange with an expert flip and a twist, such that the fruit could be tied to any handy rafter or curtain rod. Henrietta had dealt with her partners in much the same way.

Flattery, affection, an interest in the man's welfare, a semblance of friendship always bounded by pragmatism. When the gentleman grew too demanding or restless, a subtle cooling from Henrietta was all it took to nudge him out the door and add another diamond necklace to her collection.

The oranges Isabel decorated would shrivel and turn brown, then be tossed to the hogs, no matter how pleasing their fragrance now.

"I don't want to go back to what I was," Henrietta said, "but I'm not sure in what direction I should move next."

Michael Brenner's image came to mind as Henrietta had last seen him. He'd followed her out to the drive at Inglemere, bowed over her hand in parting, and remained bare-headed at the foot of his front steps, his hair whipping in the winter breeze as the coach had taken off down the drive.

He'd looked lonely. Papa had looked lonely when Henrietta had packed up her coach and taken herself to Thad's house. Her next stop would be Philip's, after Christmas, but then...

Would Michael still be at Inglemere when the new year came?

"Has Thad ever broken your heart?" Henrietta asked.

Visiting with Isabel wasn't so different from visiting with other courtesans. Henrietta had somehow concluded that decent women sat about discussing the weather or recipes for tisanes rather than men and teething babies.

Courtesans had all too many babies, and all too many men.

"He came close," Isabel said, impaling the second orange with its first clove. "The year after we were married, I thought I was carrying, though it came to nothing, and that unnerved him. He got a bit too close to Penelope Dortmund, who'd been widowed the year before. She had the knack of grieving ever so prettily."

Henrietta had not been invited to her younger brother's wedding or any of the christenings. "What happened?"

Isabel jabbed three more cloves into the orange. "I saw them in the livery, literally rolling in the hay, though Thad hadn't got under her skirts yet. When he came home, I plucked a bit of hay from his hair and told him only a very foolish man would sleep beside one woman while playing her false with another. He barely tipped his hat to the widow after that."

"You *forgave* him?"

Isabel set the orange aside and took another from the bowl, a perfectly ripe fruit. She tore a section of peel off, then another.

"Have you seen Izzy's cradle, Henrietta?"

"It's gorgeous." The cradle was made of polished oak— a heavy, durable wood that wasn't easy to work with. The oak was carved with flowers, a rabbit, a kitten, and the words *Mama and Papa Will Always Love You.*

Henrietta couldn't stand to touch it. Another one very much like it lay in the squire's attics.

"Thad made that cradle. Stayed up late, worked on Sundays. He said it wasn't labor, it was love for the child I carried that sent him out to his woodshop. He built this house for us. He puts food on my table and coal in my hearth. He's not perfect, but neither am I. The widow wanted a stolen moment, but Thad asked me for my entire future. For better or for worse means for better or for worse."

She passed Henrietta a section of orange, then took one for herself.

"You love each other." The words hurt.

"Mostly. We used to argue more than we do now. Izzy helps. Thad adores that child."

The baby was fast asleep, an innocent, endlessly lovable little being who years from now might roll in the hay with the wrong man, or disappoint her papa in a fit of indignation. Henrietta hugged the baby close, and that, of course, woke the child.

"She'll be hungry," Isabel said, wiping her fingers on a towel. "Give her to me, and you can finish this orange. So will you go to services with us on Sunday?"

Isabel put the child to the breast while Henrietta took up stabbing cloves into the thick rind of the orange.

"I don't know about attending services. I think so. I'll scandalize the entire congregation."

"If they can't muster a bit of warm-heartedness at Christmas, then they're not much of a congregation, are they?"

"I wasn't much of a courtesan," Henrietta said, wondering why she'd taken ten years to realize this. "Papa never bade me come home, I was ruined, and I simply didn't know what else to do." And there Beltram had been, just full of suggestions and bank drafts, when it was clear that a life in service would mean more Beltrams who wouldn't bother to pay for the favors they sought.

Henrietta was abruptly glad Michael had pitched the bloody book into the fire.

"You're home now," Isabel said. "That's a start. I didn't realize Thad had taken the sleigh over to Philip's."

Henrietta went to the window, because the rhythmic jingle of bells heralded a conveyance coming up the drive.

Not Michael.

"It's Papa, driving himself, and both Thad and Philip are with him. He'll catch his death if he doesn't wear a scarf in this weather."

Papa was coming to call at a house where Henrietta dwelled. She did not know what to feel, and now, unlike the past ten years, her feelings mattered. Did she want to see her father when he was being such a pestilential old curmudgeon?

Did she care that he'd come to call on a house where she dwelled just days after waving her on her way?

"You'll have to see to him," Isabel said with a glance at the baby. "Izzy does not care for the company of her grandpapa, and the squire doesn't think to lower his voice around a small child. He walks into the room and she fusses. I'll join you as soon as I can."

Voices and heavy footsteps sounded in the hall above.

"Henrietta Eloisa! I know you're here because your coach yet sits in the carriage house at the livery. Show yourself this instant and prepare to go calling with your family!"

"Has he been drinking?" Henrietta muttered, gathering up her shawl. "I cannot tolerate an intemperate man."

"He never drinks to excess. Go see what he wants, and recall that it's Christmas, Henrietta. Dredge up some charity for a lonely old man, because when you leave here, the rest of us have to put up with his moods and demands."

"You don't have to, actually," Henrietta said, taking a moment to arrange her shawl before starting for the stairs at a decorous pace. "You never did."

Michael closeted himself in the library—the last place Henrietta had kissed him—but he couldn't focus on work. He'd written to Beltram, one sentence informing his lordship that the book had been destroyed by fire before Michael's very eyes.

Had Michael's future with Henrietta been destroyed as well?

The door opened, revealing Michael's butler. "You have callers, my lord. Squire Josiah Whitlow and company. I put them in the family parlor because it's the only one with a fire."

Wright's words held reproach, for a proper lord would expect callers at the holidays and keep the formal parlor heated for the vicar and the second parlor toasty for the neighbors.

"Thank you, Wright," Michael said, turning down his cuffs and shrugging into his coat. "Please send up a tray on our best everyday service with a few biscuits or some short-bread. Did the squire bring his sons?"

"He did, sir." Wright bowed and withdrew on a soft click of the door latch. Wright would have made a good spy, except a palpable air of consequence enveloped him whether he was polishing the silver or lining the staff up to welcome Michael home.

Back to Inglemere—not home.

Perhaps Squire Whitlow was visiting for the purpose of calling Michael out, which occasion would necessitate the presence of the sons, who'd serve as seconds. Hardly a holiday sentiment, calling on a man on Christmas Eve to announce an intent to end his days.

Would Henrietta care? Other duels had been fought over her, but she was retired, and the last thing Michael wanted was to give her more cause for upset.

Then too, Michael was a baron now, and strictly speaking, a titled man did not duel with his social inferiors. He paused for one fortifying moment outside the parlor, then made a brisk entrance and stopped short.

"Mr. Whit...low."

Michael remained in the doorway, gawping like an idiot, for Henrietta graced his family parlor. She was resplendent in yards of purple velvet with red trim. Her father and brothers were so many drab grouse compared to her, none of them looking particularly comfortable to be paying this call.

Michael was pleased. Cautiously pleased.

"Welcome to you all," he said. "Squire, introductions are in order."

The squire cleared his throat, harrumphed, then stood very tall. "Henrietta, may I make known to you Michael, Lord Angelford, who has taken possession of Inglemere since last you bided in Amblebank. His lordship paid a call on me yesterday, hence our neighborly reciprocity of his gesture. My lord, I make known to you my daughter, Henrietta, and her two brothers, Philip and Thaddeus Whitlow. You can thank the mighty powers that my grandchildren did not accompany us, else they'd be climbing your curtains and breaking yonder porcelain vase by now."

Whitlow had introduced her with all appropriate decorum, even knowing Michael was not a stranger to Henrietta.

The strategy was brilliant, did Whitlow but know it.

"Miss Whitlow," Michael said, taking the lady's hand and bowing. "I am honored by your company." He bowed in turn to Philip and Thad, who were younger versions of the squire. The tray soon arrived, and much to Michael's surprise, the squire carried the conversation.

He inquired regarding crops and tenants, drainage—ever a fascinating subject to the English gentry—and game. Henrietta presided over the tea tray with perfect grace but added little to the conversation.

What did it mean that she'd come to call? Was her family treating her well, and how could Michael find five minutes alone to ask her if she'd forgiven him?

He'd watched every crumb of shortbread disappear down the gullets of the Whitlow menfolk and was about to embark on a discourse regarding the construction of a ha-ha bordering a hayfield—about which he knew not one damned thing—when Wright interrupted again.

"More callers, my lord, and I hesitate to bring bad tidings, but they've children with them. Noisy children."

"Healthy lungs on a child are always a cause for rejoicing," Squire Whitlow said. "Well, don't just stand there," he went on, waving a hand at Wright. "Get us another tea tray with plenty of biscuits and show the visitors in. You're in the household of a baron, and company will be a constant plague."

"Wright," Michael said, rising. "Who are these callers?"

"Your sisters, my lord. All of them. With all of their children, and a husband or two, if I'm not mistaken. Cook will have an apoplexy."

His sisters? *All of them?* And the children and the husbands?

The cautious joy blooming in Michael's heart lurched upward to lodge in his throat. "Make them welcome, Wright, or I'll sack you on Christmas Day. You will make my family welcome, no matter how much noise they bring, or how many vases they break."

Wright bowed very low—though not quite low enough to hide a smile—and withdrew.

"Shall we be going?" Philip Whitlow asked, rising. "Your lordship's apparently quite busy with visitors today, and we wouldn't want to overstay our welcome."

"My friends are always welcome here," Michael said, and he was smiling too, because now—finally—Henrietta was looking straight at him and appearing very pleased with herself.

Or possibly, with him?

⁓

Michael did not look well-rested, but neither was he being the unapproachable lord. As Papa bleated on about ditches and boggy ground, Henrietta considered that Michael Brenner might be a shy man. She liked the idea and, as she watched Michael draw both Thad and Philip into the discussion, admitted that she liked Michael as well.

What's more, Papa liked him.

"I'll suggest we remove across the hall to the library," Michael said, "lest the size of the company exceed the capacity of the parlor. My nephews can be rambunctious."

"So can mine," Henrietta said, offering Michael her hand. Her brothers looked surprised, but then, her brothers had been indulged by wives who'd let manners lapse amid the exigencies of domestic bliss.

Michael's grasp was firm, but fleeting. "You'll find the library a little lacking in warmth," he said, aiming his comments at Henrietta. "But the room could be gracious with a little attention."

His library was lovely, though his desk was a bit untidy, as if he'd tried and failed a number of times to write a difficult letter. Henrietta was wandering about, trying to casually work her way to the desk when a herd of small children galloped into the library.

"I get the ladder!" one boy yelled.

"First on the bannister!" another cried.

"I get the bannister," a small girl called, elbowing one of the boys in the ribs.

"Reminds me of you lot," Papa said, taking some book or other from Henrietta's hands, while Michael went to the front door to greet his sisters. "That man is in love with you, Henrietta. Properly head over ears. I had to see it for myself, and he did not disappoint. If you show him the least favor, he'll make you his baroness."

Papa's words were offered beneath the pounding of a dozen small feet up the spiral staircase in the corner of Michael's library. His lordship rejoined the group in the library, bringing four laughing, chattering sisters with him and two much quieter men.

Pandemonium ensued, with children sliding down the spiral bannister, mamas and papas clucking and scolding, Philip and Thad putting a boy each on their shoulders to reach the higher shelves, and Papa—Papa?—presiding over the bowl of rum punch on the sideboard.

"You come with me," Henrietta said, taking Michael by the hand. "We're seeing to more refreshments."

He came along docilely—brilliant man—while one of the girls snatched Henrietta's serving of punch and nipped up the steps with it.

"My sisters have come to call," Michael said. "I've been hinting and suggesting for weeks, but they never acknowledged my overtures. Now they're here, and all I want is to see them off so I can have more time with you."

"Where's the formal parlor?" Henrietta asked.

"Two doors down, to the right. My staff has doubtless lit the fire there, because they're certain the vicar will soon be joining the riot that passes for my household at present."

Henrietta escorted Michael to the formal parlor, a lovely room full of gilt chairs upholstered in pink velvet, thick carpets, an elegant white pianoforte, and a pink marble fireplace.

"The quiet," Michael said as Henrietta closed the door. "Just listen to the quiet."

The only sound was the fire crackling in the hearth, though Henrietta could feel her heart pounding against her ribs too.

"Listen to me," she said. "I don't like that you stole my book, Michael Brenner. You should have asked me for it."

He stuck his hands in his pockets, though the parlor was cozy. "Would you have given it to me? I was a stranger to you, a man you had no reason to trust."

"Then you should have taken the time to earn my trust."

"I should have, and I am profoundly sorry I didn't. I behaved badly, but Henrietta…"

From the library came the happy shrieks of children loose for the first time in their uncle's home. The sound nearly broke Henrietta's heart, though at least Michael's family had come, however dubious their timing.

"But what, Michael?"

He put his hands behind his back and approached her. "I do not regret the intimacies I shared with you. I can't, and I never will. If I'd approached you as Beltram's negotiator, bargaining that book away from you with coin, charm, or threats, would you ever have allowed me close enough to become your lover?"

She'd wondered the same thing. "I don't know."

He stepped away, and the silence grew to encompass Christmases past, future, and all the years in between. Without Michael, those Christmases would be terribly lonely, even if Henrietta became the doting aunt and spinster daughter her family now invited her to be.

A revelation, that.

"I do know," Henrietta said, "that I treasure those moments shared with you too. I should have thrown that book in the fire years ago, but hadn't the courage. I wouldn't be here, calling on you, if my father hadn't kidnapped me and demanded I accompany him on a holiday call, as a proper daughter ought. He's gone daft."

"He's apologizing, in his way. He and I had a frank talk the day after you left his household. Will you accept his apology, Henrietta?"

"You and Papa had a frank talk? What did you and he have to talk about?"

One corner of Michael's mouth lifted. "I wanted to ask him if I could pay you my addresses, but the topic didn't come up. I was too busy lecturing him."

Henrietta sat on the nearest reliable surface—a tufted sofa. "There's too much pink in this room."

"Then redecorate it," Michael said. "May I sit with you?"

"You wanted to ask Papa if you could *court* me? You're a baron, and I'm a…" A woman in love, among other things. Henrietta patted the place beside her. "This is all very sudden."

"This is all ten years too late." Michael came down beside her and took her hand. "Can you forgive me, Henrietta? I have wronged you, but I also hope I've nudged things with your family in a better direction. I couldn't think what else to do."

Michael had *had a talk* with Papa. Henrietta shuddered to think what that conversation had entailed, but Papa had introduced her not an hour past as a proper young miss, which she most assuredly would never be again.

"Whatever you said," Henrietta replied, "it opened a door that all of my wrenching and wrestling couldn't budge. Papa and I will never get back the last ten years, but you've given us the years to come, and that's miracle enough."

Michael's grip on her hand was loose and warm. "You'll allow me to court you?"

Henrietta didn't fly into giddy raptures, though she was tempted to. Ten years ago, she might have. Michael apparently didn't expect giddy raptures, and that made up her mind.

"Papa has the right of it," she said. "You will court me, right down to asking his permission before he leaves here today. You'll walk out with me, when the weather moderates."

"And join your family for Sunday dinner," Michael said. "Sunday dinners are very important."

"I'll get to know your sisters—I wrote to them, by the way."

He kissed her knuckles. "You put them up to this invasion?"

"You looked so lonely and they hadn't had a formal invitation, only hints and suggestions. They were waiting for the great baron to do the pretty, never having had a great baron in the family before."

"Thank goodness you came along to translate the brother into the baron, then. Will we cry the banns?"

This discussion was so odd, and so right. This was two people discussing a shared future, not an arrangement. This was solving problems, forgiving, loving, and moving forward, not choosing jewelry or signing a lease on a love nest.

This was what a happily ever after in the making looked like.

"We'll decide whether to cry the banns or use a special license if you propose," Henrietta said. "First, you must have permission to court me."

"No," Michael said, taking her in his arms. "First, I must kiss you, then I must gain permission to court you— provided you're willing?"

Henrietta kissed him with all the willingness in her, and not a little stubbornness, along with heaps of gratitude and bundles of hope. Desire was making the list just as the door flew open, and a small red-haired girl pelted into the room.

"Can I hide in here?"

"You may," Michael said. "But only for a short while. I'll need this room for a private chat with Miss Whitlow's father."

The child darted behind the sofa. "Good! Don't tell anybody I'm here."

So it came to pass that Michael asked Squire Whitlow for permission to court Henrietta while one of Michael's nieces giggled and fidgeted behind the sofa. Henrietta fidgeted in the library—but did not giggle—until her Papa returned from the formal parlor to offer her a cup of punch from the nearly empty bowl on the sideboard.

"He'll do, Henrietta," Papa said. "The fellow's besotted, worse even than I was with your mama. Don't make him wait too long, please. A man's dignity matters to him."

"So does a woman's," Henrietta said. "I want to be married in spring, with my family all around me, and Michael's family too. You'll give me away?"

Michael returned to the library, a little girl carried piggyback. "Nobody found me!" she cried. "I won!"

Michael found me, and I won too.

"Of course I won't give you away," Papa replied. "I'll walk you up the church aisle, but don't ever expect me to let you go again."

He passed Henrietta his serving of punch so she held two nearly full cups, kissed her cheek, then crossed the library to pluck the child from Michael's back.

Michael joined Henrietta and took one of the cups of punch from her. "If the squire made you cry, I'll thrash him, and I will not apologize for it."

"He made me cry, but don't you thrash him, not for that."

The children were thundering out of the library, every bit as loudly as they'd arrived, and mamas and papas were calling for wraps and finishing servings of punch. A game of fox and geese was being organized, and nothing would do but Uncle Michael must referee.

"Shall I return you to your family, Henrietta? Your father was most insistent that all proprieties be observed."

"You already did return me to my family, and we'll observe the proprieties only when privacy is denied us. I'll marry you, Michael, gladly, but I'd like some courtship first. Not for my sake, but for—"

"Your family's," Michael said. "You'll go from your father's household to this one. I understand."

His kiss said he did understand and confirmed for Henrietta that early spring would do for a wedding date, possibly even late winter.

Uncle Michael presided over the holiday game of fox and geese, which became a tradition that grew into a family tournament. Michael and Henrietta's own brood joined the hunt, along with cousins, aunts, uncles, and—when the snow wasn't too deep—the squire himself.

Then all would repair inside to enjoy the Christmas punch and listen to a version of the story of how Michael and Henrietta had found each other—and happiness—in the midst of winter's chill. Some of the details were edited, but Christmas after Christmas, the ending was always the same, a happily ever after, forever in progress.

Grace Burrowes grew up in central Pennsylvania and is the sixth out of seven children. She discovered romance novels when in junior high (back when there was such a thing), and has been reading them voraciously ever since. Grace has a bachelor's degree in political science, a bachelor of music in music history (both from Pennsylvania State University); a master's degree in conflict transformation from Eastern Mennonite University; and a juris doctor from the National Law Center at the George Washington University.

Grace writes Georgian, Regency, Scottish Victorian, and contemporary romances in both novella and novel lengths. She's a member of Romance Writers of America, and enjoys giving workshops and speaking at writers' conferences. She also loves to hear from her readers, and can be reached through her website, graceburrowes.com, and Twitter @GraceBurrowes.

Fall in Love with Forever Romance

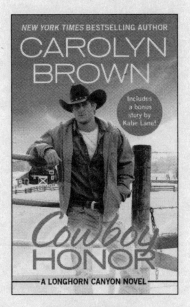

COWBOY HONOR
By Carolyn Brown

New York Times bestselling author Carolyn Brown delivers a sweet cowboy romance with a heart bigger than Texas itself! After her SUV runs off the road in the middle of a Texas blizzard and her cell phone stops working, Claire Mason is about to snap. Getting back home to Oklahoma with her four-year-old niece is top priority. And, lucky for her, help comes in the form of a true Texas cowboy...Also features the bonus story *O Little Town of Bramble* by Katie Lane!

Fall in Love with Forever Romance

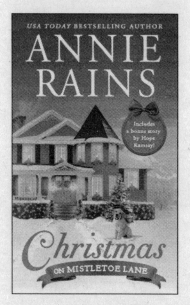

CHRISTMAS ON MISTLETOE LANE
By Annie Rains

Mitch Hargrove wants nothing more than to put his hometown in the rearview mirror, but his plans get derailed when he learns he's now half owner of the Sweetwater B&B. The fact that he's given only two months to make the inn a success is a huge problem, but it's his pretty—and incredibly headstrong—partner Kaitlyn Russo who's the real challenge. She's inherited the other half of her grandparents' charming (if a little rundown) bed and breakfast. With the grand reopening fast approaching, will Mitch keep running from the ghosts of Christmas past...or will he realize the true gift he's been given? This special 2-in-1 edition features *A Midnight Clear* by Hope Ramsay!

Fall in Love with Forever Romance

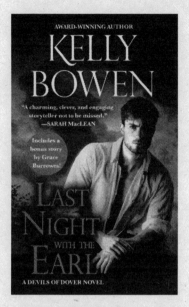

LAST NIGHT WITH THE EARL
By Kelly Bowen

War hero Eli Dawes was presumed dead—and would have happily stayed that way. All he wants is to hide away in his country home, where no one can see his scars. But when he tries to sneak into his old bedroom in the middle of the night, he's shocked to find the beautiful Rose Hayward. Eli might be back from the dead, but it's Rose who makes him feel *very* much alive. This special 2-in-1 edition features *Respect for Christmas*, a bonus novella by Grace Burrowes!

Fall in Love with Forever Romance

IT HAPPENED AT CHRISTMAS
By Debbie Mason

Out of money and out of options, Skylar Davis returns to Christmas, Colorado, seeking the comfort of the small mountain town all decked out for the holidays. There's no place Skylar would rather be...until she comes face-to-face with one of her biggest mistakes: the town's gorgeous mayor. Skye's never been able to forget her time with Ethan O'Connor. With snow in the air and the magic of the season all around them, will a Christmas miracle bring them back together at last? This special 2-in-1 edition features Debbie Mason's **never-before-in-print** novella *Miracle at Christmas*!